TO TEMPT A LADY

"I have always been taught that as a woman I had few choices in life. Most females believe that in a world they do not control acceptance is the only response," Anne said. "Yet I stubbornly cling to my independence, even if in reality it might be more illusion than fact. Pray, do not take that from me."

"Never. Believe me when I say that I will never force you."

She turned her head to look at him. She did believe Richard. In spite of her resolve to keep her distance, Anne found herself leaning closer. Her body tingled as she drew nearer. He touched her chin with his fingers and tilted her head. She watched him with luminous eyes, waiting, wanting, yet slightly afraid.

The first touch of his lips against hers was silky and sensuous. His kiss seemed like a natural action, a feather-soft touch that left her aching for more. Anne's eyelids fluttered closed and she felt a stirring of warmth invade every part of her body.

She relished the sweet, strong taste of his lips. Her hands moved from her lap to rest on his chest. She could feel the hardness of his muscles, could sense the strength of his desire, yet there was a gentleness in his manner. He increased the pressure of his lips, making the kiss intimate and unique.

"At least you want to kiss me," he whispered huskily in her ear. "That's not a bad start. I suppose the perfect solution would be for you to fall in love with me straightaway."

Anne smiled, even though a part of her wanted to run and hide from him. For deep within herself she knew the truth. She wanted far more from this man than his gentle kisses . . .

Books by Adrienne Basso

HIS WICKED EMBRACE
HIS NOBLE PROMISE

Published by Zebra Books

HIS NOBLE PROMISE

Adrienne Basso

Zebra Books
Kensington Publishing Corp.

http://www.zebrabooks.com

ZEBRA BOOKS are published by

Kensington Publishing Corp.
850 Third Avenue
New York, NY 10022

Zebra and the Z logo Reg. U.S. Pat. & TM Off.

First Printing: February, 2000
10 9 8 7 6 5 4 3 2 1

Printed in the United States of America

To my big brother Gary,
and my little brother John,
from your perfect sister, Adrienne.
Thanks ... for everything.

Prologue

Battlefield at Talavera
July 28, 1809
Late afternoon

Richard Cameron, Earl of Mulgrave, second in command of King George's 9th Light Dragoons, moved forward slowly. His eyes burned from the smoke that still hung in the air, his nose filled with the stench of blood and death. Weary and worn out, less from fatigue than from anxiety, he surveyed the carnage stretching before him.

It seemed as if the world had tumbled to pieces and everything was destroyed in the wreck. Lord Mulgrave wondered in anguish if he somehow could have done more for the men who had died under his command during this hard-won, desperately fought British victory.

"Come away now, Richard. 'Tis best to return to the house before darkness sets in."

Lord Mulgrave lifted his head and stared mutely at the man

who had spoken. Captain Miles Nightingall, the earl's boyhood friend and comrade-in-arms, sat stiffly upon his horse, his eyes filled with regret and understanding.

Miles looked unusually pale, due no doubt to the loss of blood from the sabre wound that had deeply slashed his thigh. It had been hastily attended to by a field doctor, and Richard could see the streaks of crimson that marred the none too clean bandage. Though concerned about his friend's health, in truth Lord Mulgrave was glad of Miles' quiet, capable company.

"And I need a drink," a second voice chimed in. "Better make that several." Captain Ian Simons, the other member of this closely knit boyhood trio, urged his mount closer to the earl. He was riding Lord Mulgrave's steed, having suffered a badly sprained ankle when his own horse was struck down in the heat of battle.

The earl cast a jaundiced eye toward his friend, then led the way on foot across the now eerily silent battlefield. Heaving an inward sigh, Richard forced himself forward through this waking nightmare, refusing to allow himself to feel the despair that threatened to crush his spirit. So much blood. So much pain. So much death.

It was dusk when they arrived at the house where Lord Mulgrave was billeted. Though modest in size and furnishings, it offered privacy and comfort, two things Richard felt sorely in need of.

Miles and Ian, both limping noticeably, followed him into the small front parlor and waited silently as he poured them each a large drink.

"You are exhausted, Richard," Captain Nightingall remarked, shifting the goblet in his hand. "Why don't you get some sleep? We'll see you after you have rested."

Richard hesitated, but once the words registered in his brain he experienced bone-wrenching fatigue. Miles was right; above all else he needed rest. Perhaps he was finally tired enough to close his eyes and collapse into oblivion without reliving every scream, every cry of anguish, every moment of panic and fear from today's battle.

Using the sheer stubbornness of will he was known for, Richard propelled his weary feet through the small house toward his bedchamber. He had barely reached the hall when the elderly couple he employed as servants ambushed him.

"You come now ... quickly ... la senora, she waits all day," Antonio insisted.

"La senora ... she waits," his wife echoed.

Now what? Richard thought with puzzled annoyance. Too emotionally and physically drained to summon much interest in their distress, Lord Mulgrave lifted himself up the stairs while the pair of servants followed tightly on his heels. They babbled excitedly in his ear, a mixture of Spanish and broken English that Richard found incomprehensible.

He shooed them away with his hand, but they would not relent. He opened his bedchamber door and resisted the temptation to turn around and snarl at the servants, demanding they leave him alone. Fortunately, breeding prevailed over emotion.

Lord Mulgrave entered the room and stopped cold. Someone was in his bed! The occupant's back was towards him, but judging by the slight form and figure barely concealed by the bed linens, Richard concluded it was a woman. A naked woman.

"Who the hell are you?" he barked in anger as the last remnants of civility all but disappeared.

He stomped toward the bed and yanked hard on the sheet, determined to chase the mysterious harlot from his bed and from his house.

"I do not know who you are and I do not care. Get out of my bed! Get out of my house! This instant!"

When she refused to move, refused to even acknowledge his commands, something inside him snapped. Too much was beyond his control on this day—the reasons for this maddening war, the personal loss and sacrifice of so many, the senseless death and suffering of the hundreds of men under his command—but this woman, this girl, this *creature* would do as he bid.

Richard reached out to grasp her shoulders, intending to shake her until her teeth rattled, but at that exact instant she rolled onto her back. His stomach gave a sickening lurch.

The woman was deathly pale and covered in sweat. Her eyes were glazed with pain and fear and she was breathing in deep gasps and moaning to herself.

"Juliana?" he whispered in disbelief. His fingers reached out tentatively and brushed a damp curl away from her face. Trembling, he dipped his hand lower, outlining her swollen belly. It moved beneath his palm and he jerked away in alarm. "What is happening?"

"Richard? Is that you? Richard? Oh, please, God, let it be him."

Lord Mulgrave sank down on the edge of the bed, his mind in disbelieving shock. How could this be? When he left Lisbon last fall he had no inkling of Juliana's condition. The deep depression that had clung to her since her husband's death had finally lifted and she had spoken of returning to England, perhaps to live with her brother in York.

But she had not left the Peninsula, for here she was nine months later, struggling and suffering to give birth. To his child? Of course. Why else would she have traveled this long distance to be with him in such an advanced stage of pregnancy?

"I am here, sweetheart," Richard said as he stroked her cheek softly. "Shhh . . . I am here."

Juliana's eyes fluttered open. "Oh, Richard, you have finally come home. I have—ahhh . . ." Gasping deeply, Juliana pulled her knees up and turned her face into the pillow.

Richard watched in horrified wonder as the young woman writhed on the bed, her body tensing with pain as each contraction gripped her. Guilt, stronger than any he had ever known, sliced through him.

He had done this to her. Juliana had followed her husband

to war, and when he was killed she had been inconsolable. All the younger officers of the regiment, including Richard, Ian and Miles, had made a special effort to comfort the lovely Juliana.

To them she was a representation of all the beauty and gentility and goodness they had left behind in England. She was a living, breathing reminder of what they were fighting so hard to preserve.

Yet Richard had unintentionally taken it one step further. An illicit liaison, a brief, physical affair between a sad young widow and a lonely soldier. They had given and taken comfort in each other's arms, foolishly ignoring the possible consequences of their passion.

"Why did you not tell me sooner?" he asked quietly when her breathing finally became even.

"Forgive me," she said faintly. "I should not have come here, but there was nowhere else to go."

Juliana struggled to lift her damp head off the pillow. Failing, she rolled her head toward Richard and tried to regulate her breathing.

"There is great love inside you, Richard. I have always felt it, even though it was not meant for me." She was pale and gaunt, yet her strong eyes seemed to be boring straight into his soul. "I want that love for my child. You must promise that if I do not survive you will care for my baby. Swear before God you will never let any harm befall my innocent babe."

"We will both care for him," Richard insisted, adding with a weak half-smile, "or her."

"You don't understand." Warm tears trickled from Juliana's eyes. "Please, promise me. You must promise."

"I promise," he stated firmly.

His words calmed her and she appeared to drift off into a peaceful slumber. But it did not last. She tensed suddenly and let out an agonized scream. Lord Mulgrave jumped off the bed and spun around the room. His wild eyes lit upon his elderly servants, who had thankfully remained in the bedchamber.

"She needs help. The baby is coming. A midwife. We must have a midwife."

"Sí, sí . . . midwife," Antonio repeated. He pointed to his wife. The woman bustled importantly to the bed. She poured water in a basin, washed her hands, then wiped them on her apron.

Richard turned his head away as she lifted the sheet and parted Juliana's legs. He heard her voice murmuring gently in its usual mix of Spanish and English. Cursing himself as a coward, Richard forced his gaze back to the bed, but the sheet now covered Juliana.

Teresa spoke rapidly to her husband and he attempted to translate. "It will be a hard birth. The baby is big . . . la senora, she is small."

Richard's heart raced as the reality of the situation went round and round in his head. Juliana was so delicate and fragile. How would she possibly survive this?

"I shall return in a few minutes," he choked out, pausing only a moment to lift a small leather pouch from his armoire.

Richard clattered down the stairs in a rush, bursting into the front parlor without pausing. Facing his friends with a grim expression, he stated flatly, "I must find a clergyman. Now."

It was imperative that he locate a clergyman as quickly as possible. He knew he must marry Juliana before the child was born or else it would forever be branded a bastard.

"Why in the world do you need a clergyman?" Ian asked, sitting up in alarm. "Is someone dying?"

"There is no time for lengthy explanations." Lord Mulgrave quickly assessed the condition of the two men, concluding that Captain Nightingall was in slightly better physical shape than Captain Simons.

"Miles, you must help me." Lord Mulgrave thrust the small pouch filled with gold coins into Captain Nightingall's surprised hands. "Scour the city, bribe whomever you must, but bring me someone who can perform a marriage ceremony immediately."

At first Miles didn't move. Lord Mulgrave could fairly see the questions swirling in Captain Nightingall's brain, but in the end loyalty won out over curiosity.

"I'll not return until I've found someone," Miles promised solemnly, knocking a chair over in his hasty, clumsy exit from the room.

"I can search for a military chaplain," Ian volunteered. "My ankle hurts like the devil, but I can sit on a horse."

Wordlessly Richard nodded in agreement. He hated to risk the health of his two best captains, his two great friends, but there was no one else he could call upon to aid him with this critical dilemma.

The waiting seemed endless. Richard refused to leave Juliana's side, doing what he could to distract her from the pain. Impressed by her courage and dignity, he kept up a steady stream of conversation trying to convince her, and himself, that all would be well. But it was not.

The priest arrived with Miles in barely enough time to administer last rites to an unconscious Juliana. What little remained of her strength had been used to push their daughter into the world. She had even lacked the will to open her eyes and gaze, at least once, at the red and wrinkled little bundle Richard held close to her breast.

Something inside Richard's heart twisted and broke as he stared down at Juliana's fragile body. True, he had not loved her, but he had cared about her and she had sacrificed her own life to give him the greatest gift known to man. A child.

It was difficult and costly convincing the priest to procure and sign the appropriate documents substantiating the occurrence of his marriage before the birth of his daughter, but Richard would not be denied. Money, the great equalizer of worldly and spiritual matters, succeeded in salving the priest's conscience when words failed.

Witnesses willing to sign the fictional marriage papers? The two men Lord Mulgrave trusted most, Captain Miles Nightingall and Captain Ian Simons.

Two days later as Richard frantically combed the city for a wet-nurse to feed his hungry daughter, a lone officer stood beside the freshly covered grave of the Countess of Mulgrave. Kneeling stiffly in the dirt, his captain's bars reflected the shimmering morning sunlight and sent it dancing merrily among the leaves in the trees.

At first the tears would not come, but memories of the enchanting Juliana soon brought forth the grief hidden deep in the soldier's heart.

"I failed you, my beloved. In life and in death. I should have answered your letters of distress, but I was too much of a coward to face up to my responsibilities. 'Tis fitting and proper that I shall now be forced to suffer the anguish of watching another man claim our beautiful daughter as his own."

A sharp noise nearby startled the captain and he lifted his head in alarm. Unable and unprepared to face the questions and consequences of being found, he rose to his feet and limped slowly away from the gravesite.

Chapter One

Devonshire, England
June, 1816

"You will not marry this woman, Nigel. I absolutely forbid it."

Richard Cameron, Earl of Mulgrave, stood at the library window of his ancestral home, Cuttingswood Manor, and delivered his edict to his nephew, his heir, in his usual calm, authoritative manner. And Nigel reacted precisely as the earl expected.

"I love her, Uncle Richard," Nigel protested vehemently. "She is my heart, my destiny. I love my dearest Miss Paget, my sweet Nicole, from the depths of my soul. 'I love her heartily, for she is fair and wise as she hath proved herself.' "

"I believe the correct quote is: 'I love her heartily, for she is wise, if I can judge of her, and fair she is, if that mine eyes be true, and true she is, as she hath proved herself,' " the earl insisted with a sigh. He moved from his position in front of the window and came to stand a few feet in front of his nephew.

"Mangled Shakespeare aside, I cannot permit such a liaison. Be sensible, Nigel. You have only recently met this young woman. We know absolutely nothing about her nor her family."

Nigel made an impatient sound of disgust. "That is untrue! Her name is Nicole Paget. She is the fourth of five sisters, followed by two younger brothers. Her father is the Baron of Althen, her mother, Lady Althen late of Hampshire currently residing in London."

"Never heard of them," Lord Mulgrave replied briskly.

"How could you, Uncle Richard?" Nigel declared. "You live like a monk, rarely leaving this place and never attending any society function in or out of season."

The earl lowered his chin slightly, conceding the point. "True, I prefer the quieter pursuits of country living, but I own I know something of the goings-on of town life. You are the heir to an old, respected and wealthy title. There are many eager mothers who will encourage their eligible daughters to employ any means necessary to attract your attention."

"Miss Paget is nothing like those giggling ninnies who simper and flirt with every titled gentleman unlucky enough to cross their path. Nicole is a lady. *My* lady." Nigel drew himself up to his full height, which still left him several inches shorter than his uncle. "Naturally, I want your blessing in my choice of bride, Uncle Richard. But I give you fair warning I shall marry my Miss Paget whether or not you approve. I am of age, you know."

Lord Mulgrave clenched his jaw. "I see this wondrous new love has given you a backbone. I hope it has also given you the means to support yourself. 'But love is blind, and lovers cannot see the pretty follies that themselves commit.' "

Judging from the twitching of Nigel's facial muscles the earl knew that he had scored a direct hit. Perhaps the Shakespeare quote about love being blind was a bit over the top, but it seemed so appropriate, Richard was unable to stop himself.

Lord Mulgrave genuinely liked his nephew or else he would

not have made the boy his heir, but the earl held no illusions about the young man's character.

Nigel was an impulsive young man, indulged and spoiled by a mother who fairly doted on her son. Richard knew he should have been more insistent that his sister keep a tighter rein on her headstrong son, especially since Nigel's father had died when the boy was an infant. Richard had been able to offer some assistance, teaching Nigel to ride, shoot and hunt, but he had been away fighting on the Peninsula during Nigel's formative years.

By the time Lord Mulgrave returned to England, Nigel had already developed a taste for independent thinking. Unfortunately, he also possessed a somewhat underdeveloped sense of duty and took the wealth and privilege of his lifestyle very much for granted.

The earl was certain his nephew would barely last out the month if he was cut off from his generous allowance. Eternal love was one thing, but abject poverty was an altogether different situation.

"Of course, I may be jumping to all the wrong conclusions," Lord Mulgrave said politely. "Does your Miss Paget have a large dowry perchance? Or a sufficient yearly allowance that will enable the two of you to live comfortably until you come into your majority a few years hence when you turn twenty-five?"

"I would never presume to discuss anything as vulgar as finances with Miss Paget," Nigel exclaimed hotly.

The earl smiled. "I take it that means Miss Paget has little or no money. Somehow I figured as much."

"You go too far, Uncle!" Nigel exclaimed, losing control of his facial muscles as well as his temper.

The tense set of his shoulders warned Richard that Nigel was angling for a fight. *At least he is passionate about the chit,* the earl thought with grudging admiration. *Maddeningly immature, but passionate.* Yet it was clearly unrealistic to hope that Nigel would simply abandon the notion of marrying Miss Paget merely because he disapproved. Richard decided he would have to devise a more subtle approach.

"If I remember correctly, you were head over heels for Lord Kersey's daughter at Christmas time, and last summer it was the Thornapple girl," the earl said calmly. He paced back toward the window, then turned to face his nephew. "Marriage is a commitment that spans a lifetime. The woman you choose will be the next Countess of Mulgrave as well as your lifelong companion. The mother of your children. I fear you are far too young to have fixed on a bride at this juncture of your life."

"I will be twenty-two years old in six months. You were married at twenty-three," Nigel flung out in anger. "And already a father."

"There is no basis for comparing our situations. My marriage took place during wartime. The civilized rules that govern society no longer exist at a battlefront."

"Love crosses all boundaries, Uncle. My love for Miss Paget is as strong and deserving as your love was for Juliana."

The earl did not reply. Nor did he correct his nephew's misconceptions. Everyone in society believed he had been totally devoted to his young wife who died so tragically in childbirth. Richard had worked hard over the past seven years diligently keeping Juliana's memory alive for the sake of their daughter, Alexandra.

Fortunately, his supposed obsession with his wife had been viewed as a romantic tragedy by society's most influential matrons. Little scrutiny had been given to the actual circumstances surrounding his nuptials, and female interest was directed mostly toward the depth and magnitude of the earl's suffering now that the love of his life was forever taken from him.

Richard had been uncomfortable maintaining the charade of an undying love between him and his countess, yet, as he knew they eventually would, the *ton* shifted their attention away from him the moment a new, more exciting bit of gossip came along. But they never forgot what he wanted them to believe.

Crossing his arms over his chest, the earl watched calmly as Nigel wrestled with and then mastered his temper. Lord, was he ever that young? That innocent? That full of optimistic passion? A small sigh escaped the earl's lips. No, he was not. War had quickly stolen his youth, and while he never regretted his decision to serve his king and country, Richard did regret the loss of his innocence.

"You must not dismiss this out of hand, Uncle Richard," Nigel pleaded woefully. "I know that if you had the opportunity to meet Miss Paget, to see and judge for yourself what a truly spectacular woman she is, your opinion of my marriage would be entirely different."

Feeling generous in light of Nigel's abject misery, the earl elected to be magnanimous. "I am certain there is a great deal of truth in what you say. However, as you so accurately pointed out, since I seldom travel to London there will be little opportunity for me to meet Miss Paget. The season will be ending in a few short weeks, so it would be futile to attempt to organize a trip to town at this late date.

"However, if your feelings remain so passionate in the future, I promise I shall do whatever is necessary to meet Miss Paget and her family next season."

Nigel's head shot up, revealing an expression of sheer delight. "But, Uncle Richard, it is not necessary to wait until next season. Miss Paget and her entire family are right here in Devon, staying with Sir Reginald Wilford."

"What?" the earl shouted. The chit was here? In Devon? What a scheming little wench! This was rapidly developing into a far more serious situation than he thought.

"Sir Reginald Wilford is in fact the recluse you so eagerly accuse me of being, Nigel. He seldom ventures out of his house and leaves the daily running of his estate to his agent. Even though his property borders mine, I rarely set eyes on him."

The earl stroked his chin thoughtfully. "I remember Sir Reginald had a younger brother but he died before he reached manhood. I was unaware of the existence of any other living relations."

"The connection between the two families is rather distant," Nigel admitted with a blush. "And recently renewed. Needless to say, I was over the moon when I learned that Miss Paget would be near enough to visit regularly."

Lord Mulgrave remained silent for several minutes, digesting this newest tidbit of information. He was certain Sir Reginald had no close relations, so the connection between him and Miss Paget must be extremely slight. How the devil did she manage it? the earl wondered, not believing for an instant that this miraculous kinship with his closest neighbor was a remarkable coincidence.

"Then I shall look forward to receiving an invitation to dine with Sir Reginald and making the acquaintance of his houseguests," the earl replied. "Including the infamous Nicole."

Nigel neatly pounced on Lord Mulgrave's hastily spoken offer. "I will be honored to present her to you this evening, Uncle Richard. She plans on attending the Earl of Rosslyn's masquerade ball celebrating the first anniversary of the victory at Waterloo."

"This evening?" The earl cast his nephew a shrewd glance. He suspected he had been rather cleverly set-up, but Richard realized he could easily turn the situation to his advantage. A masked ball. The ideal circumstance to test the true intentions and character of the clever Miss Paget, especially if she had no idea to whom she was speaking.

"I feel certain it will be a most enlightening experience to finally meet the sparkling Miss Paget," Lord Mulgrave stated smoothly. "Most enlightening."

* * *

"Anne, you must come at once," Nicole wailed in horror. "I have torn the skirt of my gown!"

Anne Paget, oldest daughter and mainstay of the Paget clan, answered her sister's howl with the good humor and level head for which she was known and seldom appreciated.

"Do not fret, Nicole. I have brought my basket of threads and sewing needle. Since I designed and sewed this garment for you, I am certain I shall have no difficulty repairing it."

Anne sank to her knees and began examining the damage to the costume. Nicole had decided to appear at the ball dressed as Queen Elizabeth, and it had taken Anne three weeks to create the magnificent dress. Historically accurate from the starched white ruff collar to the flared skirt that jutted out stiffly from the hips, the outfit gave the diminutive Nicole a regal, feminine look.

Nicole fidgeted impatiently as Anne expertly ran her fingers through the deep blue material. She soon discovered a substantial rip in the silk overskirt of the gown but decided that with careful, tight stitching it would be barely noticeable.

Nicole lowered her head and watched her sister's every move. "The tear is right in the center of the skirt," Nicole cried when Anne began threading her needle. "Everyone will see that my gown has been mended, especially Nigel's horrid uncle, the Earl of Mulgrave."

Nicole's china-blue eyes widened to huge proportions and her bottom lip began quivering. Without further warning she burst into tears. "I cannot wear this dress in public," Nicole sobbed. "I simply cannot."

Anne, her mouth filled with pins, sat back on her heels in surprise. She knew Nicole was especially nervous about tonight's ball, but this was carrying things a bit too far. Some, indeed many, thought Nicole was a selfish, self-centered, spoiled young girl, but Anne knew that beneath the surface Nicole had a good and true heart.

Doted on by both parents since she was a young child, Nicole had been destined to become a woman who needed pampering and protecting. On occasion Nicole became totally wrapped up in the circumstances of her own life and was oblivious to the situation of other family members, but Anne knew it really wasn't her fault that she was so demanding.

For Nicole everything must be perfect. Her greatest desire at the moment was to become officially betrothed to Nigel Gwyn, future Earl of Mulgrave. And even though she was only seventeen years of age, Nicole seldom had difficulty achieving her goals.

"No one will be looking at the skirt of your gown," Anne told her distraught sister. "Everyone will be staring at your lovely face."

"Really?" Nicole sniffed, dabbing at her eyes with a linen handkerchief.

"Absolutely," Anne replied honestly.

Nicole was by far the prettiest of the five Paget sisters. She was a true English beauty, tiny and petite with masses of honey blond curls artfully framing an oval face, fair flawless skin and blue eyes that gazed upon the world with delight and excitement. Their father often remarked that Nicole had an eager face that invited all to approach her.

Well, men at least. Being the oldest child, at twenty-five, Anne could have easily resented all the male attention and adulation bestowed upon her younger sister. But she didn't.

Oh, Anne liked men well enough when they happened to spare her a glance. She did not possess her sister's stunning good looks, few women did, but Anne's willowy slimness, warm brown eyes and light brown hair brought her an occasional request for a dance or an invitation to the theater.

For Anne it was enough. The simple truth was that Anne was not especially interested in attracting a man. For herself.

She had worked diligently and successfully for the past three London seasons securing husbands for her younger sisters. The twins, Prudence and Madeline, were now happily married, thanks in large part to Anne's scheming. Next would come Nicole and in a few years Rosalind, who at fifteen was displaying the kind of fair, blond beauty that seemed to attract men like bees to wildflowers.

"Oh, Anne, I can clearly see the ridge of fabric where you have stitched my gown together," Nicole protested as she peered closely into the mirror. "This costume is beyond repair. What am I going to do? I cannot attend the ball without a proper costume."

Anne stood beside her sister. She rustled the skirt so that the repaired section was hidden inside a fold of material. "There. It looks fine."

"No, it does not," Nicole insisted defiantly, taking a step forward and revealing the mended section. "The imperfection of the skirt appears each time I move. How can I possibly dance in this beastly dress? Everyone will notice and comment upon my mended garment. You must find me another costume."

"The ball begins in less than five hours, Nicole," Anne said with a trace of weary annoyance in her voice. "There is no other costume to be found. You must wear this dress."

"I will not." Nicole lifted her chin and shook her head vehemently. "There must be another gown somewhere in the house that can be altered for me. What are you wearing tonight?"

"I fashioned a simple Grecian gown for myself," Anne explained patiently. "There was not time to do much else since I exerted all my efforts on your dress and the Marie Antoinette costume that Mother requested."

"I want to see the Grecian gown," Nicole declared. "I do hope it is not white. I look horrid in white, rather like a ghost who is haunting a castle."

Anne's eyes moved quickly over her sister's well-endowed

curves. "The gown is pale blue, and it will be both too long and too tight across the bosom for you to wear."

"Please," Nicole said with a quick artificial smile that Anne knew was trouble. "There cannot be any harm in letting me *look* at the dress."

Knowing it was a mistake, Anne nevertheless retrieved the gown from the bedchamber she was sharing with Rosalind. The moment Nicole put it on, Anne knew they were doomed. The color was wonderful for Nicole, bringing out the blueness of her eyes, complementing her blond hair and showcasing her creamy skin. Perhaps a bit too much creamy skin.

"The bodice does not drape properly, making the neckline too low," Anne stated flatly.

"Shockingly low," Nicole breathed excitedly.

"The hem is easily six inches too long."

"If you pin it for me, I will gladly spend the remainder of the afternoon sewing it. I do not have your skill with a needle, but you did teach me how to run a proper stitch. Please?"

Their eyes met in the mirror and Anne could feel her resolve slipping. Nicole did look stunning in the outfit. Certainly far more beautiful than Anne ever could. After all, this was a most important night for Nicole; it might very well decide her future. For Anne it was merely another party.

"What will I wear if you go as a Greek goddess?"

"Oh, thank you, Anne." Nicole rushed forward and hugged her older sister tightly. "I knew you would not fail me. As for your dress, why don't you go as Queen Elizabeth? If we can shorten your gown for me, why not lengthen my costume for you?"

Anne snorted. "It will take more than a lengthened hem to make the queen's outfit ready for me."

"I'm sorry." Nicole hung her head and plucked at the golden sash tied around her waist. "You need not give me the dress if you really want to wear it. Perhaps I can find another gown. As you said, there are five whole hours before the ball begins.

And if there is no appropriate garment for me to wear then I shall remain at home. All alone.''

"Cease being so Gothic, Nicole. I already agreed to switch costumes.''

Nicole's transformation was instantaneous, as Anne knew it would be. With a delighted giggle she twirled about the room.

"I do look fetching in this gown. Nigel will be speechless when he sees me, and doubly surprised since I told him I was going to appear as Queen Elizabeth. Would it not be hilarious if he did not recognize me? Then I could flirt with him and judge for myself if his heart has truly been given to me. I certainly would not want a husband whose head is easily turned by a beautiful face.''

It seemed ironic to Anne that Nicole, a woman who made flirting an art form, would be so threatened by the idea of her beau showing interest in another. For all her supposed sophistication, Nicole was still in many ways a seventeen-year-old girl.

"If you are wearing a mask, then Nigel will not know that you have a pretty face," Anne pointed out. She motioned for Nicole to stand on the low stool near the window so she could take the measurements for the new hemline on the Grecian gown. "Besides, Nigel will most likely be too busy ogling your magnificent breasts to care what you look like behind your mask.''

"Anne! What a positively vulgar thing to say." Nicole gasped. Crouching low, she added in a whisper, "Do you really believe that Nigel will think my bosom is magnificent?''

"If he is half the man you claim he is," Anne said with a laugh. "Of course, you must remember that Nigel may *look* all he wishes, at this juncture in your relationship, but he absolutely may not *touch* until you have exchanged your wedding vows.''

"Anne!" Nicole straightened and thrust her nose in the air.

"You really must learn to curb your tongue. Whatever will Nigel's uncle think if he heard you speak so bawdily?"

Anne merely shrugged her shoulders in response. Although it was hardly a proper subject for conversation, she was more than willing to allow the discussion to continue. She had never subscribed to the notion that it was beneficial to keep women ignorant about life, and that included sexual matters.

Anne might have little firsthand experience of men to offer her sister, but years spent sitting among the older society matrons at various balls, parties and soirees had taught Anne a thing or two about males.

In her opinion it was only through ignorance that a young, or older, woman found herself ruined. Anne firmly believed it was her duty to educate her sisters. Their mother would have had a fit of the vapors at such frank talk, but Lady Althen had never been the type of parent to overly concern herself with the activities of her offspring.

It was Anne, not either of their parents, who determined that Lord Marton was a disreputable rake who had no intention of making a legitimate proposal of marriage to Nicole at the start of this year's season. So she had skillfully encouraged Nigel's interest in her lovely sister, especially after discovering he would one day inherit a respectable title and a sizable fortune.

Anne had also negotiated the favorable marriage contracts for her two married sisters, Prudence and Madeline, when it became apparent that their father, Lord Althen, was incapable of securing a fair settlement for his daughters.

In truth, Anne had assumed responsibility for the entire family four years ago when they teetered on the brink of social and financial ruin. Her quick thinking, level head and skillful weaving of fact and fiction had been the family's salvation.

In a society that was so easily swayed by scandal, Anne had performed nothing short of a miracle to ensure that not even a breath of impropriety ever touched her family. After all, the truth of their disgrace was not an uncommon one. Although they appeared to live the carefree, privileged life of the nobility, the Baron of Althen and his family were in fact nearly penniless.

Anne would never forget the moment she realized the serious extent of their financial dilemma. She had reached her twenty-first birthday with great anticipation. Her grandmother had generously bequeathed her oldest granddaughter a special inheritance, a yearly allowance that would enable her to forgo the necessity of marriage and live independently if she so chose.

And Anne defiantly chose an independent life. Her greatest dream had always been to travel to Europe and study art. Seriously study art. Yet as she sat in her father's library on that dreary winter day and heard the truth from her grandmother's solicitor, Mr. Addams, all her dreams turned to dust.

"There is no money, Miss Paget," Mr. Addams said sympathetically, clearing his throat and shuffling his papers noisily. "Lord Althen has borrowed heavily against this stipend over the years. With every good intention of repaying the loan, I am certain.

"However, he has not yet made restitution of the funds. In order for you to collect the inheritance, you must demand payment from your father. I regret to inform you that he is already deeply in debt. The only asset he possesses of great value is this estate, which is entailed and cannot be sold or mortgaged. The property will, of course, one day be inherited by your brother, William."

Anne flinched and struggled to control her breathing. It was a mistake. Some sort of horrid legal mixup that would soon be remedied. Then they could all have a good laugh over it. Anne stared hopefully at the lawyer, but he quickly lowered his gaze, refusing to meet her eyes. At that moment Anne knew deep in her heart he was speaking the truth.

"What about my dowry?" Anne inquired in a small voice. "Am I not legally entitled to that money since my father has seen fit to use my inheritance for his own purposes?"

The lawyer bent his head even lower, attempting to squirm

away from Anne's troubled eyes. "Lord Althen has spent the dowry funds also, Miss Paget."

Stifling a cry of alarm, Anne stiffened her spine. "I have four younger sisters. What of their dowries?"

"Gone."

"What has happened to all our money, sir?" Anne asked urgently. "I know that my father is not a gambler; a modest wager or two on a horse race or an occasional card game at a party is the usual extent of his wagering. How is it possible that all of our money is gone?"

"It is highly improper for me to discuss these matters with you, Miss Paget," the solicitor protested. He made a move to get to his feet.

"Sit down, Mr. Addams!"

The firmly issued command hung in the air. The lawyer pursed his lips in defiance but slowly resumed his seat, cracking under Anne's hard, determined stare. By the time he left the estate, Anne had received a full accounting of her father's financial situation. It was not a very encouraging picture.

Her parents had blindly followed the lead of the Regent when it came to matters of money. Thrift of any sort was absolutely foreign to their nature. Over the course of their twenty-six-year marriage they thought nothing of spending money they did not have on anything from extravagant clothing to expensive horseflesh.

If they continued on their current course the family would be completely ruined in less than a year's time. As oldest, Anne knew she had no choice but to accept responsibility for the welfare of the family. So on that dreary afternoon, with the reluctant aid of Mr. Addams she devised a plan of survival.

The rich, fertile farmland surrounding the family estate was leased to neighbors and the impressive manor house was rented to a rich merchant from Brighton.

She packed up the entire family along with their personal servants and descended, unannounced, on her mother's brother who lived in Cornwall. They lived with her uncle for almost nine months until early spring when the London season began. Imposing this time upon a cousin once removed on her father's side, the entire clan traveled to London, and the twins, Prudence and Madeline, were launched into Society. With one special goal in mind. To snare a mate.

Prudence succeeded that first year; Madeline the next. They each married men they liked and admired who were socially acceptable and independently wealthy. With the funds secured from their marriage settlements, Anne was able to rent a modest home in a fashionable section of London for several months. When the rent money ran out, the Paget clan simply "visited" another relative.

Anne's plan for survival was simple. Without the added burden of the family estate expenses, Anne was able to more effectively utilize the family income. By curbing her parents' extravagances as much as was humanly possible and saving the bulk of the family funds to outfit the next sister eligible for marriage, Anne was able to pay the salaries of their personal servants, meet the bills for her younger brothers' schooling and keep the family fashionably clothed. After all, appearance was everything.

Relieved of the financial burdens which had plagued him for years, Lord Althen did not interfere with his daughter's plans. Nor did he acknowledge her efforts, but Anne honestly never expected he would.

"Do you think that Nigel might declare his intentions tonight?" Nicole breathed with a sigh. "Perhaps he will make a formal offer. Just think of it, Anne! By the end of the evening I could be an engaged woman."

"No good will come of anticipating the event before it actually occurs," Anne said, clucking her tongue.

"Really, Anne," Nicole replied with some indignation. "How can I avoid it? 'Tis all well and good for you to be so calm and composed. It is not your future happiness that rests on the outcome of tonight's ball. I shall be on pins and needles all evening waiting for the odious Lord Mulgrave to pass judgment upon me.''

''I am merely reminding you to be sensible,'' Anne suggested gently. ''Disappointment is never a pleasant experience.''

Truthfully, she wasn't sure who was more excited over the prospect of an imminent engagement, her or Nicole. Seeing her sister safely married would bring Anne one step closer to her ultimate goal of independence. For as soon as Nicole was settled, only Rosalind would be left.

Then in a few short years Rosalind too would be wed and Anne would finally be free. Free! Free to indulge her passion for painting. Free to travel to Europe and see for herself the great works of art by the masters she had always admired.

Free to express her innermost feelings through her own humble sketches and oils. Free to become the artist she always imagined and experience life beyond the rigid confines of the society into which she had been born.

Still, Anne cautioned herself to heed her own advice. Disappointments were cruel enough to bear, shattered dreams nearly impossible to survive.

And yet as the two sisters prepared for the ball, Anne's naturally optimistic spirit overtook her. Nigel might very well propose this evening. Nicole was a vision in her Grecian costume; no man with red blood in his veins would be able to resist her.

''You will outshine every woman in attendance this evening,'' Anne remarked to her sister as they entered the coach for the short carriage ride to the party.

And I shall be close by to assure that all goes as planned, Anne added silently to herself. *For your success, dear sister, will bring me one step closer to my own dreams of artistic freedom.*

Chapter Two

The Earl of Rosslyn's ballroom sparkled with candlelight and lavish colors as the dizzying number of festively costumed guests mingled amongst themselves. The assembled crowd danced to the strains of lighthearted music, indulged in the sumptuous buffet of rich food and flirted with carefree abandon from behind the anonymity of their masks.

Laughter and muted conversation drifted out through the French windows along the length of the ballroom which had been opened to allow in the evening breeze. There was an atmosphere of gaiety punctuated with an air of excitement among the guests that was almost contagious.

Clearly everyone was having a marvelous time. Except Lord Mulgrave. He was the single point of incongruity in the entire ballroom as he stood alone and brooded, observing all the elegance and fanfare with growing annoyance. *Where the devil was she?*

"Must you stand so near the entrance to my ballroom, Richard?" the Earl of Rosslyn asked with a sarcastic twist in his voice. "Your expression is set with such furious determination it is frightening many of my guests."

"Shut up, Ian," Lord Mulgrave replied darkly. "I have been waiting over two hours for Nigel's darling Miss Paget to arrive. Apparently she lacks the wit to tell time correctly since she is far beyond fashionably late. I am in no mood for joviality."

Richard tried scowling at his host and lifelong friend but was unable to keep from grinning. The former Captain Simons was now the current Earl of Rosslyn, and Richard was pleased that Ian had taken on his unexpected role as an earl so seriously. With only the occasional lapse in good judgment. Such as this evening.

Ian should have looked ridiculous in the white Roman toga trimmed in gold, sandals, and laurel wreath encircling his blond head, but amazingly he didn't. He looked strikingly commanding and regal.

Of course, only Ian could have invented such a bizarre reason for a costumed ball, the anniversary of Wellington's victory at Waterloo, and gotten the entire neighborhood of nobles along with a smattering of the beau monde to attend. Most of them dressed in outrageous outfits ranging from a swashbuckling pirate to Henry VIII.

"Ahh, yes, Miss Paget." Ian signaled a passing footman and snagged two flutes of champagne off the silver tray the servant carried. He handed one to Richard. "I remember. You want to speak with Miss Paget the moment she arrives. What exactly are you planning to do to the poor thing?"

"Scare her away from Nigel, I hope. If she is as shallow as I suspect, it should not be that difficult a task."

Ian lifted his goblet in a mock salute and the two men clinked glasses. Richard sipped his champagne distractedly, his eyes never leaving the rounded archway entrance to the ballroom. The steady stream of arriving guests had dwindled to a trickle, yet Richard knew that Nigel's little darling had to descend these steps to enter the ballroom. And Lord Mulgrave would be waiting.

Surprise was the key element in Richard's plan of attack this evening. It was imperative that he reach Miss Paget before Nigel had an opportunity to introduce them. He wanted time alone with the little schemer without her knowing with whom she was speaking.

"Do you want me to distract Miss Paget?" Ian volunteered. "I met her last week at the Tollies' dinner party. She is rather attractive in a pretty, girlish way. It would not be a great hardship to lavish attention on her. I can be most charming when pressed, especially with the ladies."

"I know." Richard laughed under his breath. "From barmaid to noblewoman and across all continents."

"It might work," Ian persisted, taking a large swallow of champagne. "After all, I inherited the title of earl from my brother, God rest his soul, last year. I am already an earl while Nigel is merely a baron and will have to wait many years before he inherits. If Miss Paget throws in her lot with me, she will not have to wait eons to become a countess."

"She would have to wait an eternity." Lord Mulgrave tipped the remaining drops of champagne into his mouth. "If Miss Paget is only half as clever as I think, she will already be well aware that you are an outrageous flirt, an occasionally charming and experienced rake. The type of man known for browsing among unmarried females, but never seriously considering making a permanent selection. The prospect of marriage has always made you jittery."

"Your cruel words wound me, Richard," Ian replied lightly.

"I know from years of experience it is impossible to penetrate your foolish hide," Lord Mulgrave commented with a smile. "By the way, you look ridiculous in that getup. Julius Caesar, my arse."

"I like how my costume shows off the strength of my legs," Ian remarked mildly. He straightened his broad shoulders and adjusted the laurel wreath in his hair. "I recently discovered that women have an affinity for men's muscular bare legs. Capitalizing on that weakness left me with a choice of Roman emperor or highland warrior, but I had trouble fastening the damn kilt. That left Rome the victor."

"You are impossible," Lord Mulgrave said fondly. Ian was probably the only person in the entire room who could bring a genuine smile to his face tonight. "And I refuse to ask how you acquired this insane knowledge about female's interest in men's bare legs. Frankly, I don't want to know."

Shifting his attention away from his host, Richard once again scanned the crowded ballroom. There were actually several people he recognized, despite their costumes and masks. Of course, not all the gentlemen were dressed-up. Many, like himself, were garbed in black formal evening clothes.

"I have not seen Miles all evening. Is he here?" Lord Mulgrave asked.

The humor immediately receded from Ian's eyes. "Yes. Miles arrived last night," Ian replied tersely. "We need to discuss our mutual friend. I am worried. I have heard rumors about Miles since he returned to England, but paid them no heed. I should have. He has developed quite a reputation as a reckless gamester with a violent temper. Most recently he has been banned from White's for one full year for brawling in the card room."

"Miles? Our own level-headed Captain Nightingall brawling? And gambling? It seems impossible."

Ian shook his head. "He is not the man we knew. Miles has changed and not for the better."

Richard grabbed Ian's arm. "Why haven't you told me?"

"You have other more immediate problems to manage at present. We will both confront Miles when the time is right."

Ian stiffened suddenly. Richard turned his head, following his friend's gaze. A gaily attired group of guests were converged on the steps leading to the ballroom.

"Is it her?"

Ian smiled softly. "Brace yourself, Richard. Miss Paget has finally arrived."

"Here comes our host, the Earl of Rosslyn. Is he not handsome in that costume? He has the most enchanting smile." Nicole squealed. "Good heavens, you can see his unclothed legs!"

Anne ceased fussing with the folds of her gown and raised her head. The earl's costume did indeed afford a splendid view of his muscular calves, but after a brief admiring glance Anne's attention was drawn to the man by his side.

They were quite a contrasting sight. Although both were tall, attractive men, the stranger possessed an arrogantly commanding air. His power went beyond his obvious physical strength. Anne knew without a doubt that here was a man whose wishes were seldom thwarted.

"Who is that tall, serious man beside the earl?"

"I do not know," Nicole whispered. "He is rather formidable looking."

Conversation between the sisters ceased as the earl and his companion drew near.

"Welcome, welcome," the earl called out merrily. "I am indeed honored to count you among my guests this evening. Lady Althen, you make a positively smashing Marie Antoinette, I fear it shall be us poor gentlemen who lose our heads around you tonight."

Anne's mother snapped open her fan in response, clearly pleased with the earl's teasing flirtation. "Good evening, my lord," she said pleasantly, dropping a low, elegant curtsey. "I believe you are already acquainted with my husband, Lord Althen, and my daughters Nicole and Anne. Although I shall not spoil the surprise and tell you who is who behind their masks. I leave that discovery to you, my lord."

"Mystery has always been a female's most powerful ally."
The earl shook hands with Lord Althen and bowed to the ladies.
"I am delighted you can attend my humble gathering. May I
present a close friend who has specifically requested an introduction to the Miss Pagets."

The earl turned to his companion, and Anne saw the warning
look in the stranger's eye. Apparently so did the earl, and he
must have reacted as silently commanded because when he
began to speak, the warning look in the stranger's eyes was
replaced by appraising interest.

"Although my friend has chosen to forgo the ritual of a
costume," the earl said calmly, "at my request he has agreed
to join in the spirit of the evening by keeping his true identity
a secret until the midnight unmasking. Therefore I shall simply
introduce him as my dear friend, Lord Richard."

Lord Richard gave a proper, albeit swift bow while the earl
finished the introductions. Anne took the opportunity to study
him. Up close the stranger was even more attractive, she quickly
decided. He had deep green eyes that contrasted strikingly with
his dark brown hair. His strong, lean features were classically
handsome, and his smile, though briefly seen, was nothing short
of dazzling.

He carried himself with arrogant purpose and there was an
air of military command emanating from him even as he was
standing still. Who was this mysterious stranger? Anne wondered.

Lord Richard turned his perceptive gaze toward her, and
Anne's heart began a steady, maddening thumping. His look
was almost accusatory, but Anne convinced herself that was
impossible. She had just met the man. Determined to prove
she was merely being fanciful, Anne lifted her chin and boldly
returned his stare.

He gave her a dark, seductive smile that revealed a depth of
raw masculine virility far more appropriate for the bedchamber
than the ballroom.

Anne's jaw nearly dropped. Unnerved, she flashed a brief, restrained smile and pulled her eyes away from the stranger. Nicole was chatting animatedly with the earl and her parents, and Anne pretended great interest in their conversation. In truth she was desperately attempting to regulate her breathing.

"May I escort you into the ballroom, Miss Paget?"

His voice, deep, strong and masculine, seemed to come from far away. Yet when Anne shifted her attention toward him, he stood no more than a few feet in front of her, his vivid eyes holding her captive once again.

An abrupt silence greeted his request.

Even Nicole ceased speaking, in mid-sentence. Anne's entire family stared at Lord Richard as if he had taken leave of his senses. Anne? He had requested Anne's company? This simply did not happen, especially when she was in the presence of one of her sisters.

Anne was always the last one chosen, if at all. More often than not she sat among the elderly matrons and chaperons, keeping a sharp eye on the activities of her sisters as they danced and flirted until the wee hours of the morning.

The earl cleared his throat. "Umm, Lord Richard, would you kindly escort Miss Paget, the charming Grecian goddess, to the buffet so I may dance with the lovely Queen Elizabeth?"

Anne pressed her lips together nervously, realizing her host was probably trying to smooth over an awkward misunderstanding. Naturally, Lord Richard really meant to ask Nicole to accompany him. Didn't he?

"I would be delighted to bring Miss Paget to the buffet after I claim the first dance with our good Queen Bess," Lord Richard countered.

Anne's father coughed. Her mother began fanning herself with a short fluttering motion, launching puffy clouds of powder from her wig into the air. Nicole stood completely still, her mouth visible beneath her mask, shaped into a perfect oval.

Anne felt a trickle of sweat run down her back and hoped

the stain would not show. She hated being so conspicuous, the object of everyone's undivided attention. Yet was it so completely extraordinary to imagine that this handsome stranger had chosen her over her sister? Especially since they were both wearing masks and he could not possibly appreciate the full impact of Nicole's fair beauty.

Drawing herself up, Anne stared hard at Lord Richard. His expression was one of open innocence, but she suspected there was a very deliberate reason for his request. She was genuinely puzzled, but also intrigued.

"I would be honored, my lord," Anne replied in a soft voice.

He bowed politely before offering his arm, yet his deep green eyes did not leave her face. Anne was immediately glad the mask she had crafted for her costume was the one component of the outfit that fit her perfectly. It covered most of her face except her mouth and jaw. Combined with the elaborate red wig she was wearing, it somehow seemed to protect her from Lord Richard's penetrating gaze.

With her fingers resting lightly on his sleeve, Anne slowly descended the staircase. It was difficult to walk smoothly. The skirt of her costume was widely flared and jutted out stiffly from her hips, which were padded by great folds of cloth creating a drum shape. The stiff ruff that fanned out behind her head made quick turns of her neck impossible.

The dress might have been considered simple in Queen Elizabeth's time but it was a far more elaborate and cumbersome outfit than Anne had ever worn. She only hoped that she would be able to move about the room with at least a hint of grace.

Lord Richard brought her to the edge of the ballroom and they watched the glittering, brightly dressed crowd swirl past them. The lack of conversation should have been unnerving, but Anne felt oddly calm. When he wasn't scrutinizing her, Lord Richard's powerful presence gave her an almost protected feeling.

Then he touched her arm. The warmth of his fingers easily

penetrated the thin material of her sleeve, and pleasure flushed through her. How strange. The tingling sensations seemed to run from the top of her head down to her toes. Anne took a deliberate breath and told herself to calm down.

She was acting like a green girl, an innocent child at her first grown-up party. Lord Richard was merely leading her onto the dance floor. There was no need to be so flustered. Yet how odd that the warmth of his fingers had sent her heart racing.

Striving to gain her equilibrium, Anne muttered the first thing that popped into her head.

"Do you have an affinity for queens?" she inquired as they joined the set forming on the dance floor. "Is that why you partnered me for this dance instead of my sister?"

"Redheads," Lord Richard answered with a sly grin.

Anne felt herself blushing behind her mask. "Then I must in good conscience tell you the truth, my lord. I am wearing a wig."

"I know."

The rhythm of the music came together and their dance began. Lord Richard slid his arm possessively around Anne's waist, and she stifled the cry of surprise in her throat, realizing that their dance was to be a waltz.

Anne chided herself for being so foolish. What was wrong with her? She had never been the belle of any ball but she had danced the waltz countless times with many different men. She swallowed the apprehension in her throat and fixed her eyes on an imaginary point over Lord Richard's left shoulder. When the dance began, she was ready. Or so she thought.

It was like being awake during a glorious, exciting dream. He danced beautifully. Anne followed his lead naturally, gliding and twirling gracefully about the floor. As they whirled around the crowded room, Anne tried not to dwell on how Lord Richard made her feel. Every nerve ending was more taut, every touch more intense, every smell more pungent. He was somehow able to heighten all of her senses just by his close proximity.

He was so tall and broad and muscular. Even with her considerable height and even wider padded skirts, he easily dwarfed her. There was something intimate, almost forbidden about the way he held her in his arms. She felt like his possession and was completely puzzled why that feeling brought her an unexpected rush of excitement instead of a logical sense of dismay.

A young buck sporting an eye patch and a lace-ruffled shirt barely missed colliding with them, but on the second circuit around the ballroom he knocked squarely into Anne.

The hand at the small of her back drew her closer.

"I've got you," Lord Richard whispered softly.

Flustered, Anne raised her eyes. The tips of her breasts were touching his black evening jacket. A wave of acute tension fluttered through her chest and stomach. The voice of strict, proper training inside her head told her to pull away immediately, but Anne ignored it. Softly she pressed herself forward, helpless to control these crazy, newly awakened feelings.

The muscles across Lord Richard's shoulders went rigid beneath her fingers and his eyes grew dark. The look he gave her made Anne's skin feel hot, then cold.

He is going to kiss me, she thought wildly. Rattled by the preposterous notion, all Anne's fogged brain could register was the simple truth that she very much wanted him to do so. *And I shall delight in kissing him back!*

"Pardon me," the young pirate sang merrily, "I do hope I missed smashing your feet." He grinned sheepishly as he danced away.

The cheerful apology effectively shattered the mood. Anne pulled herself back to a respectable distance, struggling to adopt an air of nonchalance that was total affectation. She nervously flexed her fingers and felt Lord Richard's strong muscles shift beneath her hands.

How very different his body was from hers. She remembered the time she had seen a group of farm workers laboring in the fields stripped of their shirts. Bronzed backs and chests, muscles straining with effort as they lifted and hauled.

Yet Anne strongly suspected that Lord Richard's unclothed form would put them all to shame. He was the very essence of male beauty. The artist in her longed to see and feel and explore this strange, intoxicating man at her leisure, yet the woman she was did not dare.

"That clod has stepped on your gown and torn the hem," Lord Richard growled.

Anne shrugged her shoulders. "He is merely enjoying himself. The pirate and pretty young shepherdess make a rather fetching couple, do they not?"

"With feet like that he should be dancing with the sheep, not a shepherdess," Lord Richard muttered. "In a barnyard."

Anne smiled. "When the dance is finished I shall order him to be imprisoned in the tower. Will that be sufficient punishment for his accidental crime of gown tearing?"

"You should hack off all his toes and feed them to the hounds," Lord Richard insisted. "In retribution for his clumsiness and to ensure the safety of all the other dancing couples."

Anne gasped. Lord Richard turned his head sharply, as if realizing he had just expressed a graphically violent sentiment to a lady.

He cleared his throat. "Forgive my lack of sensibility, Miss Paget. When one has witnessed the type of cruelty toward humanity that war brings, you occasionally forget that gentility still exits in the world."

Anne's initial shock at his blunt words disappeared.

"Ah, but you forget, my lord, I am a warrior queen, accustomed to such violence," Anne replied in a quiet, sensitive voice. She stroked his sleeve in a calm, comforting manner. "Did you fight at the battle of Waterloo?"

"No. I returned to England shortly after the battle of Talavera. My family needed me."

The stroking hand stopped. An unexpected knot began to

curl in Anne's stomach. What sort of family had he returned to? A wife? The notion that he was married left a sour taste on her tongue, yet she could not in all honesty understand why she should care if he had a wife.

Perhaps it was because she felt such an intense attraction for him, and while it was madness to dream that perchance Lord Richard might also find her attractive, it was a harmless fantasy. If he was married, however, the situation would become utterly distasteful, almost immoral in Anne's opinion.

"Is your wife here with you this evening, my lord?"

"I am a widower."

Anne released the breath she had been holding. She was so intent upon hearing his answer that she barely noticed he spoke of his widower state without any trace of emotion in his voice.

They twirled gracefully around the ballroom one final time. Anne felt a pang of regret pierce her heart when the last strains of the music died away. She had so enjoyed being held in his arms. She curtsied low and waited to be escorted to a quiet corner where she strongly suspected she would spend the remainder of the evening craning her neck searching for Lord Richard while she pretended disinterest in his whereabouts.

But instead of returning her to the sidelines, Lord Richard steered her away from the crowd and out the open French doors. Heart thumping madly, Anne allowed herself to be led down into the garden to a secluded spot among the flowers and trees.

Now what? Would he pull her into his arms and steal a kiss? With uncharacteristic recklessness Anne secretly hoped that was his intent. Still, she cautioned herself to be sensible.

Whereas she had never been overly disappointed by her lack of male admirers, tonight she felt a strange, perplexing need for Lord Richard to find her desirable. Just once she wondered how it would feel to be wanted, especially by this extraordinarily powerful man.

If she indulged this strange temptation, however, it must

only be on this one magical night. Her future plans of freedom and independence would not be jeopardized by the complication of a male relationship.

" 'Tis a lovely evening," Anne volunteered. "Though perhaps a bit warm. Is it usually this warm in Devon at this time of year?"

"It's July."

"Well, of course I know what month it is," Anne replied with a slight laugh. "I can assure you, my lord, the summers in Cornwall are never this warm."

"Is that where you are from? Cornwall?"

Anne's step faltered slightly. "No. I grew up in Hampshire. We keep a house in London, but with the season nearly over Papa gladly accepted Sir Reginald Wilford's kind invitation to visit. He is a distant cousin of my mother's."

Anne turned her head up toward the sky, deliberately avoiding Lord Richard's sharp green eyes. She had never before questioned the unusual way her family lived. Especially since the plan was of her own devise and necessary in order for them to remain members of polite society. Yet she felt uncomfortable telling Lord Richard the half-truths she had grown so accustomed to uttering.

"I am rather surprised," Lord Richard replied. An undercurrent of accusation crept into his voice. "I have known Sir Reginald since I was a young boy. I always found him to be a somber and reclusive man, something of a hermit. I find it difficult imagining him inviting a parcel of energetic relatives for a prolonged visit."

"Goodness, you make us sound like a tribe of primitives," Anne said. Her hand fluttered to her neck and she adjusted the stiff collar of her costume.

"Sir Reginald has been most welcoming. My father has a keen eye for horseflesh and has been advising him on the acquisition of several prime mares. Mother has generously lent her assistance in the running of the household and shared some of her best recipes with Sir Reginald's cook. He remarked just last evening that he has never sat down to a finer table.''

Anne paused for a breath. Gracious, she was babbling. He must think she was the biggest fool, but Lord Richard's inquiries into her personal affairs made her very nervous.

''I stand corrected, Miss Paget. Sir Reginald is indeed fortunate in his choice of house guests. Pray tell me, what exactly do you do to enhance Sir Reginald's dull life?''

Anne decided she did not appreciate the mocking edge in Lord Richard's voice. She stiffened her spine and held his gaze steadily as she spoke.

''I keep my two sisters and my two young brothers out of doors as much as possible, and when they are inside the manor house I move them to an unoccupied section so Sir Reginald can enjoy the quiet he so treasures.''

Anne knew she had struck home with her answer by the slight frown that appeared on Lord Richard's handsome face. ''You are a most resourceful woman.''

''You need not sound so astonished, my lord,'' Anne countered. ''It takes only good manners and common sense to remain a pleasant house guest.''

They came to a secluded section of garden surrounded by hedges. Without speaking, Lord Richard grasped her elbow and sat her down on the stone bench strategically placed inside the small maze. He immediately joined her, sitting closer than was strictly proper.

Anne breathed deeply of the night air. It was filled with the distinctive scent of rose mingling with an edge of expectancy. Senses heightened with almost unbearable anticipation, she waited.

''Will you remove your mask?'' Lord Richard asked, reaching boldly for it.

Suddenly Anne felt frightened. She knew she wasn't beautiful or enticing or provocative. Fearing that once Lord Richard saw her pleasant but plain features he would no longer find her worthy of his attentions, she held up her hand to forestall the removal of her mask.

"Please?" he coaxed.

Honesty won out over curiosity. It had been an exhilarating flirtation, and if it were to end now, then so be it. She grasped the mask between her fingers and slowly pulled it away from her face.

"You are so very lovely, my dear," he whispered in a deep, strong voice.

Although seated, Anne suddenly felt weak at the knees.

Richard held her gaze and fought to keep his eyes as blank as his expression. She was not at all as he imagined. Listening to Nigel describe his darling Nicole, he had pictured a tiny woman with a provocative stare and an annoying giggle. Rather like her older sister, the busty Grecian nymph.

But she was none of those things. Intelligent, amusing, even kind. A woman who lived by her wits. He saw immediately how Nigel would be smitten with her, but what could she possibly see in his nephew? He was far too young and spoiled to stimulate the bold Miss Paget.

Lord Mulgrave reached out his hand and gently traced the curves of her face. She wasn't conventionally or strikingly beautiful, but he had been completely honest when he told her she was lovely. She had smooth, flawless skin, light brown expressive eyes, a straight nose and generous lips on a pretty mouth.

A very pretty mouth. A very pretty enticing mouth. Knowing he shouldn't yet unable to resist, Richard held her face softly between his fingers, bent his head and captured her lips in a searing kiss.

He wasn't sure how she would react. He half expected her to push him away and slap his face since she was supposed to be in love with Nigel.

He could feel her initial surprise. She stiffened and pulled back for a fraction of a second. He splayed his hand against her back and held her in place, effectively cutting off her retreat. But he did not force himself on her. Instead he waited with mounting desire for her to make the next move.

"I really should not," she choked out in a harsh whisper.

Frustration surged through him at her words. Tamping down his rioting passion, Richard shifted uncomfortably on the stone bench, resigning himself to accept her appropriate response.

Then to his utter delight and astonishment she sighed deeply, lifted herself forward and kissed him back. Without restraint.

She parted her lips slightly and Richard ran his tongue slowly, sensually across the seam of her mouth, tasting her sweetness. His heart beat in a wild pulse of need as she softened and molded herself against his chest, clearly aroused by their embrace.

His disappointment over her apparent lack of morals was quickly overshadowed by incredible sensations streaking through him. Their kiss was an intoxicating blend of pleasure and fascination. The thrust and stroke of his tongue was met with equal fire, and Richard felt the heat and coiling tension rise inside him.

She was incredible! Soft and warm, hot and sweet. Knowing it was wrong, but not caring one whit, Richard tightened his embrace.

"You are truly beautiful." He whispered the words against her neck before pressing his lips against the white column of her throat.

He set his arms tightly around her, one on her waist, the other on her shoulder. He pushed aside the cumbersome ruff collar around her neck. It crumbled like a deck of cards, revealing the luscious creamy white skin beneath. She was not a voluptuous woman but her feminine curves easily inflamed his senses.

He trailed a line of soft wet kisses down to her breasts, expertly drawing down the top of her gown with his thumbs. Her skin felt hot against the moisture of his tongue, and he could hear her harsh breathing even though her face was turned down against the top of his head.

By the time the rustling sound of clothing and footsteps approaching registered in Richard's passion hazed brain, it was too late. His immediate reaction was protection, and almost without thinking he stood abruptly on his feet, thrusting himself in front of the disheveled Miss Paget.

Ian stood before him, and alongside the earl was Lady Althen. Their expressions of stunned disbelief informed him that he had in no way concealed the fact that he had been kissing Miss Paget. Rather thoroughly.

"Good evening." It was difficult to smile with clenched teeth, but somehow Richard managed.

"What in heaven's name is going on here?" Lady Althen exclaimed in a high-pitched squeal. "Anne, are you alright?"

Anne? Richard spun around and glared at the woman on the bench. This delectable creature he had nearly seduced was not Nigel's darling Nicole?

"Gracious, Mother, I am fine," she replied breathlessly. She struggled momentarily with the neckline of her gown before succeeding in covering her lovely breasts. "Please refrain from becoming hysterical. I don't have any smelling salts with me."

Lady Althen humphed with annoyance, but her daughter ignored her. Remarkable. She had just been caught in a compromising position with a man she barely knew, yet she was lecturing her parent.

Ian spoke, but Richard was not listening. Anne? He felt his mind spiral into a dark, dizzying vortex. Who the devil was Anne, and where in the hell was Nigel's darling Nicole?

Chapter Three

Lord Richard stared hard at Anne and for a few seconds their eyes held. He was obviously puzzled and clearly annoyed. But why? It would surely be her reputation, not his, that suffered if anyone else discovered their shocking behavior.

"Who the devil are you?" he inquired in a deep, flat tone that did little to conceal his anger.

Anne took offense at his question and the attitude that accompanied it. Her heart was still racing from their passionate embrace but she gazed at him in a very direct manner and stated coolly, "You know very well who I am, sir, since our esteemed host introduced us earlier this evening. I am Miss Paget." Anne narrowed her eyes at him. "But who the devil are you? Or do you lack either a title or last name to go with the first, Lord Richard?"

His expression became unreadable as his anger lessened. Then he did the one thing she was completely unprepared for. He smiled. A brilliant, white-tooth grin of pure amusement.

"I am Mulgrave," he replied. "The Earl of Mulgrave actually, although my friends call me Richard."

"I doubt I shall be counting myself among their numbers, my lord." Anne humphed loudly to hide her shock.

How could it be? This man was Nigel's horrid uncle? The one that Nicole so dreaded meeting tonight. What an impossible mess!

"Perhaps it would be best if we adjourn to my second-floor drawing room for a private chat?" their host, the Earl of Rosslyn, suggested.

"A perfectly civilized suggestion, my lord," Lady Althen purred sweetly. She adjusted the silk shawl draped around her shoulders. "Come along, Anne. Though the air is warm it is horribly damp. I cannot imagine the havoc it is wreaking upon my wig. I am certain I must look a fright."

The Earl of Rosslyn immediately assured Lady Althen that she looked absolutely lovely.

Anne rolled her eyes. It was ludicrous, yet not surprising, that during the biggest crisis of Anne's so far rather dull life her mother was most concerned about her own appearance instead of her daughter's situation.

Lady Althen moved forward, apparently having decided she did indeed look well enough to leave the darkness of the garden. Lord Richard, or rather the *Earl of Mulgrave,* quickly imitated her mother's actions, clearly eager to also depart.

Anne hesitated. She felt the situation was rapidly moving beyond her control and she needed a few moments to marshal her wits. Her unease increased when she noted the unspoken communication that passed between Lord Mulgrave and Lord Rosslyn, but the look the two men exchanged was too brief for Anne to decipher.

At least her mother was no longer hysterical, Anne consoled herself, deciding it would be best to be grateful for small blessings. After discovering that her daughter's would-be seducer was a wealthy and titled gentleman, Lady Althen had turned nauseatingly friendly and flirtatious. It would almost be comical if it wasn't so pathetic.

Lord Mulgrave held out his arm toward Anne. Without breaking the steady gaze she held his eyes with, Anne stepped back slightly, knowing her mother would be unable to resist the opportunity. True to form, Lady Althen pushed herself forward and grasped eagerly onto Lord Mulgrave's sleeve. Anne noticed his lips twitch, but he did not utter a sound.

That left Anne with her host as an escort. She glanced suspiciously at Lord Rosslyn before settling her hand lightly on his arm. He merely smiled politely, either unconcerned or unaware of her scrutiny. In silence the two unlikely couples strolled through the fragrant garden with shafts of moonlight illuminating the way. Although a great deal of the earlier enchantment was missing, Anne could still appreciate the beauty and mythical quality of nature's nighttime splendor.

They entered the house through a seldom-used side entrance and climbed a deserted back staircase to the second floor. Upon reaching the dimly lit landing, a moment of organized confusion occurred. In all the shuffling and jostling Anne saw her mother being whisked down the hallway by Lord Rosslyn. They disappeared from view before Anne had a chance to speak.

She found herself suddenly alone with Lord Richard.

"That was rather neatly done," she complimented the earl, understanding finally the unspoken communication that had occurred between Lord Mulgrave and his dear friend Lord Rosslyn.

Silently Lord Mulgrave took her hand, drew her into the empty drawing room and shut the door firmly behind them.

The unexpected contact of his warm fingers on her bare flesh sent her nerves quivering. Shocked, Anne tried to pull away, but she could feel the heightened tension gripping the earl. Prudently deciding now was not the moment to assert her independence, Anne allowed herself to be led to a nearby settee. She gratefully sank down upon the brocade silk, feeling as though the usually solid muscles in her legs had turned into the consistency of oatmeal.

Anne neatly folded the pieces of the ruff collar she still carried and stuffed them in the pocket of her gown. There weren't many. Slightly embarrassed, she realized the majority of her collar was strewn about the garden floor. Along with most of her common sense, she thought grimly.

"I much prefer to have our discussion in private," Lord Mulgrave began. "I hope you don't mind."

Anne slowly raised one eyebrow. "And if I do object, my lord, will you release me?"

"After we have spoken," he insisted, with a sigh that was apparent, even though inaudible. He moved about the room with obvious familiarity, lighting most of the candles that were strategically placed on various tables. The room soon glowed with a brightness that resembled daylight. "I know that you are Miss Paget but I take it that you are not, as I believed, Miss Nicole Paget. You are instead one of her numerous sisters?"

"Is that what this is all about? You thought I was Nicole?"

Anne blinked against the brightness, wishing he had not lit so many candles. She felt exposed and under close examination, rather like a fly pinned beneath a quizzing glass. It was not a pleasant feeling.

Lord Mulgrave stroked his chin. "I was given to understand that Nicole was going to be dressed as Queen Elizabeth this evening. When we were introduced I naturally assumed you were Nicole. I did not discover my mistake until we were . . . interrupted by your mother and Ian."

He really had thought she was Nicole? Anne let loose a hollow laugh. How totally fitting that her one daring, exciting flirtation occurred only because she had been mistaken for her beautiful sister. Would she never learn?

Anne felt an almost overwhelming urge to cry, but she quashed it. She was determined to walk away from this insanity with a modicum of her pride and dignity. At this rather miserable juncture in the evening, it seemed all she had left.

"I am Anne, oldest of the Paget sisters. Nicole and I decided to switch costumes earlier today. Obviously, we had no idea it would cause anyone any sort of hardship."

Especially me, Anne added silently to herself. She stood on her feet and stiffened her spine, aware of how utterly foolish she must appear.

"I apologize for the . . . um . . . inconvenience," she said. "And now that we have cleared up this silly misunderstanding, my lord, I shall return to the ballroom. I daresay no one would have noticed my absence, but I am certain all the ladies in attendance will be clamoring for your company."

Lord Mulgrave smiled. "You have a flatteringly unrealistic opinion of my charms, Miss Paget," he replied softly. "Yet I confess I find your views of my desirability rather stimulating."

The smile on the earl's face became a bit lazier and more relaxed. Anne nervously backed up and stumbled against the settee. It hit her squarely in the back of the knees. She awkwardly sat down again.

His eyes never once left her face. Anne shifted uncomfortably on the plush cushions as the strangeness of the situation came sharply into focus. She was alone with a man she had only moments before been kissing with all the womanly abandonment and passion she had long denied existed deep within herself.

He stimulated and attracted her in ways she had never thought possible. Even now, as he stood a respectful distance away, every nerve ending in her body tingled, knowing that all it would take would be the gentle touch of his warm fingers for her hard-won calm to swiftly deteriorate.

Immediately Anne vowed to keep both her distance and composure. She was too wise, too experienced, to fall prey to a man, no matter how unusual he made her feel. She was not a silly young girl whose head was easily turned by a handsome face and impossibly broad shoulders. She was a sensible woman. A practical woman.

Yet she could not forget how truly wonderful it had been when the earl kissed and caressed her. She had not known she could respond so wantonly, that she could feel such blinding hunger, such desperate need. She, the practical, level-headed Anne Paget, had felt almost giddy with pleasure, alive with forbidden sensations.

Anne felt herself starting to drift away from reality. The fantasy of being a desirable woman, wanted by such a strong, powerful, attractive man, began to dominate her thoughts. Then Anne heard his voice in the distance, deep and certain, and knew she had completely, utterly lost her wits.

"What did you say?"

"I asked you to become my wife."

Anne turned her head and shot him an irate glare. "I find your joke and your humor to be in equally poor taste, my lord."

"It is no joke, Miss Paget. Forgive me for stating the obvious, but given the circumstances, I fear we have little choice."

He joined her on the sofa and touched her arm lightly. Anne muffled a cry and moved as far away from him as she could manage.

"There are always choices in life," Anne replied. Breathless, her heart racing in an irregular rhythm, Anne forced herself to remain clear and lucid. The very idea of a match between them was completely out of the question. "If you knew me better you would be aware of the fact that I seldom, if ever, make the conventional or appropriate choice."

"Good. I find your philosophy of life refreshing." His eyes touched hers briefly. "Within limits, of course. We shall provide a well-tuned balance for each other since I always take the responsible path."

"Not in this instance," Anne interjected. "I have never heard of a more radical, impulsive, ill-conceived and totally ridiculous solution to a problem in my life. We have known each other for less than four hours. You may feel honor-bound to offer for me, my lord, but I feel no such compulsion to accept your offer."

"It pleases me to discover that your passionate nature extends beyond the physical."

"Insulting me is not an effective method for furthering your cause."

"Perhaps you are right. Although my remark was meant as a compliment." The earl leaned back against the settee and folded his arms. "I am open to suggestions as to the best way to insure you will accept my offer. Do you care to offer any?"

Anne could not hold back her smile. Why must he be so charming and witty? For a brief, insane moment she was tempted to seriously consider his outrageous offer, suspecting that life with him would never be ordinary. But in the long run it would not be fair. To either of them. Anne knew her destiny lay elsewhere.

"A calm, rational examination of the facts, my lord, reveals that only two individuals witnessed our . . . our . . . moment of indiscretion." Anne cleared her throat. "My mother will never breathe a word about what she saw, once I explain the situation. I assume Lord Rosslyn can also be trusted to hold his tongue?"

Lord Mulgrave scratched the top of his head in puzzlement. "I would think that most mothers would be out for blood if they discovered their daughter in such a compromised position. Or perhaps that outrage is being reserved for your father, Miss Paget?"

"What utter nonsense! My father is many things but he would not be so foolhardy as to challenge you, especially when there is no need." Anne stopped speaking and glanced over at him. He met her glare with an expectant look. "Certainly you do not think I used this occasion to trap myself a husband?"

The earl shrugged noncommittally in response.

Anne took a short breath and called upon years of practice to maintain her composure. All she really knew about this man was that he was Nigel's uncle, his kisses curled her toes, and Nicole was more than a little frightened of his powerful influence. " 'Tis nothing personal, sir. I made my decision years ago. I will not marry. Anyone. No matter how sought after or eligible. You are an eligible bachelor, are you not, my lord?''

"Many of society's matrons consider me a great matrimonial prize.'' Lord Mulgrave frowned vaguely. "I don't often participate in town events, but I possess an old, respectable title and have a healthy income. It has long been rumored that I shall never marry again. Perversely, I believe that makes me an all the more impressive catch.''

Anne wrinkled her forehead. "You make it sound like you are a trout, sir, while the entire female population of the beau monde are a bunch of canny fisherwomen rising early each morning in hopes of landing the great prize.''

"An astute, though unflattering observation, my dear.'' The earl raised his eyebrows. "A trout?''

"True, that was an unkind comparison.'' Anne smiled mischievously. "Trouts are not known to be very intelligent. Perhaps a shark is a more apt description.''

"Sharks are predatory creatures,'' Lord Mulgrave said softly, "known for swiftly destroying their enemies. They are feared by most, including man.'' He leaned closer, caught her hand and gently lifted it to his lips. "I would not want you to think I am as equally ruthless.''

Anne did not doubt for an instant that he could be. Lord Mulgrave's manner, his bearing, his very presence all shouted that he was a man seldom thwarted. Yet thwart him she would.

She tugged on her captured hand, but he would not release it. Anne's gaze intensified as she prepared herself for battle. Yet her forceful words were lost the moment his firm lips brushed against the sensitive skin of her pulsing wrist. Anne felt an aching shudder race through her body. The need to respond was almost uncontrollable, but she somehow resisted.

She leaned away from him. He finished his marvelous caress

and lifted his head but still held her hand. The contact felt impossibly intimate. Anne sent him what she suspected was a rather poor excuse for a withering glance.

"The fact remains, my lord, I detest fishing of any sort. So you have no fear of my trying to *catch* you."

Richard knew from her dismissive tone that Miss Paget intended to bolt out the door, head high, back straight, heavy skirts swishing furiously with indignation.

So he held tightly to her hand, simply refusing to let her leave. She struggled mightily for a few minutes, then blew out her breath and waited. He waited too.

The raw, almost primitive emotions she evoked inside him were oddly heightened by her refusal to become his wife. Richard had been furious when he first discovered she was not Nicole, but Anne's no-nonsense handling of the situation had quickly squelched his annoyance. He was forced to admit, in all fairness, that it was certainly not *her* fault that *he* made a mistake.

Yet the bizarre events of the evening had set in motion an entirely new set of circumstances that neither of them had the power to stop. The loss of a reputation was almost impossible to recover from, especially for a woman. And even if Anne's mother and Ian said nothing about the glimpse of passion they had seen, he and Anne had already been absent from the ball for too long. Surely by now some gossip-minded tabby had noted that fact.

When he sensed that Anne had regained her composure, Richard opened his fingers and released her hand. She snatched it away from him as if he had burnt her and settled it on her lap.

"I understand how you might be experiencing a bit of shock over this evening's events," he began quietly. "I confess I'm feeling a bit out of sorts myself. However, like it or not, the facts cannot be changed, the past cannot be altered.

"You are a gently born woman that I have compromised

in the home of my best friend. Once this becomes common knowledge, and it will, then you shall be shunned. Ignored. An outcast, no longer accepted in polite society. There exists one honorable solution. We will marry.''

"I thought only women were given to fits of melodrama, my lord,'' Anne sneered. "I do not share your dire predictions of my future. I have neither a grand title nor a substantial fortune. I am not young, I am not beautiful. Frankly speaking, in society's eyes I am nothing. Though not shunned, I am already ignored.

"If my moment of madness becomes public knowledge, which I doubt it shall, perhaps it will briefly elevate me to a status of notoriety, but that will quickly fade. Even you must concede that society scandals come and go at breakneck speed. I insist there is no need for us to do something as foolish as enter into marriage.''

"Is there someone else?''

"Goodness, no.'' Anne jumped up from the settee and paced about the room. "I should be a very vulgar woman indeed if I allowed you such liberties while my affections were engaged elsewhere.''

"What of your family, Miss Paget? Scandal has a nasty way of touching those around it. Your sisters will suffer from your disgrace.''

Anne bit her lip in consternation, and Richard knew he had struck a nerve. Yet she locked her eyes on his and stated boldly, "My sisters and I shall brazen it out. Together. I will not be threatened, my lord. Or backed into a corner.''

Richard fought to keep an amused smile from his lips. She was magnificent in her defiance. Her eyes sparkled with life and her gentle voice was strong and sure. He admired the passion she used to defend herself and her family, anticipating the days and nights when that passion would be turned toward him.

Cowering women tended to bring out the beast in him. One

forcefully issued command and they were easily controlled. But a woman with a sharp mind and a strong will stimulated him in an entirely different manner.

Of course, too stubborn a will could become tedious. Yet Richard was confident that it would take but a short time for Anne to capitulate. She did not strike him as an impulsive creature; the idea of marrying a man she barely knew was obviously difficult for her to accept. In the end her intelligent mind would guide her to the only sensible choice.

"It appears we have reached an impasse, Miss Paget."

"An impasse?"

"I declare we must marry and you insist we should not," Richard said. "Since I strongly suspect that neither of us shall change our minds within the next few minutes, I suggest we return to the party."

"Gladly."

Her instant, pert reply stung. She was obviously thrilled at the thought of escaping his company. Deciding he could not possibly let this affront to his masculine charm go unchallenged, Richard advanced toward her.

She widened her eyes as he approached but held her ground. He smiled wolfishly. No retreat in the face of danger for his brave Anne.

"Just a parting token of my regard, my dear," he said, settling his hands over her shoulders. "Perhaps this will help convince you that there are many benefits in spending the rest of your days as my countess."

He didn't hesitate for an instant, knowing he had only a brief moment to make his point. Richard bent his head and took her mouth in a fiery kiss that left his pulse pounding and a throbbing ache low in his gut.

She did not respond at first, but he would not allow her to retreat. His hand cupped the back of her head and he held her in place, kissing her again until he tasted her answering desire.

A soft moan rose from her throat as their lips melded together.

Richard had meant the embrace to be gentle yet insistent, but it quickly turned fierce and possessive. His tongue glided inside her warm mouth, probing and teasing.

He felt famished when he kissed her, like a man tasting fresh water after spending weeks in the dry desert. He simply could not get enough of her sweetness. Protest she might against the possibility of a future life together, but Richard knew her weakness. Relished it, in fact.

She responded physically to him. Quite unmistakably, with a fierceness and honesty and pure enjoyment that set his blood to boiling.

He had not given serious thought to marrying again, assuming that at some point in the future he might find a woman with whom he could share a warm friendship and mutual contentment. But now he dared to dream of more, firmly believing that there could be something strong and lasting between him and Anne.

Richard's hand closed over her breast. His fingers eagerly stroked the delightful softness, and the nipple tightened into a firm bud. He ached to move his mouth against her breast, to suckle hungrily on her delicious sweetness. The heady combination of innocence and sensuality she exhibited drove him wild.

Yet slowly he pulled away. Richard wasn't exactly sure why he stopped. She was not struggling. The inviting arch of her back, the soft moan escaping through her lips, the fingers of her right hand laced in his hair all bespoke of her eager participation.

Yet he could also feel her other hand trembling, pressing against his shoulder in an unconscious plea for him to retreat. Her breathing was erratic and her passion was evident but so was her confusion. And even though Richard could feel the rapid hammering of her heart beneath his palm, he could also sense the hesitation in the lovely body that was pressed so intimately against his own.

Reluctantly, Richard paused and drew away from her, knowing this was not the time to pursue. This woman was to become his wife. They would hopefully spend a lifetime together. A happy lifetime. He would not seduce her into compliance. It was sneaky and unfair, especially considering her passionate nature and his superior experience.

There was no honor, no challenge in winning such a clearly mismatched battle. Richard admired her spirit and her intelligence. He would use logic and cunning to achieve his goal but he would not sink to seduction.

However, mastering his smoldering passions took several minutes. He held her loosely yet securely in his arms and waited for the physical effects of her nearness to fade. After all, it would be rather bad form to march into Ian's ballroom with the rigid proof of his desire for the lovely Anne prominently on display for all to shockingly see.

"We should return to the party," Richard said in a somewhat breathless voice.

He watched her eyes flutter open and knew the exact moment when reality registered in her brain. Her face flushed scarlet, but instead of jumping away and slapping his face, as most outraged virgins would do, Anne straightened her shoulders and lifted her chin.

Meeting his eyes squarely, she announced, "I assume you know the way, since you are such a good friend of Lord Rosslyn's."

Richard smiled approvingly. No display of maidenly temper or tears. Inwardly he congratulated himself on this incredible turn of fate, having no doubt that she would make a magnificent countess.

"Come along, Miss Paget."

She stared so long at his outstretched arm that Richard began to suspect she would not take it. Finally she inhaled deeply and placed the tips of her fingers on his sleeve. He extinguished several of the lit candles and they left the room.

Richard deliberately took the longest route back to Ian's ballroom, prolonging their time together, leading Miss Paget through a winding maze of hallways. He made an occasional comment on an interesting piece of furniture or an unusual work of art. Good manners prevented her from remaining silent and she mumbled appropriate responses without doing any more than quickly glancing at the objects.

Their return to the ballroom was somewhat anticlimactic. Richard was so certain that everyone would have noticed their absence, he half expected a hush of shock and outrage to occur when they came into view.

Yet no one seemed to take much notice of their reappearance. The music played harmoniously and dancers swirled by them in graceful patterns. Richard shook his head. Maybe Anne was right, he did seem to possess a rather excessive streak of melodrama.

"There should be at least one more waltz before the evening ends, Miss Paget," Richard announced. "You shall dance it with me."

He had not meant to sound so forceful or possessive, but now that they were in a crowd of peers he experienced an overwhelming need to stake his claim on her. To let all the others, especially the eager young bucks, know that she belonged to him and him alone.

Anne turned her head and smiled sweetly up into his eyes.

"I do believe, my lord, there is a far greater chance of it snowing in hell before I waltz again with you."

And with a final, dazzling smile she flounced away.

Chapter Four

"Where have you been? I have been searching for hours and hours trying to find you." Nicole clutched Anne's arm. She pulled her into a quiet corner of the ballroom, then broke off and stared in confusion at her older sibling.

"Where is your mask? And the ruff collar of your gown? Really, Anne, you look quite disheveled."

Anne self-consciously stroked her bare neck. "I clumsily knocked into another dancer and the collar simply fell apart. It was rather embarrassing. I suppose I didn't secure it properly after I refitted the costume for myself. And then my mask began to itch so I removed it and I can't seem to recall exactly where I left it."

Anne made a great show of looking mildly distressed and confused, hoping her sister would soon drop the matter.

"Oh. Well, I'm sorry about your dress, but I have been looking absolutely everywhere for you. When I asked Mother if she had seen you, she gave me a sly look and implied you were with the mysterious Lord Richard, but I knew that was not possible. You met the man hours ago.'' Nicole frowned suspiciously. ''You haven't been with Lord Richard all this time, have you?''

''Don't be daft, Nicole.'' Anne's eyes darted nervously about the area as she hoped no one had overheard her sister's hastily spoken words. The last thing she needed right now was to draw attention to herself. For once her reputation as a plain wallflower would work to her advantage, Anne decided.

''I knew it was impossible,'' Nicole stated knowingly. ''I worry about Mother, Anne. She has always been flighty but I have noticed lately she can be positively addle-brained at times.''

''Exactly,'' Anne agreed, but her emotions were running high and she could not seem to prevent herself from adding, ''Why would a handsome, well-dressed, titled gentleman want to spend the majority of the evening in my company? 'Tis an absolutely ludicrous notion.''

Anne's sarcastic comment drew a baffled stare from her sister. Anne sighed, realizing it was unfair to vent her frustrations on Nicole. Yet it stung deep down inside to know that everyone, including her own sister, found it nearly impossible to fathom that a man, especially an attractive one, would be interested in her.

''Where is Nigel?'' Anne asked, deliberately shifting the conversation to a new direction. ''The music is rather lively this evening. I thought you would take advantage of the masquerade and dance every dance together.''

''I have not seen Nigel for the past hour,'' Nicole said, tossing her head in a flippant manner that Anne knew meant trouble. ''I left him in the card room. I grew tired of watching him play. Half the time I couldn't even understand what was happening. 'Tis difficult following the game when they pass the cards about so quickly.

''However, when I asked him, Nigel rudely refused to leave the table. So I told him that I did not come to this lovely ball to stand behind his chair like some harem slave girl in a crowded card room and watch him make an utter cake of himself.''

"Nigel was gaming?" Anne gnawed the inside of her cheek with worry. This was an unexpected, unpleasant insight into the young man's character. "What happened?"

"Actually, Nigel was winning," Nicole admitted with a nervous smile. "But he was also drinking, more than he is accustomed to, I am certain, and the stakes were steadily rising higher with each subsequent hand of play. Even I know that is a fatal combination. How can one continue to win at cards if your wits become muddled by alcohol?"

Anne looked at her sister with new respect. Nicole always judged her beaus on the amount and variety of the compliments they spouted about her hair, her eyes, her smile, her gown, her laugh. She quickly lost interest in those who fell short in bestowing upon her the adoration she assumed was her due. Usually the more outrageous the flattery, the faster Nicole's interest in her male admirer escalated.

Nigel had always reigned supreme in his ability to utter the most ridiculous and inane compliments in a totally sincere and believable manner. And even though Anne could see that Nicole was upset at being ignored by Nigel earlier this evening, she was clearly more distressed over his reckless behavior. This surprising reaction demonstrated a level of maturity Anne had not credited her younger sister with.

"I'm sure this is a minor transgression on Nigel's part," Anne said soothingly. "He has been under a great strain lately."

Nicole gave an unladylike snort. "What about the strain that I have been under? I have been waiting half the night on pins and needles to meet Nigel's horrid uncle, knowing that I must be charming and kind to a man who blatantly disapproves of me. Does Nigel care about that? No, he does not."

Anne swallowed uncomfortably, reluctant to reveal all she knew about Nigel's horrid uncle. She could barely imagine Nicole's shocked reaction if she told her that she had been kissing Nigel's horrid uncle, rather thoroughly, just moments before, and that he had actually proposed marriage to her. Unbelievable!

"He has a name, you know," Anne said softly. "Nigel's horrid uncle? He is the Earl of Mulgrave."

"I know who he is," Nicole answered curtly, flipping open her hand-painted fan and vigorously waving it in front of her face. "I can scarcely close my eyes at night without reciting his name a hundred times over in my head, silently like a prayer. I swear it gives me nightmares."

Anne smiled patiently at her younger sister. "I just thought it would be best if you started referring to the earl by his title rather than the charming pet name you have concocted."

"You're right." Nicole sighed. She closed her fan and let it dangle from her dainty wrist. "The way my luck has been running, when I finally meet the man my mind will go completely blank and I'll call him Nigel's horrid uncle instead of my lord."

"Not exactly the impression one would hope to make on a future in-law."

"No, it isn't."

The two women stared at each other for a moment, then broke into genuine smiles.

"Let's go to the card room and fetch Nigel," Anne suggested, looping her arm through Nicole's. "I'm sure he will be most apologetic once he learns how distressed you are over his gambling."

"I'm not eager to face him," Nicole said in a small voice. "He has most likely lost his entire quarterly allowance by now."

"Then it is your duty to rescue him before he begins to gamble *next* quarter's allowance."

They started toward the card room but Nicole stopped suddenly. "Men can be quite a bother at times, can't they?" she asked in a thoughtful tone.

Anne turned and faced her sister. "Yes. In many ways they behave like overgrown boys, only men can be more difficult to control. You must always remember, Nicole, in our world a husband wields enormous power over a woman's life. It is essential that the man you choose as your partner must share a similar philosophy and expectations of life. If not, you will be faced with a difficult and unhappy marriage."

"I always thought Nigel and I would agree on everything," Nicole whispered. "At least the important things. Now I am not as certain."

"I don't think you can ever be totally certain," Anne replied honestly. "You must trust your heart but listen to your head. However, it is also unwise to make serious decisions when you are overwrought."

"There's something else." Nicole mulled over her thoughts briefly, chewing steadily on her lower lip before blurting out, "There was a man at the table gambling with Nigel. He was older, not so old as father but certainly older than Nigel, and wickedly handsome. He did not speak directly to me since we were not properly introduced, yet he stared at me. Rudely. And for a rather long time. He had the most disconcerting gray eyes ..."

Anne's senses went on full alert as Nicole's voice trailed off dreamily and a soft flush rose in her cheek.

"Did you discover his name?" Anne inquired sharply.

"I overheard one of the other players address him as Captain Nightingall," Nicole replied eagerly. "Have you ever met him?"

"Not formally, but I have heard of him." Anne frowned in concern. "He is not the sort of man I would encourage any young woman, especially my sister, to take an interest in."

"Really? Why?"

The simple, casually uttered questions did not fool Anne for an instant. Nicole was obviously intrigued by this man, and her interest was definitely heightened by her current anger at

Nigel. All Anne felt she could do now was relate what she knew about Captain Nightingall in the most unflattering light possible. Which wouldn't be hard, considering what she knew of him.

"Nightingall is the younger brother of Viscount Lindsey but aside from his noble name he has little to recommend him. He has a comfortable income that he supplements at the gaming tables. I am told he seldom loses."

Judging from the sparkle in Nicole's eyes, Anne knew she was not creating the impression she wished, but she plunged ahead.

"Nightingall is something of a war hero, though they appear to be in rather large supply these days. If only half the acts of wartime heroism I've heard tell of were true, Napoleon should have been defeated in a week."

"He is sinfully handsome," Nicole interrupted. "Captain Nightingall, I mean. I could not properly judge his height because he was seated, but his muscles looked splendidly firm beneath his coat."

"I have no doubt he is a fine figure of a man," Anne said tersely. "Jaded roués generally are attractive. It helps to offset their terrible reputations. Captain Nightingall is said to be a dedicated bachelor and known to be ruthless when it comes to women. I have heard that he divides his time equally between his mistresses and his gambling."

"His eyes are extraordinary. So very gray. I felt them stray to me again and again. They seemed to be looking into my very soul. It made my heart beat like thunder." Nicole sighed dramatically. "I've never felt this way with any man before, even Nigel. Anne, I simply must meet Captain Nightingall."

Anne scowled in frustration. Her earlier delight at Nicole's brief demonstration of maturity evaporated. Worse, she was failing miserably in her attempts to discourage her sister's interest in this blatantly unsuitable man.

"Have you listened to one word I've said, Nicole? It would

be nothing short of criminal to waste your energy thinking about, let alone spending any time with, a man who clearly lacks the character to return a woman's affections. He is a rake of the worst sort. Thus far only minor scandals have encroached on his good name, but I feel certain they will eventually give way to more serious transgressions.''

Anne wanted to say more but felt a sudden shiver of awareness streak down her back. She lifted her head and scanned the crowd in alarm. She gasped, then stepped back into the shadowy edge of the room to hide the flush she felt rise in her cheek.

Lord Mulgrave stood no more than twenty feet away. He appeared to be engaged in an earnest debate with a tall, good-looking gentleman, but his mesmerizing dark green eyes were trained squarely on her. Anne silently prayed the two men were too far away to have overheard any of her conversation with her sister.

"Egad, there he is!"

I know, Anne wanted to scream before realizing that Nicole did not know exactly who Lord Mulgrave was and thought him to be the innocuous Lord Richard. But Anne did not have an opportunity to enlighten her sister to this rather salient fact.

"It is Captain Nightingall," Nicole said reverently. "He is speaking with Lord Richard. Hurry, Anne, Lord Richard can introduce us."

"Nicole, wait—"

Anne threw out a steady arm to stop Nicole but it was a fruitless effort, as ridiculous as attempting to hold back the stormy sea. Nicole shook off her sister's grasp, deliberately removed her mask and with a mutinous expression on her lovely face advanced toward the two men.

Anne battled her feeling of panic, stealing a moment to collect herself. Then acting against her better judgment, she swallowed hard, lifted her skirts and followed determinedly behind her headstrong sister.

* * *

Richard watched the pair approach with a cautious eye. He had promised himself he would leave Anne in peace for the remainder of the evening and he truly meant to honor that vow. Yet he could not help staring at her the moment he spotted her across the ballroom.

He had felt a rush of exhilaration when he saw Anne raise her chin suddenly, her eyes searching the crowd frantically. He was certain she had sensed his nearness, like an animal sensing its mate. It was a pleasing thought. Although she had refused his marriage proposal, he guessed that an unconscious part of her had already accepted her destiny as his partner.

Richard knew that the pretty, busty young woman by her side was her sister Nicole. Nigel's darling Nicole. Yet according to the account that his good friend Captain Miles Nightingall had just given him, Nigel and his little darling had had a bit of a public tiff this evening in the card room.

The news heartened Richard. He knew that Nigel was far too young and irresponsible for marriage, and this latest behavior confirmed that belief. Richard wanted to please Anne, but not even for her sake would he approve the marriage of his nephew and heir to a mere chit of seventeen with only her lovely face and voluptuous figure to recommend her.

"Lord Richard." Nicole Paget pushed herself forward eagerly. "How lovely to see you again. Would you do the honors and present us?"

Although her comment was supposedly meant for him, Nicole's rapt attention never once wavered from Miles's face. It was a rather extraordinary and humbling experience to be ignored so completely by someone, especially a woman. Richard felt as though he were the peas on her dinner plate and Miles the dessert.

Her manner was far too bold, and Richard's initial reaction was to refuse her request, nay, demand, for an introduction.

He was far more accustomed to giving than taking orders. But the expression on Nicole's face was so intent Richard knew she would have her way in the end.

"Ladies, may I present my friend Captain Miles Nightingall," Richard said after making a brief bow of greeting. "Miss Anne Paget and her younger sister, Nicole."

The women curtsied and smiled. At least Nicole smiled. Brilliantly. Anne merely stared, with a good amount of suspicion and a dash of annoyance on her face.

"I have heard a great deal about you, Captain Nightingall," Anne said in her gentle voice.

"All of it bad, I presume?" Miles responded with a mocking grin.

"Every word." Anne looked as if she wanted to say more but changed her mind. She turned with great purpose toward her sister. "Nicole, you have not yet been fully introduced to Lord Richard."

"What?"

"Lord Richard has been having a bit of fun this evening. All in the spirit of the masquerade, of course," Anne said with a tight smile. "He is actually Lord Mulgrave. The *Earl of Mulgrave.* Nigel's uncle?"

Nicole turned her head so suddenly a blond ringlet wrenched free and tumbled to her shoulder. Well, that got the chit's attention, Richard thought gleefully. She didn't blush, but her expression was one of sheer horror.

Richard felt perversely pleased by her reaction. His eyes shone with devilment as he removed his seldom-used quizzing glass from his coat pocket. Yanking it up by the ribbon, he grasped the handle and held it to his left eye.

"Good evening, Miss Paget," Richard said in his best haughty aristocratic voice, ignoring Miles's snort of laughter. "I vaguely recall my nephew mentioning you once or twice."

"My lord." Nicole pursed her lips and made a deep, slightly unsteady curtsey. "I am honored you remembered my name.

I only wish that Nigel were here. He wanted so very much to make our introduction himself.''

''Really?'' Richard replied, rocking back on his heels in enjoyment. With an exaggerated motion he lifted his chin up and then down, all the while scrutinizing Nicole through the lens of his glass. She held his stare for as long as she could before finally blushing and casting her eyes down.

Richard smiled. It was turning out to be unexpected fun testing this young woman. ''I haven't seen much of my nephew tonight. Captain Nightingall informs me that Nigel has spent the majority of the evening playing faro in the card room. No doubt losing.''

Richard sighed for effect. ''That boy has the worst luck at the gaming tables. He leaves his vouchers all over London, hoping that I'll make good on any debts he cannot pay. 'Tis the way of most young gentlemen, you know. They thrive on reckless excitement, spending the better part of their time roaring drunk and spoiling for trouble.''

Both Nicole and Anne winced visibly, and Richard felt a slight twinge of guilt over the lies. Still, it was necessary to provide a detailed, exaggerated list of Nigel's real and imagined shortcomings to the Paget sisters. Richard was steadfast in his determination that the only alliance occurring between the two families would be his and Anne's.

An awkward and conspicuous silence ensued until Miles gamely suggested, ''Since neither of you ladies are dancing this set, perhaps we may escort you into supper?''

Unenthusiastic murmers of consent greeted Captain Nightingall's offer. Yet twenty minutes later they were all facing each other across a cozy table set for four, their plates piled high with a rich assortment of culinary delights that no one was eating.

The room was a crush of people, laughing and gossiping as they made their way around the enormous buffet table. There were many curious glances sent their way that made Richard uncomfortable until he realized the most scandalous looks were being reserved for Miles and not him and Anne. Apparently, Anne had been correct in her prediction. No one had noticed their prolonged absence from the ball earlier in the evening.

While he was glad to be able to spare Anne a public humiliation, Richard also realized this did not bode well for his matrimonial cause.

"Have you recently come down from London, Captain Nightingall?" Nicole asked. "Was the journey pleasant?"

"Anything but, I'm afraid," Miles replied. "The roads were ghastly as always, and I encountered nothing but trouble at the inns along the way. There was a sword fight in one, a fisticuffs in another and a dashedly awkward incident in the last where a local squire thought I had insulted his good wife and demanded satisfaction."

"Satisfaction?" Anne echoed faintly.

"You know, pistols at dawn and all that sort of nonsense. What passes for honor among cowards in England these days." Miles locked his gaze on Anne, but his expression revealed only mild boredom. "I briefly considered accepting the challenge but decided it wouldn't have been very sporting to kill the old boy just because his wife was an outrageous flirt. So I took out my pistol and shot the flame clean off the candle resting in the middle of their table."

"Good show," Richard declared with enthusiasm. "You always were a crack shot, Miles."

Captain Nightingall tipped his head in humble acknowledgment. Richard found himself smiling, knowing the tale must be pure fabrication. Miles was the most level-headed, cautious man he knew. And he never flirted with women. Ian on the other hand would probably have been caught *in flagrante dilecto* with the wife in the squire's own bedchamber. But not Miles. Never Miles.

"What about the poor squire?" Nicole asked.

Miles shrugged his shoulders. "The moment the flame was

extinguished, his wife fainted dead away and slid beneath the table. When I left she was being carried out to their coach.''

"My goodness, excitement must follow you everywhere, Captain Nightingall," Anne intoned tersely as she placed an empty champagne goblet on the table. A footman came by and offered to refill the glass but she waved him away. Anne lifted her chin slightly, keeping a steady gaze on Miles as she continued.

"Sword fights, brawls, pistol shots in the taprooms of quiet posting inns. How dull we must all appear in comparison. The most memorable occurrence on our journey from town was my brother becoming ill from the swaying motion of the carriage and losing his breakfast on the newly upholstered seat cushions.''

"Anne!" Nicole gasped. "How indelicate to speak of such matters. Especially while we are at the table." Nicole made a small choked sound and glanced at Miles worriedly. "What ever will Captain Nightingall think of us?"

"I suspect both Captain Nightingall and Lord Mulgrave possess strong enough constitutions to hear such a shocking tale," Anne insisted with subtle disapproval in her voice. "I doubt there is little that shocks either of them."

Richard coughed behind his hand. Her tone should have had them all straightening to attention. He glanced over at Anne half expecting her to smile smugly, but she barely acknowledged him.

She seemed tense and worried. At first he'd thought it was due to his company, but as the conversation moved to the less controversial topic of the weather, Richard noticed that Anne's eyes rarely left Miles. She studied him as if he were a fascinating puzzle that she was trying to piece together.

Richard clenched his jaw. The sudden spurt of jealousy he felt was both unwelcome and unwarranted. He, Miles and Ian had always shared a special, unique friendship, a closeness few brothers enjoyed. Their ties transcended boyhood, manhood and war. Although they competed in many of life's masculine pleasures and pursuits—cards, hunting, horse racing, marksmanship and so forth—the trio had never before competed for the affections of the same woman.

It would have been a hollow, fruitless waste of time since the conclusion was already predetermined. Ian always claimed the widest circle of admiring females no matter what the circumstances and had done so ever since they were all old enough to grow and shave off their whiskers.

It was an accepted occurrence, never spoken about, simply understood. Miles was the crack shot, Richard the expert horseman, Ian the breaker of female hearts.

Yet Richard began to wonder uneasily if Miles was now encroaching on Ian's domain. Ian had said that Miles had changed and hinted broadly of scandal and trouble in London. And even out here in the quiet seclusion of Devon there seemed to be some knowledge of Miles's unsavory reputation, judging by the sensation he was causing at the ball.

"Will you be staying long in the countryside, Captain Nightingall?" Anne inquired, her tone indicating she hoped he would be doing just the opposite.

"Ian has been generous enough to extend an indefinite invitation, but I am uncertain how long I shall stay. There is just so much fresh air and early evenings one can endure."

"Yes, I'm certain the quiet of rural life will prove a great trial to you," Anne said reflectively. "You shall be racing back to London in less than a fortnight, no doubt encountering all sorts of muck and mayhem along the way."

Miles's mouth quirked in brief amusement. "It appears you know me all too well, Miss Paget, despite our brief acquaintance."

"Nonsense," Nicole interrupted. She sat up restlessly in her chair and pushed herself closer to Miles, leaning so far over she was practically in the poor fellow's lap. "I am sure Anne is very much mistaken in her impressions of your character,

Captain Nightingall. There is much to recommend the green meadows and breathtaking landscapes of Devon. We must endeavor to do everything in our power to ensure your visit is lengthy and thoroughly enjoyable.''

Miles did not respond to Nicole's rather blatant invitation. Richard could tell by Nicole's stunned expression that this frustrated her greatly. She crumbled her linen napkin into a mass of wrinkles, then took a sip of water, her eyes cast down.

Seemingly oblivious to this drama, Miles leaned back in his chair and casually removed a gold snuffbox from his waistcoat pocket. Richard caught his friend's eye and glared pointedly at the box. Miles quirked a brow and gestured toward the pocket that housed Richard's quizzing glass, silently challenging his friend to make an issue of the snuff.

Richard treated Miles to a patronizing stare that was promptly ignored. With graceful elegance Miles flicked open the box lid, took a pinch of the contents and inhaled deeply.

Nicole chewed her lower lip and gazed off in the distance. Even though he wanted Nicole's attention diverted away from his impressionable nephew, Richard could not help but feel a dash of sympathy for the young girl. He suspected it was a rare event for her to encounter a man like Miles, a man who was so completely immune to her feminine charms.

"What precisely do you find so enchanting about our quaint little village, Miss Paget?" Richard asked, finding the prolonged silence uncomfortable.

"The excellent company, my lord," Nicole replied. "Naturally, I miss the Society of London, but the chance to meet new and interesting people is a welcome change. And the quieter pace of country hours affords me time to pursue other pleasures."

Miles snapped the snuffbox lid shut. "Whatever might those pleasures be?"

"Reading," Anne interjected in a flat voice. "Nicole has always been an avid reader."

"Really?" Richard was genuinely surprised. Nicole seemed to be the sort of woman who would avoid opening a book at all costs.

"Nicole reads just about anything she can get her hands on," Anne said. "She has already read most of the books in Sir Reginald's rather limited library. Last week I caught her perusing a dry tome on farming techniques for want of anything else new. She relishes the written word."

"Gracious, Anne, you make me sound like a bluestocking." Flushing, Nicole darted a quick glance at Miles. "Ever since I purchased an annual subscription to a small lending library in London, Anne has been under the false impression that I do nothing but read and study."

"Which subjects do you favor, Miss Paget?" Richard inquired curiously, struggling to reconcile the various conflicting impressions he had formed about this self-absorbed young woman.

"I read for pleasure, sir, not the pursuit of knowledge," Nicole insisted. "I have read several volumes on ancient history and some Evangelical fiction that is interesting but I must confess a great enjoyment of Mrs. Radcliff's Gothic tales."

"I suppose you are enraptured like most of the female population of England by the poetry of Lord Byron," Miles commented in a bland tone.

"On the contrary," Nicole replied. "I find Byron's poems very morbid and exaggerated."

"I disagree," Anne said quietly. "Although I haven't read many of them, I have enjoyed Lord Byron's poems. I was genuinely saddened to hear of his troubles. He has become a tragic figure, ostracized by society and forced into exile."

"He might have been forced from England but he had a momentous sendoff." Miles smiled wanly. " 'Tis said that Dover was filled with dozens of women trying to obtain a last glimpse of the poet as he left."

"Byron was foolish enough to test the *ton* beyond its limits,"

Anne replied. "He ignored society's rules whenever it suited him and now he must pay the price. Even for a man, they say his behavior was nothing less than shocking."

Richard nodded in agreement. "Byron was known to be an inconsiderate and unappreciative husband and had a disastrous marriage by all accounts, though I'm not surprised. I was acquainted with his wife, Annabella, before she married him. She was young and spoiled and thought a great deal of herself. Their life together was most unhappy."

"Tragic proof that marriage between two unsuitable partners ends in grief," Anne stated firmly, her features hardening in firm resolve as she stared across the table.

Richard met her gaze levelly. He was something of an expert in intimidation, but Anne never moved an inch. Even when he deepened his features into a scowl. Secretly Richard was pleased. Her challenging stare only earned his respect. And heightened his desire to have her for himself.

"Enough," Miles declared suddenly. "All this talk of unhappy marriages depresses me." Miles stood on his feet and bowed elegantly toward Anne. "Would you care to dance, Miss Paget?"

Nicole gasped softly. Anne turned sympathetically toward her sister, then back to Miles. Anne's face was riddled with indecision, but she really had no choice but to gracefully accept. Richard watched curiously as Anne gave Miles a wan smile and placed her hand in his. With polite excuses they left the table.

"I really must apologize for my sister's behavior, my lord," Nicole said, apparently unable to contain the spurt of jealousy that attacked her. "I don't know what has gotten into her this evening. She is generally the most quiet and circumspect person, as one would expect from a woman of her advanced years."

"Careful, Miss Paget," Richard said. He was well aware of Nicole's fascination with the rakish Captain Nightingall. There was no mistaking the flare of resentment in Nicole's eyes as they followed her sister and Miles from the room. But he would not have Anne maligned by anyone, even her sister.

"My lord?" Nicole spread her hands expressively in confusion.

"Trust me, Miss Paget, there is no cause for alarm." Richard leaned back in his chair, the very picture of strength and composure. "Any interest you perceive Captain Nightingall has in Anne is only temporary. Your sister is going to marry me."

Chapter Five

"He told me he was going to marry you!"

"So you have said, Nicole." Anne grimaced, then took a deep breath. "Several times."

Anne approached Nicole's bed with trepidation. The morning sun shone brightly through the bedchamber windows of Nicole's room, but Anne found little to be cheerful about on this sunny day. She had spent an oddly sleepless night, twisting and turning in her bed, her mind filled with strange exotic visions of a handsome green-eyed man with broad shoulders and a forceful nature.

Yet the coming of the dawn brought not only light but a strong dose of reality. The ball had ended, at three A.M. not midnight, yet this Cinderella had gladly returned to a life filled with chores and pumpkins. Precisely as she preferred.

However, as she tried rousing Nicole from bed, Anne admitted to herself she felt uncomfortable facing the questioning looks in her sister's eyes. Of course, if she had known her sister was going to continue harping on this marriage business, as she had for nearly half the night, Anne would have left her alone. Until dinner.

Trying her best to ignore her wide-eyed sister, Anne moved swiftly about the chamber, picking up discarded bits of Nicole's clothing. Sir Reginald's maids continually grumbled about all the extra work Nicole's slovenly habits created for them. Meredith, the young, eager lady's maid she and Nicole shared could not possibly keep up with all the mess, so the other maids were pressed into reluctant service. In a household already short-staffed this was not a welcome occurrence.

This morning Anne felt edgy about Nicole's unpopularity with the staff, very much aware that this was the worst possible time to annoy their host. She knew that the family might be forced away from Devon for any number of reasons, but it would be awkward and humiliating if their host asked them to leave. Especially since she had not yet devised a plan as to where they could next go.

"It was the most dramatic thing I have ever witnessed," Nicole continued with her repeated recitation of last evening's events. "Lord Mulgrave's expression never changed, never wavered for an instant. He spoke in a deep, dark tone and made his declaration with total confidence and certainty. 'Twas most extraordinary."

"Mmmm," Anne replied, reaching under the bed and withdrawing a dusty dancing slipper. "Sounds as though Lord Mulgrave has missed his true calling. With talent like that he should be on the stage at Drury Lane providing ample competition for Mr. Edmund Kean."

Anne held up the dusty shoe in mute accusation, but Nicole appeared uninterested. Shaking her head, Anne placed the slipper on the ever growing pile of items in her arms and reached for a white cotton stocking. If she kept moving, then she wouldn't have time to think, and if she didn't have time to think, then she would not have time to worry.

It was a sound plan but inherently flawed. Anne was too

practical a woman to hide from the truth, and more than ever she felt the sharp burden of providing a proper home for her rowdy family. Nicole's relationship with Nigel was on a most tenuous thread; her sister had barely managed a civil farewell last evening to her supposed "one true love."

Of course, the argument between Nicole and Nigel was merely one of a half-dozen bizarre happenings at last night's ball. If they continued, it was questionable as to how long the Paget family would reside with Sir Reginald Wilford. Anne was feeling most uncertain about many things but she was resolved on that matter.

"I simply could not believe it," Nicole muttered. She sat in the middle of the large bed in her nightclothes while a fully dressed Anne continued her efforts to tidy the unruly bedchamber. "Bold as you please, without blinking an eye or missing a breath, he stared at me and declared, *'Your sister is going to marry me.'* "

"Yes."

"I nearly asked him to repeat it, but I was stunned. Simply stunned. Shocked into silence if truth be told. *'Your sister is going to marry me.'* "

"Yes."

"Yes? Why do you keep saying yes? Whatever do you mean?" Nicole shrieked. She scrambled up from her position on the feather bed and leaned through the thick bed curtains. She stared at Anne in dumbfounded accusation. "Are you saying that you are going to marry this man?"

"Of course not," Anne replied quickly, almost too quickly. "It is too ridiculous to even consider. We would never suit, Lord Mulgrave and I. He has the makings of a first-class tyrant, and I despise bullies.

"His sheer presumption that I will be his wife indicates that he is far too used to having his own way. 'Tis beyond time that someone taught him the exact meaning of the word *no*.

Overall I find him domineering, forceful and at times unbearably arrogant.''

"You realize that you have just described yourself, dear sister," Nicole said sweetly. She sank back on her knees and smiled knowingly at Anne.

"I am seldom arrogant," Anne replied with a small grin, willing to concede Nicole had a tiny point. "It is an unflattering notion to be considered so similar in temperament to Lord Mulgrave, yet *if* it is true 'tis merely further proof that he and I are a mismatched pair. With two such volatile personalities living together, we would not have a dish left unbroken in our household."

Nicole smiled and rolled lazily onto her back. "Try as I might, I cannot picture Lord Mulgrave throwing crockery about the room."

"Perhaps you are right," Anne agreed. "He would probably delight in tossing *me* about the room."

Nicole giggled. Shifting again, she propped her elbow on a pillow and rested her chin in her hand. "I know you have always said that you have no wish to marry, Anne. And that you long to travel to the Continent to see and study the classic art of the great masters. Yet I think you must consider Lord Mulgrave's offer carefully. After all, he is an earl."

"His title makes no difference," Anne answered honestly. She swallowed the impatient lecture that hovered in her brain. Some things were not easily expressed or understood, and Anne's feelings about marriage was one of them. "I made my decision about marriage a long time ago. Lord Mulgrave's outrageous proposal last night did not in any way change my opinion."

"But, Anne—"

A knock at the door interrupted the discussion, much to Anne's relief.

"Come in," Nicole commanded sharply.

A chambermaid carrying two bouquets of flowers slowly

entered the room. Her appearance, and the lovely flowers she carried, immediately distracted Nicole. One bouquet was a monstrous arrangement of red and white roses while the other a small nosegay confection in various shades of pink.

"For you, miss," the maid said shyly.

Nicole gaily reached for the flowers.

"Oh, no, Miss Nicole, these are for you." The maid held out the small pink nosegay. "The roses are for Miss Anne."

"They are?" both women exclaimed simultaneously.

Anne exchanged a confused look with her sister, then carefully placed the pile of garments she held on the bed. Flowers were a commonplace occurrence for Nicole. Their sisters Prudence and Madeline had also received many a fine bouquet while they enjoyed the events of the London season as single women. But Anne had never been sent even a solitary blossom.

"Thank you, Mary," Anne finally said. Her fingers shook as she took the glorious arrangement from the maid. It was a magnificent riot of contrasting colors with a scent as sweet and gentle as the delicate blooms.

Angry with herself for having a fluttering reaction to such a florid gift, Anne nevertheless pulled out the small card tucked inside the bouquet with an unsteady hand. And nearly lost her tenuous grip on the roses.

"They are from Captain Nightingall," Anne whispered in confusion.

"What!"

Nicole carelessly tossed her bouquet to the floor and stalked across the bedchamber. She rudely pulled the card away from Anne and examined it thoroughly.

Anne's angry reprimand at Nicole's discourteous behavior remained unspoken as she noted the stricken expression on her sister's face.

"Oh, and, miss," the maid interrupted timidly, "there is a gentleman waiting in the drawing room. The butler told him the ladies of the house were not receiving callers, but he slipped me a coin and told me to bring his card directly to you.''

Anne reached for the card assuming it was also from the wild, hedonistic and unpredictable Captain Nightingall. Bribing a maid to do his bidding was precisely what she would expect of him. Yet the gold name embossed on the card belonged to Nigel.

Anne waited until the maid left before she spoke. ''It appears that Nigel waits downstairs.'' Anne pocketed the card discreetly, realizing this unexpected turn of events could work to their advantage. ''I think you should see him. You both have much to discuss.''

''Nigel?'' Nicole lifted her head and stared blankly off in the distance. ''He is here?''

''Yes, Nigel,'' Anne repeated. '' 'Tis clear he has something important to say if he has gone to all this trouble to try and see you. He cannot wait forever. Hurry now; I'll help you dress.''

Anne hustled Nicole toward the wardrobe intent on getting her sister down to the drawing room as soon as possible, knowing she could not afford to let this opportune moment slip away. Regardless of what she had learned about Nigel last night, Anne still thought he would make a fine husband for Nicole. Definitely better than the reckless Captain Nightingall.

''Which one?'' Anne asked Nicole, holding aloft two gowns, each pretty in their own way.

''I don't care.'' Nicole shrugged with disinterest. ''You choose.''

Anne ignored the jolt of alarm that flashed in her stomach. Nicole was merely tired and feeling a bit put-out because the flowers Nigel sent were not as impressive as the ones Captain Nightingall had chosen for Anne. She would perk up the moment she saw Nigel. Anne was certain.

Yet try as she might, it was difficult for Anne to reconcile the downtrodden reflection of the sister she saw in the glass with the normally confident Nicole. A woman who despite her young age knew what she wanted. Looking at her now, Anne saw only a confused, unhappy girl.

Doubt and guilt gnawed equally at Anne. Was she pushing Nicole too hard and too fast? Was her desire to see Nicole married and away from the family clouding her judgment? Her sense of fairness?

Anne had managed to hold the family together through difficult and oppressive times. She had postponed her own chance for personal fulfillment in order that her younger sisters could marry men they admired and cared for who would provide them with financial and emotional security.

Yet at this moment it appeared that Nigel could do none of those things for Nicole. Drat that Captain Nightingall! He was at the crux of this dilemma. Nicole had been perfectly happy with her choice of Nigel until Nightingall showed up. If Anne thought, even for a moment, that the rakish captain would be a suitable husband for Nicole, she would wholeheartedly encourage her sister's fascination with the man.

However, it would be a pointless endeavor. Nightingall was not interested in Nicole, and Anne feared that if he did turn his attention toward Nicole, he would most likely break her heart. Or damage her reputation. Or both.

Anne bent down and picked up the lovely pink nosegay Nicole had tossed to the floor. She placed it gently on the dressing table, then motioned for her sister to sit.

"Talk to Nigel," Anne said softly. She quickly unbraided Nicole's hair and diligently brushed out the few knots. "It would be best if you reach an understanding before things progress beyond your control."

Nicole remained silent, but Anne saw her lift the flowers and stare at them reflectively as she twirled the nosegay between her fingers.

"I will speak with Nigel," Nicole declared.

"Good. After I finish helping you dress I shall call Rosalind.

She and I will serve as your chaperons. An older sister and a younger sister." Anne smiled. "We shall keep a discreet distance, of course, to afford you some measure of privacy."

Hastily Anne pulled a handful of blond hair to the crown of Nicole's head and began to deftly pin the ringlets into place. She wasn't as skilled as a proper lady's maid in the arrangement of hair but she had fixed all of her younger sister's tresses often enough to do a competent job.

When she finished, Anne stepped back to admire her work. Nicole looked lovely as always, but the sadness in her eyes troubled Anne.

"You must be truthful," Nicole said solemnly, toying with a petal she had plucked from her bouquet. "Have you formed a *tendre* for Captain Nightingall? Is that the real reason you have refused the Earl of Mulgrave's marriage proposal?"

Anne's lips parted with shock. How was it possible that Nicole believed such an outrageous statement?

"You have misunderstood the situation completely," Anne insisted. "I refused Mulgrave because I don't want to be his wife. Or any man's, for that matter. As for the flowers, I have no idea why Captain Nightingall sent them. Probably as a joke. The man is a rogue. It would seem to fit his perverse sense of the absurd to send an old dried-up spinster like me flowers."

"You are neither old nor dried-up." Nicole looked at her strangely. "If you would take merely half the time to fuss over your own appearance as you do with mine, you would have a swarm of admirers at every society function."

Anne paused. Was that true? Had she never tried to attract admirers because she was afraid that in the end she would be unable? Anne shook her head, refusing to consider the cowardly notion.

"I danced but one quadrille with Captain Nightingall," Anne said. "It was the only time we were alone all evening. You and Lord Mulgrave provided the necessary company to qualify as chaperons. Not that it was needed. Nothing even remotely improper happened.''

Of course, Anne realized the same could not be said about all that time she spent with Lord Mulgrave. Alone. She raised her head and saw that Nicole was scrutinizing her carefully. Anne abruptly averted her face.

Lord only knew what kind of guilt was written there. Given Nicole's current volatile state, she would probably misconstrue any emotion she perceived.

Anne spun away, crossing the room with short, angry strides. ''I'll send one of the maids to help you finish dressing. Then I shall fetch Rosalind and meet you in the rose garden,'' Anne said in a far sharper tone than she intended. ''Perhaps the fresh air will help clear all our heads.''

As promised, Anne and the young Rosalind kept a discreet distance behind Nicole and Nigel as they strolled beyond the restrictive paths of the rose garden and wandered over the rolling green hills of the estate.

Rosalind skipped along beside Anne, her head bobbing with energy and excitement, exclaiming over each small detail. Was not the grass so green and the sky so blue and the small family of rabbits so adorable this morning? Her sister's delighted chattering brought forth strong pangs of guilt.

With her younger brothers away at school the better part of the year, fifteen-year-old Rosalind was often relegated to the background. Not yet a woman but no longer a child, Rosalind was forced to stay above stairs when visitors called and banished to take meals in the nursery. Usually with only a servant for company.

Anne sighed. She loved her sisters dearly, and knowing that she had neglected her youngest sister hurt. She had tried so hard over the years to be the responsible one, the one they could depend on in adversity. At times it was physically and emotionally draining, but Anne had remained steadfast in her devotion and until now believed she had done an admirable job.

Her sisters Prudence and Madeline both had happy marriages thanks to Anne's intervention. But their success was part of the past. Today Nicole seemed destined for heartbreak, and Rosalind was slowly slipping away due to neglect.

Anne closed her eyes and bowed her head. She must renew her commitment to her sister's future happiness and security. Action, not regret, would help dispel this melancholy self-pitying mood that accomplished nothing except giving her a rousing headache.

"Look, Anne," Rosalind called out. "Sir Reginald has had the boats put in the lake, just as he promised."

"So he has," Anne acknowledged, noting the appearance of two sturdy rowboats tied at the bank of the artificial lake. They rested just beyond the shade of the unusual Oriental pagoda. "Don't forget, we must ask permission before we venture out in them. We are Sir Reginald's guests and must always act accordingly."

Anne quickly realized it was now also necessary to make certain her brothers were never unattended when they visited the lake. On holiday from school, the lads had recently joined the rest of the family, and Anne wisely capitalized on their preference for the outdoors to keep them out of trouble and away from Sir Reginald. They were fascinated by water, as were most young boys, and would think it a grand adventure to go exploring the lake by rowboat. The problem was that neither could swim a stroke.

For the first time in many months Anne felt a strange longing for her own home. A fine example of sixteenth-century architecture, the sprawling estate of Anne's childhood had a character uniquely its own, an atmosphere of antiquity and elegance, the best furnishings and draperies that money could buy. In all their many travels about the countryside and in London, Anne had seen none like it.

In the last months before they left it, Anne had come to view the estate distastefully, as nothing more than a drain on their already overburdened finances. Yet it was still the home of her childhood, and mingled amidst the negative were pleasant memories of the beauty and splendor of the place. It represented a more stable and secure time in her life, a place of safety and joy.

"They are fighting again," Rosalind stated solemnly.

Anne squinted into the sunlight. Nicole and Nigel were strolling a fair distance ahead, but Anne could see that Rosalind's observation was unfortunately quite accurate.

Nigel was speaking with exaggerated gestures while Nicole remained still, almost rigid by his side. Anne was struck again by how mature Nicole appeared, forced no doubt by the precariousness of their bizarre family situation to grow up fast. Anne had done her best to shield her younger sisters from anxiety, but they had nevertheless experienced it for themselves in their own way.

The steady beat of pounding hooves and sounds of thundering vibrations alerted them all to the approach of riders. The argument between Nigel and Nicole abruptly ceased and they moved back to join Anne and Rosalind. All heads turned toward the source of the interruption.

Anne scanned the horizon curiously, knowing that Sir Reginald never ventured out on a horse, preferring to use a cumbersome old-fashioned black coach on the rare occasions he left the house. She observed two riders cresting over the hill, first at a steady gallop, then breaking down to a slower canter. They kept pace with each other admirably although the vast difference in the size of the mounts and riders was evident as they drew closer. One rider was a child, the other a man.

Anne eyed them with misgivings as they neared, her keen vision having identified the male rider. She braced herself, focusing her attention and energy on the commanding figure atop the large black stallion.

Dressed in a blue coat, buff-colored waistcoat, snowy white cravat and buckskin breeches, Lord Mulgrave was even more intensely virile than last night. Once again Anne felt that unexplainable pull as if Lord Mulgrave were some sort of strong metal and she the helpless magnet drawn to him against her will. He had a sexual magnetism that both fascinated and frightened her.

"Good morning, Miss Paget," the earl said. He dismounted from his horse, casually tying the stallion's reins about a tree, and moved to stand directly in front of Anne. "What luck finding you here. Of course, 'tis much too beautiful a day to remain indoors. I assume any sensible person would take advantage of the sunshine."

Anne did not reply but swept the earl a low, ironic curtsey. *Luck, my foot,* she thought grimly, deciding that Lord Mulgrave was not the type of man that relied on luck. He was the type that made his own.

He gave her a bright, penetrating look. The obvious delight in his eyes was a potent reminder of their last meeting. Resolutely Anne lifted her head and forced herself to hold his gaze, praying he could not tell that deep inside he was making her feel like an awkward, yearning girl.

"May I present my daughter, Alexandra." Lord Mulgrave turned and assisted the child from her horse. "This is Miss Paget."

Alexandra made a pretty curtsey to Anne, then favored her with a stare so reminiscent of her father that Anne nearly took a step back.

"Lady Alexandra." Anne acknowledged the introduction with her own curtsey. "These are my sisters Nicole and Rosalind. And of course you already know Baron Anson."

"Yes. Hello, Cousin Nigel. I thought you were coming riding

with us this morning. We waited and waited for you, but Papa became cross so we started without you.''

Nigel blushed noticeably, muttering a brief apology. Then he quickly excused himself and Nicole and whisked her away down the gravel path that bordered the small lake.

Alexandra seemed unaffected by her cousin's desertion. She turned eagerly toward Rosalind. ''Is it true you have other sisters? And brothers too? Papa told me there are many, many of you.''

Rosalind laughed. ''Yes, there certainly are a lot of us. So many that sometimes we lose count.''

Both girls broke into fresh giggles. Anne regarded the earl's daughter thoughtfully. She was dressed in a fashionable dark blue riding habit artfully trimmed in gold braid. A matching hat with a small veil was set atop her pretty red hair. It gave her a remarkably sophisticated look, though Anne judged her to be no more than seven or eight years old.

She did not remotely resemble her father in looks, but the uncanny similarities of gestures suggested they spent a great deal of time in each other's company.

''We just spotted a lovely family of rabbits,'' Rosalind told Alexandra. ''Shall we try and catch a glimpse?''

''Rabbits! They are my favorites.'' Alexandra lifted the hem of her riding habit and charged toward Rosalind. ''I have a large white bunny at home. His name is Prinny. Papa had one of the grooms build a big hutch for Prinny to live in, and we keep it by the kitchen door so I may visit him whenever I wish.''

''What fun,'' Rosalind replied with an encouraging smile. ''I've never known anyone who kept a rabbit for a pet. We had four cats and two dogs but we couldn't take them with us when we left.'' Rosalind dropped her head and tone. ''I do hope our tenant has been properly looking after them.''

Anne blinked with surprise. She knew Rosalind had always been fond of the stray cats and dogs haphazardly adopted by the family, but this was the first time she had ever expressed any emotion over them.

"You may come and play with Prinny anytime," Alexandra generously offered. "He really is the most special pet."

"He sounds quite extraordinary," Anne said, hoping to draw attention away from Rosalind. The poor girl was embarrassed by her emotions and suddenly appeared shy.

"I shall be back after we find the rabbit family, Papa," Alexandra decided. "Do you remember the exact spot you saw them, Rosalind?"

"Yes." Rosalind recovered nicely and obligingly took Alexandra's hand after receiving Anne's brief nod of permission.

"She will take good care of Alexandra," Anne told the earl as they watched the girls walk away. "Rosalind is a very responsible young lady."

"I would not have let them leave if I thought otherwise."

"Oh?" Anne expressed her disbelief clearly. "Your daughter has spirit and a direct manner of speaking, my lord. I somehow imagine she would have gone with or without your permission."

"Are you criticizing my child?" The earl's tone was calm and even but his expression was fierce.

"Merely an observation," Anne hastily assured him, pleased how quickly he rushed to Alexandra's defense. "When I was a girl the only rabbits I ever had were on my dinner plate."

"Egad, don't let Alexandra hear you." The earl cast his gaze about furtively as if fearing his life was in mortal danger. "My housekeeper once let it slip that rabbit stew was my favorite meal when I was a lad. Poor Alexandra nearly had apoplexy."

"Prinny?" Anne raised an eyebrow.

"Trust me, 'tis a most apt name." Lord Mulgrave flashed her a grin that made her uncooperative heart lurch. "You would be amazed how much that silly rabbit resembles the Regent. Down to the fleas we occasionally find on his thick, white fur."

Anne could not swallow her laugh in time. "Alexandra is

very fortunate to have such an indulgent father. Most little girls find their papas a shade daunting.''

"I am the only parent that Alexandra has ever known,'' Lord Mulgrave said. "Above all else I want her to feel safe and loved. I deliberately hired a young, progressively thinking governess for my daughter, remembering all too well the stiff-necked, unsmiling, strict woman who cared for me as a child. Miss Fraser has rather liberal opinions on discipline and encourages Alexandra to speak her mind. She feels it is more important for a child to learn common sense, dignity and integrity.

"Miss Fraser also believes, and I concur, that Alexandra can become a woman who does more than spend her days painting uninspired watercolors, playing the pianoforte and gossiping with friends and acquaintances. We don't hold with the notion that boys should learn everything and girls nothing. Actually, I think you would like Miss Fraser.''

Anne nodded. "I probably would. She sounds most enlightened and far different from other women in her profession. I remember the loud scolding and occasional shrieking of our governess. For all the good it did, poor woman. Despite her best attempts, I fear we tended to be excessively naughty.''

"Mmmm, naughty children tend to grow up to be difficult adults.''

Caught between laughter and insult, Anne chose the former. "Yes, I suppose I'm living proof of that theory.'' She looked at him askance. "Of course, spoiled children tend to grow up to be impossible adults. Despite your ogress governess, I suspect you were positively doted on by the rest of the family as a child.''

"Good Lord, do you think so?'' Lord Mulgrave laughed heartily. "I probably was.''

Against her will, Anne's gaze was drawn to his mouth with its strong, full lips and humorous curves at the corners. For one fleeting moment she imagined herself kissing those strong lips, of becoming engulfed in the heat and strength of his embrace, of entering the mysterious, sensuous world he had briefly tantalized her with last night.

Embarrassed at the strange, exotic turn of her thoughts, Anne deliberately looked away. Her mind was an ache of confusion. She had formed so many conflicting impressions of Lord Mulgrave over the past twenty-four hours it made her teeth ache. He was both funny and humorless, gentle and arrogant, kind and then demanding. He seemed to have great empathy but lacked the patience to understand another's point of view. In short, he was a total puzzle.

Yet why was he so impossible to ignore? He was only a man. Nothing more, nothing less.

It was quiet for several moments with only the sounds of rustling leaves and the trilling of birds breaking the silence. Anne took in the surrounding scenery with a false air of calmness. Standing this close to Lord Mulgrave made it impossible to act nonchalant.

Rosalind and Alexandra were near, crouching low in the tall grass. They looked like two young cats ready to pounce at a moment's notice on unsuspecting prey. Nigel and Nicole had completed one circuit around the lake and were now starting a second.

Nigel and Nicole walked quietly side by side apparently no longer fighting. Anne watched their progress for several minutes until they came to a large puddle blocking the path. Without hesitating for a moment, Nigel lifted Nicole up in his arms and carried her gallantly across the water and mud.

"He learned that from me, you know," Lord Mulgrave whispered in Anne's ear.

Her first instinct was to utter a witty, slightly derogatory remark, but Lord Mulgrave's nearness seemed to jumble her brain. While she was struggling to regain her equilibrium, he reached down and grasped her hand, turning it so it met his own palm.

Anne's breath caught. He felt so strong and solid and impossibly warm. It was rather unsettling, this immediate, intense response to his touch. She knew the sanest reaction was to pull away, but the romantic moment she had just witnessed between her sister and Nigel lingered in her mind. Pure sentiment was enchanting, romance contagious.

Lord Mulgrave linked his fingers through hers. It caused another strange sensation to flutter through her system, a curious mix of sensuality mingled with a feeling of safety and protection. He slowly raised her hand to his mouth, and Anne panicked.

She abruptly disengaged her fingers. What was she doing? She wanted no sentimental attachments to this man, no bonds of any kind. She would not allow her carefully laid plans for the future to go awry.

"I had best get the girls out of the sun before they burn," Anne said stiffly, praying he could not hear the distress she felt. "Rosalind refused to wear a bonnet, and the tiny hat that Alexandra has on is most fashionable but useless in this heat."

The earl effectively blocked her retreat. Anne saw his nostrils flare, could feel the tension vibrating from him. Clearly the very last thing he wanted was for her to go to fetch his daughter. Silence heightened the awkwardness of the moment until Anne felt her lungs begin to strain from lack of breath.

Then finally he inclined his head and let her go, just as she had requested. She escaped quickly, without a backward glance. Yet why did it make her feel so sad?

Chapter Six

The lone rider increased his speed as he neared his goal, pleased that he had finally been able to shake his companion and continue his journey alone. He rode for several miles on Sir Reginald's land before veering toward the edge of the forest. Seeking cover beneath the trees, he gracefully dismounted, then grasping the reins firmly in his left hand he led the stallion toward a little-used, little-known trail.

He walked at a brisk pace to avoid detection. Time was of the essence, and both man and animal were focused on the mission at hand. Rather like being back in the army, the man thought with an ironic grin.

The trail they followed was narrow and overgrown. The path climbed upward and the woods grew thicker, providing ample cover, just as the man had intended. Deeper and deeper he entered the woods, and it grew darker as the warm summer sun was lost to him with only an occasional glimmer of light escaping through the dense leaves.

Finding an appropriate spot to tether his horse, he tied the reins to a low-slung tree limb and continued on without his faithful steed. His passage flushed a flock of birds from the nearby undergrowth, and it startled him as they soared into the sky with their wings thumping furiously.

Steady, he admonished himself. Clandestine activities required nerves of steel, and thus far he still possessed most of his.

He soon reached his intended destination, the crest of a hill, and dropped softly to his knees in the tall grass. His neck and shoulders ached with tension knowing that he must remain very quiet and make no sudden moves. Parting the grass slowly, he looked down the hillside, choked with bramble.

Confound Sir Reginald. Did the man never have his groundskeepers clear the underbrush from his woods?

Annoyed but not deterred, the man silently removed a spyglass from his coat pocket. It was an expensive instrument of the finest quality with its brass casing polished to a high shine. A gift from Richard. How fitting.

The man raised the glass to his eye and stared below, hungering for his first glimpse of the girl. He saw Richard first; the earl's tall, broad shoulders were difficult to miss. Yet his heartbeat quickened, knowing she would be near the earl, as always.

Finally he spied her. Her face, cast in the half-light of sunshine, was partially hidden. Frustrated, he squirmed up on his belly moving higher in the tall grass. His patience was rewarded when she turned her head to laugh at something said by the young woman who was her companion.

Alexandra. His lovely little girl. She had inherited her mother's good looks, the thick red hair, deep blue eyes with a sprinkling of freckles across an upturned nose and pure sunshine in her smile. She was a beautiful child. A true delight. His daughter.

The man's heart ached. She was his one connection to the past, and he clung to her tenaciously. He shook the long hair that had fallen down on his forehead out of his eyes. He readjusted the spyglass, eager for another glimpse of his precious little girl.

Eyes wide with wonder and cheeks flushed with excitement, she rushed across the valley and launched herself at Richard. The earl caught her up in his arms and swung her around in a wide arc, the sound of their laughter carried by the cruel wind up to his ears.

He averted his head. He had no wish to see their happiness, to witness their mutual joy. It only increased his melancholy mood.

He met her socially, of course. She even called him Uncle, and he liked to think that they shared a special bond, a secret friendship, but in somber moments he knew it was merely his imagination. He was a close friend of her father's who brought her treats and gifts that she occasionally played with and always properly thanked him for after a bit of prodding from her governess.

There was always a distance between them. Distance was what he remembered most when he thought about his little girl, and it hurt. Badly.

Richard was her father and she adored him. The earl spoiled and petted her and gave her all the love and attention any child could ever want.

It hurt unbearably at times. And even though he knew it was irrational, deep inside he felt betrayed by the love they shared.

He heard a noise and jumped, the tall grass whispering as he whirled around. There was no one about, only the rustling of the leaves and the chirping of the birds. Still, it was unwise to remain too long.

Crouching, he eased down into the woods, waiting until he had once again reached the cover of the trees before standing on his feet. He started down the hill toward his horse wearily, suddenly feeling drained and exhausted.

How long could he keep the secret of being Alexandra's true father from her? How much longer could he bear to remain a casual presence in his child's life? The unanswerable questions whirled in his brain as he mounted his horse and rode quietly away.

The small clearing of trees soon gave way to an old orchard of apple trees, their trunks gnarled and twisted. The sweet scent of ripening fruit permeated the breeze along with the faint buzzing of insects. It was a tranquil setting but did little to enhance the somber mood of the young couple entering this peaceful valley.

Nicole hesitated, not wanting to move completely out of sight from her sister and Lord Mulgrave, then changed her mind and continued walking by Nigel's side. She deliberately avoided touching him. They had been arguing steadily for what seemed like hours, and the air between them was raw with tension.

"Enough of this quarreling. It serves no purpose." Nigel slowed his stride. "We need to make some important decisions, Nicole."

Nigel's serious tone jolted her into awareness. She had suspected this was coming, and what she had previously anticipated with joy and excitement she now dreaded with equal passion. She slipped her hand under Nigel's forearm and held on tightly, as if seeking escape from the pain that was sure to follow. Nigel stroked her hand comfortingly, and Nicole nearly burst into tears.

"My uncle has asked me to travel to Scotland to investigate the condition of several properties he owns in the area. I am to leave by the end of the week." Nigel gave her a shrewd look. "The earl phrased his demand to sound like a request, but I'm not a fool. It was an order, plain and simple. He has always been opposed to our marriage and has apparently decided the means to achieve our breakup is to separate us. Naturally, it will not succeed."

Nicole opened her mouth automatically, immediately at the ready to voice her distress, her anger, her outrage at Nigel's unjust, unfair treatment by his horrid uncle. But the words would not come. She slowly pressed her lips back together.

They stopped walking, and Nicole stared down at the hand that was covering her own. She must speak, yet a weight seemed to be pressing against her chest, making it difficult to breathe, let alone talk. She had never felt such turmoil.

"Distance will make little difference between us," Nicole finally said tonelessly, knowing in her aching heart she spoke the truth.

Distance would not make any difference. Near or far, now or later, Nicole knew she could no longer give Nigel her whole heart. It had quite inexplicably been stolen by another man. A man who appeared to have not the slightest interest in it, Nicole thought bitterly.

"Perhaps it would be best not to openly defy Uncle Richard," Nigel agreed readily, his voice sounding strained to her sensitive ears. "I'm not afraid of him, mind you. But it remains the sensible decision to cooperate with him. To a point."

Nigel pulled Nicole's hand up to his chest and squeezed it between his own. "I want to announce our betrothal before I leave. I shall speak to your father this evening."

No! The word hovered on Nicole's tongue. "I'm not sure that would be wise," she managed to utter. "I would not want to anger your uncle. He seems a most fierce man."

Nicole felt on the verge of complete panic. What was she going to do? She could not possibly marry Nigel feeling the way she did about Captain Nightingall. What was she going to do?

Don't be rash, an inner voice commanded her. Nigel was the right sort of man for her. Everyone thought so, especially Anne, who had both experience and success in picking husbands for her sisters. Nigel was kind and handsome and madly in love with her. Just what she had always dreamed a husband would be.

Tell him you will wait. He had a title and a fortune and a reputation for being honorable. He would spoil her and indulge her every whim and always be faithful to his marriage vows. She should feel lucky that such a fine man would have her as his wife.

Nigel released her hands and set his own tightly on her waist. "I am sorry, Nicole," he said with a boyish blush. "I bungled that rather badly. It was hardly the sort of romantic proposal you deserve."

Still clutching her waist, Nigel went down on one knee.

"Oh, no," Nicole said in a panic-stricken voice that was little more than a whisper, "please do not."

He smiled in blissful unawareness. "I adore you and love you, my dearest, even when we quarrel. Having you in my arms brings me the greatest happiness a man can experience. Quite simply you have captured my heart. I pledge you my loyalty, my fidelity and my good name until my dying day. Would you do me the great honor, Nicole, of becoming my wife?"

He had spoken the words. She had asked him not to but he had gone ahead and said them. She could feel the rhythm of her heart changing. She had no choice now. She was trapped. Nicole closed her eyes and bowed her head.

"Forgive me, Nigel. I cannot marry you." Nicole could hardly believe what she was saying. "Forgive me."

She had decided months ago to marry Nigel. The second time she had danced with him she knew he was the perfect mate. He was all the things she had always thought she wanted in a husband. Young, rich, titled, handsome and full of fun.

An image of Captain Nightingall came to Nicole's mind. She almost hated the man at this moment. He was at the heart of all her pain and confusion. Nigel might be the ideal man of her girlhood fairy tales, but Nightingall brought the woman inside her to life.

The warm hands clutching her waist slid away. Nicole could hear Nigel stiffly return to his feet. She opened her eyes but continued to stare at the ground, her heart squeezing with a strange pain. She noticed the stain on his trousers left by the damp grass. Her eyes filled with tears.

"Is it my uncle? Are you afraid of his disapproval?"

"Not exactly." Nicole took a deep breath and forced herself to look into Nigel's hurt-filled eyes. She owed him as best an explanation as she could give.

"I do care for you. Above all else you must believe that," Nicole whispered sadly. "But I cannot be your wife."

"I don't understand, Nicole. You said that you loved me." His brow furrowed as if trying to absorb her words.

Ashamed, she bowed her head again. "I did love you. I *do* love you, but not completely as a proper wife ought. 'Tis painful for me also, Nigel, yet I have come to realize that you deserve far more than what I can give you. I hope in time you can come to forgive me." She raised her head hopefully.

His jaw hardened for an instant. "I hardly know what to say."

Dear Lord, it was worse than she thought. Knowing that she was to blame for the bruised look in his eyes made her angry at herself, angry at her own shortcomings. She was too impulsive and immature, too easily dazzled by passion and romance, yet seemingly unable to change.

"I do wish I could become your wife," she said quietly. "Yet my heart has other ideas when it comes to love. I am so very sorry."

He looked taken aback at her words. His expression changed from hurt to closed anger. Nicole could almost feel the barriers being erected between them.

"Since you suddenly find my company so odious, I will not inflict myself upon you any longer. Goodbye, Nicole."

Nigel made a stiff bow and turned. Nicole's throat closed over and the tears in her eyes spilled down her cheeks. *I'm so sorry.* Standing on shaken limbs, she watched him walk away.

She tried to convince herself that it was all for the best. In time he would forget about her and find someone else to love. Rejecting Nigel was the only way to ensure that someday he would find the happiness he deserved.

But what of her own marriage prospects? Anne had already warned her that Captain Nightingall was not the sort of man who would embrace marriage. Nicole's heart filled with hopeless longing. How desperately she wanted the dashing captain to fall in love with her, to feel the same unbridled joy and restless anticipation that engulfed her whenever he was near. Yet she was not so deliriously in love that she didn't realize it was an almost impossible wish.

Fall in love? The man barely looked twice at her.

The sun moved behind a cloud and everything became shrouded in gray. A fitting chill shuddered through Nicole. By dismissing Nigel she had probably thrown away her best chance for a peaceful, contented married life. Her future never seemed more bleak and unsure.

The earl pulled his horse to a slow trot, matching pace with his daughter. Alexandra sat tall in the saddle, chattering excitedly. She had barely caught her breath since they had left the Paget family moments ago.

"Rosalind said I may come to tea one afternoon this week. Probably on Friday. She asked Anne if we could have a special tea, just the two of us, and Anne said that we could."

Richard sighed. Still a few weeks shy of her seventh birthday, Alexandra seemed remarkably grown-up for a young girl. Where had the time gone? It seemed only yesterday that she was swathed in diapers and crawling about on the library carpet, her chubby hands reaching in curiosity for everything within her grasp.

She had been so tiny when she was born, and after losing Juliana in childbirth Richard thought for certain Alexandra would also perish. Yet with the help of his loyal friends Ian and Miles and the maternal fussing of his Spanish servants, the infant soon thrived.

When she was old enough to travel, the earl had resigned his commission and brought his child back to England. It had been a rough crossing but she had been a sturdy traveler, sleeping and eating well despite the rocking ship. They had received a joyous reception from family, servants and tenants upon reaching home. Alexandra was treated like a little princess, the poor motherless waif, spoiled and adored by all.

She was a happy baby who seldom cried, and he remembered staying beside her crib for hours, singing silly songs and letting her grip his fingers in her tiny hand. She would coo and stare at him solemnly with her deep blue eyes, and his heart felt as if it would burst with love when she smiled her toothless, gummy grin.

As soon as she had mastered her first steps, they would go out for walks together, her little dainty hand clasped trustingly in his. Alexandra would run to him when she fell and scraped her knee, depending on him to soothe the hurt and put everything to rights in her small world.

Richard taught her to ride, training her first pony himself, not trusting the grooms to do a thorough job. Even now the earl never let his daughter ride beyond the stable yard unless he accompanied her. Her physical well-being was too important, her safety uppermost in his mind at all times.

"I take it you had fun this morning meeting the Paget sisters?" the earl asked his daughter.

"Yes," Alexandra replied enthusiastically. "Isn't Rosalind pretty? Her hair is a most beautiful color. Miss Fraser has blond hair but it isn't nearly as pretty. Rosalind's curls are the color of the sun. I wish my hair was yellow, not red."

Richard smiled indulgently. Alexandra was clearly taken with the lovely Rosalind. Best to make sure there was no sort of hair dye around she could use to make her wish of golden hair into a reality. Alexandra was cunning enough to gather the items needed and bold enough to try it.

The distinct sound of riders approaching interrupted Richard's thoughts of his daughter.

"Someone is coming!" Alexandra cried excitedly.

The earl scanned the horizon. He pulled back his horse before reaching into his coat pocket and reassuringly touching the butt of the pistol he carried. He seldom encountered trouble on his outings, but it was wise to be prepared. Years of army life had taught him that a cautious approach was always best even when riding on his own lands. These days he never ventured beyond the sight of the manor house unarmed.

The countryside was still overrun with former soldiers and vagrants who had retired from His Majesty's service with little more than the clothes on their backs. Just last week he had found several such men on the northern edges of the estate. He had given them permission to camp on his land for a few days and offered them temporary work as farm laborers, but they had expressed no interest.

His steward had wanted to run them off immediately, insisting they were nothing more than a gang of cutthroats who in all likelihood were waiting for the appropriate moment to attack. Richard had shrugged off this dramatic supposition, yet he rode with an extra degree of alertness. And a loaded pistol in his pocket.

"Oh, it is only Uncle Ian and Uncle Miles," Alexandra commented as the two riders neared. "I was hoping Rosalind had decided to go riding."

Richard was surprised that Alexandra sounded so disappointed. Miles and Ian both spoiled her with special treats and lavish, occasionally inappropriate gifts even though she saw them infrequently, especially Miles. Alexandra always seemed to enjoy their attention and teasing.

"Enjoying this fine weather?" Ian asked, reining in his horse beside Alexandra. "You look especially fetching this morning, Lady Alex. Is that a new hat?"

"Uncle Ian." Alexandra scrunched up her face. "You are always asking me about my bonnets. I thought only girls liked clothes so much. I am starting to think you would like to wear one of my hats yourself."

"She's got you there, Uncle Ian." Miles hooted with laughter as he saluted his greeting. The heavy gold signet ring on his right hand glinted in the sunlight. "Why *do* you take such an interest in ladies' apparel?"

"Anything of importance to a lady becomes an interest of mine." Lord Rosslyn glared at Miles and his tone changed. "I should have left you wandering in the woods," he commented dryly. "As it stands, I'm not exactly sure what possessed me to bother looking for you."

"For the last time, I wasn't lost," Captain Nightingall insisted with an exasperated grin. He shifted the reins from one palm to the other in a nervous rhythmic pattern. "I had a good hard ride, then spent the rest of my time searching the area for you. It wasn't easy tracking you down."

"Tracking me down? I found you!"

"You did not."

Ian gritted his teeth. "Miles and I started out together on our morning ride, but he had great difficulty keeping pace with me and we lost each other for a while. I'm still not quite sure how we became separated."

"It was hardly a tragedy," Miles drawled. "I might be hungover from last night's joyous festivities but am in no need of a nursemaid. I spent enough school holidays visiting you and Richard when we were boys to know my way around this countryside. I could probably show Alexandra a secret place or two that neither you nor Richard remember.''

"Really?" Alexandra perked up in the saddle. "What sort of places?"

Miles shrugged. "Trees that are perfect for climbing, the richest, sweetest blackberry bushes in the county, a small, quiet pond where the does bring their fawns for a drink. However, you might not be interested. I sometimes forget you are not a strapping young lad but a tiresome lass.''

"Stop teasing, Uncle Miles. I like those things," Alexandra assured him earnestly. "Especially the deer.''

Richard smiled at his daughter's eager look of wonder. Miles had successfully tapped into her innate sense of adventure and her love of animals. She would be quick to badger the good captain into proving his word and showing her some of these exciting locales.

"Perhaps I can be persuaded to share my secrets," Miles announced, giving Alexandra a considering glance. "If I am asked very prettily.''

Alexandra glanced first at her father, then shifted her gaze to Miles. She gave him a sweet innocent look that appeared to melt Captain Nightingall's resolve but didn't fool her father for an instant.

"Shall we race to the fence, Uncle Miles?" Alexandra challenged suddenly, her eyes glinting with mischief. "The winner must grant the loser a wish.''

Without waiting for a reply, Alexandra kicked her horse and bolted forward leaving a cloud of dust in her wake.

"You little cheater!" Miles shouted. Turning to the earl, he commented with a grin, "I see you have taught your daughter some of your old horse-racing tricks, Richard. She is as bad as you were when we were boys.''

The earl laughed. "You had best hurry, Miles. She rides like the wind.''

"I shall show no mercy when I catch her." Miles's stallion

reared, and with a cry of delight Captain Nightingall set off in hot pursuit.

"Alexandra is turning into quite a little hooligan," Ian said mildly as the two men watched the impromptu contest. "I thought you ruled your household with an iron hand."

"Appearances can be deceiving." The earl frowned. "You are the second person this morning to remark upon Alexandra's bold behavior. I must either learn to curb my daughter's exuberant spirits or get more tolerant friends."

"Who else dared to criticize our darling Alexandra?" Lord Rosslyn questioned, his voice suddenly tight with emotion.

"I was merely jesting, Ian," the earl replied. "Miss Paget made a brief passing comment about Alexandra's manner. Actually it was more of an observation."

"I think she secretly approves of my daughter's free-spirited ways. After all, Miss Paget is not exactly the most conventional young woman I've ever met. She knows as well as anyone that there will be time enough for Alexandra to become acquainted with the endless maze of society rules that guide the *ton* when she matures."

"Ah, so that is where you have been this morning," Lord Rosslyn replied with a sly grin. "How is the lovely Anne?"

Richard was dismayed to feel the color creep into his cheeks. He felt like a child caught pinching treats from the cupboards. How utterly ridiculous.

"Anne is fine," Richard said in a clipped tone, hoping to cover his unexplained embarrassment. "As are the rest of the Paget sisters. We also met Nicole and young Rosalind this morning. Alexandra was quite taken with Rosalind. She now aspires to have hair the exact shade of yellow as her new heroine. I believe she'd dye her own if given half the chance."

"Egad, I hope you'll put a stop to that immediately."

Richard's jaw firmed. "I am a tolerant father, Ian, not an imbecile."

The earl's horse slowed its already leisurely pace and veered toward a tasty patch of clover. Ian's chestnut mare followed closely. Since this route avoided a water-filled ditch, Richard allowed the detour. Up ahead he could see Alexandra and Miles together by the fence post. His daughter's merry laugh carried across the meadow, and he realized she must have won the race. The little minx.

Ian smiled at the uninhibited, joyous sound Alexandra made, then cleared his throat.

"The Paget women are an interesting breed. Miles had my gardener up at some ungodly early hour this morning searching for the perfect flowers. The poor man cleared out a whole section of roses before Miles was satisfied with the bouquet that was made," Ian offered, ignoring the sudden glint of anger in Richard's eyes. "One of my footmen delivered the masterpiece this morning. I do hope Anne enjoyed them."

"Miles sent Anne flowers?"

"Yes."

Richard's earlier embarrassment faded. He was suddenly glad that Miles had ridden ahead with his daughter, realizing that the thoughts he now had for one of his oldest, closest friends were no longer friendly.

"Clearly Miles does not understand the situation. I shall speak with him shortly," Richard declared softly. Staring into Ian's puzzled face, he added forcefully, "Miss Paget is mine."

"Really?" Ian dipped his head, and a devilish gleam lit his eyes. "I had no idea. Granted, Anne is a pleasant enough woman, but frankly I do not understand what you and Miles find so damn appealing about her.

"She is too intelligent and outspoken for a woman, a lethal combination in my opinion. The younger sister Nicole is far more attractive and seems infinitely more manageable. Are you certain you have selected the right sister?"

That comment drew a shrewd look from Richard. "Don't push me, Ian," the earl warned, trying not to pay any attention to Ian's baiting. He wasn't about to make any more of a fool of himself over Anne than he already had.

Yet hearing his friend's criticism of her made Richard feel even more protective and possessive of the wench. Exactly why he wasn't certain. Actually it was damn confusing.

"Anne will become my wife."

Ian gave a low whistle. "You sly devil. I had no idea things had progressed so far. How extraordinary. So tell me, when is this blessed event to occur? Soon?"

"We'll send you an invitation," Richard replied tightly. "If you behave."

Seeming to realize he was overstepping the bounds of their very long friendship, Ian wisely let the matter drop.

Richard directed his horse away from the clover and steered it back on course across the meadow. Once again Ian's mare followed closely. If only Anne were half as cooperative a female, life would be far more pleasant, Richard thought grimly.

"It will be Alexandra's birthday in a few short weeks," Ian said, deliberately introducing a new topic. "Have you planned any special activities in celebration of the event?"

"The usual friends and family will be in attendance and Cook will no doubt prepare a feast of all of Alexandra's favorite treats. Beyond that I have made no additional preparations."

"Sounds splendid. I've chosen a rather special gift for her this year. A miniature tea set designed just for a child. I do hope she likes it."

"A tea set?"

It was Ian's turn to blush. "A friend, a lady friend, helped me select it, assuring me it was the perfect gift for a proper young lady."

"Mmmm, proper young lady might be a bit of a stretch for Alexandra, but she will be able to organize her own tea parties and boss everyone around. She'll like that," Richard decided with a grin.

"I believe she will." Ian sighed with obvious relief. "I must remember to personally thank my dear friend when I next return to town.''

"I can only speculate what that will entail," Richard muttered under his breath.

Ian turned his head. "Why such a disapproving tone, Richard? When did you turn into such a Puritan?"

"When I became a father. To a female child," the earl responded. "Trust me, Ian, it gives you an altogether different perspective on the male/female relationship."

"I really shouldn't be all that surprised," Ian smirked. "You were always the most responsible one amongst us, the one who could be counted upon to choose duty and honor above frivolity."

"Lord, am I really such a prig?"

Ian laughed heartily. "Compared to Miles and me you are a virtual saint, Richard."

Ian's words brought the earl up short. He suddenly felt more than a bit guilty over the incident with Miss Paget at the ball. He had behaved thoughtlessly, without consideration for her feelings, without actually considering her at all. Originally he had been determined to prove her unworthy of his nephew's regard, believing she was Nicole.

True, he now intended to make honorable amends for the incident, once the stubborn Anne could be brought to reason. Yet that in itself did not excuse his behavior. The thought disturbed Richard for the rest of the afternoon.

Chapter Seven

Absorbed in the intricate design of the patterned marble floor she was sketching, Anne heard but decided to ignore her brother's angry screams.

The marble was an unusual subject for a painting, but Anne was bored with landscapes and pastoral scenes. She was searching for greater artistic challenges and had found them by focusing on the odd, small beauties in life. The sinuous veining in the marble suggested running water, though Anne doubted anyone else would notice the subtle resemblance. Yet she did. It was probably part of what made her an artist.

Crouched comfortably in a corner of Sir Reginald's grand hall, Anne painstakingly copied the floor pattern, experimenting with the light, angles and proportions of the marble to change the feel and mood of the drawing. She worked with the small canvas positioned on her lap, bending close to add details, wiping furiously with her rag to remove mistakes.

Anne painted what she saw with her eyes and her imagination. Lifting the canvas, she held it at arm's length, scrutinizing her progress. It was a decent start. Of course, she realized that she'd probably have to place something on top of the floor to make the work interesting to anyone else.

A vision of Lord Mulgrave immediately came to mind. Wearing only his buckskin breeches fitted snugly into glossy polished knee-high black boots, his arm muscles powerfully flexed and a fine sheen of sweat glistening off his bare chest. A lock of dark hair could be falling carelessly across his brow, drawing attention to the intense green eyes that viewed the world with supreme confidence. And a secret, knowing grin curving the edges of his mouth. The perfect portrait of a male animal. Virile, tempting, forbidden.

A strange heat flashed over her. Mortified by her wayward imagination, Anne shook her head as if to clear the tempting vision. It was real enough in her mind to give her heart palpitations. She brought her hands up to her flaming cheeks to cool the warmth and swallowed hard. Sounds of a scuffle and angry young male voices reached her ears.

"You idiot! I hate you, William!"

"You are such a baby, Edmund."

"I am not!"

"Baby, baby, baby!"

"Go to hell!"

"Be quiet," Sir Reginald called out loudly. "Is there no peace to be had this morning? Even within my own study?"

"Not now," Anne muttered in frustration. She diligently bowed her head toward her canvas and continued painting. The voices became louder. And closer. Anne tried ignoring the discord but her concentration was broken.

Besides, who would cope with this problem if she did not intervene? Her parents? Not likely. They were either still abed or off on some private adventure.

Anne sighed. Would there never be more than a stolen hour or two to work at her art? The resentment bubbled and brewed inside. Why must she always be interrupted? Why must she always be the one to be called away from her work, her passion, to cope with the trivial matters of everyday life?

Someday soon, Anne promised herself as she stood on her feet. *In a few short years I shall gain my freedom and have the luxury of following my own aims. Without interruption.*

"Anne! Anne!" Sir Reginald bellowed.

"Here, sir," Anne replied.

Sir Reginald entered the hall, dragging her brothers by his sides, each on a separate arm. At twelve and eleven years of age that presented a bit of a physical challenge for the older gentleman, but his obvious anger had given him the additional strength needed to control the unruly lads.

Sir Reginald's features were lean and sharp. They reminded Anne of a hunting dog. Although he preferred to limit the amount of time he spent with his house guests, when he did attend them his shrewd brown eyes missed nothing.

He was not a heavyset man, but he wore clothes that were twenty years out of fashion and neck collars that were so tight that when he bobbed his head all the condensed skin around his neck moved. Anne watched now in morbid fascination as the flesh jiggled back and forth with each angry step he took.

"I have asked repeatedly for quiet in the house at all hours but most especially in the mornings," Sir Reginald insisted with barely restrained impatience. "Is that so difficult to understand?"

"Of course not," Anne replied. " 'Tis a most reasonable expectation, my lord."

Sir Reginald gave each boy a hearty shake, then released them. "I cannot locate your father. I expect you to deal with this problem, Anne. Immediately." He pushed William and Edmund toward her as if he thought they were truly loathsome creatures.

Anne blew out her breath in frustration. She knew her brothers could be rambunctious at times but they really weren't bad children. The problem was that they easily became bored, and when they were bored they fought. Loudly and physically.

Still, Sir Reginald had a right to quiet in his own home. For his benefit Anne studied her two brothers with a harsh gaze. They lowered their heads and tried to look appropriately remorseful. Edmund inventively began wringing his hands together. Anne had difficulty keeping a straight face.

"You are disgraceful. The pair of you," Anne exclaimed, clucking her tongue in blatant disapproval. Sir Reginald nodded enthusiastically.

"It wasn't my fault. Edmund started it."

"I did not! William started it."

"And I shall finish it," Anne declared sternly. Knowing Sir Reginald's eye was upon her, Anne trained a frigid gaze on the two boys. "Since you have seen fit to behave so inappropriately *inside* the house, you shall spend the remainder of the day in a productive manner *outside* the house.

"I am certain the grooms could use the help of two strapping lads in the stables today. I expect you to muck out the stalls, attend to the feeding and grooming of all the animals and complete any other tasks assigned to you in a speedy and competent way."

The boys exchanged a look, then nodded reluctantly.

As punishments go it wasn't very harsh. Both boys were mad for horses and would like nothing better than to have an excuse for spending the rest of the morning in the stables. Fortunately for Anne, Sir Reginald was unaware of her brothers' preferences. He would most likely feel this sort of hard, physical labor was appropriate compensation for having his peaceful morning shattered.

"Now apologize to Sir Reginald for your rude and inappropriate behavior," Anne commanded.

Edmund's eyes flashed with rebellion and William sent her a resentful look. Anne held up her hand, hoping to forestall any additional outburst. There was a brief silence.

"Beg pardon, sir," William finally muttered. He elbowed his younger brother in the ribs.

"I'm sorry, Sir Reginald," Edmund squeaked out.

The older man narrowed his eyes. "See that it doesn't happen again."

"Go on, get to the stables," Anne said, dismissing the boys with a final fierce glance.

They turned tail and ran, escaping before any additional tasks could be assigned. Clearly the most difficult part of their punishment was having to apologize to Sir Reginald. Neither boy liked him very much, and as was typical of males they disliked being bested by a female in front of an enemy.

"Little heathens," Sir Reginald muttered after the boys had gone. "What they really need is a good caning."

The very idea appalled the tenderhearted Anne. Strike a child for making noise and being a child? How cruel. Yet she repressed her annoyance over the eccentric Sir Reginald's views on child rearing. It would hardly improve matters if she said anything truly insulting to the man. After all, it was thanks to his somewhat reluctant generosity they even had a roof over their heads.

"I shall strive to keep the boys occupied and out of your way, my lord," Anne promised.

"I've heard that before," Sir Reginald mumbled, unable to mask his disapproval. He turned to leave the hall, stopped, then pivoted back toward Anne. "If I forget, be sure to tell your parents about all this."

He looked at Anne as if his possible lapse of memory were her fault. She lifted her chin slightly and stared back.

"I'll inform Father the moment he comes downstairs."

"Ha, ha!" Sir Reginald crowed in triumph. "All this noise and commotion truly does addle my wits. Thanks to the lads' tomfoolery I completely forgot that your father told me he was taking a trip into the village this morning. Your mother wanted to do a bit of shopping and your father agreed to accompany her. Can't understand why. There's nothing more agitating in the world than standing about in a stuffy store while a fickle female tries to make up her mind over a purchase.''

"Shopping?" Anne paled. "When did they leave?"

"Aren't you listening to me, girl? I already told you, some-time this morning," Sir Reginald said with an exasperated groan.

Somehow Anne managed to hold back the cry of despair that rose in her throat. She knew this moment was coming. The family had left London over two weeks ago. Her parents rarely went more than a week without buying something new and useless. With all the anxiety over Nicole and the bizarre situation with Lord Mulgrave, Anne had simply not been paying attention.

"I think I'll join them," Anne said. "It's a lovely day for a drive. I hope you don't mind if I borrow a horse and cart, Sir Reginald. I'm sure I'll return it by luncheon."

There was no time to waste waiting for a reply. Anne rushed out of the house while a sputtering Sir Reginald pontificated. She sincerely hoped he had given permission for her to use one of his rigs, but, realizing that she would take the vehicle even if he objected, Anne decided it was best not to know.

Taking only a moment to don her bonnet and gloves, Anne quickly arrived in the stables. Edmund and William were already hard at work with a pitchfork and a shovel cleaning out the stalls. Not understanding the magnitude of her trip, they cheerfully abandoned their task and assisted the groom in harnessing a mean-looking horse to the cart.

With a brief nod of thanks, Anne took the reins and carefully guided the rig through the stable yard and onto the road. She had not yet been to the village, but the head groom assured her that all she needed to do was follow the well-marked path.

There was a thick heaviness in the air, an uncomfortable combination of heat and moisture that matched Anne's mood. She wondered briefly how it would feel to have parents whose life was not solely devoted to their own selfish pleasures. Anne sighed. It was ridiculous to speculate about the impossible. Better to concentrate on the inevitable.

She tried not to think overmuch of the financial disasters her parents were likely to wreak once loose in a shop. Attempting to keep full-scale panic at bay, Anne reminded herself that this would be a relatively small country village with few shops. Hopefully these establishments would hold a limited amount of expensive merchandise that would appeal to either her mother or father.

Anne allowed the horse to set a fast pace as they traveled the winding path through dense trees and lush green foliage. She wiped her brow as the moist heat enveloped her, breathing deeply the musky rich scent of the woods with its damp soil and abundant ferns carpeting the earth. The steady clop of the horse's hooves and crunching of the carriage wheels were a familiar, comforting sound.

Glancing at the gray sky, Anne noted the low, dark clouds. She smiled ironically, remembering how she told Sir Reginald it was such a beautiful day for an outdoor ride. A thunderstorm was sure to hit. Anne only hoped she would arrive in town before becoming drenched.

As she approached the picturesque cluster of dwellings, Anne kept the reins taut, slowing the enthusiastic pace of the horse to a reasonable trot. The village was larger than she expected and prosperous, judging by the recently thatched roofs on the cottages and the leaded casement windows of several shops.

The feisty horse danced excitedly, distracted by the sights, sounds and smells of the village. Anne increased her grip on the reins, struggling to keep the horse under control while she carefully negotiated the main street. She received many curious stares from the surprisingly large number of people strolling the lane at this late hour of the morning. She drove past the blacksmith, cobbler, butcher and cooper, who made barrels, without stopping.

At the end of the street she could see the village church with its proud tower and large windows. She had better sense than to head in that direction, knowing her parents certainly would not be there.

Anne continued down the lane, her head whipping from side to side as she read the passing shop signs. One immediately caught her eye. *R.F. Firmin & Son, Shopkeepers.* The huge arched windows and stone tile roof of the building housing this fine establishment proclaimed its Tudor origins. The assortment of goods displayed in those windows—combs and brushes, children's toys, bolts of fine fabric and common articles of jewelry—told Anne this would be the place to find her wayward parents.

She climbed down from the carriage and tethered the horse to a hitching post. She approached the shop cautiously, hesitating to go inside, not fully prepared for what she might discover.

Balancing on the balls of her feet, Anne tried peering into the window beyond the displays, searching for a glimpse of today's customers. She did not immediately spy either of her parents, but the interior of the shop was vast. There was ample room for them to be tucked away in a back corner, no doubt making expensive and by-and-large useless purchases.

Anne felt a familiar pain clutch at her heart. With a sense of foreboding she entered the establishment. A bell attached to the top of the door announced her arrival. The short, round gentleman behind the counter glanced up at the sound. He smiled broadly in anticipation of a sale.

Anne smiled wanly and turned away to avoid making further eye contact with the clerk. She made a quick perusal of the shop's interior, discovering there were but a few customers. There was no sign of her parents. Yet the constant scribbling of the clerk's quill made Anne very nervous. It was obvious he was writing a bill for a rather substantial purchase.

Hoping to catch a glimpse of either the name or address on the parchment, Anne sidled closer to the counter. Keeping her eyes downcast and her movements slow, so as not to draw attention to herself, Anne inched nearer. She stretched her shoulders, lifted and craned her neck, then finally angled her body toward the counter.

Slow, steady, just a few more steps. *Hummph.* "I do beg your pardon," Anne stammered, raising her eyes to look at the person she had accidentally smashed into.

"There is no cause for concern. I am fine," a stout female voice began, but when the gray-headed matron looked closely at Anne her whole demeanor altered dramatically.

The woman's former friendly regard was replaced with a frosty chill of accusation. She gave Anne a thoroughly insulting perusal from head to toe, then pulled her skirt back as if trying to avoid contact with some loathsome object. Anne nearly shrank away from that fierce stare until she recognized the woman.

"I beg your pardon, Mrs. Havlen," Anne repeated her apology. "I believe we met the other evening at Lord Rosslyn's ball? I am Miss Paget, daughter of Lord and Lady Althen."

Mrs. Havlen's nostrils flared. She looked down her rather long nose at Anne in an accusatory manner. "You do not need to remind me who you are, young woman. I know perfectly well. And I prefer not to renew our brief acquaintance. Any female who would carry on so blatantly with Lord Mulgrave is not fit company for a gentlewoman. You might think that we are only provincial county folk, but we hold ourselves to a higher moral standard than that of London society. Here in Devon we have a *horror* of scandal."

Anne's palms started sweating. Mrs. Havlen had not bothered to cloak her remarks in even the barest of social courtesies. Her disapproval was most tangible. It hung in the room, inviting all to take a scandalous look.

Though the shop was not overly busy, there was enough of a crowd to increase Anne's discomfort. The clerk had ceased all pretense of writing and was obviously absorbed in every word exchanged. An older woman whispered something to her female companion, whose mouth dropped open in surprise. Both women glanced over at Anne in shocking disgust.

Deciding her only choice was to try and brazen it out, Anne met Mrs. Havlen's eye with unflinching directness.

"I danced but one waltz with the earl," Anne replied evenly. "We also shared supper together with my sister and Captain Nightingall."

"Nightingall!" Mrs. Havlen rolled her eyes. "I know all about that rogue, you can be sure. I refused to let my daughter dance with the man, no matter how much she pleaded. He is sinful. Hardly an appropriate chaperon. Spending time with him is scandalous in itself, yet I was told that you spent a considerable amount of the evening somewhere alone with Lord Mulgrave."

Mrs. Havlen lifted an eyebrow as if daring Anne to challenge her words, smug as a cat who's just captured a tasty bird for its dinner.

Anne breathed slowly through her mouth, imposing an iron control on her tongue. A flicker of unease swept through her. How in creation did Mrs. Havlen discover her shocking secret?

Mrs. Havlen was several inches shorter than Anne yet she still managed to look down her nose at her. Anne glanced away trying to avoid the older woman's glare. The contempt she felt directed toward her was most unsettling. Anne licked her dry lips. While she certainly could not pretend a demure modesty, given the truthfulness of Mrs. Havlen's statement, Anne also could not allow herself to be so publicly demeaned.

Anne felt her back stiffen. "The truth of the evening has been greatly misconstrued and I want no part of whatever malicious gossip you have heard, Mrs Havlen," she retorted. Anne spoke loudly enough for the clerk and the other women to hear her. "Repeating such drivel is simply hurtful and mean. You may consider yourself a gentlewoman, madame. I, however, am a lady."

"Indeed you are," a deep masculine voice intoned.

Anne swayed on her feet. Lord Mulgrave! Just how long had he been standing there? And more importantly, how much had he seen and heard of her humiliating encounter with Mrs. Havlen?

The earl moved beside Anne, linking his arm with hers. Mrs. Havlen's eyes widened. Grateful yet embarrassed, Anne could think of no way to refuse his support. She had never imagined the time would come when she was glad to see him. The warm sense of relief was rather brief, however, lasting only until the earl opened his mouth.

"My conduct and that of Miss Paget is absolutely no concern of yours, Mrs. Havlen," the earl said with cold ruthlessness. "Someday soon she will become my wife, and I expect everyone in the county will welcome her as my countess. Including you. If I am guilty of any social crime, it is in hoping to avoid the wagging of vicious, ill-bred female tongues. You have badly shaken my faith in the women of our community."

"There has been a grave misunderstanding, my lord," Mrs. Havlen sputtered, her mouth growing pinched.

"I think not, madame." The earl's gaze lifted to Mrs. Havlen's blustering face, and something nearly violent erupted in his intense green eyes. "It has always been my experience that females of compassion, propriety and good manners have highly disciplined tongues, Mrs. Havlen. I sincerely hope that, given time, yours will improve."

The older woman looked so despondent that for a moment Anne nearly felt sorry for her. But there was no time for sympathy or anything else. She and Lord Mulgrave sailed out of the shop without a backward glance. Anne did not awaken from her dazed state until they reached the cobblestone street.

She felt the earl's warm hand on her arm and realized that he was supporting her. "I'm fine," Anne insisted, trying unsuccessfully to shake him off.

"In a pig's eye," he muttered. The earl gestured toward Anne's humble cart. "Did you drive that into town?"

"Yes."

"I'll tie my horse to the back and drive us both to Sir Reginald's," the earl declared.

Anne opened her mouth to protest, but the fierce glow was still in his eyes, warning her not to interfere. Without comment she took her seat and waited while the earl tied his stallion to the rig.

Anne managed to hold her tongue until they had left the main street. "I thank you for your assistance, my lord. I was taken quite by surprise. You dealt with Mrs. Havlen in a most direct and cutting manner, although I'm not certain that lying to her was the most effective approach."

"I did not lie."

The earl's deep voice made her jump. Anne gritted her teeth against the tingles that coursed down her back. Turning her head, she announced boldly, "You most certainly did lie, my lord. We are not planning to marry."

His reaction was slow and deliberate. Lord Mulgrave guided the rig off the well-worn path and settled it in a secluded section beneath a towering oak. He dropped the reins and turned to face her. Anne tilted her chin, bracing for the confrontation. Their gazes locked.

"My dearest Miss Paget. We are two sensible adults who both know the proper solution to this dilemma. Why can you not simply accept your fate as inevitable and be done with it?"

His words crushed her. *The proper solution. Accept your fate as inevitable.* Was there ever a more cold, depressing, unromantic reason to marry?

"As I have already tried to explain, sir, I refuse to enter into a marriage merely to satisfy the preposterous rules of a hypocritical society. A society, I might add, that does not openly embrace me as a member unless it is trying to censure me. As for local opinion, Mrs. Havlen will simply have to apply her higher moral standard to someone who actually cares what she thinks.''

''Higher moral standard? What rot,'' the earl snorted. ''Mrs. Havlen's first grandchild was born a scant six months after her daughter's wedding. She is hardly fit to be casting the first stone.''

''What!'' Anne barely held onto her temper. ''Why, that old hypocrite. Well, her rude actions this morning merely enforce my position. Society is corrupt. I would be twice a fool to follow its dictates.''

''A noble sentiment, my dear, that I completely agree with in theory, but I'm afraid I must take the more realistic path.'' Lord Mulgrave propped his booted foot against the dropped front of the rig. He kept his voice firm and his eyes steady.

''There are others to consider. My daughter for one, your sisters for another. I choose to limit my contact with the *ton,* but as you can plainly see, those of the beau monde are not the only ones with strong moral opinions.

''Reputations and families have been ruined on far less than what occurred between you and me. At least we can take solace in the fact that we had a few stolen moments of pleasure, however brief. I should hate to be condemned for something purely fictitious.''

Anne's brow lifted cynically. ''You marry every woman that you kiss?''

He smiled roguishly. ''I marry every woman I am *caught* kissing. A subtle but important difference.''

''How reassuring.''

A smug, superior look entered the earl's green eyes. ''So it is settled. You will marry me.''

''I will not.'' Anne heard her voice starting to break, so she waited until she felt under control before continuing. ''I would ask you not to address me in such an authoritative, arrogant manner, yet I fear it is too much a part of your nature for any permanent change to occur. I do not know how I can make you understand . . .''

Anne's voice trailed off as she continued with her disjointed muttering. She raised her eyes to the gray sky, searching among the clouds for heavenly guidance.

"Am I really that objectionable?"

"No! Yes! Ahh . . ." Anne felt like stomping her feet in frustration. Yet how could she explain her feelings? He was appealing to her on so many levels, yet accepting his proposal— well, it wasn't exactly a proposal, it was more of a command— would change her life forever.

This morning's unpleasant encounter with Mrs. Havlen might have shaken Anne, but she was not cowed. And the physical temptation she felt for the earl was strong but not enough to entice her to surrender her uncertain future to a man.

Nerves wound tight, Anne attempted once more to explain her position. "It is not only society's dictates I object to, 'tis your dictates, my lord. You make me feel as though the decision for us to marry has already been determined and you absolutely refuse to deviate from this course of action. My objection, it appears, is quite immaterial."

Anne bit her lower lip and glanced out at the thick, dense woods. "I have always been taught that as a woman I had few choices in life. Most females believe that in a world they do not control, acceptance is the only response. Yet I stubbornly cling to my independence, even if in reality it might be more illusion than fact. Pray, do not take that from me."

"Never." He spoke gently, as if he sympathized with her feeling of helplessness. "Believe me when I say that I will never force you."

She turned her head to look at him. She did believe him. In spite of her resolve to keep her distance, Anne found herself leaning closer. Her body tingled as she drew nearer. He touched her chin with his fingers and tilted her head. She watched him with luminous eyes, waiting, wanting, yet slightly afraid.

The first touch of his lips against hers was silky and sensuous. Then he touched her with his tongue. Anne whimpered. His kiss seemed like a natural action, a feather-soft touch that left her aching for more. Anne's eyelids fluttered closed and she felt a stirring of warmth invade every part of her body.

She relished the sweet, strong taste of his lips. Her hands moved from her lap to rest on his chest. She could feel the hardness of his muscles, could sense the strength of his desire, yet there was a gentleness in his manner. He increased the pressure of his lips, making the kiss intimate and unique. All too soon he pulled away.

"At least you want to kiss me," he whispered huskily in her ear. "That's not a bad start. I suppose the perfect solution would be for you to fall in love with me straightaway."

"My lord." Anne smiled, even though a part of her wanted to run and hide from him. For deep within herself she knew the truth. She wanted far more from this man than his gentle kisses. Those sensuous thoughts were scandalous enough to make her blush, hot enough to even put Mrs. Havlen's gray head spinning.

Anne rubbed her forehead with the tips of her fingers. What was needed was a change of subject.

"I have been thinking about my unpleasant encounter with Mrs. Havlen. What disturbs me the most is her uncanny accuracy in the retelling of the events. I should very much like to know the source of her information."

The earl's expression was all innocence. "Don't point the finger at me, Miss Paget. I have better ways to spend my mornings than trading insults with Mrs. Havlen."

"It was something of a battle." She smiled impishly. "Be honest, who won?"

" 'Tis too soon to tell." The earl's smile faded. "I tried to warn you the other evening that this was a close-knit and inward-looking community."

Anne inhaled slowly. " 'Tis all so ridiculous. Everyone will be properly aghast at my social impropriety once the tale has been spread. Yet no one thinks twice about a married woman having any number of dalliances."

"Shocking."

"Don't mock me, my lord."

"Richard."

"Beg pardon?"

"Call me Richard. I shall call you Anne." He tilted his head to one side and looked at her for several moments without saying anything. "I was most sincere in my promise not to force you into an alliance you find objectionable. However, I must confess I have not changed my mind about our marriage. Spending time alone together, becoming better acquainted should allay your apprehension."

Anne uttered a sound of frustration. "That is idiotic. Spending time alone is precisely what got us into trouble in the first place."

"We will be discreet." Lord Mulgrave inclined his head. "I too have a reputation to protect."

Anne heard the amusement in his voice. Her cheeks began to color as she imagined hours spent alone in his company. He would keep his word and not force her, that much she believed. Yet she also knew the exact form of persuasion the earl would employ to have his way.

Long, soul-melting kisses. Sweet, forbidden caresses. Hot, sensuous desire. Anne gulped her embarrassment. She bent and retrieved a stray piece of hair ribbon from the floor of the rig. Anything to avoid those worldly, perceptive eyes.

"If I agree to pursue our . . . our friendship, will you promise to accept my decision?" Anne inquired.

"Yes."

It was almost too easy. Anne glanced suspiciously at Lord Mulgrave. He met her gaze unflinchingly as if he had nothing to hide. Anne folded her hands in her lap and leaned back against the seat in what she hoped looked like a carefree attitude.

Perhaps it was only an illusion that she was able to make her own decisions. At this moment she wasn't sure about anything.

Anne felt a great surge of relief when the earl took up the reins and maneuvered the cart onto the road. Conversation was stilted at first but became easier with each passing mile. Lord Mulgrave—Richard—had a wicked sense of humor. Anne found herself smiling with genuine amusement several times. Miraculously the storm clouds that had threatened so menacingly earlier in the morning simply blew away.

As Richard held her hand and assisted her out of the rig, Anne glimpsed a ray of sunshine breaking through the clouds. An eager groom stepped forward to untie Richard's horse from the back of the small rig, then led the cart away.

"Alexandra will be coming to have her special tea party with Rosalind tomorrow," Richard said calmly. "Though my daughter prefers to ride, I shall send her in my carriage. I expect you to use the vehicle to return to my home for an afternoon visit. Bring your maid, of course, for the sake of propriety, decency and gossip."

Anne did not reply, but he appeared not to expect an answer. He took her hand and raised it to his lips. His kiss was brief since they were being observed by more than one curious servant. Still, it set her heart racing. With a slight blush Anne pulled her hand back and hid her fingers in the folds of her gown.

He gave her one final bow, then swung onto his horse with muscular grace. "Until tomorrow, sweet Anne."

Richard smiled at her, a very private smile, then turned and disappeared down the road.

Chapter Eight

The earl's open-air black carriage traveled the mud-spattered road at a leisurely pace. The rains that had been threatening yesterday had arrived in the middle of the night with a vengeance, washing the air clean of the lingering heat but leaving the ground a muddy mess.

Anne, seated across from her maid Meredith, kept her gaze firmly fixed on the surrounding countryside. Although she had journeyed through sections of the area before, she was immediately struck by the pastoral beauty of the landscape and the acute difference between the green, lush farmland here in the south of Devon and the untamed and hilly terrain of northern Devon.

Anne remembered once hearing that the difference between north and south Devon could be seen in the cows. Those of the south, happy and content cream producers, grew fat on the abundance of green grass, while the cows of the north were angular and tough, chewing the wild cud of the moorlands.

Always one who embraced the unconventional, Anne was

surprised to discover that she far preferred the peacefulness found in the south of Devon. The set rhythm of an agricultural life with the planting of seeds and harvesting of crops and the breeding and raising of animals was in many ways a simpler, more direct existence.

If only there was some way the serenity of the countryside could influence and miraculously correct the chaos of her own life.

Anne sighed softly. She had spent yet another sleepless night of agonized indecision, not quite understanding how her carefully thought out plans had run so completely astray.

Sir Reginald's house was far from the safe haven Anne had anticipated, a place of excellent location and privacy that would bring Nicole the marriage proposal she'd dreamed about for months, and the rest of the family a much-needed respite from their continuing money troubles. Instead Nigel had left, apparently without declaring himself, and Nicole was sullen and withdrawn, refusing all of Anne's attempts to discuss the matter.

Anne was worried about her sister. Nicole had become a virtual recluse, haunting the rooms of the manor in a depressing, untidy state. She declined any and all social invitations, and Anne greatly feared that by the time her sister was ready to rejoin the colorful social Devon whirl, the invitations would no longer be forthcoming.

Her parents were an altogether different matter of concern. In an amazingly short time they had managed to form a solid bond with a local shopkeeper. This shrewd businessman was able and willing to procure any number of frivolous items, at outrageous prices, they desired.

Anne shuddered to think of bills that were rapidly mounting at this very moment. If she didn't find a new diversion for her mother and father quickly, the creditors would soon be pounding at the door demanding payment.

Both of Anne's brothers were having a good sulk today. They had been confined to the nursery, copying pages of hated

Latin and Greek texts as punishment for yesterday's ruckus. Their father had been fawningly apologetic to Sir Reginald over the lads' behavior and had assigned the punishment to make amends, although it was truly unnecessary since the boys had already been corrected.

What Anne's father failed to realize, however, was that William and Edmund would most likely behave twice as badly tomorrow after being held indoors all day today.

Only Rosalind appeared happy. She was clearly pleased with the worshiping attention of young Alexandra and had prepared for their upcoming tea party with all the unstinting abandon of a great hostess.

"This sure is a grand carriage, miss," the young maid Meredith suggested shyly. She ran her hand over the richly upholstered seat. "Soft as butter. Wait till I tell the others I got to ride in His Lordship's shiny new coach. They'll all be pea green with envy."

"It was most considerate of the earl to provide us with transportation," Anne replied. They sat comfortably side by side in the conveyance that was similar to a traditional phaeton but much larger and had an additional front bench to accommodate the driver. "I'm sorry that I was unable to greet Lady Alexandra and her governess when they arrived. Perhaps when we return to Sir Reginald's there will be an opportunity to visit with them."

Meredith nodded agreeably. Anne smiled faintly, then shifted nervously on the plush squabs, tightening the already strong grip on the sketchbook she held on her lap. She had brought it along on impulse. Yesterday Lord Mulgrave—Richard—had declared his wish to become better acquainted with her.

Anne decided it might be prudent to indulge him. Hence the sketchbook. Perhaps if he learned just a bit about her eccentric interests and her serious artistic desires, he would understand the futility of suggesting a matrimonial union between them.

For once her peculiar ambitions would work to her advantage.

Marriage was impossible. How could she willingly surrender all rights to her life, her future? The only notion that had kept her sane these last four years was the knowledge that once Rosalind was safely married Anne would be starting a new life, one of her own choosing. She could not possibly relinquish her freedom when she was so near to finally gaining it.

Anne shifted again on her seat, then straightened her narrow-brimmed dove gray bonnet. It contrasted nicely with her lavender walking dress and gave her confidence a much-needed boost. She had taken great care with her appearance today, choosing the least dowdy and most flattering costume from her meager wardrobe. With its simple lines and lack of adornment, the gown was hardly in the height of fashion but it suited Anne.

She adjusted the sketchbook on her lap and smoothed a small wrinkle from the skirt of her gown. They must be getting close to the earl's home. They had been traveling for nearly thirty minutes and with each subsequent turn in the road Anne's stomach lurched in anticipation. She flicked a glance at her maid, wishing she could feel just a tenth of the joyful excitement of the younger girl.

Meredith obviously viewed this afternoon as a great adventure. Anne thought of it as a necessary evil. She drew a deep breath, though the warm air did little to repair her nerves. Finally the coach made a sharp turn off the road, slowly negotiating a less worn path.

Anne craned her neck in open curiosity but the area was too densely forested with mature trees for her to see the manor. They approached the house down a narrow, winding lane with high hedges on either side, then eventually passed through a massive stone archway with open wrought-iron gates and two fierce granite lions standing guard.

As the carriage entered the gravel driveway, Anne could see the ornamental garden stretching before them. Beyond the gardens stood the manor house, and just beyond it a rich green valley of crops waiting to be harvested come fall. Anne won-

dered briefly if it was just her imagination but the light of the
sun seemed whiter and more brilliant here.

While the driver brought the carriage into the open courtyard,
positioning it at the impressive front entrance, Anne seized the
opportunity to study the house. Since it was an inherited property, not newly commissioned, Anne knew it would reflect the
taste of some long-dead ancestor, not the personality of its
current occupant.

Built in the traditional Elizabethan E pattern with long wings
projecting out on either side of the entrance court, the honey-
colored facade and its generous mullioned windows shimmered
golden in the sun. There were twisted finials and chimneys
reaching skyward from nearly every gable, creating a flamboy-
ant roof-line that resembled a forest of stone fingers. It was a
unique blend of romance, fantasy and age.

Once the carriage stopped, things became eerily quiet. The
earl was nowhere to be seen. A liveried footman came forward.
He put down the carriage step and held out his hand respectfully.
Anne balanced herself in the swaying coach and climbed down
with the servant's assistance, motioning for Meredith to follow.
The young maid giggled nervously as she descended.

The footman escorted them to the huge double oak doors,
which were immediately opened by the butler. He was a square,
stout individual with curly black hair and like many of his ilk
remained stone-faced and stiff-backed.

"Good afternoon, Miss Paget," the butler said. "His Lordship is expecting you."

The butler gazed expectantly at the sketchbook in her arms,
but Anne hugged it closer to her side, conveying her desire to
keep it in her possession.

She had only a moment to study her surroundings. Her artistic
eye was immediately struck by the vastness of the entrance
hall in which she stood. Directly ahead was a magnificent
staircase with an elegant iron balustrade curving gently upward,

drawing one's mesmerized gaze to the delicate plasterwork ceiling subtly colored in pink, lilac and green.

"Welcome to Cuttingswood Manor, Miss Paget. I hope you had a pleasant ride."

The earl entered the hallway with a congenial smile on his handsome face. His strides were long and firm. The tight buckskin breeches he wore molded the strong muscles of his thighs, which flexed powerfully with each step. Anne had difficulty not staring as her ridiculous heart started its customary madcap thumping.

"The weather and scenery made the journey most enjoyable, my lord." Anne colored slightly, then dropped a deep curtsey.

He took her hand and kissed it lightly. "Have you brought me a gift?" He smiled charmingly and inclined his head toward her sketchbook.

"No."

She pulled her hand back, not realizing how rude her answer sounded until she heard the butler's none too discreet cough. By sheer force of will Anne managed to keep the sudden flush of warmth in her chest from reaching her face.

The earl's smile deepened as if he guessed her secret. "I'm sure your maid will be more comfortable in the kitchen having tea with my staff. Roberts, escort Miss Paget's maid below stairs. I'll ring when we are ready for tea to be served."

Anne turned and caught a glimpse of Meredith who was being shepherded away, her eyes wide and her mouth agape at the splendor spread before her.

Anne turned back to the earl and for a moment she found it hard to breathe. He was a stirring sight. In these opulent surroundings she was suddenly more aware of his aristocratic bearing. Dressed in a dark green tailcoat, silver brocade waistcoat, white linen shirt and snowy white cravat, Lord Mulgrave was every inch the lord of the manor. In Anne's opinion it only served to enhance his obvious sexuality.

"I hope Alexandra and her governess arrived at Sir Reginald's home without mishap,'' Lord Mulgrave said. He placed his hand in the small of Anne's back and gently guided her through the hall. ''It was kind and tolerant of Rosalind to extend the invitation. Alexandra considers herself quite important now that she has such a mature friend.''

Anne smiled stiffly, very aware of his warm touch. ''Rosalind is equally delighted to have the company. It is rather stuffy and boring at Sir Reginald's and she sees little of other children. Though at fifteen I suppose I can hardly call Rosalind a child.''

''Rosalind is a very pretty young woman,'' Lord Mulgrave remarked. ''The young bucks and dandies will be swarming around her the moment she enters society.''

Anne frowned at the thought. She had enough problems coping with the beautiful Nicole at the moment. Adding Rosalind to the mix was almost too much to contemplate.

Anne resolutely pushed those troublesome thoughts aside as they passed through an elaborate drawing room and beyond that a smaller, cozier sitting parlor. The earl offered his arm and Anne latched onto it. She felt relieved to have the intimate touch at her back disappear, but Lord Mulgrave was close enough for her to still feel the sensual warmth radiating from his long, lean body.

The muscles of his arm felt strong and solid beneath the soft cloth of his coat. The tingling sensation that washed over her was promptly ignored. She drew a tight breath, then realized her mistake. The earl smelled alarmingly masculine, like leather and spice. It was an enticing aroma.

Anne again ignored her curious senses and made herself meet his eyes. ''Your house is spectacular, my lord. Did you spend much of your boyhood here?''

''Yes.'' He glanced down, assessing her with those worldly green eyes. ''And please, call me Richard.''

Anne swallowed, then turned her attention to the huge carved marble fireplace dominating the drawing room. It was so elaborate in detail it could take months to properly study each carving.

The artist in Anne appreciated the eagle with outstretched wings that formed the focal point of the fireplace, and the various depictions of pheasant, partridge and woodcock darting and perched amidst sycamore, oak and maple trees.

There was evidence of luxurious tastes in each room they entered, from the silver irons set before the many fireplaces to the exquisitely crafted inlaid furniture.

"This is most unusual plasterwork," Anne commented as she studied the walls of the blue salon, illustrating seventeenth-century village life. Her immediate favorite was the one showing a henpecked husband being berated by his wife as he drew ale from a barrel rather than attending to the baby he clasped in his other arm. "These are utterly charming."

"I had a suspicion you would like that one," Richard said with a smile. "Actually, I'm rather pleased to discover that a few of my ancestors had a sense of humor. Most of them were very serious, somber men."

"There is much to be said in favor of sobriety," Anne said primly.

"Hmmm, I find somber men a trial. All that clicking of tongues and cold, disapproving stares. Very tiresome."

"Is that why you retain the friendship of the Earl of Rosslyn and Captain Nightingall? To avoid the company of somber men?"

"Absolutely," Richard replied with a twinkle in his eye. "Compared to Ian and Miles I am the dull, boring member of the trio."

"A most terrifying thought." They shared a quiet laugh and Anne felt an absurd warmth. Knowing that he was most dangerous when he was being charming and agreeable, Anne deliberately shifted to a neutral topic. "Would you please relate some of the history of your beautiful home?"

"If you wish," Richard responded politely. "Sir Charles, the man who was awarded this house, wisely backed the right king in the War of the Roses and later served the Tudors by becoming Henry VII's ambassador to France. He had great political ambitions, as did most of the following generations, and enjoyed great royal favors."

"Do you also have political aspirations?"

"Not at all. I don't even sit at Lords when the House is in session. Politics annoys me. Perhaps when Alexandra is older and clamoring for more excitement and variety I will spend part of my year in town. For now I far prefer the country to London."

Anne pursed her lips. His indulgent tone agitated her. How casually he spoke of his political power. "Only a man used to a life of command and privilege would take such a cavalier attitude. Politics might be annoying and even unscrupulous, but at least you are afforded the opportunity to have your views and opinions heard. That is quite a bit more than most men, and certainly more than all women."

He gave her a charming, practiced smile. "I am not totally lacking in a sense of political duty. I have voted, more than once, to approve the army budget. Beyond that I find the Lords are mostly concerned with haggling over absurd questions of local government, such as whether or not a particular road should have a turnpike. An issue I'm sure even you would find boring.

"However, I applaud your political interests. When we are married I shall happily subscribe to the *Times* so you can keep abreast of all the current political intrigue. If you happen upon an issue of great concern, I will gladly consider your view and even vote your conscience, if it agrees with my own."

"Such liberal thinking!" Anne lowered her head for a moment, unable to decide if the fluttering in her stomach was anger or nerves. His easy self-confidence was infuriating and jealously coveted. "Must you continually be so annoyingly condescending? *When we are married,* indeed! Is it so impossible for you to humor me a bit? Can you at least say *if* we are married?"

"If we are married?" He looked bemused.

Anne drew a slow breath. "Better. Marginally."

His intense gaze captured hers. Anne stiffened her spine and waited for the argument to begin. But Richard merely smiled softly. "Come. I want you to see some of my gardens. They are among the most splendid in the county."

He looked so cool and composed, so arrogantly sure of himself that Anne wanted to scream. Her nerves were wound tight as a drum and she could feel the tension between them escalating.

She stared for a long moment at the bare hand he held out to her. He had long, elegant fingers and clean, short nails. The hand of an aristocrat, certainly, but it was equally evident there was the strength and power of a man who was not idle. After a brief hesitation Anne placed her fingers across his.

He led her out of doors and Anne pondered her situation. As usual, things were not progressing exactly as she had planned. Of course, that seemed to be the normal course of events whenever she was in the earl's company.

It took several minutes out in the sunshine for Anne to regain her equilibrium and relax enough to become aware of her surroundings. The earl certainly had not exaggerated the beauty of his grounds.

The enchanting formal gardens were laid out as a series of outdoor rooms within the warm brick Elizabethan walls. The first garden they entered boasted raised beds bordering the centrally located fountain with a riot of wallflowers, marigolds and dahlias flowering orange and red in vivid display.

They serenely followed the brick path leading through an arch to another garden. In this one there was a profusion of flowering pink, blue and purple plants expertly positioned around a sundial. They strolled next by apple, pear and plum trees thriving in the sun that were trained along the high brick walls of the large kitchen garden.

Richard proved to be a surprisingly knowledgeable guide,

answering all of Anne's questions and offering tidbits of interesting facts as they strolled.

Beyond the walls of the kitchen garden was yet another cozy
spot, festooned with roses and honeysuckle. Richard guided
Anne to a secluded garden bench and they sat together in
silence, listening to the hum of insects as time gently slipped
by.

" 'Tis glorious," Anne said, thoroughly enjoying this lovely
spot, the perfect place to sit on a pleasant afternoon, gazing
over the lush countryside. "One can almost feel the presence
of God amongst so much bountiful splendor."

"Utter perfection," Richard whispered.

Anne did not have to turn and look at him to know he was
staring intently at her. She could almost feel his eyes upon her
face. How ridiculous to call her plain features perfection! Yet
she felt her cheeks color. "The view, my lord. I am speaking
of the lush countryside."

"We each appreciate beauty in our own way, my dear."

He placed his arm along the solid wood top of the bench
and leaned closer. The air felt tight and sparse. Not quite sure
how she would react if the hand so perilously close to her back
suddenly came to rest upon her shoulder, Anne pulled out her
sketchbook and placed it solidly in her lap.

"Would you care to see my drawings?" she asked, opening
the book and displaying two of her more recent efforts. One was
a detailed rendering of the unusual pagoda near Sir Reginald's
ornamental lake and the other was a whimsical sketch of one
of the housemaids.

Richard reached over and positioned the book on his lap.
He bent low, peering closely at the sketches. Anne bit the inside
of her cheek as she awaited his reaction. It really shouldn't
matter what he thought. She had brought the sketches to reveal
her unsuitability to be his countess, yet as the quiet stillness
stretched on, she felt exposed and vulnerable.

"These are quite extraordinary." He pulled back and gave her a curious stare. "Did you really draw these?"

"Yes." Her cheeks heated. He sounded amazed.

The earl leafed carefully through the book, asking a myriad of questions. He appeared genuinely impressed by her work, and his praise was honest and complimentary without the offhanded tolerance Anne usually received from her family.

She had deliberately left her favorite drawings behind, feeling insecure about sharing something so intimate as her art with anyone. Now for a brief moment she wished she had included those special pieces that revealed more of herself.

"I can hardly believe you have done all these beautiful drawings. Have you studied for many years?"

"No. Never." Anne shook her head. He liked her work! "I have always longed for the opportunity to study art seriously. On the Continent. I can only hope that after my sisters are grown and married I will be able to fulfill my dreams."

She had chosen her words deliberately, hoping to convey to the earl the depth of her feelings and commitment to her art.

He lowered the sketchbook. "If you have never had a tutor, then I do not understand the need for you to study. The beauty of your work speaks for itself. Take this young sparrow." He lifted the book and repositioned it so they both could view the drawing. "You have somehow managed to make this humble bird seem majestic. It's delightful."

Anne exhaled slowly, trying to temper her pleasure. He really liked her work! Yet he failed to understand her commitment. "These are only sketches. I wish to paint in other mediums, specifically oils. And I ache for a true challenge. An unclothed human form in all of its God-given glory."

"Unclothed?" Richard raised an eyebrow.

"Of course." Anne had spoken impulsively. But she did not retract her words. "Are not some of the greatest works of the old masters done in the nude?"

"I have seen a few." The expression on his face turned

speculative. He gently returned the sketchbook to her lap. "But there is no need for you to leave the English shores to find a willing model."

"Indeed?" She knew him too well to be surprised, or even shocked, by his next remark. Still, she caught her breath to hear him speak the outlandish words aloud.

"I feel it is my duty as an English gentleman to offer myself as the subject of your next work." His eyes sparkled like newly fallen snow in the moonlight. "Lest you get the wrong impression, I must add that I am willing to make this supreme sacrifice only for the purpose of furthering your remarkable artistic talent."

"Naturally." She smiled ironically.

"I don't think you understand, my dear." The corners of his mouth turned up in a wry grin. "My offer is sincerely and honestly given. I would be honored to pose for you. In whatever state you require."

Anne's smile vanished. She stared disbelievingly at him, a mixture of terror, excitement and gratitude coursing through her at the realization that he was serious.

Was it possible? Would he really do this? Perhaps he was testing her? Or even mocking her?

His handsome face revealed little beyond a hint of challenge. His suggestion was highly improper. Outrageous. She should be burning with shame. A genteel lady would storm away in an indignant huff. Or slap his chin.

Posing nude? Indecent! Unthinkable! And so irresistibly wicked. She had never been offered anything so dangerous in her entire life.

Without fully considering all the implications, Anne found herself saying quite calmly, "I've never had a male pose for me, with or without his clothing. 'Tis a scandalous notion, but I suppose it could remain a private matter between us. And it would be a great artistic challenge." She glanced away and took a deep breath. Gathering her nerve, she concluded strongly,

"I would be most pleased to accept your very kind and generous offer, Richard."

The sudden silence was deafening.

What had she done? Anne opened her mouth to rescind her impulsive words but stopped when she beheld Richard's astonished expression. He looked far more shocked than she could possibly feel.

They stared at each other for a long moment, taking each other's measure. It seemed as though now that the offer had been made and accepted, the real challenge was about to begin.

"Shall we start today?" The earl leapt from the bench and strode about the edge of the garden, as if searching for an appropriate location. "The weather is promising and the garden totally secluded. You have the sketchbook with you. Do you need a pencil?"

"I have one." Anne dug through the small reticule that hung from her wrist and produced a stubby but adequate pencil with a surprisingly fine point.

"Excellent." He smiled broadly, giving her the full force of his charm. "Shall I stand here? Or would you prefer these thick hedges for a background."

"Near the hedges is fine." Anne was suddenly finding it difficult to breathe evenly. He was actually going to go through with this. And so was she.

Feeling an almost detached sense of disbelief, Anne watched the earl casually remove his coat, waistcoat and cravat. His eyes never left hers as he began unbuttoning his shirt, revealing the hairs on his broad chest. The atmosphere between them rippled with escalating heat as he opened the final button on the shirt and carelessly dropped the fine linen garment to the grass.

Unclothed, his shoulders looked broader, his chest more muscular, and his waist leaner than beneath his finely tailored garments. There was a silky mat of darker hair in the center of his chest, and flat male nipples nestled within those tufts immediately drew and held Anne's gaze.

Just the sight of his naked chest was enough to make a maiden's heart flutter. His potent masculinity had a wild, primitive beauty she had never seen, and Anne worried that she would be unable to capture that spirit and excitement on canvas.

Especially since there was something about all that strong male skin that left her with an unfamiliar, fierce need to press her fingers to it, to spread her hands lovingly across the warm expanse of hard muscle.

Anne remained perfectly still while this unfamiliar tension vibrated through her. She watched his movements in an almost dreamlike manner, yet when Richard reached for the first button at the top of his breeches, she came vibrantly to life.

"Stop!" She pressed her lips together, and her teeth nearly bit through her bottom lip. "That is enough. I shall sketch your upper torso first, and I certainly have plenty to work with for the moment."

"Are you sure?"

His tone was so calmly nonchalant Anne almost envied his ease. Apparently, males were just more natural and casual about nudity than females. Although she briefly wondered what his reaction would be if she was standing before him bare from the waist up. Shock? Desire? Amusement?

How ridiculous to speculate on something that would never happen. Anne returned her complete attention to her noble model, hoping she would at least be able to properly grip her pencil. Now was not the time to turn into a silly, fluttery girl. She was an artist.

For a long moment Anne didn't move or speak. She just stared. Then with shaking fingers she began sketching the broad expanse of the earl's shoulders. After a few quick strokes she realized the shoulders were so far out of proportion there would hardly be room for the rest of him on the page.

With a sigh she flipped the parchment and began anew. She

tried focusing her attention on small details, although there was not much on the earl's person that was diminutive. The problem was she needed to calm her racing heart and view the earl less as a wholly desirable man and more as an artistic subject.

"Shall I alter my pose?" Richard inquired, obviously noting her distraction.

"Not until I tell you."

"As you wish."

Anne smiled. What a rare position she found herself in. It was a heady feeling to realize that this powerful, commanding man would do her bidding. Follow her direction. Succumb to her will.

Feeling empowered, Anne turned her attention entirely to her work. Richard was an excellent model; he held his position still, yet naturally. Her pencil and imagination flew across the page.

Anne became totally absorbed in her task, barely noticing when a fat, round bee flew swiftly from the fragrant border of flowers and came to rest precariously on the earl's shoulder.

"Take care, Richard," Anne called out in warning, observing a second too late the insect's interest in her model.

The earl turned sharply at Anne's words, but his sudden movement served only to anger the curious insect. It fluttered down his naked chest and then stung him, rather viciously, in a most indiscreet location.

Chapter Nine

Richard yelled with surprise and pain. He swatted at the bee but the damage had been done. Well, it was probably exactly what he deserved for strutting about the garden half-naked and acting like a fool. Still, it hurt like the devil.

"Oh, Richard." Anne raced across the small expanse of lawn with surprising speed and agility despite her long, cumbersome skirts. "I tried to warn you, but it was too late. That nasty creature! Are you alright?"

His lips twitched. Good Lord, it was only a pesky insect bite. He had seen and endured far worse during his years as a soldier. But it gave his weary heart a lift to know that the almost frightened, concerned expression in Anne's eyes was on his behalf.

" 'Tis a bee sting, Anne."

"I know, but they can be serious. Are you certain you feel alright? No difficulty catching your breath? Are you having any strange or unusual twinges?" She moved closer and searched his face with anxious eyes. "When I was a girl the gardener's young helper was stung by a fat bee and the poor lad nearly died. His neck swelled and his breathing became so labored we all thought he would perish. 'Twas a miracle he survived.''

"I am fine." Richard shifted uncomfortably. She was close enough that he could feel the brush of her soft curls against his bare chest. He noticed that a certain part of his anatomy was indeed starting to swell. And it definitely wasn't his neck. He took a small, modest step away from his anxious nurse.

"Oh, dear, it is growing larger," Anne gasped. "And turning red."

"What?" Richard sputtered.

"I'll get a wet cloth."

She scurried away and Richard belatedly realized she was referring to the bee sting. He lifted his shoulders, sucked in his already flat stomach and looked down, searching for the spot where he had been bitten. Near his navel he noticed a slight, red bump.

Richard grinned. Ahhh, the infamous injury.

"Come, sit on the bench," she said, returning.

Because it seemed so inexplicably important to her, and because he was in truth enjoying all of her flustering attention, Richard allowed himself to be led to the garden bench.

She wrung out the wet cloth she had cleverly dunked in the ornamental fountain and folded it neatly. Richard noticed the finely embroidered monogram and realized it was her handkerchief.

"This should bring you some relief," Anne stated seriously, carefully pressing the wet cloth against the small bite.

Richard groaned, then quickly tried to disguise it as a cough. It was a mistake to let her touch him, he'd realized the instant her warm hand came in contact with his stomach, but by then it was too late.

He fixed his stare on the far end of the ornamental rose bed and tried counting the flowers within each cluster to distract himself. Silence filled the garden. Not even one lone insect buzzed.

What sort of spell was she weaving over him? Richard wondered. With each encounter, he felt the need to possess her grow stronger and more certain inside him. But she seemed steadfast in her determination to refuse his honorable offer of marriage.

She was probably the only woman of society he had ever met who did not feel the need for the security of marriage. After viewing her sketches and hearing her speak of her dream to paint and study, he felt he was at last able to understand a part of her reluctance.

Yet why couldn't a married woman pursue her artistic gift? Her talent would surely not disappear upon the reciting of her marriage vows.

He set one hand beneath Anne's chin and raised her face.

"I feel much better, my dear. Thank you."

"Are you sure?" Her gaze was still anxious with concern. "Shall I go to the house and get some salve?"

Richard smiled. "I fear you would have made a shockingly poor nurse if you followed the drum, fussing and worrying over such a trivial wound as my bee sting."

She reached up and smoothed back a stray lock of hair from his forehead. Her lovely eyes were filled with compassion. "It must have been horrible on the battlefield. I can barely imagine it. So much death and brutality."

A lighthearted response sprung instantly to his lips. He was so accustomed to lying about the war, especially to a female, but somehow the words became lodged in his throat. Something inside him urged Richard to share just a bit of the truth with her.

"Even after all this time, 'tis the sounds I remember most vividly. Bloodcurdling screams of anguish that were so alien you would wonder if it was the cry of a man or a beast."

Richard swallowed hard at the memory. "It was, I believe, an accurate representation of hell itself."

She was quiet a long time. He was beginning to fear he had truly shocked her speechless until she whispered raggedly, "It pains me to think of you enduring all that suffering."

He pulled in a heavy breath. "I was among the fortunate ones. I returned to my home and family, alive and whole. Far too many did not, including several young men under my command." Richard cleared his throat loudly, mortified to feel moisture in his eyes. He turned his head away, hoping Anne had not seen his weakness.

But she must have seen something because she reached for his hand and lifted his clenched fist to her mouth. Richard tensed, but she gently kissed each finger until he slowly relaxed and turned toward her.

"I'm sorry," she said. "So very sorry."

Anne buried her head against his shoulder and he enfolded her in his warm embrace. She felt solid and real, and the light touch of her tender caress down his forearm was like a soothing balm.

He held her loosely against his naked chest and marveled that her simple understanding could bring him such comfort. Richard did not consider himself an overly demonstrative man. He hugged his young daughter often, embraced his good friends Ian and Miles on occasion, and even gave his nephew Nigel a hearty hug once or twice a year. But there was something unique about holding Anne so close to his heart that brought a feeling of serenity to his soul.

Richard allowed himself a few more moments of quiet reflection before the absurdity of their situation registered in his mind. He was sitting half-naked in his garden embracing an unattached, unchaperoned female. His servants were well trained and would never dream of disturbing the earl's privacy, but that could change in an instant if a friend or neighbor decided to make an afternoon call, as was often the case.

Though he was loath to disturb the gentleness of the moment, Richard knew they should return to the house. Soon. He sighed with regret, then lowered his head and brushed his lips lightly across Anne's temple, just below the rim of her bonnet. He felt her inhale sharply.

"Will you come visit me again tomorrow?" Richard whispered against her ear. "You may continue with your sketching, though perhaps it would be wiser if I pose for you inside the manor house, in one of the more private salons. Bees are strictly forbidden there."

He heard her small laugh. Then she turned her head until their lips were separated by a mere breath. "I will return," she promised before pressing her lips lightly against his.

Her kiss was full of sweetness and some emotion he had not yet deciphered. It would have ended as gently as it began had she not pressed herself forward for a second kiss. And then a third.

Richard found himself lingering over each kiss, savoring the flavor. Anne's mouth clung to his. Sweet, warm and inviting. Richard felt his body grow hard, responding as it always did to her nearness.

Her kisses stopped his mind from racing, his brain from thinking, and allowed his ardor to carry the moment. Anne started stroking his bare chest, her nimble fingers creating an aching void deep inside him. Richard fought to hold back the emotions that swamped and controlled him but soon lost the battle.

With a half groan of surrendered frustration he greedily accepted all she freely offered him.

He took his time, molding her soft lips to his, enticing her mouth open so he could touch her teeth with his tongue. Her breath mingled with his as she welcomed his invasion, and he kissed her hard and deep.

It was remarkable how her body softened to fit so exactly and easily against his. The comfort her nearness had brought was now replaced with an aching, spiraling urgency that shimmered between them. With each kiss it gained in strength. Built in intensity.

Richard dropped his hand to the swell of Anne's breast, closing it possessively over the sweet mound. She moaned with encouragement. He rubbed gently. Her nipple stiffened against his palm and she gasped, pressing herself closer. The elemental heat they seemed to generate so easily between them burned hotter.

Anne was melting in his arms, her passionate nature and lack of experience combining to make her an easy target for seduction.

Richard's fevered brain raced. He could teach her. She was clearly eager and ready to learn. He could succumb to temptation and arouse the natural passion within her. He could give them both the piercing excitement and shattering closeness of a shared climax. A shared loving.

"Have you changed your mind?" he asked breathlessly, pulling himself reluctantly away from her warmth. "Will you become my wife?"

"Oh, Richard." Anne's lashes fluttered as her eyes slowly opened. She blinked several times, but the motion did not fully remove the passion from her eyes. "Marriage is an irrevocable step that I fear I am not, nor will likely ever be able to take."

"Yet you feel ready for this?" His hand tightened about her hip and he strained fully toward her, pushing himself back and forth against her upper thigh, letting her feel the hardness of his erection.

"No," she whispered. "But I am bold enough and curious enough and probably foolish enough to want it. To want you."

He stared into her luminous eyes and realized she was as shaken as he. There was a yearning in her voice that bespoke the surrender of her will and the seduction of her body.

His own body went rigid. He wanted to comply. His loins were aching, throbbing for the fulfillment that only Anne could provide. Yet Richard refused to succumb. He would not allow their passionate natures to rule them.

He knew he was fighting for something very important. He wanted more than her lovely body. He wanted her heart. And her mind. Permanently. It was unthinkable to consider anything less.

A stream of foul curses hovered on the edge of his tongue. He swallowed them, hardly believing he would actually utter these words to a lovely woman who had just expressed her desire to couple with him. Yet Richard nevertheless found himself saying reluctantly, "I do not want to be your lover, Anne."

"I see." She blushed but did not lower her eyes. "I apologize for my unseemly behavior. I was under the apparently false impression that you desired me."

"Stop being idiotic, Anne," Richard snapped. He could hardly credit that such an intelligent woman could be so dense at times. Not want her? Was the woman daft? "You cannot possibly mistake my desire."

Anne licked her lips. "I fear that I must have," she replied softly.

"Bloody hell!" Frustration careened through Richard's veins. Grasping her wrist roughly, he pulled her hand toward the front of his breeches and crudely placed it on his fully aroused, straining erection. "There! Can you feel, my dear, how very much I do not want you?"

Her mouth formed a perfect, silent circle of shock. Richard immediately regretted his action but he had no time to offer an apology. For instead of yanking her hand away in maidenly horror, Anne began a tender, curious exploration.

It was sheer torture. Her head was bent low, but he caught a glimpse of her stunned expression before her fingers closed around him. Slowly, deliberately she began stroking him.

Richard froze. And grew larger.

"It moved," Anne gasped.

Richard closed his eyes. "This particular part of the male anatomy often seems to have a will of its own, yet I can assure you that my will is stronger," he murmured in a strained voice. His eyes snapped open. He gave her an intense look that had been known to wither the resolve of many a hardened soldier. " 'Tis only fair to warn you that I have decided that I shall not be your lover unless I am also to be your husband."

Her hand abruptly fell away. "I understand."

Richard felt a ripple of anguish pass through him. It was damned inconvenient at times to have a conscience. The ache in his groin was now an acute pain. He took a slow, deep breath, fearing that any sudden movement would surely burst the buttons on his breeches.

He waited several minutes before moving away from Anne and began to slowly clothe himself. The distance and silence provided a much-needed respite from his temper and frustration. Feeling calmer after retying his cravat, Richard propped one elbow on the top of the garden wall and placed his other hand on his hip. He considered his companion carefully.

Anne had trouble meeting his eyes. "I promise that I shall seriously consider your offer of marriage. Yet I doubt my answer will be changed."

Richard nodded his head curtly. Knowing he had little choice, he accepted her answer. For now.

"Time for tea," he said, offering his arm.

He escorted his guest into the drawing room and they spent the remainder of Anne's visit discussing matters of trivial concern. Normally Richard acted from instinct when it came to women, but his unconventional experience with Anne forced him to reassess his strategy. For the rest of the afternoon he opted to allow politeness and good manners to rule the day.

When it was time for Anne to depart, Richard escorted her outside. He kissed her hand briefly and properly and watched as his coachman assisted her into his carriage. She did not look into his eyes as she muttered her goodbye nor look back once after the carriage pulled away.

Richard held his position, feet braced apart for balance. While observing the coach's progress, he continually wondered why her somber mood affected him so deeply.

Anne wondered too. Why she felt such a deep sense of regret. Or rather what exactly was she regretting? That she had acted cheaply, and offered herself to the earl like some tavern wench? Or that he had refused? Did she truly regret that they hadn't become lovers?

Was that what she really wanted from the earl? To become his . . . his mistress for a brief time? If that happened, there would be no romance, no love, no true intimacy between them. Would she be content to settle for that sort of relationship? One that lacked tenderness and emphasized the frenzy of physical passion only?

Most confusing of all to Anne was the fact that despite all of her conflicting emotions, her determination to remain unmarried was barely shaken. She would reconsider his proposal, but her reasons for remaining single were unchanged. The earl might have given her mind, and body, a new direction of thought, but he had failed to erase her old resolve.

Apparently, the question of her becoming involved with Richard was a moot point anyway. She could speculate and wonder long into the night whether or not she would be satisfied with a merely physical affair, but he had made his position abundantly clear.

It was marriage or nothing.

Anne smiled. His control amazed her. She had become so quickly heated by their passion it seemed as if her body had become quite separated from her mind and emotions. But Richard had remained in command of his will, if not the reactions of his body.

How wickedly male he had felt to her hands. Hard and strong, yet his skin was so hot and silky. His body had been rigid and tense with need, and it ignited the fires within her. He was the first man, the only man, she had ever touched with passion, and she feared that once aroused it would be difficult to let her ardor lie dormant.

Yet, ever practical, Anne realized it must.

Shivering thoughts and remembrances of the earl consumed her so completely on the return journey that she was startled to realize the coach had arrived back at Sir Reginald's.

Anne was visibly flustered as the footman assisted her from the carriage, but at least she had the presence of mind to send her maid to quickly fetch Lady Alexandra and her governess.

It was imperative that they set out for home at once. The sky had turned gloomy, and Anne feared that the earl's daughter would become soaked in the open carriage.

An impending crisis in the nursery involving her two younger brothers and a cricket bat regrettably prevented Anne from greeting young Alexandra and meeting her progressively opinionated governess, Miss Fraser.

Anne hoped there would be another opportunity. Yet she wasn't certain there would be, since during her long carriage ride Anne had once again reached the inevitable conclusion that she could not marry the earl.

It would be a monumental mistake. Still, it was a great temptation. *Richard* was a great temptation. Anne knew she would never receive a better offer from a better man. Perhaps if she liked the earl less she might seriously consider his offer of marriage. No, that wasn't right either.

Anne had honestly never thought she would have an opportunity to marry and had set the course of her life accordingly. Consequently, she was simply unprepared for the sacrifices, especially on the part of a woman, that marriage involved. Thus far Anne had already made far too many sacrifices and compromises with her future.

However, one persistently nagging thought played over and over in her mind. Lord Mulgrave could ease some of her burdens. He was a wealthy man and could provide a great many things for her family.

Nicole would be assured a second season and a second chance to find a proper husband if Nigel failed to propose. Rosalind's future would also be secured, and in the meanwhile she would be thrilled to be related to her new young friend, Alexandra.

The boys would have an opportunity to continue their studies without Anne having to scrimp and save for the tuition, and her parents could at least remain debt free for a portion of the year.

It would in truth solve a great many problems if Anne became the earl's wife. Yet for each problem solved, a new one was likely to be created. Anne sighed as her innate honesty took hold. Good heavens, what would Richard think if he knew his marriage proposal would encompass all of that?

The family was her responsibility. She had no right to shackle someone else with that burden.

With that somewhat depressing thought repeating in her head, Anne took herself off for the front salon to join her parents and sister. Sir Reginald kept country hours and ate supper ridiculously early in the evening, but since their arrival he had begun the pretentious ritual of an adult gathering for cordials and conversation before the meal.

He claimed it improved his digestion to have a civilized discourse at the start of his supper. Anne decided that Sir Reginald's definition of *civilized* was rather loose, since she found these conversations awkward and stilted. By and large they had a most adverse effect on her own appetite.

Yet though Anne found it a tiresome routine, as an uninvited house guest she had little choice but to comply. She arrived a few minutes early and found only her mother and Nicole waiting.

Her sister, Anne noticed, looked pale and tense, but her mother seemed in boisterous spirits.

"Ahhh, Anne, there you are," Lady Althen chirped the moment her daughter entered the room. "I've hardly set eyes on you all day. Come and see the lovely ring your father has given me. Although I must confess I did help him make the final selection. Is it not precious?"

Anne hesitated. Not another ring! She looked at her mother, then glanced outside. A cold fist of tension clutched at her stomach. It was not so much the gaudy ring her mother was so clearly eager to show Anne that made her angry. She was far more concerned over the unknown number of items that would remain hidden until the bills had to be paid.

Just thinking about them made Anne's jaw lock.

For a long moment the only sound in the room was from the soft crackle of wood burning brightly in the fireplace. Lady Althen waited expectantly. Anne finally relented and with a deep sigh moved forward to dutifully gaze at the ring her mother proudly displayed. It had a large, square-cut ruby stone and was set with gold and diamonds. It glittered expensively on the woman's finger.

"That must have cost a pretty penny," Anne said tersely. "Yet if I recall correctly, both you and Father have already spent this quarter's allowance."

"Oh, posh, what do a few more baubles matter?" Lady Althen insisted, lifting her hand toward the light of the flickering fireplace. She spread her fingers and openly admired her latest gift. "Besides, it is vulgar for a woman to discuss money, even amongst family."

Anne felt fury explode in her brain but she forced herself to remain calm. She should be used to this sort of reckless behavior by now, but it still hurt. Her mother did not seem to understand about consequences. Or responsibility. She never had. Actually, she did not seem to understand about anything other than getting her own way.

"We have discussed often the need to be prudent in our spending, Mother," Anne muttered between tight lips. "Especially while Nicole and Rosalind remain unwed and the boys are so young."

"Enough!" Lady Althen declared, raising her voice. "I have grown weary of your endless lectures on responsibilities. It is most tiresome. Sometimes I think you forget exactly who is the parent and who is the child."

"So do you, Mother," Anne whispered defensively.

"My word!" Lady Althen raised her head. "You always were a bossy little girl, but you have grown into a positively dictatorial woman. I cannot imagine what a handsome and dashing gentleman like the Earl of Mulgrave sees in you. 'Tis no wonder the man has not yet made you a proper offer."

The Earl of Mulgrave? Anne felt her eyes widen. Why on earth did her mother mention him? Lady Althen had never said anything about him or the passionate embrace she had witnessed between Anne and the earl on the night of the masquerade ball. And now she spoke of him and marriage. All in the same breath.

She exchanged a nervous glance with Nicole. Anne was astute enough and experienced enough to recognize trouble when she saw it. When their mother became fixated upon a subject, it was close to impossible to shake her from it. Heaven help them all if Lady Althen ever discovered the earl had in fact proposed marriage to Anne. And that she had refused.

Anne straightened and met her mother's eye. Lady Althen's mood was clearly unsettled, but that did not deter Anne. "We were not discussing the earl. We were discussing your new ring."

"I would think that a girl of your advanced age and limited prospects would be far more concerned about getting a ring, a wedding ring, properly placed on her finger." Lady Althen considered her daughter long and hard. "Fortunately, you are blessed with a mother who takes more than just a passing interest in her daughter's future. I take action.''

Anne felt her nerves jump. Her mother was taking action? Now, that was a truly terrifying notion. "What . . . what exactly have you done?" Anne inquired cautiously.

"Well, let us just say that I have whispered a word or two in the right ear. I shall be much surprised if an offer is not made very soon for your hand in marriage.''

The smug look of satisfaction on Lady Althen's face was a telltale sign of imminent disaster.

"Who? Who have you been whispering to?" Anne demanded frantically.

"Mrs. Havlen. Sir Reginald told me she is the biggest snob and most efficient gossip in town. Your father and I met her in Mr. Firmin's shop. I thought it a great oversight that Mrs. Havlen had not heard of all the particular attention the earl lavished upon you at Lord Rosslyn's ball.'' Lady Althen smiled slyly. "She was fascinated by the information.''

"Oh, Mother!" Anne wailed. "How could you do such a thing?" She felt a shudder of anger race through her body. "I met Mrs. Havlen quite by accident soon after you left Mr. Firmin's shop. She acted horribly. I was practically shunned.''

Lady Althen shrugged expressively. "Then all is going according to plan. Perhaps now that the earl knows what an enormous scandal he has created, he will finally act like an honorable man and marry you.''

Anne almost bit her tongue. It took all her strength to suppress her anger and outrage. How could her mother be so foolish? And so devious?

Anne prepared to give her mother a scathing lecture, but a tiny voice of conscience intervened. By what right did she cast the first stone? Had she in fact been honest while scheming to find husbands for her sisters? Were they all not in truth living a lie of wealth and prosperity thanks to Anne's clever manipulation of several unsuspecting relatives?

Anne bowed her head in shame. For the first time she felt a sharp pang of guilt over her deceptions. She had dragged her family to Devon specifically with the intention of securing, under somewhat false pretenses, a marriage proposal for Nicole.

Wasn't Lady Althen now doing the same thing for Anne? Perhaps Anne had not gone to the extremes her mother had. After all, she had never deliberately caused a scandal to force a proposal, but frankly, that hadn't been necessary. But in the end were her actions really so different from her mother's?

"I was initially concerned that if you marry the earl and Nicole marries his heir, well, clearly only one of you can be a countess at a time," Lady Althen declared with a puckering frown. "And then I decided if *Anne* can somehow manage to land herself an earl, then Nicole should certainly set her sights higher. Why, even a duke would not be beyond her reach, I should imagine."

"Really, Mother," Nicole blushed.

" 'Tis the truth," Lady Althen insisted. "And now that you have turned Nigel away and refused his proposal, then we must keep our eyes open for an appropriate nobleman. One who is worthy of you."

Anne frowned in puzzlement. "I was unaware that Nigel had made an offer. And that you rejected it." Anne studied her sister's beautiful face. "I thought your heart was set on the match. Why did you not tell me? And why have you sent Nigel away?"

"Please do not be angry with me. I don't think I could bear it." Nicole's eyes filled with sudden tears. She bit her upper lip and dropped her head dejectedly. "I simply could not agree to be Nigel's wife. Not feeling as I do about another. I'm very sorry, Anne. I know that I have made a complete mess of everything."

Anne sat down hard on one of Sir Reginald's upholstered chairs. Nicole's hurt was so genuine, her unhappiness so real. Anne knew that Nicole had been upset but had not pressed her sister hard enough to discover the reason. She felt a jolt of guilt. Her preoccupation with the Earl of Mulgrave had left her blind to the depth of her younger sister's suffering.

"Are you certain, Nicole?" Anne inquired softly. "You were very taken with Nigel in London earlier in the season. And 'tis plain for all to see that he is quite smitten with you. Perhaps you will reconsider his offer?"

Nicole struggled to draw a deep breath. "I cannot."

Anne felt disgust. Thorough and absolute. With herself.

They had followed Nigel here so Nicole could find a husband and happiness. She had found neither.

Anne wasted no time. She strolled with great purpose to the far side of the drawing room. She gathered parchment, a quill and a pot of ink from the compact writing desk in the corner of the room and set about composing a letter to their great-aunt Sophie who lived in Bath.

Anne had never met nor corresponded with this woman who was the sister of her grandmother, but it didn't matter. Everything was at sixes and sevens. There seemed to be no simple way to make it right, so Anne resorted to the only solution she knew would work. It was time to move on. It was time to leave Devon.

Chapter Ten

"I thought I would surprise Alexandra and take her riding this afternoon but I was told by her governess that she is once again visiting the Pagets," Captain Miles Nightingall complained to the earl. "This is the third time that has occurred this week. Egad, Richard, is it necessary to make an appointment in order to see your daughter?"

Propping his shoulders against the mantelpiece of his drawing room, Richard smiled at his friend. "Alexandra is extremely fond of you, Miles. But she is completely besotted with Rosalind Paget and seizes every opportunity to spend time with her idol."

"Pity." Miles arrogantly lifted his brow. "Alexandra is probably the only female of my acquaintance that I eagerly anticipate spending any length of time with. And now even she has deserted me."

"Have a seat," Richard offered his friend. "I shall pour you some fine French brandy to drown your sorrows."

"I will not refuse a glass, although I must insist that I am not one to moon over a woman,'' Miles declared, sprawling comfortably on the brocade settee beneath the mullioned windows. ''I believe that honor belongs to your nephew Nigel.''

''Alas, no longer. My nephew must now sulk without an audience.'' Richard handed Miles a drink. ''I have sent a rather subdued Nigel off on an extended tour to inspect my estates in Scotland.''

''Excellent decision. Separating Nigel from the source of his imminent downfall is his only chance at salvation. You always were a first-class tactician, Richard, in military strategy as well as in chess.'' Miles lifted his glass in salute before taking a healthy gulp. ''I imagine the younger Miss Paget is now devastated by Nigel's absence?''

''I'm not certain. I haven't seen Nicole since Nigel departed, though some interesting gossip has reached my ears.'' Richard gave his companion a shrewd glance. ''In hindsight I'm not all that certain it was necessary to send Nigel away. It appears that the lovely Nicole has shifted her attention from my nephew and lined you up in her sights.''

Miles rolled his eyes expressively. ''Lord save me from enthusiastic virgins.''

''That is not what I have been hearing.'' Richard lifted the stopper off the crystal brandy decanter and poured himself a generous portion, having an inkling that this discussion might require some fortification.

''Reports of the London exploits of Captain Miles Nightingall have even reached us here in sleepy Devon. Frankly, I'm at a loss to understand it all. Your behavior has been both reckless and dangerous, even when taking into consideration that probably no more than half the stories are true.''

''Bloody hell, not you too, Richard.'' Head snapping back, Miles sat up. A deep black scowl lined his handsome features. ''It has been difficult enough listening to Ian's poorly disguised lectures on decorum these past few days. Ian talking about proper behavior! The man who in a crowded ballroom, on a dare, once asked the Duchess of Penwick if he could try on her false teeth.''

"Ian always did have a high-spirited attitude with certain members of the *ton,*" Richard said with a chuckle, remembering the incident all too clearly.

"High-spirited! Ian has slept with more women, run from more irate husbands, and wagered more coin on horses and cards than any man I've ever known. I should be insulted by his little talks if it weren't so downright laughable.''

"I am not trying to be condescending,'' Richard said mildly. "Ian may be wild but he is never reckless. You have been. We are both worried about you, Miles.''

"Don't be,'' Captain Nightingall huffed. He gazed out the window, then turned back to the earl. "I've come here searching for a bit of peace. If I wanted a lecture I would go home. My esteemed older brother has a wide variety of discourses he enjoys repeating. All about chivalry, appropriate behavior befitting a man of my rank, and upholding the family honor that has never once known a trace of scandal. They are each tiresome in their own unique way.''

For the first time Richard heard the edge of irate weariness in Miles's voice. It disturbed him deeply. "I only want to help,'' Richard said firmly. "As does Ian.''

"Thank you.'' Miles graciously inclined his head. "If I require your assistance, I shall ask for it.''

Richard said nothing. He took a drink of his brandy, fully appreciating Miles's anger. If the situation were reversed, he would probably react in much the same manner. For now Richard conceded there was nothing more that could be done. He had offered his help. Sincerely and in good faith. He could only hope that Miles would indeed ask for it, if it was required.

"I've been thinking about having a party,'' Richard tossed out, deciding a change of subject was in order. "Nothing as grand as Ian's ball, but a simple gathering of local society.''

"A party?'' Miles shook his head. "I believe all these years rusticating in the country has muddled your brain. I can remember when we would do just about anything to avoid the constant crush of people, the petty gossiping and the crafty matchmaking matrons that frequent these affairs. And now you are hosting these torturous events. First Ian and now you. It's positively maddening.''

"I take it you were not enamored with Ian's ball?''

Miles snorted. ''Ian might have thought the anniversary of the battle at Waterloo was cause for celebration, but since I was the only one of the three of us that was actually in the fighting, my perspective is quite different. In all honesty, my greatest wish has always been to forget, not remember, the horror of that day.''

"I have heard a few men speak of the experience.'' Richard observed his friend closely. Miles's eyes seemed to glow with an intense pain Richard hadn't previously noticed. ''Was it terrible?''

Miles's jaw tightened. ''Do you remember how after a battle we would scour the area searching for the wounded? And if we happened upon a brother officer from another regiment we would anxiously inquire, 'Who has been hit?' ''

"I remember,'' Richard replied solemnly. ''Far too well.''

Poker-faced, Miles met his eyes. ''Then all I shall say is that after Waterloo upon meeting a brother officer the greeting was changed from 'who has been hit' to 'who is still alive?' ''

"I did not realize.'' Richard fought to keep any manner of sympathy from his expression, fearing Miles would feel weakened by it. ''Thank God it is finally over.''

"Yes, it is over.'' Miles's smile was filled with irony.

Richard assessed his friend for several moments, but Miles's expression did not alter. The hurt must go very deep indeed, he realized with growing understanding. It might just explain some of Miles's erratic behavior.

They had all suffered some effects from the war in varying degrees. Miles had fought the longest, seen more devastation, experienced greater personal loss. It would stand to reason that his demons would be harder to tame, more difficult to control.

It seemed strange to think that events occurring years ago would cause Miles to act so out of character and so contrary to all that his family and peers expected. Yet having experienced it himself, Richard understood a small part of Miles's dilemma. He sincerely hoped he could do at least something to ease Miles's burdens.

Distraction seemed an excellent place to start.

"Well, since you are unable to go riding with my daughter this afternoon, I suppose you must settle for my staid company," Richard said in an inviting tone. "I fancy a long, hard ride along my western borders. Care to join me?"

"Why not?" Miles stood on his feet. He cocked his head and gave the earl a calculated stare. "If I recall correctly, your western boundaries are adjacent to Sir Reginald's property. Still chasing the spirited Anne?"

"Yes, and don't forget it," Richard added firmly, feeling the residual effects of jealousy over the flowers that Miles had sent her after Ian's ball. "Anne will be my countess."

"At least you are showing some sense with your choice of women," Miles replied. "Unlike Ian, who seems to take perverse delight in encouraging any number of vapid, simpering creatures. Several of them giggle. The rest are predatory, a few are somewhat slyly seductive.

"Anne appears intelligent and has enough spirit to engage in stimulating and serious conversation beyond the state of the weather or the latest fashions." Miles placed his empty brandy snifter on the Pembroke table. "Although why you would willingly set foot in the parson's mousetrap is a total mystery to me."

"I shall take great delight in reminding you of those words the day you become leg-shackled," Richard said with more than a hint of humor. "You forgot to mention that Anne also disapproves of your roguish antics."

A deep laugh rumbled from Miles's throat. "I told you she was a smart woman."

Equilibrium restored to their abiding friendship, the two men ventured out to the stables. They waited patiently while the grooms saddled the horses. After quickly mounting their stallions, they thundered out of the stable yard side by side, the clop of hooves ringing loudly on the cobbles.

The afternoon sunshine greeted them, warming the air pleasantly. By unspoken agreement Richard and Miles rode off at a gallop, giving their eager mounts liberal rein. At that pace it didn't take long to reach the earl's western border.

Once there the men slowed to a sedate trot, taking time to enjoy the ever-changing views. The creak of their leather saddles and the shuffle of the horses' hooves on the soft grass echoed through the quiet meadows. Miles commented on the green growth of the fields they passed, while Richard silently admired the robust crops and healthy, abundant herd of cows in the far pastures. The few tenants they encountered were respectful and friendly, doffing a cap or bobbing a quick curtsey in greeting.

Richard felt his heart swell with quiet joy as he surveyed his domain. He wondered if most men felt as strongly about their property as he did about his estate. Richard worked hard, and took great pride in his home, his land and the accomplishments of his people.

Some members of his class might consider it a dull existence, living in the country away from all the excitement of town. But Richard had discovered a part of his identity and the best part of himself here at Cuttingswood. He knew it was a good life, filled with substance and meaning. A life that was meant to be shared.

After another mile of comfortable travel, Richard heard the splashing of the sizable stream that ran from Sir Reginald's property onto his own. Swelled with moisture from recent rains, the water rushed swiftly, muffling out the sounds of the surrounding woodlands.

Richard exchanged a conspiratorial grin with Miles and allowed his companion to lead the way across a narrow section of the stream.

"Ahh, we have spotted our prey," Miles joked soon after they crossed onto Sir Reginald's land.

Richard glanced through a gap in the tree line and saw two women making their way slowly across a small bridge. They turned onto an overgrown path that curved and followed the direction of the water, continuing with their stroll. They walked arm in arm, with their backs toward the riders.

Richard immediately recognized Anne's willowy figure. She had not been out of his thoughts for more than a few minutes these six long days since he had last seen her.

Initially he had been worried when she did not return to Cuttingswood Manor to continue with her scandalous sketching as she had promised.

She had instead sent a short, polite note of regret explaining that family obligations prevented her from calling on him. Richard remembered smiling when he read the final line of her letter, inquiring sincerely after his health. The nasty bee sting had healed much sooner than his wounded pride.

He had been sorely tempted to visit Anne but had managed to hold off his enthusiasm until today. Of course, Richard knew in his heart why Anne had stayed away from him. He had pushed too hard again for marriage. She wasn't exactly frightened of him; Richard sincerely believed there was little in this world that scared Anne, but she was cautious and perhaps a tad suspicious.

He admitted to himself that he was disappointed she hadn't returned to continue with her sketch. Richard had greatly enjoyed their private time together, despite the bee sting and the heightened sexual frustration. He had hopes these private meetings would afford him an opportunity to further his matrimonial cause. It appeared that a different tack would now be needed.

The earl's horse began to dance beneath him, impatient at the slow pace. With an expert pull of the reins Richard quieted the animal. Undetected, he and Miles took advantage of the opportunity to observe the women for several minutes.

They appeared deep in conversation, and Richard soon realized that Anne's companion was her sister Nicole. He glanced covertly at Miles, wondering if his friend was aware of her identity.

Suddenly Anne stumbled on a large tree root and reached for her sister's arm. Richard watched Nicole steady Anne, but then Nicole unexpectedly began to teeter. Anne attempted to lend assistance, but with a soft cry of distress Nicole fell onto one knee. Anne swayed also and barely managed to stay on her own feet.

Richard reacted instinctively, jabbing his heels to the horse's ribs, galloping forward to help. But he found himself staring at the rear end of Miles's horse. The ever gallant Captain Nightingall's reflexes were apparently far superior and he handily beat the earl to the rescue.

When she first glanced up, Nicole was uncertain if her eyes were being truthful. Thundering across the short expanse of woodland as if he were leading a calvary charge rode Miles Nightingall. She blinked. Was it possible that the sharp pains in her leg had also addled her wits? Or had she become so totally consumed by the idea of Captain Nightingall becoming the most important man in her life that she had lost them completely?

"Anne?" Nicole cried softly.

"I see them," Anne replied calmly. " 'Tis the earl and Captain Nightingall. Are you badly hurt?"

"I'm not sure," Nicole replied. She glanced up again at the

approaching riders and tried to untangle her thoughts. They advanced steadily, with Captain Nightingall still in the lead. All he needed was an unsheathed sabre to complete the frightful warrior image.

Drawing in a deep breath, Nicole let it out slowly, then stared hard at this man she could not shake from her thoughts no matter how hard she tried. He was a man who acted rashly. A reckless man who immersed himself in gaming and drink and duels and women.

In truth, he was no more than a handsome, distant stranger. An unfriendly one too, at least toward her.

Nicole was distressed to realize that despite all of that, her feelings about him had not altered. In fact, they had grown stronger.

A small shiver slid through her. Seeing him now, in all his warrior's glory, Nicole suddenly believed every critical word she had ever heard about him.

There was a harshness and dangerous intensity about Captain Nightingall that Nicole found almost frightening. It should have warned her away, but it drew her to him like a siren's song. This unusual, unique man haunted her dreams and her waking hours with equal fervor.

"Please, Anne, help me stand," Nicole cried. "I must look like a half-witted child sprawled in the dirt." She chewed her bottom lip with worry. "Do you think they saw me fall?"

"Probably," Anne replied, bending to give Nicole assistance.

Nicole groaned with embarrassment. She clutched her sister's arm and managed to unsteadily regain her feet. She tried walking a few steps but winced with pain at the movement. The burning on her knee must be a scrape, Nicole decided, and her ankle hurt fiercely when she applied even the slightest pressure.

Trying to reclaim her dignity, Nicole leaned against a strong oak, standing awkwardly to avoid putting any weight on her injured ankle. She lifted a hand to remove a strand of hair that clung to the corner of her mouth. She was certain her face was unattractively red—heavens, there might even be a bit of sweat glistening on her upper brow.

"You took a nasty fall, Miss Paget," Captain Nightingall declared as he swung down from the saddle. "Are you in much pain?"

"I'll be fine in a moment," Nicole protested weakly. She tried taking a few tiny steps and nearly crumpled from the effort.

With a muffled cry Anne leaped forward, but Captain Nightingall was already there.

"Lean on me," he commanded.

Nicole gave Anne a small apologetic shrug, then allowed Nightingall to help her over to a nearby tree stump. His arm held her steady as he guided her, but she forced herself to remain rigid. Still, she experienced a slightly dizzy sensation that she knew was not being caused by the pain in her ankle.

With his help Nicole managed to seat herself gracefully. The pain in her leg was now a dull, insistent throb. Captain Nightingall shifted his position and knelt down on one knee in front of her. Nicole closed her eyes. It was so like the image in her dreams, she almost believed she might be imagining these bizarre events. Then he pulled up her skirt.

"Sir!" Nicole reached down to push his hands away and encountered the solid warmth of strong, bare fingers. He had apparently taken a moment to remove his riding gloves before touching her leg.

"I am trying to determine if anything is broken, Miss Paget."

"You are touching the wrong limb, sir," Nicole stated frostily. " 'Tis my left ankle that has been injured."

"My apologies."

He actually smiled. Nicole was so astonished she almost lost her seat. Then his hand closed around her injured ankle and her brain seemed to freeze.

Every nerve in her body came alive. Fiery shivers coursed

through her. There was something so unbearably sensual about his touch that Nicole forgot the pain of her ankle, forgot the stinging in her knee, forgot that her sister was standing but a few feet away. Forgot everything but him.

She wanted to kiss him. She wanted to feel and taste the lips of this man who so easily controlled her emotions. The craving grew stronger, quickly becoming an uncontrollable obsession. She placed her hand on his broad shoulder but he did not raise his head. Frustrated, Nicole leaned forward, bending closer. Closer. Closer.

"Ahhh!" The sharp pain in her ankle jolted her back to reality. Thank goodness. Cheeks flaming with emotion, Nicole managed to grasp at her last few wits and pulled away just in time.

"I'm sorry," Captain Nightingall muttered gruffly. He took a deep breath. She felt his long fingers once again on her injured ankle, but they were gentle and careful as they examined her.

"Does that hurt?" he asked.

"Not there," she answered. "A bit lower, near the joint."

He slowly moved her foot. Nicole tensed and held her breath, then slowly released it when she determined he wasn't going to accidentally cause her any additional pain.

His warm fingers moved higher. She lowered her chin, ever at the ready to offer him a coquettish smile, but he never glanced up from his task. Piqued at his apparent lack of interest, Nicole narrowed her eyes and closely observed her gallant rescuer from beneath the brim of her straw bonnet.

She was forced to admit to herself that physically he was superior to all other men she had ever met. So handsome, so engaging, so impossibly perfect. His tall, muscular figure was lean and fit; his expensively tailored clothes merely enhanced his boundless physical beauty.

He was so self-possessed, so supremely male. He had not offered his assistance nor asked permission; he had simply taken charge. She wondered briefly if it was his military training, then decided it was more likely his natural inclination.

"Is it broken?" she asked stiffly.

"No, but it is very swollen." He stood on his feet, towering ominously above her. "We should return to the house as quickly as possible so you may rest the sprain. And the scrape on your knee must be cleaned and bandaged. If the dirt becomes embedded, it could cause a nasty infection."

"Well, I am quite relieved to hear that you are not seriously injured. Thank you for your help, Captain," Anne said, pushing herself forward, stepping between Nicole and Nightingall. "I had no idea you were so knowledgeable."

"It doesn't hurt as much as it did before," Nicole said in a small voice, noting her sister's less than subtle attempts to separate her from the good captain.

Anne smiled wanly at Nicole, then turned to the earl and asked, "May Nicole ride back to the house with you, Lord Mulgrave? I fear it is too far for her to walk. Captain Nightingall and I will follow on his stallion."

"No!"

"No!"

Nicole's energetic protest was uttered nearly simultaneously with Captain Nightingall's objection. Her heart leapt. She met his eyes with great excitement and offered him a dazzling smile. He stared blankly at her for a mere half-second before pivoting toward Anne.

"I believe that Richard would run me through if I dared to place my arms around you," Captain Nightingall said to Anne with a rakish smile. "Even if I embraced you only to prevent you from falling off my horse."

Nicole hissed in a breath. What a blow to her pride! He rejected Anne's suggestion only in order to avoid angering the earl. Nicole's anger heated. She leveled her eyes at Nightingall, searching his face for a hint of mockery, not fully believing his insulting remarks.

Again his expression betrayed nothing. Feeling flustered and frustrated, Nicole was preparing to fling his less than gallant offer coldly back in his face when Anne's voice cut into her thoughts.

"Perhaps a ride on horseback would be too difficult for Nicole. I must beg another favor of you, Captain Nightingall, and ask that you ride to Sir Reginald's stable for assistance," Anne said forcefully. "I'm certain one of the grooms could bring a cart back for Nicole. It will be far more comfortable."

Nightingall shrugged and turned to leave. Lord Mulgrave stopped him.

"I have decided on a better plan," the earl announced. "Anne shall ride ahead with me and Miles will escort Nicole. Come along, Anne."

"I don't think—" Anne began.

The remainder of her words ended in a shriek when the earl suddenly seized Anne and tossed her onto his horse.

Nicole's eyes widened in shock as she watched her sister, breathless with surprise, barely manage to lock her fingers around the pommel before the earl mounted behind her. Anne screeched in alarm and started sputtering indignant protests.

The earl ignored her. He wrapped a muscular arm about her waist and pulled her against his chest. Anne squeaked.

"We shall send for a physician the moment we reach Sir Reginald's," the earl declared. "He should arrive soon after you return to the house."

With a cordial nod to a grinning Captain Nightingall and a thoroughly astonished Nicole, the earl turned his horse and trotted away.

Nicole could faintly hear her sister's indignant cries echoing across the meadow as they disappeared from view.

The sounds of rushing water from the nearby stream suddenly became monstrously loud. Nicole twitched nervously. They were alone, and for the first time in her life she couldn't think of a single thing to say. Any other time she had stolen a few private moments with a gentleman, and there had been quite a few moments, her legion of admirers were busy flattering and flirting with her. Trying hard to steal a kiss.

Nicole glanced over at the captain and shifted uncomfortably. There would be no sweet compliments or coy remarks from him. A stolen embrace? Hardly. He appeared more eager to kiss his horse.

"Ready, Miss Paget?"

He did not wait for a reply and approached her with purposeful strides. Nicole forced herself not to look away from his sharp, determined eyes. A strong part of her pride desperately wanted to reject his help, but Lord Mulgrave had already ridden off with Anne. It was Nightingall or nothing.

"Put your arm around my neck," Captain Nightingall commanded in that rough voice that sent shivers through her body.

She placed her arms gingerly about his neck and gasped when he lifted her from the ground. He carried her the short distance to his mount easily, as if she weighed no more than a small child.

"If I place you on the saddle, can you keep your balance on my horse?"

Nicole nodded. He gave his horse a quiet, stern command, then lifted her atop his stallion, taking extra care not to jolt her bruised leg. Once she was securely seated, Captain Nightingall expertly vaulted up behind her. He enfolded her in a casual embrace and picked up the reins, holding her loosely in his arms as they rode.

Nicole swayed slightly with giddiness. Her back was pressed tightly against his broad chest and shoulders. Physically, this was the nearest she had ever been to him. She felt his powerful male body through the thin layer of her muslin gown. Strong and solid and warm.

Nightingall set the horse to a brisk pace. Nicole struggled a bit to stay upright. They made their way down a small hill, and Nicole bounced awkwardly in her sidesaddle position. She drew in a deep breath and clutched at the arm across her waist. He tightened his grip but did not slow down.

"Try to relax," he whispered into her ear. "I won't let you fall."

Nicole closed her eyes as the shivery tremor coursed down her spine. That deep, low voice could lead a saint down a sinful path. But her cold shivers soon turned to heat. With every step the horse took, she rubbed against the gallant captain, feeling the muscles in his hard thighs and firm chest stroking seductively against her hips and waist and lower back.

Nicole stiffened. It was wicked. Distracting. Arousing. The heat inside her increased, and along with it came an odd sort of tingling in her stomach. It made her feel restless. She fidgeted in the saddle, pressing herself backwards, closer to the source of torturous heat.

Nightingall remained rigidly in place. She heard him make a low, growling sound deep in his throat but she couldn't distinguish any words. Then he fell silent.

Nicole's mind began to drift. If he moved the arm around her waist merely an inch higher, her sensitive nipples would brush against it. How would that feel?

A drop of perspiration trickled between Nicole's breasts as she dwelled on that sinful thought. What a truly scandalous rake he must be to make her feel and think these completely unfamiliar and shocking notions.

Nicole swallowed hard. The tension inside her increased with the silence. She searched her mind frantically for something to say, but speech failed her. Sensations, anxious, pulsing and forbidden, had silenced her tongue. Her mind was spinning, yet the one thing Nicole clearly realized was that she desired this man in ways she couldn't imagine, in ways she didn't fully understand.

Things had always come easily for Nicole, thanks to her beauty and manipulative nature. She had never made any hard choices in her life until she had been forced to refuse Nigel's marriage proposal.

Even as a child she was rarely denied her will, and as she grew older the men who crossed her path were overeager to indulge her. Nightingall had been the only adult male she had ever shown such blatant interest in who had not pledged unfailing devotion.

In fact, he had taken it one step further by pointedly ignoring her. She was at a loss to understand why it mattered so much to her, but the plain fact was that it did.

Nicole had taken the captain's rejection to heart and instead of employing her usual method of rushing forth and taking what she wanted, she had held back. Overcome and uncertain because of her emotions, feeling vulnerable over her one-sided interest and regard, she had brooded and sulked.

Well, no longer.

Anne had once told her that painful lessons in life were learned harder but lasted longer. Nicole suddenly realized that was true.

She shifted her position in the saddle, twisting and tilting her head back so she could look squarely into those slumbering gray eyes.

"I have not properly expressed my gratitude for your noble assistance today, Captain Nightingall," she said breathlessly, no longer feeling so totally rattled by her emotions toward him. "You have been extraordinarily kind."

"I acted only as any gentleman would," he protested.

"Oh, no, sir," Nicole insisted with a sly smile. "You have gone far beyond the actions of a gentleman. I must confess I shall greatly enjoy the many hours I spend deciding on the perfect manner to express my feelings of thanks."

"That is not necessary, Miss Paget," he said gruffly, with his eyes looking shrewdly back into hers.

"But it is, Captain Nightingall," she replied sweetly. "It absolutely is."

Nicole could tell by his fleeting expression that she had startled him. Good. It was about time he began to understand that she would not be so easily bested, so quickly dismissed.

"We will be arriving at the house shortly," Captain Nightingall announced suddenly.

"I am in no hurry," Nicole replied.

She shifted her position again and settled intimately into his embrace with a familiarity that was both bold and improper.

A look of naked desire flared unexpectedly into his eyes. It was fleeting but she saw it clearly. Nicole nearly shouted with triumph but managed a sweet smile instead.

The determination to become the woman of his heart grew even firmer in her mind. It would not be an easy victory. His resistance was strong, but the kink she had just seen in his armor gave her great hope.

If she listened to the sensible part of her head, she might abandon her difficult quest, but, alas, the mind cannot always rule the heart. Her heart had chosen this man. And her mind and cunning would win him.

She knew it was a great risk. What if she chased and failed to capture him? It would be a tremendous blow to her already shaken pride. Her self-confidence. Her womanhood.

Yet in Nicole's considered opinion, Miles Nightingall was worth taking that risk.

Chapter Eleven

Anne gazed fretfully at her sister. Nicole was stretched out like a martyred saint upon the bed with an abundant amount of pillows behind her shoulders and a rolled blanket propped beneath her wounded leg. The physician had come and gone, declaring her injuries minor ones. He had cleaned and bandaged Nicole's scraped knee and poked and probed at her swollen ankle until Nicole had cried out for him to stop.

With a superior air common to many men of his profession, the physician had departed, promising to return in a few days to check on the patient's progress. Once alone with her younger sister, Anne had wanted nothing more than to sit and listen to a detailed account of Nicole's ride back to the house with the rakish Captain Nightingall, but the good doctor had prescribed a sleeping draught that Nicole had obediently swallowed.

It put her promptly to sleep. Feeling restless and hesitant to leave, Anne observed Nicole silently as she slept. How sweet and young Nicole looked. How naive and innocent. Anne's mind churned. How long would Nicole remain that way?

Anne sighed and stared blankly at the green velvet pleats that graced the elaborate canopy over the bed. Nicole turned onto her side, whimpering softly. Her eyes did not open. Anne felt sympathy for the obvious pain Nicole was suffering but admitted she was more concerned about her sister's future injuries than her current ones.

The flushed expression on Nicole's lovely face and the sly half-smile on her lips when Miles Nightingall had carried her into the house a few hours ago had brought on feelings of near-panic in Anne.

"Where is her bedchamber?" Captain Nightingall had inquired.

"My goodness," Anne exclaimed in a high voice. His question flustered her completely even though his voice was toneless and his handsome face marred by a persistent scowl.

"Upstairs," Nicole whispered sweetly. "In the west wing."

Anne stared at them, mesmerized by the intimate portrait they presented, the very picture of an eager groom and his beautiful bride on their wedding night.

"The doctor will arrive shortly. It is unnecessary for you to bring Nicole above stairs," Anne was finally able to say, after taking a few moments to gather herself together. "It would be best to leave her in one of the front drawing rooms. The couch in the gold salon is rather long and plush."

"I prefer to be examined in the comfort and privacy of my bedchamber," Nicole stated firmly. She smiled flirtatiously at Captain Nightingall. "Do you mind carrying me upstairs, sir?"

Anne went speechless with horror. It was almost beyond improper for him to enter Nicole's bedchamber.

"I'll call for a servant," Anne improvised quickly. "It will take but a moment."

"No need," Captain Nightingall replied. "I have matters well in hand."

With the grace of a born athlete he strolled casually past Anne. Nicole rested easily in the cradle of his arms. The sound of his booted heels clicking loudly on the black and white marble floor in the large foyer were a stark reminder of his superior strength and will.

Anne caught only a fleeting glimpse of her sister. Nicole's face was no longer pale and set as it had been these many days. She glowed with charm and beauty and mischief.

While Anne was inwardly pleased at the apparent reinstatement of Nicole's spirits, she was annoyed that her sister had chosen now as the time to stand firm on an issue.

Frantic, Anne turned to Richard for support, but Lord Mulgrave merely shrugged his shoulders, conveying clearly the message that it was none of his business. She could expect no help from that quarter.

"Nicole is far too heavy, Captain Nightingall," Anne blurted out in desperation, wondering if they could feel her growing agitation. Deciding they most likely didn't care. "You will certainly strain your back climbing the long staircase. Please wait for assistance."

Nightingall turned toward Anne. He lifted one dark brow arrogantly. His eyes were grave. He stood stock-still for a full two minutes as if he held no burden at all. Not one muscle moved or even quivered. Anne shivered, then sighed with defeat.

Words were superfluous.

The captain resumed his task, ascending the stairs steadily. Anne sprang back to life, following on his heels, chattering mindlessly, doing everything she could possibly think of to shatter this sudden intimacy between her sister and this dashing rake that seemed to be growing before her very eyes.

Her words, as well as her blatant disapproval, were all but ignored by the couple. As they reached the landing, Anne saw Nicole twine her arms even tighter around Nightingall's neck and hide her face against his broad shoulder. She made a noise that Anne thought sounded suspiciously like a giggle.

"Which is your door?" Nightingall asked Nicole. The timbre

in his voice was so smooth and seductive even Anne felt a shimmer of warmth.

"There." Nicole pointed a delicate finger.

Captain Nightingall looked over his shoulder at Anne. She glowered at him. He didn't react, just continued to stare pointedly at her until she realized with a blush he was waiting for her to open the bedchamber door.

There were manners and polite civility to be observed even in these bizarre circumstances. Anne only wished that her sister understood that rather salient point.

Nicole was looking at the captain as if she wanted to devour him, bite by bite. Anne felt another burst of panic at the prospect. Nicole was no match for Nightingall. She would be playing with fire if she tried to tease and flirt with him. He had been capturing female hearts long before she was even out of the schoolroom.

Anne's initial concern over Nicole's fascination with the roguish captain had begun to fade over the last few days. There had been no contact between them, and both Anne and her sister seemed to have accepted the notion that Nightingall was uninterested in Nicole.

Perhaps that had not changed, Anne told herself somewhat desperately. Captain Nightingall had seemed immune to Nicole's charms the night of the ball. And he had not made any overt advances toward Nicole today. At least not any that Anne could see.

Perhaps he was just acting as a proper gentleman ought to by taking care of Nicole in her time of need. Perhaps.

Anne's panic began to abate. Maybe she was overreacting. Captain Nightingall seemed oblivious to the looks Nicole gave him, those melting glances and coy smirks that promised so much.

Still, the moment Nicole was placed upon the bed, Anne rushed forward, fully intending to separate Nicole from Nightingall's physical magnetism. Ever prudent, Anne decided it would be wiser not to tempt the fates.

But Captain Nightingall's fingers were already assisting Nicole with the ribbons of her bonnet. Short of being abdominably rude, Anne had no choice but to wait until he finished.

Anne watched in fascination as he gently lifted the bonnet off her sister's head. Nicole's eyes lit up. She giggled softly, nervously. He smoothed the hair back from one side of Nicole's face where her hat had crushed the fine golden curls. Before he removed his hand he ran his knuckle slowly along her jaw line.

Anne thought she might have imagined the flicker of desire in his eyes since she was observing him so closely. It was subtle and well controlled. But then she caught a glimpse of the energy charge between them. It was an unusual, unreal moment.

Anne clamped her teeth together. Fortunately, the physician arrived at that precise moment. Amid the jostling and confusion, Anne succeeded in placing herself between Captain Nightingall and Nicole.

But it was too late. Anxiety filled Anne. Anxiety and fear. The damage was already done. For all her flirtatious manner and legions of beaus, Nicole was still an inexperienced young woman. She wore her heart plainly on her sleeve for all the world to see.

Anne felt tears spring to her eyes. Nicole was in love with the most notorious and dangerous rogue in England.

Anne stopped in the kitchen and ordered tea to be served in the gold salon. In spite of all the harried commotion and turmoil that occurred when Captain Nightingall carried Nicole to her bedchamber, Anne had noticed Lord Mulgrave being led in the direction of the gold salon by one of Sir Reginald's footmen.

She assumed the earl was still there, along with the infamous Captain Nightingall, awaiting word of Nicole's condition.

Anne was not thrilled with the prospect of facing either man. She had no inkling of how to cope with the potentially disastrous situation between her sister and Nightingall, and she was still harboring a healthy dose of resentment toward the earl for the stunt he pulled earlier.

If she had been able to remain with Nicole, Anne felt certain that some of this difficulty might have been avoided. Instead Lord Mulgrave had interfered, precisely at a time when Anne did not want his assistance, and decided that Nightingall would be the one to care for Nicole.

Lord Mulgrave had then compounded that mistake by throwing Anne upon his horse and carrying her away like some barbarian conqueror.

The worst part of the encounter was that the moment she and Richard had ridden away from Nicole and Nightingall, Anne had lost the lion's share of her anger. The mere touch of Richard's solid muscles had warmed not only the places where their flesh met but her entire body. There was no escaping the fact that Anne had felt safe and protected in his arms.

There was something magical and mystical about the earl, and Anne felt it more strongly each time she was with him. Deep in her heart she knew her resistance toward him was weakening. Another potentially dangerous occurrence.

Well, it was high time she regained control of the situation, Anne decided. She entered the gold salon grandly, smiling as serenely as she could. Her chin went up a notch as she searched the room for Captain Nightingall.

Her courage restored, Anne intended to look him in the eye, explain that Nicole was a young, naive and thoroughly impressionable young woman. And many a young woman was ruined by an inappropriate fascination with a totally unsuitable man. But most of all Anne wanted to tell Nightingall to stay away from her sister at all costs.

"I hope that scolding look is not meant for me, Anne."

Lord Mulgrave spoke from the shadowed corner of the room.

" 'Tis no less than you deserve after acting like some sort of barbaric pirate and kidnapping me this afternoon," Anne readily retorted.

"Kidnapping?" The earl's brow lifted. "I was offering assistance to a fair damsel in distress. It made me feel rather useful."

Anne folded her arms. "Nicole was the one who needed help," she insisted. "You chose the wrong damsel."

"I chose the right one." Richard smiled charmingly. "I chose you."

Anne pursed her lips and struggled to hold onto her anger, but failed. She blushed and soon found herself grinning back. Those words might have sounded foolish and insincere coming from any other man. But not from him.

Anne instantly decided the most irritating aspect of this entire situation was that her ire could be so easily and rapidly deflated. It was positively maddening to realize how difficult it was becoming to stay angry with Richard for any sustained length of time. Even when she had every right to be.

"Where is Captain Nightingall?" Anne asked the moment she realized that her anger toward the captain had not been affected by her softening feelings toward Lord Mulgrave.

"Miles left soon after the physician gave us a report on Nicole's condition," Richard replied. "Dr. Smythe is a pompous ass but reputed to be the most skillful doctor in the area. I suppose that means a fewer number of his patients die." The earl widened his grin. "Since Nicole's injuries were hardly life-threatening, I'm sure she has been given the best of care."

"Yes. She was sleeping comfortably when I left," Anne commented, considering his words thoughtfully. Lord Mulgrave's opinion of the doctor mirrored her own. It was strange how she was noticing more and more things they agreed upon.

The observation started her mind churning. Lord Mulgrave might be just the person to shed some much-needed light on

Nightingall's character. Knowing more about the rakish captain might very well be the key to keeping Nicole safe. Anne wasn't precisely sure of the relationship between the two men, but she had seen them together on two occasions. They must be friends of a sort, or at the very least good acquaintances.

Deciding it was worth a try, Anne closed the door behind her and crossed the room to sit on one of the high-back chairs near the fireplace.

"How well are you acquainted with Captain Nightingall?" Anne inquired directly, after she was seated.

Lord Mulgrave seemed surprised by her question but he answered readily. "Your dour expression and obsessive need to keep him away from Nicole suggests that you have heard some of the rather shocking tales that are eagerly told about Miles."

Anne delicately cleared her throat. "One does tend to hear things. Especially when a man has a great affection for the races, gaming, duels and women," she said, not bothering to remove the disapproval from her tone.

"Good Lord, Anne, you have just described half the men of the beau monde," Richard replied irritably. He moved from his position near the window to take the matching chair opposite hers.

"I have known Miles since we were boys. I consider him and Ian to be my brothers in all but name. Miles is one of the finest people I have ever had the privilege of knowing. He is noble and decent and kind." The earl bent at the waist and leaned forward in his seat. "I will hear no slander against his character. From anyone."

Anne smiled faintly. "It is heartening to learn that Captain Nightingall commands such loyalty among his friends. I do not doubt he makes an excellent companion for a male. I am far more concerned, however, about the sort of companion he makes for a female."

"There are those that would label him a rake, yet I can

honestly say I have never seen him treat a woman with anything other than respect," Richard declared. "From ladies to barmaids, and even those women that society deems undeserving of even the most common courtesies."

Her eyes widened. "Do you mean prostitutes?"

The earl's expression turned distant. "We were soldiers, Anne. It was wartime."

It was neither a defense nor an apology. Anne nodded her head absently, admitting she couldn't have cared less if Captain Nightingall had bedded half the whores in Europe, but the thought of Richard being intimate with just one soiled dove left her feeling cold.

She leaned back and tried to refocus her mind on the problem of Nicole. "I am very concerned about Nicole's future and her feelings. 'Tis obvious to anyone with eyes in their head that my sister's affections are already engaged by Captain Nightingall. My greatest worry is that he will callously reject her. Or even worse, take advantage of her. Based on what I have seen this afternoon, that wouldn't be difficult. She is reckless and foolish where he is concerned."

Her words did not appear to shock or even surprise Richard. "I have always heard that women fall just a little bit in love with a rake the first time they meet one," he said lightly. "Perhaps this infatuation will pass."

"I cannot take the risk." Anne nodded her head forcefully. "If I thought that he would consider giving up this wild existence and settling down with one woman, I would not say a word. But I am not that much of an optimist."

"Is it not said that rakes make the best husbands?"

Anne snorted. "What rot! Who says that? Women who have already made the insane mistake of marrying one?" Exasperated, she gave him a quick, hard stare. "Nicole needs a man who can provide stability in her life. Nightingall is a gamester, known for playing deep in the pockets. He might very well have a substantial fortune today, but what about tomorrow?

"I know my sister. She would not do well as a poor man's wife."

A polite knock and the arrival of tea halted the conversation. It was probably for the best, Anne decided as she silently watched the servants set out the china cups, delectable plates of sandwiches and sweets, and heavy silver service. Richard was unable to supply her with the insight she needed. His loyalty toward Captain Nightingall had shaded his opinion, just as her love for Nicole colored hers.

Anne poured Richard and herself a steaming cup of tea. They spoke politely of proper, inconsequential matters until the servants were dismissed.

"I appreciate your candor in discussing Nicole and Captain Nightingall with me," Anne said the moment they were alone. "Still, I shall feel at greater ease once we have left Sir Reginald's."

"You are leaving?"

"Yes." She hadn't meant to blurt out that information, suspecting that Richard would be displeased. Suddenly feeling tied in knots, Anne struggled to summon a small smile. "We plan to go to Bath and visit with our Aunt Sophie. The arrangements should be finalized no later than the end of this week.

" 'Tis all for the best. I fear that the longer we stay in Devon, the greater the chance that Nicole will throw all sense of caution to the wind and do something utterly reckless."

Anne lowered her gaze, nearly forgetting to breathe as she awaited the earl's reaction to the news. She studied the back of her hand with great interest as her heart began thudding, pounding inside her chest. She felt Richard move closer. He placed his fist beneath her chin and lifted her face.

"Running away, Anne?" His voice was low but his eyes had turned cold and hard.

"No." She turned away from his touch but did not lower her head. "Making a dignified retreat."

He frowned. "What of our marriage?"

"There will be no marriage," she said, making her best attempt to answer calmly, but the blood was pounding so fiercely in her ears it dulled the sound of her own voice.

Anne expected anger. Bellowing. Perhaps some stomping of feet. She braced herself.

The earl let out a long breath. Then he cocked his head to one side and stared at her with a skeptical expression on his face. "You need a little happiness in your life, Anne. Why won't you allow me to provide some for you?"

Anne blushed. For the first time she admitted to herself that a part of her wanted to accept his offer. Despite all her misgivings about marriage and the sacrifices involved, she knew that life as the earl's wife would be a far better existence than life without him. If only it were possible! "You are talking nonsense, Richard."

"I know how much you have dreamed of going abroad. I shall take you to the Continent," he continued, changing the pitch of his voice to a seductive tone that glided through every pore in her body. "There are a few areas that hold unpleasant memories for me, but there is much I would like to show you. And there are so many places I've yet to explore. We can see them together. As man and wife."

"No," she said softly. But not very forcefully.

He must have sensed her weakening. He leaned forward eagerly, clasping her hands between his own. "Art lessons, Anne. I can arrange for an art instructor to come and live at Cuttingswood. He could teach you whatever you wish, although I still contend that a woman with your natural talent does not need any lessons."

"Oh, Richard." Her fears and objections to marriage seemed very foolish at the moment. Dare she hope that it was possible? So much in her life would be easier if she became his wife. And harder. Yet as Anne gazed into those heated eyes, all she could think of was how much she felt like a true woman when she was with him.

Deep inside she felt a primal craving for this man who was so strong yet could be so gentle. Who was relentless yet not ruthless. Her desire for him went way beyond the physical, but the practical obstacles they faced could not be so easily dismissed.

He was offering her a chance to realize a part of her artistic dream. It was almost too much to consider. But what of her family? What would become of them if she left? How would they survive?

And what of Richard? How would he react if he knew the truth about them? Would he be so generous and indulgent once he discovered the true state of her family's affairs? Once he realized the extent to which her sisters and brothers and even her parents depended on her?

"Not too long ago you promised me that you would accept my decision about our marriage. I humbly ask you now to honor that promise," Anne said slowly. She bowed her head. It was harder than she ever imagined to say those words. Sadness deeper than she had ever known invaded her soul. But the crisis of conscience she suffered quickly swept away any lingering doubts lurking at the back of her mind.

He released her hands. "I find it difficult to accept such a cold dismissal from such a passionate woman. Only a few short days ago you embraced me in the garden and offered to become my mistress. I believe that entitles me to some sort of explanation." He spoke calmly, but she noticed his fists were now clenched.

Anne took a deep breath. She had reached the end of her options. He would not relent. Not without good reason. Anne realized she had only one choice remaining. Tell him the truth. The unsavory truth.

"You have left me no choice," Anne said with a sigh. She closed her eyes briefly. While she was not exactly ashamed of what she had done over the years to protect her family, she was not proud of her actions either.

"We are fortune hunters, my lord," Anne said bluntly. "We came here by exploiting an extremely distant relationship with Sir Reginald, expressly for the purpose of securing a proposal of marriage for Nicole from your nephew Nigel."

The earl's eyes turned dark but he made no comment. After a deep swallow, Anne continued.

"Nicole met Nigel in London early in the Season and they appeared to share a mutual affection. I made detailed inquiries into Nigel's financial background and future prospects. When I discovered he was a man of property, and the heir to your title, I encouraged my sister's inclination."

Richard's eyes narrowed. "I know that," he stated in an exasperated voice. "Why else would I have chased my poor nephew off to the wilds of Scotland?"

"You know!" The impassive expression Anne had struggled to maintain fled.

"Of course." Richard raised his brows, seemingly pleased by her confusion. "Did you think me a fool?"

It was a question that required no answer. She never had thought him to be an ignorant man, but she realized that she had severely underestimated his powers of observation and deduction. Feeling decidedly unbalanced, Anne reached for her cup of lukewarm tea, needing the distraction to gather her thoughts.

An unnerving twinge of guilt slithered through her. Anne had hoped to surprise and disgust Richard thoroughly with her admission of fortune hunting. Now it would be necessary to reveal everything.

"There is more." Anne's stomach tightened. She placed the teacup back in the saucer. It rattled and nearly tipped over. "We are not merely fortune hunters. We are a fraud. A complete sham. A family teetering on the very brink of financial disaster masquerading as respectable members of society."

He laughed softly. " 'Tis the curse of the aristocracy to live above their means. It has been so for generations. Is not the

Regent the ultimate example? All noble families go through their share of financial highs and lows. It is a normal occurrence."

"I dare anyone to classify our financial or family situation as normal," Anne said in a sharp tone. "We have no financial highs. Only lows. Always lows."

"Surely you exaggerate," he said mildly, eyeing her with disbelief.

Anne stiffened. "I cannot begin to count the number of nights I have lain awake and prayed that I was wrong. But numbers do not lie." She wrapped her arms tightly about her waist and hugged, feeling a need for comfort. "My parents are very self-indulgent people. They like to buy . . . things."

"Things?"

"Yes. All sorts, all kinds, all manner of things. Clothes, furniture, paintings, vases, the odd bit of jewelry." Anne smiled grimly. "I have studied it closely over the past few years, yet cannot decipher a particular pattern. There is seldom any rhyme or reason to their purchases. One week it is jewels, the next rare wines.

"I have come to finally understand it is the excitement or freedom of buying that brings them the greatest joy. The actual item they buy is usually a secondary consideration, although Father went through a period last year when he consistently bought horses. Race horses. He lost interest, however, and never actually entered any of them in a competition."

Richard frowned. "I don't understand."

Anne pursed her lips. "The fact that my parents cannot pay for the many and varied items they purchase has never been considered more than a very minor detail."

A light of understanding sparkled in the earl's eyes. "Are there a great many creditors now pressing your father to settle his debts?"

"Not as many as in previous years," Anne admitted. "When my two sisters married, their husbands generously agreed to settle the oldest outstanding accounts. Some went back nearly twenty years.'' She tried to laugh. It was difficult, but the alternative was tears.

''Quarterly payments are now being made to a variety of London merchants to cover both older and newer purchases, which still leaves the purchases from the Devon shopkeepers to be settled,'' Anne continued. ''I strongly suspect I have seen less than half of those bills.''

''It is most unusual for a daughter to be this involved with the financial dealings of her family,'' the earl commented. ''Why doesn't your father's lawyer or man of business attend to these matters?''

''We really can't afford to employ one.'' This time Anne actually did laugh.

The earl stroked his jaw thoughtfully. ''I assume you have already sold off whatever portable assets were available?''

''Yes, although there weren't many,'' Anne replied. ''The manor house and surrounding farmlands of our estate are currently leased. The income we receive allows me to keep the worst of the creditors at bay. Even though we no longer live there, my parents are forced to ship their larger purchases to our home, supposedly for safekeeping. Unbeknownst to them, I have made an arrangement with our steward to get rid of the stuff as soon as it arrives.''

The earl raised his brow. Anne felt the color rise in her cheeks. This was by far the most unusual conversation she had ever had with a man. Yet it felt oddly cathartic to finally discuss this bizarre situation with someone.

''The steward tries as best he can to resell these treasures,'' Anne continued. ''I use those funds to offset the next round of buying, but since our steward usually sells the merchandise at a loss, I can never catch up or break even, let alone get ahead. It is an endless cycle, seemingly forged in iron.''

''Are the items that inferior?'' Richard asked curiously.

Anne considered his question carefully. ''Actually, no. My

parents both have a keen eye for quality and beauty, and some-what extravagant, overblown taste. The problem lies with my father. He considers it far beneath his dignity to question or haggle with a merchant over the price of goods. Consequently, he and my mother pay exorbitantly inflated prices for just about everything they buy.

"There is of course no possible hope of recouping that money during resale." Anne shrugged her shoulders. "I find it vastly ironic that two people who spend such a disproportionate amount of their time shopping are so exceedingly bad at it."

Richard gave her a measured glance. "Do you share your parents' passion for hummm . . . acquisition?"

Anne's mouth dropped in horror. "Absolutely not!"

"Then I fail to see how their difficulties affect our future together," he said calmly. "I will naturally assume the most pressing of your families debt, as did your brothers-in-law."

"And then what?" Anne interrupted, shaking her head in frustration. For all his kindness and sympathy, Richard still did not comprehend the enormity of the problem. "Who will pay for the next round of bills? Nicole's husband? Or Rosalind's? How will my sisters even find decent men to marry if I am not there to protect them?

"Nicole is wildly impulsive, and Rosalind is still so young. My parents would marry them off to the first man with deep pockets who looks at them twice. I have always promised myself that I would stay until the girls are safely wed so that I may protect them from a disastrous husband. I would not be able to sleep at night knowing I abandoned them."

"And your brothers?"

"Hopefully, they will be nearly finished with school when Rosalind becomes a bride. As the older son, Will shall inherit. I will then turn the responsibility of the estate over to him, knowing that I have done all I possibly could to keep his inheritance safe.

"Perhaps Edmund will wish to enter the church or the military, as do many second sons. I shall also do everything within my power to aid him. Yet both boys will have a decided advantage over my sisters. As young men they will be afforded the opportunity to earn their fortunes. A woman has little choice but to marry hers.''

Anne rose to her feet and began to pace in front of the long gold sofa. Her recital continued, her agitation gaining momentum as she outlined each problem, one more difficult than the next.

''But that is all in the far distant future. What of today? Where will the family live? Sir Reginald is not the only relative we have foisted ourselves upon. We save a considerable amount of money by moving from place to place every few months.

''Since it was my idea, I am the one who writes the letters, asking to renew acquaintance with our unsuspecting relations, securing accommodations with our reluctant hosts, acting as shameless beggars when we have overstayed our welcome but have nowhere else to go.''

Anne finally stopped moving. *Dear Lord, what had come over her?* With a shaky hand she smoothed back the wisps of hair that had loosened from the tight coil on her head. Gathering her courage, she risked a quick glance at Richard.

The earl had also risen to his feet. She expected him to be racing toward the door. Any sane man would have ridden halfway to the borders of Sir Reginald's estate by now. But not Lord Mulgrave. He appeared oddly calm.

''I believe marriage to be a partnership, a sharing of joys and sorrows, burdens and rewards. Do you agree?''

''Yes,'' she rasped out. The timbre of his voice and intensity of his gaze caused a tingle of excitement to dance over her skin.

''Then be my wife.''

Anne gasped loudly. She felt giddy, almost lighthearted with relief. Deep in her heart she had feared he was saying goodbye.

She had challenged him with the truth and he had accepted it, and her, without hesitation.

It was impossible. Given the choice, no man would burden himself with in-laws practically running from debtors' prison. Yet the earl appeared not the least bit concerned by what she had just revealed. He was willing to take the risk. Did she share his courage?

"Will you be my wife?" Richard repeated, louder.

"Yes." Anne let out her breath. She waited for the doubts to assail her, the fear of making a horrendous mistake overtake her. But it did not happen. Perhaps it was finally time she learned that depending on Richard could indeed make her a stronger, not weaker woman. Anne broke into a wide grin. "I will marry you."

Chapter Twelve

Richard poked at the dim fire barely blazing in the large fireplace of his bedchamber. The night was warm and the fire unnecessary, but he needed a task to occupy his mind, so he had built a fire. Then he prudently opened a window to let the heat escape.

It was long past the time he should have retired to his bed. The hour grew late and the house remained quiet, but sleep eluded the earl.

Tomorrow was his wedding day.

Richard sat down in his favorite chair and laced his fingers behind his head, stretching out before the fireplace in a relaxed manner that belied the turmoil of his mind. And heart.

He had kissed Anne senseless after she had finally agreed to become his wife, partly from delight, partly from shock. Her revelations about her family's finances were a somewhat unpleasant surprise, but they had not overshadowed his obsessive need to claim her for his bride. In hindsight, however, they might prove to be far more of a challenge than Richard originally supposed. That thought concerned him greatly.

The Paget family had left Sir Reginald's home almost immediately after the announcement of Richard and Anne's intended nuptials had been made the following morning at the breakfast table. The surprised and delighted reactions of the family convinced Richard that Anne had kept her word and not spoken to anyone of their plans, but it had been Sir Reginald's reaction that caused the most excitement.

The old gentleman had shouted and bellowed at Richard, accusing the earl of trying to insinuate himself into the family expressly for the purpose of gaining control of Sir Reginald's property.

It was a preposterous notion. Yet no manner of argument from either Anne, Richard or Anne's father could convince Sir Reginald that he was mistaken. The old man vowed to set fire to his lands before allowing Richard to claim so much as a blade of grass. He even went so far as to forbid the marriage.

Given the disapproval and rantings of their host, there remained no alternative for the Paget family but to leave. Quickly. They packed up and departed within the hour, and since they had nowhere else to go, they invaded the earl's home. At his hesitant invitation.

Richard sighed and glanced over at the full decanter of brandy resting on his night table, trying to decide if a drink would lighten or darken his mood. Miles and Ian had jokingly offered to spend the evening with him on this his last night of freedom, exploring the vices of bachelorhood.

He had refused the invitation, having no intention of appearing hung-over with bloodshot eyes and green-tinged pallor at his wedding ceremony. Besides, Richard realized he needed to keep his wits sharp when dealing with both his bride and future in-laws.

The announcement of their marriage should have been handled quite differently. Anne had insisted that due to her advanced age there was no need for him to speak with her father and ask permission for her hand. They could make the announcement together to the entire family while they were gathered for breakfast. It would be easier and perfectly proper.

Richard had disagreed but graciously deferred to Anne on this point only because it seemed so important to her. He also made it abundantly clear this would not become a pattern in their married life.

Anne's eyes had grown dark and wary. Eventually she had nodded her head in acknowledgment and he had kissed her again. Hard. She resisted for a moment, then melted against him with her usual honest passion. Along with his rising desire, Richard had felt a stirring of hope for their future life together.

There was no need to wait to be married. Neither of them was interested in an elaborate or involved ceremony. In a strange twist of fate, the earl had once again found himself in need of a special marriage license. Fortunately, this time it was not an urgent matter of life and death. The wedding would occur tomorrow, three days after her acceptance of his proposal.

While he had great hopes for the success of this marriage with Anne, there were doubts too. Could their life achieve the happiness celebrated so joyously in many of the fairy tales Alexandra enjoyed having read to her each night? Would they eventually come to love each other and live happily ever after?

Richard frowned. He suspected he was more than half in love with Anne already. It worried him. Mostly because he was so unsure of her feelings. In his opinion, there was nothing more pathetic than unrequited love. Especially from one's mate.

An unfamiliar noise at his bedchamber door interrupted Richard's musing. He turned in curiosity at the sound and his tired eyes widened with surprise.

Anne appeared suddenly, seemingly conjured up magically by his thoughts. Richard blinked, assuming she was a product of his exhausted imagination. But she did not disappear. She remained standing calmly with her back pressed solidly against his door, dressed in a simple nightrail and matching robe. Then she took a step forward.

She startled him, moving quietly as a ghost in her long white dressing gown with her hair hanging loose and free. She looked lovely. Fresh and innocent and womanly. His throat tightened.

"Forgive me for disturbing you at this late hour," Anne whispered. "I needed to speak with you."

"Can it not wait until morning?"

"I would not have come if it could wait."

Richard smiled softly. Only his Anne would beg forgiveness in one breath and release her indignity in the next.

He stood politely and indicated the chair opposite his own. "Please, join me."

Her eyes crinkled in an expression of puzzlement. Richard was unsure if it was due to the unnecessary fire burning in the grate or her realization that he wore only his breeches, stockings and linen shirt. He watched her closely as she glided across the room. Her spine was stiff and straight, and the hands at her sides were clenched into tight fists. She was clearly nervous.

After Anne primly seated herself on the very edge of the chair, Richard resumed his seat. He tried catching and holding her gaze, but she seemed to have great difficulty keeping her eyes from staring at his naked throat.

He was forced to lower his head considerably in order to snag her attention. Anne hissed in a startled breath and lifted her gaze. Her expression revealed her mortification at being caught staring and she blushed soundly.

Richard shifted uncomfortably in his chair. Thank God they were going to be married tomorrow. Her open sexual curiosity and heightened desire were surely going to kill him. His erection was already throbbing uncomfortably between his legs, straining against the fastenings of his breeches. His balls felt heavy and full, like they were ready to explode.

The earl crossed his legs to hide the evidence. Anne might be bold but she was still innocent. For the moment. He owed her respect and intended to give it to her, even though he had not experienced a single thought that was not completely lustful since she had entered the room.

"I have been speaking with my mother," Anne finally got out after taking several dry swallows. "She has been rather eager to impart a varied collection of matrimonial advice."

"Matrimonial advice from your mother?" Richard barely managed to contain his shudder. "The mind boggles."

For a fraction of a second Anne looked confused and defenseless. "I admit it was probably not the best idea on the eve of my wedding to listen to anything she has to say. My mother is not known for her common sense or good judgment. I suspect she experienced a sudden burst of maternal instinct, and it seemed cruel not to at least pretend to listen."

"What precisely did she have to say?"

"Not very much worth repeating." Anne folded her arms beneath her breasts. "Yet she did dwell on how a wife must understand her husband and devote all her energies toward making him happy and content. And she repeatedly mentioned that a man of your age would naturally be considering his own mortality and the need to perpetuate his line."

Anne took a slow breath before she continued. "I truly had not considered the possibility of us having a baby. I suppose I have thought of Nigel as your heir for so long it did not occur to me that you would want or need additional children."

Richard's heart sank. His daughter, Alexandra, was the one person in the world who loved him unconditionally. And he loved and adored her beyond measure. She was, without question, the greatest joy of his life. The possibility of additional children had long been a distant hope burning in his heart, yet since he was unmarried, Richard had chosen not to acknowledge that desire. Until now.

He had never forgotten the agony of watching Juliana struggle to give birth to their daughter. Those feelings of helplessness were among the strongest he had ever had, and he still occasionally suffered pangs of guilt over Juliana's death. Yet time had lessened the horror and he had eventually come to accept the tragedy as God's will.

"Alexandra's mother died giving her life," Richard said solemnly. "I was present at my daughter's birth and am not eager to thrust that experience upon you, Anne, especially if you are unwilling. I feel no burning desire to beget a nursery full of heirs.

"But I would be lying if I did not say that I had hoped we might have at least one child together. Son or daughter, it truly would not matter, as long as the babe was alive and whole."

Anne seemed to consider her words very carefully before she spoke. "I never thought to marry, therefore I never thought I would have children. And the idea of going through life childless did not distress me overmuch. For some women, like my sisters, finding a good husband and having a family is their greatest wish, their only course toward achieving happiness.

"I never shared that feeling. I also have never been a woman who longed for children. It troubled me for many years until I finally concluded I lack the maternal instincts that naturally possess so many females. Besides, taking charge of my family has left me feeling very much like a mother, albeit a somewhat reluctant one."

"You have experienced all the responsibilities of motherhood with few of the joys," Richard observed. "It would be different with a child of your own."

"Perhaps." Anne's expression turned reflective. "I do not dislike children, although I own I know next to nothing about infants. Quite frankly, the idea of being wholly responsible for a tender new life terrifies me."

"You will not be alone, Anne." Richard reached over and clasped her hand firmly in his own. Her fingers were cold, despite the warmth of the room. "I will share in the responsibility of raising our child, far beyond the traditional expectations."

"Oh, Richard." She squeezed his hands tightly. "Will you

carry the infant inside your body, give birth and then nourish it from your breast?''

"If I recall my anatomy lessons correctly, I do not believe that is precisely the male's role,'' Richard replied lightly, trying to both understand and allay her misgivings.

"Unfortunately for me.'' Anne laughed softly and shifted restlessly in her seat. "You must think I am a most unnatural female. Yet I am glad that we can joke and discuss these matters so openly.'' She moved her head closer to his. "I have thought long and hard about becoming a mother and searched within myself for an honest answer. My fears and uncertainty have not miraculously vanished, but I know in my heart that you are the only man whose children I would willingly bear.''

He smiled, pleased by her words.

"Yet I must beg an indulgence of time from you,'' Anne continued solemnly, releasing his hands. She cast him a sidelong glance. "I do not wish to be like so many other brides and give birth a mere nine months after we are wed.''

Her request wounded him. He had not realized how much he yearned to see Anne's body grow and swell with their babe. How much he longed to experience the mystery and wonder of life from the very moment of creation. How much he wanted to be a part of all the things he had missed by being separated from Juliana during her pregnancy.

"There are ways of preventing conception,'' the earl said slowly. After Juliana's unexpected pregnancy, he had made it his business to learn as many of them as possible. "They are not, however, foolproof.''

"I understand.''

"The only way to be absolutely certain a woman does not get with child is to abstain from the pleasures of the marriage bed.'' Richard narrowed his eyes as a thought struck him. A most unpleasant thought. "Is that what you are asking?''

"No.'' Anne's head shot up. "If I am going to be your wife, I want a complete marriage.''

"Good. Then we are in agreement." Richard decided it was unnecessary to inform her that he would not have tolerated a marriage of convenience or marriage in name only. Under any circumstances. "I will employ the necessary precautions to delay getting you with child. Although I cannot guarantee the outcome."

"Thank you."

He stood on his feet. Anne also rose. The mood turned awkward. Even though they had just rationally discussed the most intimate of subjects, Richard felt a distance, a remoteness between them. He didn't like it.

He expected Anne to now drop a quick curtsey and bid him a hasty good night. He sincerely hoped she did not want a good-night kiss. As much as his body desired her—she did look so serenely pretty in her flowing robe—his mind and heart and male pride were still stinging a bit.

"There is one other matter I need to discuss with you." Anne fumbled in the pocket of her dressing gown and brought forth several small objects. She held them out silently for his inspection.

Richard glanced down curiously at Anne's open palm. She held a silver fork, a man's quizzing glass and a gold snuff box. Each item looked vaguely familiar.

"What is all this?" he asked.

Anne sighed. "I recognize the pattern on the handle of the fork; I believe it is a part of Sir Reginald's table service. If I'm not mistaken, the snuff box is Captain Nightingall's property. Do you recognize the quizzing glass? I think it belongs to—"

"Me." Richard lifted the quizzing glass by the black silk ribbon and dangled it above Anne's palm. It twirled merrily, reflecting odd bits of light from the flames in the fireplace. "Where did you find these things?"

"Aunt Sophie's room."

Richard frowned. *Aunt Sophie's room?* In a most ironic turn of events, the very relative that Anne had pinned her hopes on providing the next home for the family, one Aunt Sophie of Bath, had arrived on Sir Reginald's doorstep the morning they had announced their betrothal.

The poor woman had been so excited when she received Anne's letter that she had misread it. Instead of issuing an invitation for the Paget family to visit her in Bath, Aunt Sophie had packed her carriage and come posthaste to Sir Reginald's home to meet her long-lost relatives.

When the rest of the family beat a hasty retreat from Sir Reginald's and moved into the earl's home, Aunt Sophie had come along. She was teary-eyed and emotional over the prospect of attending Anne's wedding and it seemed cruel not to include her.

To Richard she had seemed similar to many other lonely gentlewomen he had known. Harmless, flighty, bossy with the servants, prone to gossip and forgetting people's names. She was yet another colorful addition to the already unconventional Paget brood.

"How in the world did Aunt Sophie come to have these items in her possession?" Richard asked.

"I do not know." Anne drew in a deep breath. "She wanted to stroll in the garden with my parents this evening after dinner. It was damp outside so I went to her bedchamber to fetch her favorite shawl and discovered these things on her nightstand. It wasn't as if she were trying to hide or conceal them. They were out in plain view."

Richard ran his thumb absently over the surface of the quizzing glass. "I knew a boy at school who had a similar affliction. If anything was ever missing, his was the first room searched. He suffered many a stiff caning from the headmaster for his deeds and eventually was expelled from school for stealing. Yet oddly enough, the items he took were rarely of any value."

"Goodness." Anne's lips twitched. "What an abomination."

The earl rubbed his chin thoughtfully. "Alexandra was complaining to me this afternoon that her favorite bonnet has gone missing. I assumed she had carelessly misplaced it. By chance, you didn't happen to notice it in Aunt Sophie's room?"

"No. But I shall look again early tomorrow morning." Anne went rigid and pale. "I am so very sorry. I will write Sir Reginald a note and have a servant deliver the fork to him. I would bring it myself, but given his current mood over our marriage, I doubt Sir Reginald would receive me.

"I will, however, personally return Captain Nightingall's property, and I shall then make certain that Aunt Sophie is sent back to Bath immediately. Before the wedding."

"It is not necessary to be so harsh," Richard decided with a wry grin. Despite everything, his smile held a small amount of humor. Her courage amazed him. It was no wonder she was skittish about having children. For Anne, family meant nothing but trouble. "Aunt Sophie has done no real harm."

Astonishment and disbelief crossed Anne's face, and for several moments she simply stared at him.

"My family is nothing more than a thinly disguised band of schemers and thieves," Anne declared in a distressed tone. Spreading one hand over her heart, she solemnly inquired, "How will you ever tolerate being married to me?"

It was a fair question. Yet Richard had already concluded that some situations were unavoidable. In order to have Anne, he must contend with her family. His heart suspected it was well worth it.

Richard held out his hand toward her. She walked into the circle of his arms without a moment's hesitation.

"I expect there will be some compensations having you for a wife," Richard stated quietly.

"Really?" A tentative smile touched Anne's lips. "Try as I might I cannot think of one."

"I can," he whispered wickedly.

Richard threaded his fingers through her silky hair and tilted her head back, lowering his own until their mouths touched.

The kiss consumed him. Richard moved his tongue beyond her soft lips and into her sweet mouth. The heat inside him ignited and flared until it nearly burned him. He felt Anne reach blindly for his shoulders and he tightened his grip on her waist to steady her. Then he kissed her again.

His lips were firm and seductive. His tongue teased and dared her until Anne succumbed to the moment. Hunger burst upon them in a hot flood. The scent of passion and desire permeated the air.

Finally he broke away. Breathing heavily, Richard set his forehead against hers. Anne tried to press herself closer against him, elevating the tension between them, enticing him with her luscious curves. With amazing strength of will, Richard resisted and heard her sigh in frustration. He raised a slightly unsteady hand to stroke her hair.

"You had best be returning to your room," he said reluctantly. "I don't want my bride appearing pale and wan on our wedding day."

She lifted her gaze. He could feel the tension vibrating through her. It seemed to beat in sympathetic cadence with the persistent throbbing in his groin, but that, Richard prudently decided, was merely his oversexed imagination.

"I want to stay." Anne clutched at his shoulders, pressing her fingers into the solid muscle. "May I sleep in your bed tonight?" she whispered, adding unnecessarily, "with you?"

Richard's eyes blazed. "My dear, if you stay with me tonight we shall do everything but sleep."

"I know."

He smiled tightly, clearly hearing the tremor running through her voice. "Are you sure? There will be no half-measures, Anne. If you stay we will join our bodies fully, completely. I shall bury myself so deeply inside you it will be impossible to feel where I end and you begin. Wouldn't you rather wait one more night until we are properly wed?''

''No.'' A blush stole into her cheeks. ''I am expecting my . . . my monthly courses. They are already two days late. I fear if we wait any longer . . .''

Her voice trailed off and her blush deepened. Ahhh, his ever practical Anne. Perhaps their passion had not totally caused her to lose her head. But he suspected that with just a little extra effort on his part it would. After all, he had not yet given free rein to the intense desire he felt for her. Until now.

''Then I shall take you tonight. Several times. It should be a safe time to avoid conception.'' He captured her lower lip between his teeth, stretched and then released it. ''And hopefully I will have you again tomorrow night.''

He swept her up into his arms. She squealed with surprise. He carried her to his bed and they tumbled onto the mattress together. Anne rolled over twice and landed on her back in the center of the large bed. Richard smiled and crawled after her, pinning her beneath his hard body.

''I cannot breathe,'' she cried.

He braced himself on his arms and loomed above her. ''Better?''

For an answer she twined her arms around his neck and strained her body up to him. She grasped his lower lip, imitating his earlier move, but instead of nipping she sucked at it. Hard.

Every muscle in Richard's body went stiff and the blood started pounding in his veins. It was wonderful to no longer be fighting the need he felt for her. To allow free rein to his tightly suppressed desire. All he had to do now was somehow control and guide that passion until they both achieved fulfillment.

With a joyful grin of anticipation, the earl pulled at the ribbon fastening Anne's robe, then started on the tiny buttons of her nightgown. Urgently he pushed the fabric off her shoulders, beyond her arms and down to her waist, baring her totally.

He pulled back to stare at the magnificent splendor spread before him. Anne's gaze swung up to his face. She gasped self-consciously and crossed her arms over her breasts, attempting to cover herself.

"No!" Richard shifted his hand and held her arms at her sides. "I know you feel shy and uneasy but you must never hide yourself from me. There will always be truth and honesty between us, Anne, and nowhere is that more important than here in my bed. In our bed."

He thought she might protest. Her eyes darkened and she stared belligerently at him for several seconds. But then her confusion seemed to give way to common sense. Anne nodded tightly and said, "I shall expect the same of you, Richard."

"Of course."

They shared a smile. Slowly he released his grip on her hands. She swallowed hard but kept them by her side. A thrill went through him. She was beautiful. Her skin was creamy and lush, her nipples dark and rosy. Pride and an odd sensation of possession rushed over Richard. She was his. At last.

Deep in his groin, Richard felt a surge of excitement. Even the smell of her skin excited him, driving out the very last remains of hesitation and flooding him with desire. His hand skimmed over the delicate, pale skin. Anne shivered.

"Remove my shirt," he commanded softly as his mouth glided along her throat, caressing and licking the tender flesh.

She did not need to be told twice. Eagerly she yanked on the linen garment and pulled it over his head. His broad naked chest with its mat of dark hair must have pleased her greatly for Anne made a purring noise deep in her throat and slid herself up against him, letting every portion of her softness rub intimately against his hardness.

Richard gritted his teeth and moaned with pleasure as he experienced a new and exhilarating sense of Anne's need for him. He tilted her head back and kissed her throat hungrily, cautioning himself to remain in control.

For Richard the physical act of love was a form of communication in which his own pleasure was intensified by giving his partner pleasure. But Anne's obvious passion and delight nearly made him forget that she was still a virgin.

His hand slid through her silky hair, down her neck and shoulders and settled over her breast. While his thumb and forefinger played with the nipple, he leaned close and whispered in her ear, "How does that feel, sweetheart? Good? Does it feel good?"

Her heavy-lidded eyes closed briefly and with a groan of pure delight Anne pressed herself closer. He chuckled softly and increased the pressure. Her breasts felt heavy in his palms, lush and full and ripe.

His lips soon followed his hands, kissing, caressing, and finally sucking on the nipple until Anne began to moan. He laved her nipple gently, lovingly, then lightly blew a warm breath over the wet tip. She cried out with pleasure.

Bending his head, he caught the other nipple between his teeth. Closing his lips, Richard sucked hard. Anne screamed and whimpered, moving her upper torso frantically.

With a groan he grasped her hips and pulled her against him. His taut erection pressed into the lower part of her belly, and Anne undulated her hips in an awkward rhythm, barely noticing when Richard removed her robe and nightgown completely.

Her muscles were quivering with longing. Richard realized she was terribly aroused and he needed to bring her to climax before he disgraced himself and left them both unsatisfied.

Rising to his knees, Richard deftly unbuttoned his breeches. Eyes wide, Anne watched as he revealed himself to her, fully erect and aching for her sweetness.

"Oh, my." Anne licked her lips. Her eyes remained fixed on his groin. "It is far larger than I expected."

Richard smiled wickedly and felt himself grow even bigger. He reached for her.

Yet the small break in their lovemaking had tempered her

eagerness, replacing it with hesitation at the unknown. He sensed that immediately. So with gentle determination Richard kissed and caressed Anne until he once again saw the hunger and fiery passion in her deep brown eyes. Then he knelt above her. Pressing her thighs wide, he moved between them.

"Try and let your body relax," he commanded, sliding his hands beneath her buttocks and lifting her toward him. Her legs opened even wider as he positioned himself.

Slowly, with an effort that brought a fine sheen of sweat to his brow, Richard began pushing himself inside her. She felt so incredibly wet and tight that for a moment he felt the strongest urge to abandon all control and tear into her. His body was heavy and rigid with need, but he remained in control. Barely.

Anne's fingers threaded through the dark hair on his chest and she held on tightly to him. Her trembling touch served to ignite the raging heat that was tearing through Richard's body. She was so sweet, so dear, so desperate to please him.

He kissed her again, slowly, languidly as he thrust his hips forward. The most exquisite sensations coursed through him. Anne's hands moved to his shoulders and she arched her back in a gesture of total surrender.

"Curl your legs around my hips," he commanded in a tight voice. "Hold onto me."

She did as he asked and he felt her take him even deeper inside her warmth. Richard continued slowly, lengthening the strokes as he thrust inside Anne, claiming more and more of her for himself with each penetration. It was pure bliss. It was total agony.

Richard soon reached the thin inner veil of her womanhood but continued with the rhythm he had established. Anne's face grew tight with the lines of passion, and he whispered in her ear, words of dark desire and longing. His body and his words helped her forget her nerves and fired her passion. When he breached her maidenhood, she barely cried out.

Once pressed fully inside her, Richard's reason began to

slip. The heat consumed him totally, the pleasure so intense it made his teeth ache.

Captivated by the moment, he thrust deep and hard repeatedly into her, feeling her inner muscles tightening. She whimpered and pushed back against him, faster, more frantically. The tension built to an almost unbearable ache. Richard could tell that Anne was coming closer to climax but her movements were awkward and inexperienced. He realized she needed greater stimulation.

He flexed his elbows and lowered most of his weight onto her body, trying to stop her frantic movements. It took a few moments before Anne's body stilled. Her arms, wrapped so tightly around his back, fell limply to the mattress. She tilted her chin and gazed at him with wild, passion-filled eyes.

"That is all? It is over?" Her voice was a breathless whisper aching with disappointment.

"I have saved the best till now." He grinned affectionately and kissed the tip of her nose. "But you must trust me."

Slowly he withdrew from her. Flexing his hips, he pressed hard inside, watching her face intently. He continued to build a slow, deep rhythm until she began to move her head restlessly against the pillow.

He moved his hand down between their bodies, sliding his fingers through the damp, springy curls, searching for her inner core. He rubbed the sensitive spot gently with his thumb.

"Richard!" Anne jerked violently.

He set his cheek against her damp temple. "Let go, my love," he whispered in her ear. "Come for me. Come for me."

He pumped deeply into her softness. With a strangled cry she lifted her hips up to him. When he felt her coming closer, closer to the edge, he brushed his fingers lightly across her most sensitive flesh to complete the act.

Suddenly Anne stiffened, arching her back off the bed as fulfillment overtook her. Richard held her tightly as she shuddered beneath him, drinking in the glorious expression of wonderment and ecstasy on her lovely face.

His own release was far more subdued compared to hers, but overwhelmingly satisfying. Once he abandoned his control, it took only a few deep, swift thrusts until his hot seed flooded her womb. Along with the intense pleasure of release, however, came a strange stab of regret knowing there would be no child created from this particular act.

After his body ceased its shuddering, he collapsed against her and they lay motionless for several long minutes. Richard rolled onto his side to spare her his weight but somehow managed not to disengage himself from her body. He held her thus and waited for her reaction, knowing he had pleased her but feeling an unaccustomed need to hear that confirmation from her lips.

The room was bathed in silence and moonlight. Gradually, naturally, Richard's body shrank from Anne's. With a sigh of loss, he shifted his position and turned over onto his back. He rested one arm across his eyes and hauled Anne closer to his heart with the other arm. She made a small sound of contentment and burrowed her head against the side of his chest.

He waited again for her to speak, but after several minutes her deep, even breaths confirmed his suspicions. She was asleep.

Richard smiled in the darkness. Ahh well, they would have a lifetime together to converse. And make love. With a philosophical shrug he pulled Anne's warm body closer to his heart and drifted off into an exhausted slumber.

Chapter Thirteen

"And so, dear friends, I shall ask at this time if there is anyone who objects to this marriage, who can in good faith show just cause why these two people may not be lawfully joined together in holy matrimony, let them speak of it now or forever hold their peace."

All was silent in the earl's drawing room. The close friends and family members gathered to witness the Earl of Mulgrave's marriage ceremony all seemed to collectively hold their breaths as if waiting for at least one objection to emerge from some quarter.

Captain Miles Nightingall noted with wry humor that the earl gave his bride a rather obvious questioning look. All heads turned anxiously in her direction, including the vicar's. Anne blushed to a pretty shade of rose, but refused to lower her chin or gaze.

"Please continue," she instructed the vicar in a quiet, calm tone. "The earl is growing impatient."

Miles bit back his chuckle. She was outrageous! And precisely the sort of woman that Richard needed. Strong in a subtle manner, intelligent as well as wise, Anne would soon turn the earl's world on its side.

Miles was forced to admit to a measure of envy. Anne, with her plain-speaking tongue and attractive though not beautiful face, would be a good wife. And an even better lifelong companion.

Though he seldom thought of marriage, Miles regretted that he had been denied the opportunity to pursue Anne, but Richard had staked his claim first. In Anne, Miles saw a level of comfort and ease so rarely seen in women of his acquaintance. She could make a man feel relaxed and calm in her presence without necessarily meaning to, unlike her sister Nicole who seemed to take great delight in pushing a man's patience and emotions nearly beyond control.

Miles liked Anne, even though she had never made any pretense to approve of him. Perhaps that was why he admired her so much. There was no womanly guile in her attitude, no hidden innuendo in her remarks.

She had a frankness of manner that was often lacking in members of the female gender, and he acknowledged that she was one of the few women he knew whose respect he was interested in earning.

Anne had spoken to him prior to the ceremony, returning the gold snuff box he had not even realized was missing with a sincere apology and blushing explanation about her Aunt Sophie's affliction.

He had accepted his property and her apology with casual grace, hoping to ease her embarrassment, and been rewarded with a true smile. It was, Miles concluded, a good beginning for what he hoped would be a long friendship.

"I pronounce you man and wife. What God hath joined together, let no man put asunder. You may kiss your bride, my lord."

The earl pulled Anne into a heated embrace. Miles noted

that her blush heightened to an even deeper shade of red as Richard not only kissed her, but seemed to take possession of her lips. Yet she made no move to pull away, appearing more than willing to stay in her husband's arms.

The serious mood in the drawing room turned jubilant. Miles exchanged a quick glance of amusement with Ian, then the two men moved forward to join the crush of guests who rushed forward to congratulate the newlyweds.

Without being quite aware of it happening, Miles found himself standing beside Nicole Paget.

"Hello, Captain Nightingall," she said in a throaty voice. "It is wonderful to see you again. Did you enjoy the ceremony?"

"It was charming. Both pious and brief, the best combination. I find, however, that I appreciate a wedding ceremony mostly because some other lucky fellow is the groom."

She gave him a cryptic smile. Miles found himself somewhat disappointed in her mild reaction. He had hoped to see a bit more of her temper shine through.

Still, it was best not to linger too long in Nicole's company. Miles bowed politely, then deliberately shifted his body away from hers. He could feel her gaze upon him, so intent it made the hairs on the back of his neck rise, but he refused to glance in her direction. If she thought him rude, then so be it.

He had been on the receiving end of those looks from her since entering the drawing room. He was not a vain man, and initially he supposed he could be misinterpreting Nicole's covetous glances. But after a few minutes his rake's soul told him the truth.

Nicole desired him and she made every unsubtle attempt to let her feelings show. It became something of a contest of wills throughout the ceremony to ignore her stares, which bordered on the edge of propriety, yet once again Captain Nightingall emerged the victor.

He congratulated himself and insisted that he was unaffected by her, even though Nicole Paget was tiny and delicately beautiful with a feminine luminescence that drew the eye of every man in the room.

Beauty was an overrated asset in Miles's view. In his experience far too many a beautiful face hid a treacherous and deceitful heart.

"My dearest Anne, I am so blissfully happy," Lady Althen cried noisily. She embraced the bride and her new son-in-law dramatically. "This is the day that every mother hopes and dreams and prays for, seeing her daughter so happily wed. My heart is nearly bursting with so much joy it has turned me into an emotional watering pot. Oh, bother, what an impossible moment to misplace my handkerchief."

Lady Althen continued her loud sniffling until Lord Althen pressed a large white linen square in his wife's hand. She dabbed at the corners of her eyes, then placed it daintily over her mouth and tried, with limited success, to muffle her cries.

"Thank you for your solicitations." Anne's expression remained strangely blank when she spoke to her mother.

Lord Althen bowed his head and gave the bride a quick kiss of congratulations. Anne's expression appeared to be frozen, for it did not alter one whit at the touch of her father's lips upon her cheek.

Captain Nightingall was puzzled. Based on his observations of sisterly affection and concern between Anne and Nicole, he had assumed that the Pagets were a loyal, closely connected family. Watching Anne with her parents certainly belied that theory.

Miles saw that Ian managed to worm his way through the crowd to soundly kiss the bride. Finally she came to life. She smiled with genuine delight at Ian and joined her husband in a hearty laugh at some comment he whispered to them.

Of course, it was Nicole's that was the loudest voice of congratulations. It did not escape Miles that she somehow managed to be heard above even Lady Althen's caterwauling. Nor did it surprise him. He firmly believed that Nicole was the sort of woman that always needed to be the center of attention no matter what the occasion. Even her sister's wedding.

Anne and Richard were still being hugged and kissed and cried over by the Paget brood, so it took some time before Miles was able to make his way to their side. He felt an unexpected burst of emotion as he offered his good friend a handshake of congratulations.

"I wish you every happiness, Richard. You deserve it."

The earl's grin widened. "It means a great deal to me having you here this morning. Thank you for coming, Miles."

"It was my pleasure." He turned from the earl to address the bride. "My lady," Miles said elegantly, taking Anne's gloved hand and raising it to his lips. "May I offer you my sincerest congratulations? And add my wishes for a lifetime of happiness together."

"Thank you," Anne replied with a sparkle in her pretty eyes. "I am pleased you were able to attend the ceremony on such short notice."

Her voice was sincere and she smiled at him with gentle warmth. Perhaps the tide of disapproval was finally beginning to turn.

"There you are, Captain Nightingall. I'm so glad I found you."

Nicole again. Miles did not need to turn around to identify that particular female voice. He immediately decided it was time to change tack. Since she clearly refused to be ignored, he would remain politely formal and determinedly reserved. Perhaps that would do the trick.

Eventually she would lose interest in him. Or realize that he meant to keep his distance. Though there was much about her Miles thought he knew and much more he supposed, one thing he had determined with certainty was that Nicole Paget was not a fool.

He took a deep breath. "Miss Paget."

"May I introduce my father, Lord Althen?"

Miles was momentarily disoriented. Nicole smiled sweetly at him. Now what game was she starting to play? Captain Nightingall bowed formally in greeting but held his eyes firmly on the mischievous Nicole.

"So glad to finally meet you," Lord Althen said with an enthusiastic handshake. "Nicole speaks of you often." A cold shiver went through Miles at those words, but Lord Althen continued talking. "My little girl tells me you have an outstanding stallion, Nightingall. She says he rides like the wind. Don't like to brag, of course, but I've got a keen eye for horseflesh. Where did you buy this splendid specimen, if you don't mind my asking?"

"Actually, my lord, I did not purchase the beast. I won him. In a game of faro."

"Haaah! Aren't you the sly one?" Lord Althen let out a yelp and slapped Miles on the back. "I like a man who can hold his cards. And his liquor. It's disgraceful watching all those young bucks make fools of themselves at the gaming tables. You shouldn't drink or gamble if you don't know what you're about, that's what I always say."

Miles sighed inwardly. One of the quickest ways to discourage a romantic flirtation with an unsuitable young miss was to earn the disapproval of her family. Forbidden fruit might be tempting, but most young women lacked the courage to defy their parents.

Yet Miles's hopes of putting Lord Althen off by eagerly admitting to his fondness for gambling had fallen flat.

Of course, the fact that he had won might be clouding the older man's judgment. Miles briefly wondered if getting deep into his cups this afternoon would alter Lord Althen's favorable opinion of him, but he instantly rejected the idea. He could never embarrass Richard by getting drunk at his wedding.

Hell, what was the point of having a disreputable reputation if one couldn't use it to advantage when circumstances warranted?

Miles absently scratched his chin. He should incite Nicole's temper. Anger would prove to be an excellent antidote for infatuation. Or perhaps he could do something so shocking that Nicole would succumb to a fit of the vapors. He gave her a speculative glance and after taking careful note of her outfit realized that her sensibilities were not that delicate.

The dress she wore was cut round, low and wide around the bodice. The light blue color enhanced the striking creaminess of her complexion. He concluded she had an excellent modiste, although to be fair he admitted she would probably look stunning dressed in rags. The beautiful silk fabric she wore clung flatteringly to her rounded curves. Time and again Miles's eyes lingered appreciatively on her lush bosom.

Nicole had a great deal of flesh displayed, certainly far more than was proper for a late-morning family wedding. Well, if she wasn't above showing, Miles most certainly wasn't above staring at it.

Miles's contribution to the discussion of horses dwindled as he began to find it increasingly difficult to concentrate on Lord Althen's conversation. Reluctantly he pulled his eyes away from all the luscious, satiny flesh that Nicole so brazenly showcased, but it did no good. Her heady scent engulfed his senses.

He reminded himself fiercely that he did not find her appealing.

"Everyone has been called to the dining room. Will you escort me in to luncheon, Captain Nightingall?" Nicole asked. "Please?"

"I would be honored." Miles's lips twisted wryly. He listened for any hint of flirtation or suggestion in her voice but found none. He couldn't very well refuse her outright. It would be insufferably rude.

Nicole took his arm possessively but kept a respectable distance between them as they walked into the dining room.

The bride and groom led the way. There were many oohs and ahhs when the guests entered and beheld the lovely setting for the nuptial feast. Even though it was not yet noon, numerous candles had been lit. The tiny, glittering flames reflected against the sparkling crystal goblets and gold plates, and beams of light shot merrily throughout the room.

There were elaborate arrangements of fresh flowers in soft pastel shades adorning the long table, and their subtle aroma wafted through the air. Mingling with their scent was the sugary smell of marzipan which covered the impressive three-tiered wedding cake prominently displayed on the sideboard.

Miles found his place at the table. Nicole was seated to his left, Aunt Sophie to his right, and Lord Althen directly across. The bride and groom sat at the head of the table facing their guests. Alexandra was appropriately seated by her father's other side.

Miles settled Aunt Sophie in her seat and turned to help Nicole. She reached for her chair the same moment that he did and their bodies collided. She made a soft noise and he pulled back like a scalded cat.

Recovering rapidly, Miles deliberately scraped back Nicole's chair. She stared at the upholstered brocade cushion in solemn confusion for a moment, then gracefully sank down. A quick glance about the dining room confirmed to Miles's vast relief that no one had noticed the incident.

As soon as everyone had taken their places, Lord Althen stood and offered a toast to the bride. Anne blushed noticeably as everyone raised their glasses of chilled champagne in salute to her before drinking.

"It tickles my nose, Papa," Alexandra announced with child-ish delight. She took another gulp, effectively draining the glass. "May I have some more?"

"Only half a glass or you'll fall asleep in your soup," the earl decided with a laugh.

Miles followed Richard's advice and took a small sip from his goblet. There was a time not too long ago when he spent the better part of his day in an alcoholic haze. He drank to excess for a variety of reasons. To pass the time, to dull the pain, to drown out the visions and voices of battle.

It never helped. So he had stopped. Pity, no one seemed to notice.

Ian offered the next toast, and after him, William, the elder of Anne's brothers, gave a solemn speech about the bonds and sanctity of marriage. There seemed little that could be added after that dry recitation and the table soon grew quiet.

Nicole's eager voice broke the silence. "Gracious, that reminds me of an incident I witnessed while attending an afternoon gathering a few months back in London. The writer Matthew Lewis, or rather Monk Lewis as he is known in society because his first published tale was entitled *The Monk,* was there. He dotes on the Duchess of York, and before leaving the salon she whispered something to him that brought tears to his eyes.

"Someone asked him what was wrong and he replied, 'Oh, the duchess spoke so very kindly to me.' So Colonel Armstrong piped up and said, 'My dear fellow, pray don't cry. I dare say she didn't mean it.' "

Everyone joined in the laughter, William loudest of all. With high spirits once again reigning, the servants brought out the first course, a cold vegetable soup. Nicole dipped into her soup with her silver spoon and casually leaned toward Miles.

"Be careful of Aunt Sophie," she whispered. "She is a dear old thing but has a rather annoying habit of acquiring items that do not belong to her."

"I shall make certain to count the coins in my pocket before I leave the table," he whispered back, surprised and touched by her warning.

"Best count the number of gold buttons on your waistcoat too," Nicole entreated. "She seems to like anything that glitters."

Miles allowed himself a quick smile before remembering that he had planned on ignoring Nicole. But it was impossible, for she sparkled throughout the meal. One would think that she, not Anne, was the bride. Yet instead of being resentful or displeased by her behavior, the bride appeared content to allow her sister the spotlight, laughing hardest at Nicole's retelling of a childhood tale.

Miles forked up a mouthful of lobster patty and admitted that whenever Nicole was around, conversation would never be strained or sparse.

Nicole finally paused for breath, and Ian assumed the role of lead entertainment, launching into a much-censored tale of a Peninsula escapade. Nicole smiled graciously, not resentfully as Miles assumed she might.

He watched her take a sip of champagne and roll it sensuously around her tongue to savor the taste. An acute pang of longing seared his gut. Shaken, he jerked his head away and rubbed his hand over his eyes, needing a moment to collect his thoughts.

She is a mere girl, he reminded himself as he struggled for common sense. A seventeen-year-old chit who had long ago perfected the art of simpering and flirting and teasing. He was a man with far more experience than she could even begin to imagine. Miles fortified his spirits with those thoughts as he speared an asparagus stalk with his fork.

Over the last year female companions had often accused him of having no feelings. And in most cases they were correct. It hurt too much to care. He did not relish the alternative much either, but thought it was the lesser of two evils. Consequently, Miles felt alone almost all of the time, cut apart, separate from those around him.

He preferred it that way. Or so he had always believed. And that was why, he finally realized, Nicole Paget was so dangerous. For when he looked at her, he felt deep within his heart that he didn't want to be alone anymore.

Nicole had been unable to tear her eyes away from Miles from the minute he had entered the drawing room only moments before the wedding ceremony started. She had not seen him since the afternoon he had carried her up to her bedchamber at Sir Reginald's manor house. That was three days ago. Her eyes had been starved for a glimpse of him, her ears hungry for his voice. When he finally appeared, she feasted on the sight of him.

He was flawlessly garbed in a closely fitted dark jacket of the finest cloth stretched across muscular shoulders, a stark white linen shirt along with an intricately tied cravat, a subtly patterned cream-colored waistcoat.

His breeches were form-fitted and spotless, his boots so highly polished she could see her reflection. He was the quintessential picture of the perfect gentleman. But Nicole saw beyond the trappings of his expensive clothes. Beyond the facade of a careless rake to where his raw virility spoke to her restless heart.

She had been warned. There were many who believed that Nightingall possessed neither heart nor soul. Why, just this morning Anne had cautioned her again to keep her attention away from Captain Nightingall.

Anne proclaimed him a totally unsuitable companion for any young woman. She even promised Nicole an elaborate London Season next spring as a further enticement to stay clear of the dangerous Miles Nightingall.

Nicole had smiled prettily and remained silent while her sister lectured, knowing no words would ever have the power to sway her. Besides, it was Anne's wedding day and the very last thing Nicole wanted was to distress her sister on the morning of her wedding.

Miles had pointedly ignored her throughout the ceremony, but now that they were seated together at the table he was not so distant. She knew he watched her. She could feel his scrutiny, his weighing of her comments, his judgment of her behavior. Surprisingly, it did not anger her, for she welcomed the attention.

Nicole took a sip of her champagne and risked a quick glance. She caught him gazing at her with such naked emotion she almost dropped her goblet. She blinked with surprise and the look fled. But she had seen it. Bleak and stark. Loneliness. So potently real and painful she nearly burst into tears.

Her throat tightened. More than anything she wanted to wrap her arms around him and hold herself close to his heart. To offer comfort and love, to chase away the aloneness she had earlier sensed and now seen in him.

Her fingers shook with the force of her emotions. She gripped her fork tightly and attacked the pheasant on her plate with all the turmoil she dared not show to anyone.

The remainder of the meal passed in a blur. The champagne flowed freely and there were more toasts and much laughter. At long last the beautiful marzipan fruitcake was cut and served. Nicole seized the opportunity.

"Shall we take a stroll in the garden?" She placed her fingers on the sleeve of Miles's coat. "The grounds are especially lovely this time of day."

She could feel his lean muscles tensing beneath her palm. He disengaged her hand, and Nicole's heart started jumping when she realized he might refuse. For instead of politely rising to his feet and offering her his arm, he leaned back in his chair, folded his arms across his chest and stared at her.

"You don't have any ulterior motives for asking me out-of-doors, do you, Miss Paget?" he asked in a sarcastic tone. "After all, one does have a reputation to maintain."

"I know all about your reputation, sir." Nicole laughed prettily. She knew she was testing his patience, but she didn't much care. "Now, you must not be overly flattered by my request. My new brother-in-law, Lord Mulgrave, looks as though he has had enough of this sumptuous banquet but he is far too well-mannered to leave the table while his guests are having such a delightful time.

"I thought if we led the way out of the dining room and

into the garden, the rest of the guests would follow. I have never been married, but I do believe that Anne and Lord Mulgrave would prefer to spend a portion of their wedding day alone.''

His quizzical expression told her she wasn't adequately explaining herself. Nicole lifted her hands in a gesture of frustration, but continued talking.

''Since my entire family is staying at Cuttingswood, the earl does not have the luxury of whisking his bride away whenever the mood strikes him. However, if the newlyweds were left alone they at least may choose between rejoining their guests or venturing off on their own. I know my family rather well, and you must trust me when I tell you they will never leave unless they are shown. Now, shall we show them, Captain?''

His handsome face took on a suspicious expression. *He is going to refuse.* Nicole's heart constricted. Then she saw the suspicion change to curiosity and finally to resignation.

''It would be my pleasure to escort you through the gardens,'' he said, offering her his arm.

They immediately drew the attention of everyone in the room. Anne seemed to go on instant alert, but Lord Mulgrave nodded approvingly at them and then whispered into his bride's ear.

Nicole linked her right arm through Captain Nightingall's and for extra measure placed her left hand on his arm too. Now that she was finally going to have him to herself, she was taking no chances. When they reached the gravel path, Nicole glanced over her shoulder.

''Have we been successful?'' he asked.

Nicole smiled. ''Yes. Nearly everyone is out on the terrace. Except Anne and Lord Mulgrave.''

They exchanged a conspiratorial grin and continued walking, soon outdistancing the rest of the guests.

They walked in silence. At first Nicole welcomed the quiet.

It was calming and comforting in a strange way. But eventually the prolonged silence gave way to coldness. And distance.

How would she ever get through to him if he remained so icy and remote? Frustration simmered inside her with each step, and as they began to turn the corner on the gravel path, all the pent-up emotions she had been holding at bay came bursting out.

She ceased walking. Captain Nightingall pulled her gently along for an additional step before noticing. He turned to her in surprise and she seized the moment.

Nicole leaned forward, surging up on her toes, and kissed him. Full on the lips.

It was the boldest thing she had ever done.

At first he went as rigid as one of those marble statues Anne so enjoyed sketching. Hard, solid, unyielding. Nicole placed her arms clingingly around his shoulders to retain her balance and bring herself closer to his chest. She could feel the restrained power of his broad muscles beneath her hands as she continued kissing him, waiting anxiously for some kind, any kind, of response.

Suddenly she felt his hands grasp her waist. For a split second she feared he was going to push her away, but instead he lifted her upward so her soft body pressed into his hard one. And then he kissed her back.

It felt like a soft stroke of silk. Smooth and fine and gentle. Then the kiss deepened and her world became centered completely on him. Miles's tongue plunged inside and Nicole welcomed him eagerly. Joyfully. He tasted forbidden. And familiar, which was impossible, because this was their first kiss. Emotions clamoring in her heart, Nicole lost herself in the magic of his embrace.

Then suddenly the warmth was gone. He lifted his head and pulled it away. His arms and body soon followed. Nicole felt a lonely gust of warm wind brush across her cheek.

"If I had known you intended to kiss me half senseless, I

would have searched for a more secluded spot," he drawled. "Or was it your intention to be discovered in a most compromising embrace?"

A sarcastic retort was almost beyond Nicole's tongue before she successfully bit it back. She would not act like a rude and spoiled child in front of this man no matter how sorely tested.

Captain Nightingall managed to keep his gaze shuttered, his face expressionless, but Nicole saw the slight tremor of his hand and knew he was equally shaken.

Nicole smiled. Captain Nightingall did not.

She knew that he meant for her to find no encouragement in his hooded gaze. Still, his glowering, indifferent looks did not prevent her heart from racing. With steadfast determination she reached for his hand and lifted it toward her face, much as a gentleman would when greeting a lady.

But instead of chastely brushing her lips across the top of his knuckles, Nicole boldly placed her open mouth over his wrist and caressed his beating pulse gently with her tongue. Once, twice, three times. Then she released his hand. It dropped to his side.

His eyes flashed fire at her. Nicole was frightened just for an instant, but she wasn't about to show it.

"Good afternoon, Miles," she said softly. "I shall look forward to meeting you again. Soon."

"Good day, *Miss Paget.*" He turned stiffly and marched away from her, never once glancing back.

Nicole shivered. Realizing her knees were about to give out, she scurried to a nearby garden bench and sat down. Her champagne-filled stomach churned.

My Lord, did I really just do that? Be so bold and daring, so commanding and in control? It was wicked, scandalous behavior, but what better way to capture the attention of a rogue than with scandalous actions?

Nicole pressed a fist into her stomach, hoping to calm the persistent gurgling. Well, things hadn't gone precisely as she had planned, but she refused to be discouraged. This was a victory. Miles had felt something for her. Something strong enough and powerful enough to make him flee from her.

Her resolve hardened. She would have him. At any cost. Despite the objections and warnings of her family. Despite even Captain Nightingall's reluctance.

Anne had warned her that there was no wishing for what could never be. Perversely Nicole agreed. She had no intention of merely wishing for the good captain. She would convince him of her affection and worthiness. Or perhaps coax him. And if all else failed, force him to at least acknowledge her feelings.

Because somehow Nicole knew that this man was her destiny.

Chapter Fourteen

Anne wasn't precisely certain how it came to pass but suddenly she was alone with her groom. The dining room, which just moments ago had been filled with laughter and the sounds of the guests enjoying a sumptuous feast, was now silent.

"It appears we have been abandoned, my dear," Richard remarked in a light tone. "Was it something we said?"

"Or didn't say," Anne countered with a smile. "I noticed you were rather quiet during the meal."

"As were you." Richard dismissed the anxious servants hovering near their chairs with a curt nod. "There. Now we are completely alone."

Anne continued to smile but no longer felt quite so jovial. This was the first time they had been together without anyone else to act as a buffer or distraction since the wedding ceremony. She felt foolish admitting to herself that she was a tad nervous.

Richard appeared to be in a contented mood, but she suddenly wished he would smile at her. He had such an engaging, comforting smile. She had sat close, probably too close, to him throughout their nuptial feast and he had smiled often. At the other guests. Never directly at her.

Anne scolded herself for being so uncharacteristically sensitive. Ridiculous, actually. Yet it unsettled her, having no clear sense of how Richard was feeling. Was he happy that they were finally wed? Or did he have doubts? Or even worse, regrets?

Unaware of Anne's inner turmoil, the earl ceased drumming his fingers on the table and poured them each a glass of champagne. He raised his goblet. "To my bride."

"To my groom." Anne touched her glass to his and they drank. She watched him openly over the rim of dainty crystal, but instead of lifting her wineglass in a toast, what she really wanted was to reach out and caress his freshly shaven jaw.

Yet Anne quashed her longing. It was simply too intimate a gesture, too presumptuous a notion, even though he was now her husband.

Taking a fortifying breath, she drained her goblet in three long swallows and looked expectantly toward Richard. The earl pushed away from the table and stood on his feet. "Shall we make good our escape before our guests grow tired of my gardens and return?"

Anne stared at his offered hand and felt a rush of pure lust run through her. She had been thinking about entering his bedchamber from the moment she had been seated at the table and felt the press of his muscular thigh against her own. Her mind might not have fully accepted her new role as wife, but her body was well-pleased by her choice of husband.

It was scandalous. A bride standing before the vicar reciting her marriage vows not pure and innocent as she ought to be, but feeling the telltale effects and soreness throughout her body after being well and thoroughly bedded.

Anne had awakened in her own bedchamber this morning having no memory of how she arrived there, yet the memories of where and how she had spent the majority of the night were clear and vivid. Naked in Richard arms, his body pressed intimately inside hers, loving her until she had been totally sated, until she had fallen into a contented, exhausted slumber.

And now it was going to happen again, Anne thought with a quickening breath. In the middle of the afternoon with the room bathed in bright sunshine, with her family and the wedding guests mingling in the gardens and the lower rooms of the house. How would she ever be able to face them again without blushing herself silly?

Would it be different between them today? Last night she had gone to Richard of her own free will, had offered herself to him by choice. Today she was bound by duty and obligation to grant him conjugal rights. Would it somehow alter the bliss they had shared?

"Anne?"

She lifted her chin and met the earl's possessive gaze. The tension between them tightened and a streak of anticipation shot through her entire being.

" 'Tis the middle of the afternoon," she said lamely. "Won't our guests wonder at our absence?"

"I don't care."

Neither do I, Anne realized, but she did not speak her thoughts aloud. The earl was already starting to wield far too much power over her person. She had noticed since moving into his home a few days ago how she was starting to look to him for approval or suggestions or advice whenever she did anything. She did it naturally, almost without thinking.

It worried her. Anne was uncertain and fearful of this mysterious power he had so easily obtained. She was anxious to keep a piece of herself apart from him. For her own safety.

Yet she was honest enough to acknowledge that her physical appetite for him had only been whetted after last night. She found their lovemaking to be a wondrous, unbelievable act of intimacy that she could not imagine engaging in with any man except for Richard. She hungered to learn more.

"If you wish, then we shall retire, my lord," Anne said quietly.

Still, it took a far greater effort than she thought to place her hand in his. Trust did not come easily to Anne, especially with men. She stiffened her spine and rose gracefully to her feet, deliberately putting a distance between her overheated body and her husband's.

Richard raised her hand to his lips and brushed a gentle kiss across the knuckles. Anne's knees felt weak as a strong ripple of desire seized her. She found herself wanting a kiss on the lips too, but felt awkward, then foolish asking for one.

She smiled faintly at the earl as he led her out of the dining room. They climbed the beautiful staircase in silence, passing several footmen along the way. Anne avoided their eyes, knowing she would blush furiously and gauchely. Above all, she didn't want to embarrass Richard in front of his servants.

She turned left toward her bedchamber when they reached the landing, but the earl gently tugged her to his side. "Our rooms are this way, Anne."

Anne blinked with remembrance, then blushed hotly when she noticed the young footman standing guard at the end of the long hallway. Naturally, he was fully aware of what she and Richard were about to do. Doubting she could hide her embarrassment, Anne nonetheless felt compelled to at least try. She tilted her chin aristocratically in an outward sign of courage while her stomach tensed into knots.

They entered the master's chambers, and Anne was vastly relieved there was no valet waiting to assist the earl. Yet there were signs that the servant had recently been in the room. A midnight blue robe was placed carefully upon the bed, and though not lit because of the warmth of the day, kindling was laid in the grate for a fire.

There was a vase of fresh flowers placed on the dresser and two upholstered chairs arranged around a small table set with glasses, wine and a tray of sweets.

Anne had been too nervous, too agitated last night to fully appreciate the beauty of the earl's bedchamber, so she glanced about now in genuine curiosity. Done in shades of green and gold with rich dark wood furniture and several artfully painted landscapes that echoed those colors hanging on the walls, the bedchamber was elegant and refined. Rather like the man who occupied it.

Anne's feet sank into the luxurious carpet as she disengaged herself from Richard's arm and walked to the windows, away from the massive bed that dominated the north side of the bedchamber.

"The windows overlook the gardens," she commented. "I can see Alexandra and Rosalind racing on the lawn."

"They look as though they are having a delightful time," Richard remarked as he peered through the glass. "It was kind of you to include Alexandra in today's festivities. It made her feel very grown-up."

Anne turned to him in surprise. "Alexandra is your daughter. And now mine. Naturally, I wanted her present at the ceremony and the luncheon afterward."

"Many women would have objected to having so young a child sharing our table. Not all females are as tolerant as you, Anne." The sound of girlish giggles drifted up to the room and they both turned their attention back to the garden. "I hope Alexandra doesn't become too mischievous this afternoon. She tends to run amuck without Miss Fraser keeping a watchful eye on her activities."

"Don't worry about Alexandra. There are more than one pair of eyes to follow her every move. Rosalind is especially adept at keeping her young friend from harm." Anne ran her finger lightly over the leaded window glass. "I am sorry that Miss Fraser felt too ill to attend our wedding. Alexandra seems very fond of her governess, and you speak so highly of her. I look forward to making her acquaintance."

"I suspect you will approve of Miss Fraser. She is a most accomplished woman."

Anne nodded, then smiled with forced brightness. "This is a lovely chamber."

"I have always liked it," Richard agreed. "Except for some new draperies, 'tis very much the same as when my father occupied these rooms. Come, let me show you the rest of the master's apartment."

Anne knew her hands must feel cold against Richard's warm fingers, but if he found them so he made no mention.

"The house has always been well maintained, and through the years we have added as many modern conveniences as possible. There is a private bath over there." Richard gestured toward the far side of the room. "And through that door is a sitting room that connects my room with your bedchamber."

"How convenient." Anne tugged her hand away from his warm grasp and moved back to the large window that offered the fantastic view of the garden. Her mind whirled with indecision.

Should she ask to see her new bedchamber? Or did he expect her to just go there? But it was the middle of the afternoon. Anne worried her bottom lip between her teeth. Perhaps a maid was already there, waiting to help her change out of her wedding gown.

There were so many tiny buttons down the back of the dress it would take a while to properly disrobe. Would the earl become frustrated if he tried to unfasten them all himself? Would he not prefer his bride to present herself to him in a nightgown and robe? Even at this hour of the day? Anne frowned, knowing she would feel ridiculous changing into her nightclothes this early.

She bowed her head in confusion and studied the stitching on the skirt of her lovely yellow gown. The dress was a gift from Richard, the first she had worn in many, many years that she had not sewn with her own hands. It was a lovely garment that fit her well, flattering her figure and her coloring. She felt almost beautiful while wearing it.

Anne heard the earl move close beside her but did not raise her head. His nearness made her heart quicken. She feared that if she spoke now her voice would be breathless and quivering. How gauche.

She felt the whisper of his warm breath on her neck. Her spine went rigid and every muscle in her body seemed to stiffen as she waited for the feel of his lips upon her tender skin. But it never came.

She missed the darkness of last night. The darkness that had hidden her and protected her from his too keen gaze.

"Is anything wrong?" he inquired gently.

"No."

"Anne?"

For an instant she resented the sound of his deep, rich voice. Must she tell him all, now that he was her husband? Did she no longer have the right to her privacy, to her inner soul? Had she given up that along with her name and her freedom?

She turned to answer him, and the angry retort died on her tongue. There was only puzzlement in his eyes. And concern. She became acutely aware of his kindness and gentleness and the sacrifices he had made. For her.

"May I have some wine?" she asked in a desperate whisper.

"Of course, my dear. Come, sit down."

Finally he smiled at her. Anne let out the breath pent up in her lungs. He had such a handsome, elegant smile. She had missed seeing it flashed at her in genuine good humor.

Anne relaxed slightly as she obediently sat down in the upholstered chair. Accepting the crystal goblet with a quiet thank you, she placed it untouched upon the table. "You know that I was very reluctant to enter into this marriage, but now that I have made my vows to you, I promise that I shall try with all my heart to make a success of it. I want so very much to be a good wife, Richard. Yet I feel so ill-prepared. I deeply fear I shall be a great disappointment to you.''

She spread her fingers in her lap and stared down at the wedding ring of gold and diamonds that seemed so foreign and bright.

''We might not be considered a perfect match, but I truly believe we are well-suited to each other,'' Richard declared, framing her face tenderly between his hands. ''I do not expect it shall be easy for either of us, but I have always been a man who relishes a challenging experience. I also took vows today and made promises before God and our families and friends. For better or worse, Anne.''

She could hear the conviction and sincerity in his voice. It made her feel ashamed of her selfishness. ''I shall try my hardest to ensure there is far more better than worse,'' she whispered truthfully.

''As will I.'' Richard's fingers glided softly across her cheek and came to rest upon her shoulders. ''We must give it time, Anne.''

She nodded her head sharply. His hands traveled down her arms and encircled her waist. Richard lifted her toward him and Anne allowed it, finding comfort and enjoyment in his nearness. She nestled in his lap like a child, yet the distinct swelling against her bottom told her that was certainly not how Richard thought of her.

What God hath joined together. Anne shivered. It had felt strangely exhilarating at first to realize she was now a married woman. A countess. His countess.

But along with the title came both responsibility and expectation. Responsibility did not faze Anne; she was a master at accepting and shouldering a great many burdens. Expectations, however, were another matter. She had never been very adept at fulfilling them, especially the traditional female role.

A sudden ache seized her throat. She didn't want to fail at this marriage. She wanted very much to succeed. Anne decided she too could accept a challenge. She would strive to make a success of this marriage and somehow manage to keep a part of herself, her individuality, whole and alive.

Anne tilted her head up and kissed Richard, hoping to convey the depth of her promise and commitment to their life together with her lips instead of words. She tasted his surprise and then delight as his lips parted to accept her offering. Her breasts tightened almost instantly. Here at least was an area where they could find common ground, shared pleasure.

She squirmed in his lap, shifting her body closer to his. Richard's arousal grew and thickened, jabbing into her softness. He groaned, then whispered fiercely in her ear, "Can you feel what you do to me, love?"

"Yes," she said breathlessly, wondering if he could feel her desire as easily.

"Are you well enough to share my bed, sweet Anne?"

Her mind went blank for a moment until she realized what he was asking. When she came to his bed last night, she had told Richard she was expecting her monthly courses at any time.

"I—I am fine," Anne stammered, hating that she sounded so weak and flustered.

"Then come," he whispered wickedly in her ear. "Come to my bed."

How she wanted to. Anne's insides began to melt but her gaze wavered. "The room is so bright," she implored weakly.

Richard lifted her high in his arms and stood up. For an instant Anne feared he was going to carry her to his bed, but instead he gently set her upright. Then he crossed the room and yanked the drapes closed. The room was instantly plunged into the soft, warm glow of twilight.

"Better?"

Even in the faded light she could see the stark passion on his handsome features. She was aware of his heat and desire.

She could fairly smell his passion. It excited and titillated her. Yet still she hesitated.

Moistening her dry lips, Anne took a step forward. She was acting ridiculous. Like a frightened virgin, which she no longer was, who was terrified of her husband, which she definitely was not.

" 'Tis very romantic," Anne said softly. This time she did not wait for him to come to her. She walked to him. Directly into his outstretched arms.

She pressed herself flat against his broad chest. The warmth of his body flowed into hers, even through the barrier of their clothing. It was the sort of intimate gesture that spoke of affection and respect and love between a couple. It was, Anne realized with a start, how she felt about Richard.

The truth did not shock her, for it was always there, close in her heart merely waiting to be acknowledged. Anne always knew Richard was different. More tolerant of her eccentricities, more accepting of her oddities. Yet who would have ever believed she would come to care for him so strongly? So completely?

These feelings didn't exactly frighten her, but they made her feel more vulnerable. Where had the sensible, practical, staid woman she had always been gone?

Richard's hand began a languid caress down her spine. Anne stiffened and went still. It was a subtle reminder of his power and control over her body. And her heart. The hand continued its sensual massage, and she lifted her chin.

There was no mistaking the sparkle of desire in his eyes. Shyness swept over Anne but she forced herself to conquer it. She slowly turned her back toward him and asked, "Would you unfasten the buttons on my gown, my lord? I am loath to call a maid to interrupt our privacy and I find that I cannot reach them on my own."

She didn't need to ask twice. Richard's fingers felt light and delicate on her back as he unlooped the many tiny fabric-covered buttons. He didn't rush, seeming to enjoy performing this intimate act for her.

Then Anne felt the caress of his tongue, warm and damp on the column of her throat. A shivery warmth raced downward, pooling in her lower belly. Anne closed her eyes and leaned back into his strength, into his hardness.

His arms reached up and he caressed her breasts through the fabric of her gown, slowly, gently. She smiled when she felt his fingers untie the ribbons at the front of her chemise and his exploring hand slipped inside. He ran his fingertips over her breast. The nipple hardened and rose and a jolt of sensation shot through Anne.

She made no protest when he pushed down the loosened bodice and short puff sleeves of her gown, for she craved the gentleness of his warm touch on the rest of her body. He caressed her for several long, languid moments until she turned to face him and lifted her head yearningly for a kiss.

Their lips met, and Richard's tongue stroked hers with slow, deliberate movements. He tasted wonderful. Her hands worked at the intricate knot of his cravat, and there was a rush of triumph when she at last got a tantalizing glimpse of his bare throat. She pressed her tongue eagerly against the rapidly beating pulse on his neck. Richard's breathing grew deep and heavy.

Anne could smell him, the fresh, exotic scent of an aroused male. It was wanton and wicked. Intoxicating.

"Anne."

The deep timbre of his voice rolled through her body. It made her knees feel like melted wax.

"Hmmmm?" she murmured breathlessly.

"Come to bed so I may love you properly."

Anne sighed. She kissed his jaw, then licked the spot where his neck curved into the broadness of his shoulder.

Richard swung her up in his arms. He carried her to his bed and dropped her onto the mattress. She shrieked as she rolled on the soft feathers, nearly becoming tangled in the bedcovers and her own disheveled clothing.

Before she could right herself, Richard was again by her side. He began tugging at her clothes and she reached for him, eager to remove his garments too. Richard proved far more adept than Anne, for she was soon naked while he sported all of his garments save for his coat and neckcloth.

With a sexy smile of sensual promise, the earl backed away from the bed. Richard quickly stripped off his clothing until he wore only a shirt and breeches. A memory stirred in Anne's mind of him last night, his beautiful hard body naked against hers, holding her tight as he pumped inside her softness.

She waited anxiously to again feel the length of his strong body against her own heated flesh, but Richard did not cover her body with his own. He settled beside her and began a trail of hot, moist kisses across her breasts, down to her stomach and beyond. His cheek felt rough against the sensitive curves of her belly. Anne tried to catch his hair in her hands, but the silken strands slid through her fingers as his head sank lower.

"Richard!"

Anne's breath caught in her throat as he started kissing her upper thighs. He rolled her onto her back. Startled, she sprawled out on the bed, too overwhelmed to move. His questing tongue dipped even lower, boldly parting the curls that hid her inner core. Anne shrieked.

The earl raised his head and smiled lazily. "Relax, my dear. I promise I shall stop if you do not enjoy yourself."

Anne's wits were far too scattered to think of any sort of reply. Taking her silence for acquiescence, Richard returned his skillful tongue to its shocking task and began a wicked caress of her most vulnerable spot.

A part of her wanted to close her thighs and push him away, to deny him this complete access to her body, to her person. Yet a larger part of her womanhood welcomed him lovingly along with this burning torment he brought.

The war within her mind was quickly won by her heart and her overstimulated body. Anne arched against Richard, opening her legs wider, lifting herself closer to him. Mindlessly her hands reached out and she stroked the sculpted, muscular contours of the arms that held her so rigidly in place.

It was too much, she thought feverishly, moving her head from side to side as the tension spiraled tighter and tighter. His tongue slid deeper and she cried out, her fingers digging into his forearms. He slid his hands beneath her buttocks to hold her in place and she whimpered louder.

Ripples of sensation washed over Anne with each flick of his expert tongue, and the tension within her continued to grow to an almost painful level.

Good Lord, she had never imagined that such openness, such intimacy could exist between two people. She could feel her heart pounding with excitement, throbbing inside her breast. Just when Anne thought she had reached the very limit of her endurance, the rhythmic stroking of his tongue increased.

Anne screamed and nearly threw herself off the bed, but Richard held her firmly in place. Then the wave of tightness finally broke and for a brief moment she felt suspended in pleasure. Tears filled her eyes as release claimed her body and she dissolved into a limp pool of quivering sensations.

Anne barely had time to catch her breath before she heard his voice calling her, luring her again with its magical seductive powers.

"Look at me, Anne."

Eyes fluttering, she gazed up into his beloved face. In the twilight glow Richard loomed above her sated body like some ancient Roman god—powerful, masculine, magnificent. He pressed a kiss against her damp temple and she nuzzled her chin against his jaw.

"I want to be inside you, sweet Anne. Spread your legs for me, my darling."

Without hesitation she obeyed his command. Anne felt the

moist pressure and stretching deep inside as he began to push. It would have been so simple, but he did not use his strength to overpower her. He took her slow and easy, although she could tell by the sweat on his brow and the rigid set of his muscular forearms that he was exerting supreme control over his passion.

At last she felt the fullness of his heavy length deep inside her. She wound her fingers in his hair and pulled him even closer. The sensations were unbelievable, a mixture of physical and emotional desire. A yearning for completion that only felt right now that their bodies were joined as one.

Following his hoarsely whispered commands, Anne wrapped her legs around his strong hips. Richard thrust deep and hard and Anne arched up to meet his heavy strokes. Their bodies soon grew slick with perspiration, and Anne savored the sweetness of her rising desire.

She risked a quick glance down to see what he did to her, to see how their bodies joined and mated. Richard pulled himself completely from her body and preened before her curious eyes. His arousal was thick, hard and glistening with moisture. From her body. From his body. From their lovemaking.

After she had looked her fill, Richard once again thrust his engorged shaft inside her. Anne felt his need become primal as his thrusts grew stronger and deeper, harder and faster. He crushed her against his broad chest and she tightened her inner muscles instinctively, longing to bring him the same pleasure he had so generously given her.

The room grew quiet except for the sounds of Richard's labored breathing. Anne tilted her hips to bring him deeper, closer to her. He thrust harder, quicker, repeatedly. She heard him groan against her hair as she imitated his movements, matching him stroke for stroke.

Suddenly she felt his body tensing. He broke their rhythm and began to shudder. Anne opened her eyes and looked up at him. Their eyes met at the exact moment she felt the heat and wetness of his seed erupt deep inside her.

"Some day I will plant our child within your body," he said in a voice filled with emotion.

Tears came unexpectedly to her eyes, and her emotions threatened to overtake her. Anne felt torn. She wasn't nearly as frightened at the idea of motherhood as she had been but she hardly felt ready to wholly embrace it either.

Anne closed her eyes. She felt his lips gently kiss her forehead and then both cheeks. With a final kiss on her lips, Richard disengaged his body and moved off her. The silence was broken only by the short, uneven breaths he drew.

Anne turned to look at him. He lay on his back, close but not touching her. In the shadowy light, Richard's handsome face showed not the slightest emotion. She felt again how far apart their expectations of life were, how very different the worlds they longed to inhabit really were. Her love for him felt strong and right and good, but the barriers between them began to loom as an insurmountable obstacle.

Anne knew that she would do whatever was necessary to make Richard happy, but at what price? By loving him would she lose a part of herself? In her attempts to please him would she become the wife he wanted and needed and deserved yet lose the woman she was, the woman she had always longed to be?

Fearful, Anne cuddled close to the magnificent male body that lay sprawled across the large bed. Inexplicably, it gave her comfort to be near him. Equally afraid and hopeful of the future, Anne rested her head against the crisp curls of her husband's broad chest and allowed the steady beat of his heart to lull her into slumber.

He sat and watched the sunset from the privacy of his sitting-room window, his arms lovingly cradling a slightly crushed bonnet. The golden streaks of color that had so brilliantly lit the sky soon gave way to dusk, but he did not rise to light the candles in the room. The gloomy darkness fit his mood. He sat in silence and in darkness. And he brooded.

Richard had taken another wife. And while he would never deny his friend a chance at happiness, for he loved Richard as a brother, his first thought was of Alexandra. His little girl.

How would she fare now that Richard had brought another woman into the household? A woman who would hold power over the little girl's actions, her behavior, her very future. A woman who would directly affect all aspects of her life. For better or worse? Only time would answer that question.

He sighed and closed his eyes, willing away the fear that took hold of him and refused to let go. What would happen to Alexandra if Richard and Anne had a child of their own? Would dear Alex be cast into the shadows? Relegated to a lesser position? Denied her share of love and affection?

His hands clenched into fists at the very idea, his strong fingers crushing the fragile piece of precious straw as if it had no weight or substance. Gritting his teeth in anger, he slowly released his deadly grip and sighed when he saw the damage his loss of control had wrought. He blew out a breath in agony, angry with himself for nearly destroying this small part of his daughter. This precious little reminder he had of her.

He never should have taken the bonnet, of course. It was foolish and risky. Yet it had been an impulse too strong to resist, too impossible to ignore. He was having them more frequently, these impulses that propelled him into unseemly acts. It momentarily frightened him to realize he could so easily lose his control, but he rationalized his behavior by recalling the depth of his pain.

Alexandra had seemed quite happy at the ceremony this afternoon. Balancing a large bouquet of flowers in her delicate hands, she had stood beside her idol Rosalind and watched her father repeat his vows with barely concealed excitement.

She had enjoyed the luncheon afterwards and her first sip of champagne. For her, it had all been a great lark, a grand adventure. And why not? She was merely an innocent child. She did not fully comprehend the ramifications of her father's remarriage nor how it might usurp her position in his heart.

He bowed his head and inhaled deeply. The bonnet had a sweet smell, like fresh soap and little girl. His eyes welled with tears. She was his daughter, the child he had been too much of a coward to claim. But he would not abandon her. He would watch and wait and be ever at the ready. If she needed him, he would not hesitate for an instant.

He would save her.

Chapter Fifteen

Anne knew the moment she shifted restlessly awake that she was alone in the bed. The earl's bed. It was the morning after her wedding day. Well, late morning. She had spent the entire night in her husband's bed, by his side. Was that how it was usually done on one's wedding night? Anne wasn't sure. Her parents had always slept in separate chambers, as did most other married couples of Anne's acquaintance.

Yet thoughts of adjourning to her own chamber sometime during the night had never been more than a flickering notion in the corner of her mind that was quickly extinguished. There had been comfort and warmth to be found beneath Richard's bedcovers, passion and fulfillment above them.

Once unleashed, it seemed as though their craving for each other would never cease. They had made love four times, sleeping for short periods in between, rising once well past midnight to devour the tray of sweets and drain the bottle of wine. Then Richard had lit a fire and pulled her down onto the soft rug.

Anne had grinned with delight, letting her hands roam freely over his hard muscles, brushing her lips eagerly against his. The kiss had aroused their passions once more and Richard had pleasured her with deep, slow strokes until she lost herself in the delightful sensations.

Even in her inexperience, Anne had recognized Richard's strong, sensual appetite. His insatiable desire for her made her feel beautiful and womanly for the first time in her life. And his skill and generosity, his careful regard for her pleasure before his own, made her feel almost cherished.

After their interlude on the rug, the earl had carried her back to his bed. She once again curled against his solid warmth and they dozed. But when the dim light of early dawn crept into the chamber, Anne had felt a gentle hand on her shoulder. She had opened her eyes and found Richard raised above her. Instinctively she opened her thighs in welcome.

He had cupped her buttocks and held her steady while he lowered himself onto her, thrusting slow and deep inside her warm, wet passage. He buried his head in her hair and whispered in her ear, sweet words of passion and desire. Silly phrases that brought a smile to her lips. Earthy phrases that made her catch her breath.

It had been another beautiful, shared experience of giving and taking, leaving them both well satisfied. For Anne it had been more than just sexual fulfillment and physical pleasure. It had been love. Pure and elemental. He had engaged both her emotional and spiritual self, leaving her tied to him on the most basic human level.

Yet she could not speak of her love to Richard. Could barely even acknowledge it to herself. They had married without fuss or romance. Without declarations of love or promises of passion. Strangely, it seemed unfair to burden him with these feelings she did not completely understand herself.

Still, they had shared a physical form of love last night that was pure and honest. It was only one aspect of their relationship, but it raised Anne's expectations for the future.

More significantly, it gave her hope. Hope that their union might one day become something more than two lives bound together by duty and responsibility. It could very well develop into a lasting, loving relationship of mutual respect and caring.

But where was her new husband now? Anne rubbed her tired eyes. Streaks of bright sunlight shone through the partially opened drapes. It must be close to noon, she decided. She sat up, pulling the rumpled sheet to her neck just in case one of the earl's servants came into the room.

Clucking her tongue in dismay, Anne pondered the best route to her bedchamber. At Richard's insistence, she had slept naked for the first time in her life, luxuriating in the unfamiliar sensation of soft sheets against her bare flesh. It had been wicked and wonderful. Yet now she faced the challenging prospect of finding something to cover herself so she could walk across the vast chamber, through the sitting room and into her own room.

A maid might very well be patiently awaiting her arrival, and Anne decided that arriving stark naked was not the most appropriate way for a countess to make an appearance. She was trying to decide how to best secure the bed linens around herself when she spied Richard's blue dressing gown carelessly thrown on the floor near the bed.

Anne leaned over and scooped up the garment. Her body groaned in protest. Her legs felt stiff, her breasts sore and sensitive. The lower parts of her body still throbbed with a sensation that recalled with great clarity the various acts of intimacy she had shared with her new husband.

Ignoring the aches, Anne donned the robe. The rich brocade fabric felt delicious against her skin. She pushed the satin lapels up to her face and inhaled deeply. The garment smelled vaguely of Richard. Anne first cuffed the long sleeves, then tied the belt securely about her waist.

She found it was necessary to hold the front of the robe off the carpet to avoid tripping as she ran lightly across the room.

The movement brought more than a twinge of soreness between her legs.

Anne smiled despite the discomfort. It was a good pain. A womanly pain. It made her feel well and truly married. To think that she had been fully prepared to spend her life as a spinster, happily forgoing the intimacies of marriage! How foolish.

There was indeed a young maid waiting for Anne in her bedchamber, a competent and fortunately not chatty girl. A bath was prepared and Anne soaked for long minutes in the warm water. But she felt too restless to linger, too unsettled to enjoy a leisurely morning toilet.

Taking far more care than normal, Anne dressed with the help of her maid. Pleased with the simple but flattering upsweep of hair the girl cleverly pinned into place, Anne dismissed her with a nod of thanks.

She hoped Richard had not yet left the house. She was unsure what time he had risen from their bed but realized it must have been hours ago. Still, it was not unrealistic to suppose the earl was at home. After all, it was the day after their wedding.

With a final glance in the mirror, Anne eagerly left her chamber, descending the stairs quickly. However, her nerves caught up to her when she reached the closed doors of the dining room. Several voices could be distinctly heard conversing on the other side of the doors. Anne's light step faltered.

What was everyone doing in there? Her family had never been the type that lingered overlong at the morning meal. Yet it sounded as though her entire family was crowded into the dining room, talking and laughing and eating up a storm.

A young footman opened the dining-room door for her. With an apologetic look, Anne held up her hand to forestall his announcing her arrival. She had never been comfortable with such formality. It gave her a momentary feeling of power and control knowing she had every right to dictate the servant's behavior. This was her home now, her domain.

Unannounced, Anne entered the room with a calm smile. She searched among the many familiar faces that cheerfully greeted her, feeling a keen sense of disappointment at not finding the one person she was longing to see. Her husband.

However, Anne stiffened her spine and kept the smile in place. The day would not be ruined. If nothing else, she would at least see Richard at the evening meal. Needing time to gather her emotions, Anne busied herself at the sideboard, filling a plate from the warming trays with a variety of tempting foods that she had no intention of consuming.

Her father looked up from the morning paper. "I didn't think you were ever coming downstairs. Thought we'd have to send up a search party to find you," he said jovially. "Mulgrave's been up for hours, no doubt attending to all manner of business. Doesn't look right for an industrious man to have such a lazy girl for a wife."

"Father!" Nicole said, looking at Anne in dismay. "Anne and Lord Mulgrave are newly married. 'Tis expected that she stay abed most of the day." Nicole held her hand against her mouth. "Not that I mean to imply you've spent the whole day in bed, Anne. Why, 'tis almost a full hour until noontime."

Nicole's voice trailed off into silence. The momentary feelings of power and control Anne had enjoyed abruptly faded. She shook her head, not knowing how she could possibly comment. She felt herself begin to blush with acute embarrassment, realizing that everyone was most aware of the reason she had uncharacteristically spent so much time in bed.

The notion upset her normally steady equilibrium so totally that Anne did not even notice the gentleman entering the dining room. Concentrating on adding more food to her already crowded dish, Anne first saw through the corner of her eye a strong masculine arm, clothed in an elegant blue coat, reach for a clean plate on the sideboard. Her head shot up.

"Good morning," the earl said pleasantly.

"Hello, Richard." She swallowed uncertainly and schooled

her face into a blank mask. It was not as though she wished
to intentionally hide her feelings from her husband, but it was
hardly appropriate to engage in intimate conversation with
nearly her entire family present.

"Did you sleep well?" Richard inquired, leaning close to
whisper in her ear.

Anne's stomach lurched at the question. He looked so very
proper and regal. So much like a stranger. Not just handsome
but compelling, dressed in his casual country gentleman's attire.
Yet the smile in his eyes was familiar.

"Yes, I slept well, my lord." Anne lifted her chin. "And
you?"

"Tolerably." The smile dancing in his eyes moved to his
lips. "I was most relieved to discover you do not snore, my
dear. I confess it had worried me."

Anne could not hide her smile. "Alas, I cannot say the same
of you, my husband," she declared in mock sincerity. "The
windows fairly rattled from the noise you made."

"Ahh, would that I had the chance to demonstrate the kind
of noise you truly inspire me to make when you are in my bed,
dear wife." He gazed at her with such a sexy, wolfish gleam
in his eye that for one reckless moment Anne desperately wished
they were alone, away from the intrusive eyes and ears of her
relatives.

Consciously pulling herself away from the earl's hypnotic
charm, Anne lowered her eyes. She placed several broiled
kidneys on her plate. To her vast relief, Richard offered her
his arm when she finished, then led her to a place at the table.

Anne felt pleased when he took the chair beside hers. As he
pushed his chair nearer to the table, he shifted closer to her.
Through the thin material of her gown she could feel the press
of his stiff leather boot against her calf muscle. She cast him
a covetous glance, but the expression on his face was unfathom-
able.

Steady and courteous conversation resumed among the family. Anne remained silent, feeling no compulsion to entertain or lead the discussion.

"Eat up, girl," Lord Althen commanded his daughter. He folded the newspaper and placed it on the table. "You'll need your strength if you want to keep your husband happy."

"Her strength?" Aunt Sophie repeated quizzically, wrinkling her brow. Then gasping with understanding, she whispered a shocked, "Oh, my goodness."

Aunt Sophie took a great, gulping breath and turned the most peculiar shade of red. Nicole pulled the napkin off her lap and began fanning the older woman energetically.

"Really, Father," Nicole admonished in a stern tone, "have a care for Aunt Sophie's delicate sensibilities." She leaned across the table and softly hissed, "And need I remind you that there are children present?"

"Sorry," Lord Althen mumbled gruffly. He snapped up the paper once more and hid himself behind it.

"I am certain that your father meant no offense," Lady Althen tried explaining to no one in particular. "He has always been a man who speaks his mind."

Not sure whether she should feel mortified or amused by her father's indelicate behavior, Anne turned to her husband, curious about his reaction. She watched him casually fork up a serving of sausage, acting as though he had not heard the exchange.

Yet Anne stared deliberately at Richard until she caught his eye. He smiled briefly, then winked at her.

The spoon in Anne's hand fell to the table and clattered noisily on the polished wooden surface. All heads turned in her direction.

"Is everything alright?" Lady Althen inquired.

Anne nodded, not trusting her voice.

"Well, then, what have you planned for yourself today, Anne?" Lady Althen asked. "Anything special?"

Anne stared blankly at her mother.

"I'm afraid I must lay claim to Anne's time today, Lady Althen," Richard replied smoothly. "My housekeeper, Mrs. Creech, would like to show her new mistress the household accounts, and I intend to take my bride on an extended tour of the manor. If the weather holds, we shall also visit some of my tenants. They are all anxious to meet my countess."

"Naturally, duty calls," Lady Althen agreed. "Anne has never been one to shy away from her responsibilities. I promise that the rest of us shall do our best to keep out of your way." She turned her head and smiled shrewdly at her new son-in-law. "I thought a ride into the village might be a pleasant diversion for me."

"The village?" Lord Althen tossed his newspaper down. "Excellent notion, my lady. The weather is perfect for an open carriage ride. I believe I will accompany you."

"Splendid." Lady Althen beamed with delight.

A cold sweat broke out on Anne's brow. She opened her mouth to protest, but Richard was quicker.

"It does indeed look to be the perfect day for an outing," he agreed smoothly. "I insist that you take one of my carriages. Just inform my butler when you are ready to depart. He will send a message to the stables and arrange everything with John, who is unquestionably my best coachman."

"How delightful." Lady Althen smiled broadly. "You are most kind." She lifted her china teacup, took a dainty sip, then returned it soundlessly to the saucer. "I believe I shall retire to my rooms. There are a few items I wish to attend to before we leave."

"I'll come along," Lord Althen quickly volunteered. He noisily pushed his chair back from the table and hurried to his wife's side. "We'll see everyone at supper."

"Richard." Anne turned pleading eyes upon the earl. "They are going to the village," she whispered harshly. "You know they will go directly to the shops. We must stop them."

"Don't fret, I have matters well in hand." He covered her

knuckles reassuringly with his warm fingers. "My driver has strict instructions to take the most circumspect route imaginable while driving into the village. I can assure you that your parents will arrive a good half-hour after all the shops have closed for the day, no matter what time they depart from the manor."

"Are you certain?" Anne asked in an anxious whisper. "My parents can be most persuasive. If they realize how late the hour is growing, it wouldn't be beneath them to offer your coachman all manner of coin to race the carriage to the village."

"Wouldn't that be a sight?" Richard smiled, but his grin disappeared. Anne did not even try to conceal her distress. "You must not worry, Anne. My coachman has received explicit instructions. I have every confidence he will carry out my commands to the letter."

Anne glanced down at her plate. She so very much wanted to believe that Richard's scheme would work, but years of dealing with her parents had left her skeptical. Yet there was little she could do but accept the earl's decision. After all, if he was proved wrong, he would be the one responsible for paying the many shopkeepers' bills.

With a final pat of reassurance, Richard removed his hand and resumed eating his meal. If he noticed Anne's discomfort, it was not apparent. He began a friendly conversation with her two brothers, questioning them about how they best enjoyed spending their school holidays.

"Is it true that you stock your lakes with fish every spring, sir?" William inquired.

"Yes."

The boys smiled and Anne noticed her brothers exchange conspiratorial glances.

"I've always liked to fish, and Will and I are rather keen to try our luck as fishermen," Edmund announced grandly. "That's what we'd like to do today."

"I'm sure the earl stocks his lakes for fishing parties with his gentlemen friends, not for the amusement of young boys,"

Anne admonished in a gentle tone. "You must not pester the earl with endless requests. Please remember that you are guests in his home."

Will's eyebrow's knitted together. "But it is your home now, Anne," he said in a befuddled tone. "And you are our sister. Lord Mulgrave won't mind if we fish in his lake, will you, sir?"

"Of course not," Richard insisted. "Just ask one of my grooms to show you where the fishing poles are kept."

"I told you he'd let us," Edmund exclaimed in triumph. He jumped to his feet and after a brief bow raced for the door. William was already there.

"Don't go digging up any worms until you've asked the gardeners," Anne called to their retreating backs. "I don't want you ruining those lovely flower beds while searching for bait."

Her only answer was the distant echo of fading footsteps.

"I apologize for my brothers, my lord," Nicole spoke up hastily. "I fear that in their excitement their manners have gone begging."

"I took no offense," Richard replied. "I enjoy having the lads about. It feels good to have some male companionship. This has been too long a household of females."

"That reminds me," Aunt Sophie put in. "Your daughter and Rosalind went riding with the governess, Miss Fraser, this morning. I was supposed to tell you."

"And so you have," Richard said graciously. "Thank you, Aunt Sophie."

The older woman blushed with pleasure at his familiarity.

"Well, we had best get going also," Nicole announced in a cheerful tone as she stood up. "Aunt Sophie and I will attend to her packing today. She will be leaving tomorrow morning."

"I have so enjoyed my visit with all of you," Aunt Sophie said. "It was such an unexpected joy to renew acquaintance with my family. And being able to attend your wedding, dear

Anne, was a great honor. I feel so blessed to have discovered such wonderful relations.''

Anne stared down at the spoon in her hand. She turned it several times before lifting her head and meeting the older woman's eye. Shame engulfed Anne. She had only contacted her aunt because the family needed an escape from Devon. If things had worked out differently, they might all be traveling to Bath to impose on this unsuspecting woman.

''We hope you will visit us often,'' Anne managed to choke out.

''You are always welcome,'' Richard echoed warmly.

Tears pooled in Aunt Sophie's eyes and Anne felt even worse. With a few dramatic sniffs of gratitude, Aunt Sophie was helped to her feet by Nicole. The still teary-eyed older woman was led from the room by a solicitous Nicole.

The moment they were gone, Anne's waning appetite completely deserted her. What a strange, emotional morning it has been, she thought. When Richard asked if she was done with her meal, she nodded enthusiastically. Though it had only begun, it already felt as if the day was unbearably long.

''We shall go to my study,'' the earl decided.

Anne held onto his arm and kept a proper distance as they walked through the house, feeling the curious eyes of the many servants they passed observing their every move. It was difficult for Anne to remain impassive under so much clandestine scrutiny. For so long she had been an unnoticed, often unwelcome guest in another's home.

Taking her cue from her husband, Anne managed, with effort, to hold herself aloof. Yet she worried about the formality of Richard's life. It did not at all fit in with her expectations. Being raised in a far more relaxed atmosphere made her a woman who lacked the rigid adherence to protocol and tradition.

She knew it would take a good deal of adjustment for her to learn exactly what was expected of her as Richard's wife. It would take time to understand her many duties and obligations. She was fully prepared to assume them, although she did hope there would be moments to steal for herself and her art.

Anne felt certain that Richard would not begrudge her that, knowing how important her work was to her. Besides, he had promised her before they married that she could continue with her painting. Still, there would be much for her to do and learn as his countess.

Though the household was clearly an efficiently run establishment, there were all manner of details to make sure that daily life ran smoothly for the residents of the manor. The majority of whom were Anne's relatives.

She preceded the earl into his study. She assumed he had chosen this room so they could discuss how she was to spend this and many other days to come. It was proper and correct.

He seated her on a small chair at one side of a massive oak desk, then lounged against it, crossing his ankles. His relaxed stance and casual attitude sent her senses on alert. She tried adopting a similar demeanor, but from her seated position she had an excellent, nearly scandalous view of the earl's lower torso.

Unable to resist, Anne let her gaze fall to his muscular thighs. She heard Richard cough discreetly. The sound brought Anne abruptly back to reality. Face flaming, she somehow managed to find the courage to lift her head and meet his gaze.

"I regretted that you were asleep when I left this morning," Richard said quietly. "I made as much noise as I could, but you didn't stir so much as a muscle. It was as if you were dead to the world."

Anne felt the heat rise higher in her cheeks. "You wore me out, husband," she said boldly, determined to somehow hold her ground.

The earl raised his eyebrow. "Complaints, my lady?"

"Quite the contrary, my lord."

The words were barely beyond her lips before he reached out and hauled her to her feet. Anne's body began pulsing with awareness as he pulled her closer. It was as though her physical self recognized him. Her partner. Her mate. Her lover. She allowed him to press fully against her.

They touched from breasts to hips to thighs. His strength surrounded her. It was glorious. A quickening began in Anne's stomach that she knew was not caused by her small breakfast.

The earl lowered his head and their lips met. Anne parted hers slightly and Richard's tongue thrust inside. The tingling feeling that had started in her stomach dipped lower. He broke the kiss and began to nibble on her neck. On impulse she tipped her chin and blew in his ear. He growled low in his throat and claimed her lips in another passionate kiss.

It took a moment for her fevered brain to recognize the noise in her head as a knock on the door. It was followed by a rattling sound as someone persistently tried the handle. Reluctantly, Anne pulled away from Richard's intoxication.

"Don't worry," he whispered huskily, "I've locked the door."

Anne lowered her forehead to his shoulder and sighed. She waited for the inquisitive intruder to go away, deciding she could use this time to refocus her thoughts before Richard resumed his mind-numbing kiss.

"Hobbs said Father was in his study, but I can't get the door to open," a young voice whined from the other side of the door. The handle rattled again.

"Alexandra!" Anne whispered loudly, springing back from the earl as if someone had thrown a bucket of ice water over her.

Richard frowned at her. Anne paid him no heed as she tidied her skirt and smoothed back the few wisps of stray hair. She lifted her head expectantly. "Open the door, Richard, before our little girl knocks it down."

Exhaling harshly, the earl obeyed his wife's commands. Alexandra veritably spilled into the room.

"There you are," Alexandra cried excitedly. "I told Miss

Fraser and Rosalind you would be in the study but they didn't believe me. Why did you take so long to answer the door?"

"I was busy working," the earl declared with a straight face. "I thought you had gone riding."

"We did, but now we are back." Alexandra whirled toward Anne. "Maybe you will join us next time. Tomorrow? Rosalind says you ride splendidly."

"I would like that," Anne replied. "Thank you for the invitation."

Alexandra beamed. "We are going to have our watercolor lessons. The light is very good in the rose garden today. But first Miss Fraser said she must speak with you, Papa, and . . . and . . ." Alexandra tipped her head to one side and stared at Anne. "What shall I call you?"

Anne considered the little girl's earnest expression. Her first thought was to say *Mother,* but that seemed presumptuous. Besides, if Alexandra really wanted to call her *Mother,* she would have stated her opinion. The earl's daughter was anything but shy.

"My name is Anne. You may call me that, if you like."

"Really?" The corners of Alexandra's mouth turned up in a sweet smile. "Rosalind calls you Anne. I cannot wait to tell her that now I may too."

With a hasty curtsey and an even quicker goodbye, Alexandra bolted from the room. Amused by the girl's enthusiasm, Anne exchanged a small smile with Richard. If only all her tasks as his wife were so easy to master.

A second knock interrupted their privacy again. Anne returned to her chair by Richard's desk while he quietly bade the person to enter. He returned to Anne's side and placed a reassuring hand on her shoulder.

"Anne, may I introduce Alexandra's governess, Miss Fraser."

"Lady Mulgrave." Miss Fraser dipped into a low curtsey. " 'Tis an honor."

Anne rose politely from the chair, but the smile of greeting on her lips melted away the moment Miss Fraser tipped her chin up and looked Anne full in the face. Anne felt glad for Richard's supporting hand on her shoulder as drawing breath suddenly required a concentrated effort.

She tried valiantly to steady her wits. *This woman is a governess?* Anne's mind screamed breathlessly. It was impossible! Governesses were dull, gray, drab creatures. Middle-aged, dumpy, colorless. The sort of person one seldom noticed. They blended into the background like a piece of nondescript furniture.

To say that Miss Fraser was beautiful would be a gross understatement. Physically she was far beyond beautiful. Dressed in a plain gray gown befitting a woman of her station, she nonetheless glowed with youth and vitality and utter loveliness.

The face that launched a thousand ships. Anne's artistic eye could easily imagine this young woman as a reincarnation of Helen of Troy. A beauty so rare and true that men would fight and die just for the chance to win her love.

They were speaking, Richard and this enchanting creature. They even tried to include her in the conversation. Anne smiled faintly and tried to listen, but, seemingly unable to stop herself, her gaze continually wandered to Miss Fraser. She stared at her beauty with almost morbid fascination.

Though pulled back in a severe hairstyle, the flaxen splendor of the governess's hair could not be hidden. Her features were dainty and delicate and perfectly proportioned. Her blue eyes revealed the color of the sky and her complexion looked as if it could be carved from marble.

In spite of the warm sunshine that flooded the room, Anne shuddered. She held her breath as she changed her focus from the governess to her husband. Anne could not help but wonder at his normal speaking tone, his cavalier attitude toward this exquisite woman.

Why was he not fawning over Miss Fraser's beauty? Was he not struck dumb by her heavenly appearance? He seemed so calm, so casual, so indifferent to the perfection displayed before him. How utterly remarkable.

The part of her brain still capable of rational thought told Anne she was acting idiotically. Like a frightened, jealous girl. Richard did not in any way behave unseemly toward Miss Fraser. He had known her for years. She was merely a woman he employed, a woman under his protection. He treated her with the same polite diffidence he showed all females. No more, no less. Gradually Anne began to relax.

"I have those papers right here," Richard said.

He left Anne's side and started rummaging through his desk. Uncomfortable, Anne glanced out the window wishing she had been paying closer attention to the discussion. Then at least she would know what the earl was searching for so diligently.

Anne had heard snippets of the conversation. Enough to know that Miss Fraser had acted as more than a mere governess these past few years. She had helped the earl with household matters that normally would have been dealt with by the lady of the house. The idea did not sit well in Anne's mind. Nor her heart.

Unconsciously, Anne's attention returned to Miss Fraser. Stunningly beautiful, intelligent and competent. Was there anything the woman couldn't do?

"Ahhh, here they are," the earl declared, holding up the errant parchment in triumph.

Miss Fraser gave him a wide smile of approval. He returned it. Anne's heart sank as all her old insecurities came rushing back to haunt her.

'Tis a shame that poor Anne is so plain while her sisters are all so pretty, yet she seems resigned to her fate. Still, it must be hard to be the weed among the lilies. Well, with five girls to marry off, it's a sure bet one of them will remain a spinster. At least the oldest daughter seems competent enough

to care for her family. She'll bring comfort to her parents in their old age.

Remarks overheard at social gatherings made by acquaintances and strangers echoed in Anne's head. She swallowed hard as she tried to reconcile these abysmal thoughts with the truth of her situation. Yet there was no use trying to hide from the fact that in the presence of Miss Fraser, Anne felt woefully inadequate to fill her role as Richard's wife, as Richard's *woman.*

But the greatest revelation was yet to come. The earl reached for a quill and scribbled a few notations on the papers. Believing she was unobserved, Miss Fraser now gazed openly at the earl. A tender, unguarded, wistful expression, full of caring and devotion and longing.

Anne somehow swallowed her gasp. She sternly told herself that she was wrong. But the look was unmistakable. Easily identifiable. It was love.

It shouldn't matter. Miss Fraser was an employee in this household. Richard had known her for years. *Had known and admired her for years.* She was not a threat to Anne, nor to Anne's marriage. *She is intelligent, accomplished and heart-breakingly beautiful. And in love with my husband.*

The nagging feelings of doubt that Anne had been trying so hard to suppress blossomed into full-blown alarm. She squeezed her eyes shut for an instant. There was no denying the quiver of uncertainty that slithered down her spine.

The room suddenly seemed a mile wide with Richard and Miss Fraser standing on one side, together, while she stood alone on the other. The distance between them seemed vast, unconquerable. Anne felt surrounded by emptiness and coldness, all alone on her side.

Miss Fraser was in love with Richard. How would Anne ever be able to cope once he realized it?

Chapter Sixteen

"You must get rid of Miss Fraser, Anne," Lady Althen admonished. "The sooner the better."

An uncomfortable silence followed her mother's remarks, but Anne preferred it to hearing the words, spoken with such a strong note of censure. She slowed her pace, hoping that none of the other women in their party had heard her mother's hastily spoken comments.

Knowing that as hostess she should be leading the small group of women, Anne instead hung back until the others had reached the drawing room. She turned to confront her mother.

"I cannot simply dismiss the poor woman out of hand," Anne said with a weary sigh. "I have no just cause."

"You don't need any," Lady Althen bristled. She adjusted the silk shawl she wore over her evening gown with a jerky motion. "Must I constantly remind you that you are now Lady Mulgrave? Household matters fall under your domain. Dismiss Miss Fraser immediately, before she causes any difficulties."

Anne rubbed her forehead wearily. Would this day never

end? This day after her wedding that had begun with such hope and excitement had degenerated into a series of small disappointments and misunderstandings that were adding up to one colossal headache.

The promise of spending at least part of this day alone with her husband had never materialized. Anne had been so rattled by the meeting with Alexandra's governess that she had retreated to the privacy of her bedchamber for the rest of the morning, needing time to sort through her confused emotions.

Recovered by early afternoon, Anne had searched for Richard only to discover he was away from home. The earl returned by tea time, but several neighbors and friends had dropped by to pay their respects to the earl's new bride.

All the close scrutiny did little to enhance Anne's already bruised self-confidence. The one saving grace was that Miss Fraser was not among the guests. Still, the minutes crawled by interminably. As the afternoon visits at last drew to an end, Anne had once again longed only for some quiet, private time alone with her husband.

Not in their bedchamber where his attentions were lavish and intense, but somewhere outside their bed where they could converse, exchange ideas, get to know each other better.

Anne toyed with the idea of asking Richard to pose for her again, remembering how mischievous and fun he had been during their other sketching session. But duty called and the opportunity never presented itself.

Disheartened, Anne had still dared to hope they could share a private supper together, but the earl had invited several of the neighbors along with the vicar and his wife and his good friends Lord Rosslyn and Captain Nightingall to join them for the evening meal.

Anne had nearly screamed with frustration. Only years of ingrained civility had enabled her to continue playing her part as the gracious hostess. Yet what had disturbed her most was that it seemed that the more she schemed to be alone with

Richard, the harder he worked to keep them surrounded by people.

Dinner had been a long, tiresome affair with the entire family in attendance, along with the added company. Local matters were the main topic of conversation, leaving Anne with little to contribute, although her parents, Nicole and even Aunt Sophie had little trouble voicing their thoughts. If not for the kindness of the vicar's wife and the special efforts of both Captain Nightingall and Lord Rosslyn, Anne would have barely spoken at all.

Near the end of the meal Anne had led the women out of the dining room in order to allow the men to indulge in brandy, port and cigars. Feeling a great need for a few quiet moments to gather her thoughts and jumbled emotions, Anne tried to slip away, but her mother attached herself to Anne's side the minute they left the dining room.

Anne pressed her lips together in a firm line. She was tired of hearing her mother's disapproval, for which she normally cared not at all. Yet the matter of Alexandra's beautiful governess had badly shaken her self-confidence, and she found herself listening and, almost against her will, agreeing with Lady Althen's reasoning.

"I shall write to my dear friend Lady Martin tomorrow morning," Lady Althen declared. "She is a much admired member of society, with many female friends and acquaintances. She has successfully raised three daughters, all of whom have made excellent marriages. I'm sure she would be delighted to make inquiries on your behalf. I feel certain Lady Martin will be able to recommend an older, experienced governess to care for your new stepdaughter."

"I will not fire Miss Fraser on a whim," Anne stated clearly, determined to cling to some principle of fairness despite her own fears.

"You are deliberately being difficult," Lady Althen huffed.

She studied her daughter with a hooded gaze. "And you shall regret it."

Anne was speechless for the moment. Her knuckles went white as she clutched the folds of her gown. She followed her mother into the drawing room and was much relieved to see Nicole immediately take up a position at the pianoforte.

Her sister's playing would provide her guests with the appropriate genteel atmosphere. And it would save her from having to make extended conversation with her female guests. If Anne could persuade her mother to sing, then she would at long last find some peace. But it was not to be.

"I recognize that stubborn look on your face," Lady Althen commented the moment she and Anne were seated. She leaned forward. "Just because you refuse to acknowledge the truth, Anne, doesn't mean it does not exist. Listen to me and heed my words of warning. Do not dismiss this as fanciful female nonsense. I am older than you and have far more experience of life and men. I know of what I speak. You must send Miss Fraser packing without delay."

"Mother, please!" Anne clasped her hands together tightly. "Can you not save this discussion for a more private location? Or better still, drop the matter altogether?"

She motioned to a footman to fill her mother's glass with a healthy portion of brandy. The other women were being served tea, but Anne decided her mother needed stronger spirits. If she could have tolerated the taste of the liquor, Anne too would have indulged. This was certainly the day for it.

"It would not only be unfair but irresponsible to dismiss Miss Fraser without due cause," Anne declared with as much force as she could muster. "She is an excellent governess and Alexandra adores her."

Lady Althen took a sip of her drink and glanced reprovingly at her daughter. "Mark my words, Miss Fraser will cause trouble in your marriage," Lady Althen predicted ominously. "She is stunningly beautiful. Properly outfitted she would even put Nicole to shame. You don't stand a chance against that kind of beauty. Frankly, I cannot understand how the earl has resisted her charms thus far.''

''You insult my husband,'' Anne replied hotly, feeling ashamed that she had thought the very same thing. It was almost beyond imagining to think that Richard could prefer her to Miss Fraser. Yet Anne stoically defended him. ''The earl is a man of honor. He would never make advances to a woman in his employ. Especially now that he is married.''

''Don't be naive,'' Lady Althen snapped. ''Married couples often lead separate lives, and gentlemen dally with married women, mistresses and servants.''

''Not in my household,'' Anne stated emphatically.

''Don't be so certain,'' Lady Althen humphed, taking another swallow of her brandy. ''This is not at all the efficient, competent establishment that it appears on the surface. Gracious, the earl's coachman couldn't even get your father and me into town at a reasonable hour this afternoon.''

Anne refused to comment. Perhaps if she remained silent, her mother would finally be quiet. Anne smiled vaguely at the vicar's wife, who sat patiently beside Nicole, dutifully turning the pages of music. How much longer would the men remain in the dining room?

''You must learn how to please your husband,'' Lady Althen lectured. ''I noticed that you were very quiet during the evening meal. I approved. You are often too clever in your conversation, too opinionated in your ideas. Men, especially husbands, do not approve of those qualities in a wife. Men love to be admired by their women. They like nothing better than receiving a look of almost witless admiration.''

Anne groaned, rolling her eyes skyward. ''Please spare me a demonstration.''

Lady Althen humphed in exasperation but mercifully refrained from bestowing any further unsolicited, unwelcome advice. Anne sighed heavily. She might be able to override her mother's errant tongue for the moment, but she could not completely suppress the doubts her mother's words had brought to her mind.

Anne so desperately wanted to believe that Richard had never done anything even slightly improper to kindle that look of unabashed adoration in Miss Fraser's beautiful eyes. Yet that nagging doubt was lodged firmly in her mind from the moment she had seen the look of unbridled admiration upon the governess's stunning face.

Anne did not like this jumbled mix of feelings. Uncertainty. Insecurity. Even fear. A deep foreboding swept over her. Perhaps she shouldn't have married. It appeared she was ill-suited to it, although after being married less than a day it was really too soon to judge.

Anne looked anxiously at the gilt clock on the mantelpiece, wondering if the men would be much longer. She needed a distraction.

She had never been a woman prone to self-pity. She had faced the most adversarial conditions of financial ruin head-on for the last few years with determination and a refusal to accept failure. Yet she had done nothing much more than feel sorry for herself after meeting the ravishing Miss Fraser. It was time for a change in attitude.

Bolstering her lagging spirits with determination to spare herself all manner of gloomy, dire thoughts, Anne excused herself from her mother's company and assumed her role of hostess.

With much laughter and high spirits the gentlemen joined the ladies. Anne resisted the urge to glance over her shoulder at her husband, not wanting to appear overanxious. Yet she could feel his eye alight on her more than once.

She lifted her head to meet his gaze, and his handsome smile deepened when their eyes met. Instantly she felt transported back to those glorious moments she had spent locked in his embrace. Her body began tingling as she remembered being joined with his, being as close as any two people could be.

Anne could vividly recall the scent of him, his strength and heat, the way his gentle hands had felt against her body. It had been the most amazing night of her life.

No other man would ever touch her body. For as long as she lived, Richard would be the man who came to her bed at night, whose body would penetrate her own, whose seed would perhaps one day enter her womb and take hold.

Sadness swamped Anne. They would have to abstain from that intimacy tonight. And for the next few nights. Even her body had betrayed her, for the monthly courses that had been late these past few days were now upon her with a vengeance.

Their physical union was the one aspect of her marriage that she felt secure about, the one aspect she considered successful, and now that would be denied. Anne shivered though the room was pleasantly warm. She belatedly realized her shudders came from fear.

Try as she might, she could not deny it. She was terrified. Of a most uncertain future.

Richard watched Anne from across the room, subtly aware of her every move. As much as he wanted to be by her side, he resisted the urge. He would not be one of those fawning husbands that hung on to their wife's every word. He suspected that Anne would not like that at all. She had resisted his offer of marriage so hard and for so long, the last thing he wanted was for her to feel trapped.

Still, the fierceness of his own sense of triumph took Richard by surprise. She was his wife. She belonged to him and to no other. Their wedding night had far exceeded all his expectations, yet left him with mixed emotions. He had departed their nuptial bed reluctantly but with the need to place some distance between himself and his bride.

He had waited all morning, then all afternoon and finally most of the evening for his sense of balance to return to some semblance of normalcy. And when it hadn't happened, Richard had laughed at his own foolishness, realizing with some degree of certainty that he would never feel the same again.

She had changed him. With some indefinable, mysterious power she had brought a completeness to his life, a comforting harmony to his soul. She released a fierce male protectiveness inside him that he had never suspected he would feel for any female other than his daughter.

Richard had contrived to spend some private moments with Anne, no easy task with a house full of family. She had greeted him pleasantly and seemed happy to see him this morning, but household matters had taken precedence over personal contentment. He sensed Anne's withdrawal and it disturbed him.

She was an enigma to him. Independence and self-reliance had carried her through a difficult life. She was a woman not easily daunted, yet there had been moments today when he clearly felt that she was hesitant and unsure.

His bride's unease disturbed Richard. Above all else he wanted her to be happy. Hell, he wanted them both to be happy. The problem was, he wasn't exactly sure how to accomplish that feat.

"Miss Paget is a talented musician. She plays the pianoforte rather well and looks damn pretty doing it," Ian remarked, joining Richard in a cozy corner of the drawing room. The other guests were clustered in small groups enjoying the conversation and entertainment. "Your household will soon be overrun with eager young swains, all vying for Nicole's attention. I daresay your nephew Nigel will have a fit when he returns to the manor and discovers this little beauty in residence."

"Fortunately, Nigel will be in Scotland for quite some time," Richard replied steadily. He too had been concerned about his nephew's reaction to his sudden marriage and Nicole's presence in the manor. "I'm hoping that by the time he returns his infatuation will be part of his past."

"Well, if he comes back too soon, you can always ship him off on an extended tour of the continent," Ian suggested with a grin. He took the offered goblet of brandy from a passing footman after Richard had refused a glass. "Nothing broadens a young man's horizons more than travel."

Miles joined them, full glass in hand. The three friends stood together thoughtfully observing the occupants of the room, well aware of the many eyes that were trained on them.

"I cannot fail to notice how Lady Beachamp's daughter, Clara, keeps gazing in your direction, Ian," Richard commented with deliberate levity in his tone. "Don't say you've been holding out on us, old boy. Is there a forthcoming announcement you wish to share with your old friends?"

Lord Rosslyn nearly choked on his brandy. Miles threw back his head and laughed loudly.

"The Beachamp chit! Why, that infant is barely out of the schoolroom," Ian bristled with feigned indignity once he recovered his breath. He looked closely at his friend. "Egad, just because you are firmly ensnared in the bonds of matrimony, there is no need to try and drag me into the fray of insanity.

"I have many solid years of bachelorhood to indulge myself in before I have to contemplate setting up my nursery. If you are so keen on playing matchmaker, I suggest you try finding a wife for Miles."

"Me!" Captain Nightingall's eyebrows shot up. "With Lady Beachamp's daughter? She practically squeaks if I come within five feet of her. Besides, she has the features of a cocker spaniel, poor girl. And nothing else to recommend her. Neither intellect nor talent nor conversation."

They all three turned to discreetly observe the lady in question. Preening, Clara grasped the fan that dangled from her wrist by a ribbon, snapped it open and waved it flirtatiously in front of her face.

Miles cleared his throat loudly. Ian swallowed awkwardly. Richard smiled broadly.

"They say she has a sizable dowry," Richard taunted as the girl's attention was claimed by her overprotective mother. "Nearly fifteen thousand a year."

"She's going to need it," Miles muttered, looking down into his goblet. "Although both you and Ian have been determined to brand me a reckless wastrel, my financial future is quite solid. Thankfully, I possess the resources to be far more discriminating in my choice of females. If the time ever comes, I shall not need to marry for money."

Richard closed his eyes with satisfaction. That was precisely the remark he had hoped to hear. For if Nicole ever succeeded in capturing the elusive Captain Nightingall, as Richard deeply suspected she was trying to do, her unusual family financial circumstances would not present a problem.

"My God, can you imagine trying to close your eyes with young Clara resting her face on the pillow beside you?" Ian shuddered. "And that laugh of hers is beyond irritating. It takes every ounce of self-control I can muster not to throttle her when without any prior warning she begins to cackle uncontrollably."

"How about Lady Caroline?" Richard said a few moments later. "She is a lovely creature. A more mature woman, to be sure, but very comely."

"Enough! You are as nagging as a sore tooth. I demand a change of subject," Ian said impatiently. "If you insist on continuing this ludicrous conversation about prospective brides, I shall no doubt break into a severe case of hives."

Richard answered with a short chuckle. "All right, I shall stop. Actually, I do have something of importance to discuss. I need to find a good art instructor for *my* bride. Since you've been in town recently, Miles, perhaps you can recommend someone?"

Miles shot him a quick, sidelong glance as he lifted his glass of brandy and took a small sip. "Creating projects for your wife already, Richard? I would have thought a man with your talents and imagination could find a far better way to occupy the new countess's time than with paints and watercolors.''

''Who is going to be needing paints and watercolors?'' Lord Rosslyn asked, turning his attention away from the fresh-faced young maid he had been discreetly observing.

''Lady Mulgrave,'' Miles supplied. ''Richard wants her to take art lessons.''

Richard restrained his hand from thumping Miles on the back and braced himself for a good ribbing. He soon discovered that smiling over clenched teeth was not easy.

Ian whistled. ''Art lessons? For Lady Mulgrave? Bit of a waste of such an interesting woman, in my opinion.'' With a sly half smile he added, ''If she were my wife, I would find other, far more enjoyable things to occupy her time. Of course, Richard never did know how to appreciate the finer qualities of the weaker sex, did he, Miles?''

''Not usually,'' Captain Nightingall agreed with a devilish grin. ''As his closest and oldest friends, I feel it is our duty to put him on the straight and narrow path to marital bliss.''

''An admirable notion,'' Ian readily answered. He stroked his chin thoughtfully. ''Our experience is, however, somewhat limited in the matrimony arena.''

''True,'' Miles conceded with an exaggerated frown. ''But we are highly superior, highly intellectual men. Who better than we to solve Richard's problem?''

''You are half-wits,'' Richard pronounced with affection. ''The pair of you.'' He gave an exaggerated sigh of exasperation. ''For your information, gentlemen, my wife is already an accomplished artist.

''Personally, I don't think she needs any lessons to improve her work, but I have made a promise to my bride and I intend on keeping it. Now, do you know of any artists with talent and reputation who might be persuaded to come to Devon and give Anne lessons?''

"I guess he is serious," Miles remarked to Lord Rosslyn.

"Apparently," Ian agreed with a smirk. He appeared to give the question some serious thought. "Have you ever heard of Joshua Quimby?"

"No," Richard answered.

"I met him once, early last season," Ian said. "He's a tad eccentric, as are most artists, but Quimby has been stirring up a lot of interest in London with his landscapes and portraits. As far as I know, he is still much in demand."

"Quite," Miles confirmed. "Quimby's all the rage in London. If I recall correctly, the Regent has purchased one of his earlier works for the pavilion at Brighton."

"Well, Quimby might be in demand, but is he any good?" Richard asked. "I don't just want someone who is fashionable, I want someone who is talented."

"I've never seen any of his paintings," Miles admitted. "But someone did point him out to me at the Worthingtons' ball last month. He is a handsome, striking young man with Mediterranean looks. Very tall, olive skin, dark eyes. He had swarms of admirers."

"He's reputed to have quite a reputation for indulgence," Ian chimed in. "Or rather overindulgence. Actually, I'm not sure he's the type you would want to have about the house. He might be inclined toward overstepping his boundaries."

"I want Anne to have the best," Richard said emphatically. "She deserves an instructor who will appreciate and nurture her talent. But I'll tolerate no disrespect toward my wife. From anyone, least of all a man in my employ."

"You misunderstand," Ian said with a twinkle of mirth in his eye. "Lady Mulgrave will be perfectly safe from Quimby's attentions. You, however, might have to fend off his advances."

Richard's brow furrowed with puzzlement. "Really?"

Miles and Ian managed to hold onto their somber expressions for only a moment before bursting out into fresh laughter.

"If the rumors are to be believed, Quimby should be much taken with you, Richard." Ian smiled broadly. "Many consider you a handsome man, although personally I don't understand why. Shall I make inquiries as to Quimby's current address so you may write to him?"

"He sounds perfect." Richard met Lord Rosslyn's gaze. He struggled to keep from breaking into a smile. "I trust my wife completely, and Quimby's uhh ... hmmm, preferences will save her from any unnecessary distractions. As for myself, I am quite capable of defending my person with fist, sword or pistol. I will eagerly await the information on Quimby's current residence. And I sincerely thank both you and Miles for your assistance in this most important matter."

"We live to serve," Ian said. With a mocking bow and a parting grin, Lord Rosslyn left to join a group of ladies on the far side of the drawing room.

" 'Tis only wild rumors and speculation about Quimby, you know," Miles volunteered after Ian left. "If he does become her teacher, Lady Mulgrave might need guarding from unwanted attentions."

"I protect my own," Richard said calmly. "Rest assured that if Quimby does enter my household he shall be carefully watched." The earl pushed aside his coat and rested one hand casually upon his hip. "Speaking of watching, I cannot help but notice you have done your fair share of ogling Nicole this evening."

Deep furrows appeared between Captain Nightingall's eyebrows. He turned his chin upward and gazed with seemingly rapt interest at the white plaster scrollwork decorating the drawing-room ceiling. He didn't say anything.

"Now that Anne and I are married, I find myself in a rather awkward position. You are my friend, Miles, and I trust you with my life. But I cannot ignore Anne's distress," Richard continued in a mild tone. "On more than one occasion she has expressed deep concern about your intentions toward her sister.''

Miles turned his head sharply. ''My intentions toward Miss Paget? I'm afraid you have gotten your facts turned around. 'Tis Miss Paget who has a wholly unsavory interest in me.''

''Has she made you an indecent offer?'' The earl's eyebrow lifted skeptically. ''I must apologize. I shall make it my business to have a word with my new sister-in-law as soon as possible. Though I doubt it will have much effect. Those Paget women are known to be an unconventional lot.''

''Unconventional!'' Miles ran his fingers impatiently through his hair. ''Nicole is the most irritating, irrational young woman I have ever met.''

Richard nodded his head in sympathetic understanding. ''I had rather similar feelings about Anne. Seemed like the only sensible solution was to marry her.''

Captain Nightingall managed to hold onto his glass of brandy. Barely. ''Lord, Ian was right,'' Miles exclaimed in a growl of disgust. ''You have marriage firmly embedded in your brain, like some sort of sickness.''

''I am not suggesting that you marry Nicole,'' Richard stated clearly. ''She would no doubt drive you mad within a week. All that female adoration and regard can become most tiresome. I must confess, however, that I should not like to find myself forced into a situation where I would have to defend her honor.''

''Her honor?'' Miles spat out. ''What of my honor?''

''I leave that to you to defend,'' Richard replied, noting that the cold indifference that so often haunted Miles's eyes disappeared completely when he spoke of Nicole. If nothing else, the girl had succeeded in bringing passion and feeling back into Captain Nightingall's life.

''I regret to inform you that your absurd rambling speculations are quite mistaken. I have no interest in Miss Paget. Honorable or otherwise,'' Miles declared hotly. He circled around behind Richard. "You must excuse me. I suddenly find myself in need of a fresh drink."

Not at all discomfited by Miles's resentment, Richard watched his friend stomp across the drawing room. He could not help but notice how Captain Nightingall kept a deliberately wide berth from Nicole.

Richard smiled slyly. As the bard said, the lady, or in this instance the gentleman, doth protest too much, methinks. Still, no matter what should occur between Captain Nightingall and Miss Paget, the earl knew his conscience would be clear. He had not been remiss in his duties to either his wife or his sister-in-law. Or for that matter, even his friend.

The sounds of laughter drew Richard's attention back to his guests. He spoke briefly with a few neighbors, then exchanged a cool greeting with Lady Althen. Apparently, Anne's mother was annoyed with him about something. She most likely blamed him for the unfavorable outcome of her afternoon journey into the village. The earl's coachman had reported that both Lord Althen and his wife had been incensed when they arrived at the village only to discover the shops closed and all the shopkeepers gone from their establishments.

Bemused at the thought, Richard reminded himself to mention it to Anne later tonight. He noticed she was no longer seated where she had been ten minutes prior. He searched her out among the small crowd, his gaze wandering about the room until he captured Anne's eye.

She was engaged in earnest conversation with Lord Beachamp, but when Richard's eyes met hers for a fleeting moment, she managed to lose her impassive expression. Richard suddenly felt filled with nervous energy. He wanted their guests to be gone. Immediately.

After what seemed an eternity but in truth was no more than an hour, the visitors departed, the family vanished, and at long last Richard was alone with Anne.

The earl dismissed the servants and waited patiently at the

drawing-room doors. With a small smile curving his lips, he watched his ever frugal wife move gracefully around the blue striped silk-cushioned chairs, gold brocade sofa and mahogany tables with clawlike legs carefully extinguishing the remaining lit candles.

Richard kept Anne close as he led her upstairs and toward their chambers, feeling an eager sexual need building inside him, rising higher and higher with each step he took. The primal, elemental need to once again claim her as his own took hold and held fast to his mind and body.

As they reached the upper landing, the earl realized his hand was trembling. It seemed impossible that merely standing this close to Anne could make his pulse race wildly and his soul ache. Hopeful that all the feelings and emotions he had difficulty expressing with words he could express with his hands and his mouth and his body, the earl led his bride to their chambers.

But she slipped off his arm, walked quickly beyond his door and continued to her own.

"Good night, Richard."

Her hasty farewell shocked him into temporary paralysis. But the moment she turned the handle on her bedchamber door he found his voice.

"Good night?" He cocked his head to one side and stared at his wife in the dusky glow of the candles that illuminated the hallway. "If you have no wish to come to my bed, then I shall join you in yours. In half an hour."

It wasn't a request. It was a statement of fact. She was acting like a polite stranger and it rankled his pride. Even more ridiculous, it hurt his feelings.

"I must sleep alone tonight." She paused, her breath catching. "I am indisposed. I will see you in the morning. At breakfast, perhaps?"

He should have been solicitous. Concerned for her health. Instead he only felt enraged. At her. At himself. He thought he knew her. He believed she enjoyed the physical side of their marriage. Nay, he *knew* she enjoyed the physical side of their marriage.

Yet she now denied him. Bitterness pierced him. He wanted his wife. Naked in his bed. Now.

"You are ill?" he asked. "A headache?" His eyes narrowed. "Or worse?"

She blushed and pressed her hands to her cheeks. "Yes. A slight headache," she whispered, edging toward the door.

For all her years of stretching the truth, Richard was surprised to discover that Anne was an exceedingly poor liar. Even moving her hand to her brow and rubbing furiously at the temples seemed an artificial gesture.

"I don't believe you."

"What?" Anne's head shot up and her hand dropped to her side. "How dare you say that to me!"

"Ahh, I see you have recovered enough to raise your voice," the earl mocked. He rushed forward until he gained her side. With strong fingers he caressed her hip in a proprietary manner. "Perhaps if I ignite your temper your headache will vanish completely."

"You fool." Anne stiffened and pulled away. "I am indisposed, and will remain so for several days."

"Several days!" Even as the words exploded from his mouth, the dawning light of understanding began to illuminate his mind. She had already told him that her woman's time would soon be upon her.

Richard laughed without humor, unable to believe his own stupidity. And thoughtlessness.

Anne seized upon his distraction and escaped. Dropping him a brief curtsey, she disappeared behind her bedchamber door and with a forceful bang, shut it tight. Richard's laughter quickly ceased.

His anticipated eagerness at finally being alone with his bride was now a mocking taste of defeat. It seemed as though the fragile bond between them had been destroyed.

It was suddenly cold. And lonely.

Richard stared at the polished wood of his wife's closed bedchamber door, and an ache seized his throat. His only hint at her forgiveness was a softly muffled, barely audible ''good night,'' spoken from behind the closed door.

Chapter Seventeen

Nicole dressed with care. Captain Nightingall was expected for an afternoon visit and it was imperative that she look her best. Her new gown, a stunningly simple blue silk dress with puffed sleeves and a darker blue satin ribbon tied just below her breasts, was freshly pressed and ready. With her maid's help Nicole donned the lovely garment, then turned anxiously to the mirror to view the effect.

She smiled with true delight as she took in all the subtle nuances of her appearance. The color was perfect. It brought out the blue in her eyes and the pink in her cheeks and gave the exact appearance of frail female beauty she desired.

"I have the rest of your outfit right here, miss," the maid said, coming up behind her.

Nicole glanced over at the frilly lace modesty piece the maid held, then down at her round-necked bodice. With a determined flick of the wrist, Nicole waved the servant away. "I don't need that. You may put it back in the wardrobe."

The maid didn't even try to hide her shock, but Nicole paid

the woman no heed. Her impressive bosom was among her finer features, and Nicole was determined to refrain from adding the modesty piece to the low-cut bodice. Besides, it ruined the line of the dress.

Under the maid's disapproving eye, Nicole tied her matching straw bonnet beneath her chin and carefully pushed back the wisps of blond hair peaking out from beneath the edges. There. She was ready.

She picked up the book of poetry she had been reading last night before going to sleep and sauntered out the door. It had taken a while, but eventually Nicole had figured out that if she sat on a particular bench in the rose garden closest to the drawing room on the east wing, she could see any approaching carriages or riders the moment they entered the front drive. It was here she waited for her first glimpse of Captain Nightingall.

As usual, there were a great number of people coming and going through the earl's front door at this time of day. It sometimes amazed Nicole that her sister Anne, a person who had shunned society and deliberately kept to herself, was now the most popular and prolific entertainer in the county. It seemed as though the manor was constantly filled with people. Family, friends, guests. Living at Cuttingswood Manor was almost as busy as spending time in London.

Nicole arranged the skirt of her gown prettily on the wooden garden bench, lifted her book to eye level to shield her identity from those who might happen to glance her way, and waited. The minutes crawled by. Then suddenly a noise. She craned her neck anxiously at the sound of crunching gravel stones, her heart filled with excitement.

Nicole's face fell with disappointment as she peered over the top of her book and saw a large black carriage roll to a stop. Two of the earl's footmen hurried out to assist the guests in the cumbersome coach. Her heart sank. It wasn't Miles. When he came, if he came, he would arrive on horseback.

Heaving a languid sigh, Nicole watched with limited interest as Lady Beachamp and her daughter Clara alighted from the vehicle. Lady Beachamp stepped down first, followed by Clara, a sour-faced young maid and finally a manservant.

Lady Beachamp barely waited for all the occupants of the carriage to disembark before turning and delivering a variety of instructions to her daughter, her maid and the manservant.

Her shrill voice carried on the slight breeze. Even though Nicole could not distinguish the exact words, she understood from the tone that Lady Beachamp was not a happy woman. The majority of Her Ladyship's commands were for the manservant, who was carrying a fat, stubby little dog on a royal blue velvet cushion. It lay so silent and still, Nicole briefly wondered if the dog was a living creature or a stuffed hide.

No longer even mildly interested in the Beachamp party, Nicole returned to her book, but Shakespeare's sonnets did not hold their usual appeal. A sudden gust of wind fluttered the edge of her bonnet, distracting her.

She readjusted it, hoping it did not leave her looking wind-blown and disheveled. She would have walked the short distance to the ornamental fountain to gaze at her reflection in the water and check on her appearance, but was afraid of missing Captain Nightingall's arrival.

At last came the distinct sound of hoofbeats. Nicole's heart filled with hope. It was all she could do to refrain from tossing her book onto the bench and rushing to the garden wall. Instead she risked a cautious glance over the top of her book. Her heart skipped a beat. 'Twas him!

Miles arrived as he did all things, with unique style and flare. Set astride a massive black stallion, Captain Nightingall approached at a steady gallop. Even at this distance Nicole could see the muscles bunch in his forearms when he pulled back on the reins and halted the beast in the middle of the earl's front drive. The footman cautiously circled the animal as it danced nervously.

With a few deep commands and a powerful press of his

thighs against its flanks, the horse was quieted. Nicole waited until she saw Miles dismount, then she hastily lifted her book higher, hoping he had not seen her spying on him.

All became still and quiet. Slowly, cautiously, Nicole peaked around the edge of the book. And met his eyes. Her breath caught, and she struggled to control her breathing. But she did not look away. His gaze was penetrating. Mesmerizing. Yet his expression remained impassive, showing not the slightest hint of emotion.

Her heart in her throat, Nicole lowered her gaze to the book. The print blurred and wobbled thanks to her trembling hands. She prayed that she was far enough away so he could not see how she shook at the mere sight of him. Tense, nervous, her ears strained for any additional sounds. Finally she heard the footman offer Captain Nightingall a polite greeting of welcome. Then the telltale sign of the massive front door closing. He had gone inside.

Nicole let out her breath. Knowing it might be a while before Miles ventured into the garden, she settled down for a long wait. But her heart was too restless, her excitement too intense to relax.

As of late Miles had been spending more time in her company, though it almost seemed as if he did it against his will and better judgment. On the surface they conversed politely, correctly, impersonally, yet underneath, the tension and desire simmered and smoldered.

It was difficult and frustrating waiting for that tension to overflow into passion. But after each encounter there were subtle, albeit unintentional signs of encouragement. Nicole, never known for patience, was quickly becoming a master of it.

She was aware too of Miles's opinion of her. Unworldly, naive, even silly. He thought her too young, too spoiled, too frivolous to be taken seriously. Well, perhaps she was all those things. It still did not change the fact that she was in love with him. And would be for the rest of her life.

Abandoning the pretense of reading, Nicole made a short stroll along the garden path to stretch her legs and distract her mind. But she did not wander far.

With noiseless footsteps, Captain Nightingall entered the garden. She sensed his nearness first, then confirmed it with her eyes. It amazed Nicole how a man of his size, wearing heavy boots, could move with such quiet grace. She quickly resumed her seat on the garden bench. Picking up her nearly forgotten Shakespeare sonnets, she assumed a casual pose, reminding herself fiercely to breathe.

This time she arranged her book so she would have an unobstructed view of the only garden path that led to her bench. Again she waited, hoping for a glimpse of him, hoping also he would not linger too long on the other side.

It seemed like forever but in reality it was only a few minutes before he came into her sight. Nicole had difficulty containing the thrill of excitement that seized her heart. As always, her eyes were eager and observant. Though she had seen and spoken with him only yesterday, he seemed to have grown taller, broader, more commanding in that short span of time.

Her position was not totally hidden, but she was in a some-what secluded spot on the edge of the garden. Nicole was unsure if Miles had seen her. He steadily walked down a different path, parallel to her position. Stopping, he reached down and softly fingered the petals of a rose. Plucking the delicate flower, he lifted it to his face and breathed deeply. Eyes trained on his every move, Nicole too inhaled as if she were smelling the lovely rose.

She must have made a noise, for he straightened suddenly, turned toward her and smiled.

For an instant the world tilted. If she didn't know better, she might actually have believed he was pleased to see her.

"Taking some afternoon air, Miss Paget?" Captain Nightingall inquired. In four long strides he was by her side. "Be careful not to stay too long in the sun or you shall bring out an army of freckles across the bridge of your nose. I am given to understand that can be something of a tragedy for fashionable young ladies."

Nicole bit back her resentment at being spoken to as if she were a girl, not a woman. Yet she took comfort in the knowledge that he was speaking to her and by his own instigation. She told herself she should be flattered by his teasing remarks. By all accounts, this was indeed progress.

"How gallant of you to be so concerned about me, Captain Nightingall," Nicole said softly, studying him through the screen of her lashes. She glided slowly, gracefully to the end of the bench. "There. I shall sit back here beneath the shade of the towering oak and protect my delicate complexion."

He grinned. His smile sent a most peculiar thrill through her. She blinked, then let her gaze fall to his lips, watching in fascination as they thinned to an even broader smile. She remembered how they had felt pressed against her mouth and was unable to stop the quiver of sensation that raced through her.

Miles must have sensed it too, for she heard him catch his breath and saw his gray eyes darken. *Oh, glory, now he will kiss me,* she thought wildly, but the powerful undercurrent was shattered by the pattering sound of light, rapid footsteps.

Nicole and Miles glanced up simultaneously and beheld a bizarre sight. Running directly toward them, as fast as his short, stubby legs would carry him, was Lady Beachamp's little dog.

"Good Lord," Miles exclaimed, shaking his head. "Has Alexandra gotten herself another pet? I cannot imagine Richard allowing that animal the run of the house."

The pup sniffed loudly at Miles's boots, shook himself vigorously, then tried Nicole's slippers. She smiled. Tail wagging furiously, the little pug placed himself by her feet and danced merrily, reveling in his newly acquired freedom.

" 'Tis Lady Beachamp's dog," Nicole explained, reaching down to give him a gentle pat on the head. Up close the pug was so hideously ugly she found him absurdly endearing. "I wonder how he got out here."

Miles stared down at the animal with a jaundiced eye. "Indeed. I'm surprised the poor thing is capable of actually running and wagging his tail. Whatever does Lady Beachamp feed him? He is so round and fat 'tis a miracle he can even move on his own."

"I believe Lady Beachamp prefers that he be carried," Nicole remarked. "He arrived in the arms of her servant, perched on a blue cushion."

"Ridiculous," Miles snorted. "I thought only lonely childless dowagers treated their pets like beloved infants."

"Apparently not." Nicole looked down at the ecstatic pup and smiled. "Perhaps he is not overly fond of all that attention, either. He does seem rather happy to be out here with us."

"Reggie! Reggie!"

The dog's ears perked up when he heard his name. But instead of letting loose a bark of recognition or running toward the sound, he scooted behind Nicole and tangled himself in the fabric of her gown. Her skirts barely hid him from view.

"Oh, I didn't know anyone was out here." Lady Clara Beachamp stopped short at the sight of Miles and Nicole. "Good afternoon, Miss Paget. Captain Nightingall." She dropped an awkward curtsey of greeting.

"Hello, Lady Clara," Miles said with a cordial bow.

Nicole merely smiled and nodded her head, knowing that if she stood on her feet the little dog would be discovered.

"Have you by any chance seen my mother's dog, Reggie?" Clara asked. "He raced out the door when one of the servants carelessly left it ajar. I am charged with the responsibility of bringing him back. Mama is fearful he will catch a chill out in the garden. Reggie is most delicate. Especially now. He has only recently recovered from a nasty cold."

"Oh, dear." Nicole gave Clara a weak smile and glanced at Miles for help. She could feel the dog's hot breath on her ankles. She had expected him to come running from his hiding place the moment he heard a familiar voice, but apparently he had no intention of moving.

"What does the dog look like?" Miles finally asked in an interested tone.

His inquiry appeared to stump Lady Clara. She bit her bottom lip between her teeth and seemed to consider his question thoughtfully. "Well, he is a small, round little dog. Light brown in color. With a white patch on his stomach and a splash of white on his paws." Her forehead wrinkled in puzzlement. "Have you seen another dog running through the garden, Captain Nightingall?"

"Ahhh, no, we have not seen another dog, have we, Miss Paget?"

"That's correct," Nicole answered truthfully.

"Well, in that case I shall ask one of the footmen to help me search the other gardens," Lady Clara decided. She gave them a strange look before bobbing another curtsey. "Excuse me."

The moment she left, the pug emerged from his hiding place. "Aren't you a sly little dog," Nicole said with a laugh. Turning to Miles, she added, "We should really bring him back to Lady Beachamp. I would feel dreadful if anything happened to him. I had no idea that dogs could catch colds."

"Pure nonsense," Miles insisted.

They both glanced down at the fat little pug. He seemed to give them a mournful glance. That woebegone expression did the trick.

"We have conspired to give Reggie a reprieve from his fate. The least we can do is indulge his freedom," Miles decided. "Let's take him on a short stroll before he is recaptured and forced to spend the rest of the day on some blasted cushion."

Nicole obligingly stood up, tucking her Shakespeare sonnets

under her arm. "We should take the path to the left, since Lady Clara went right."

Captain Nightingall whistled. "Come along, Reggie, time for a walk."

The little pug looked from Nicole to Miles in confusion, but the moment they moved he followed eagerly in their wake. Before long he was sprinting ahead of them, running as fast as his short legs would carry him, puffing and blowing out his breath with each step.

"Are you sure we are not overtaxing the poor creature?" Nicole inquired with concern. "His breathing does seem very labored. Perhaps we should return him to Lady Beachamp."

"She will only fuss and coo over him like some demented matron," Miles replied. "It would be a greater kindness if we let the poor creature have some fun. He is rather happy at escaping from all that unnatural attention."

"Well, 'tis on your conscience if anything happens to him." Nicole decided with a grin.

"I shall add it to my very long list of sins," Miles replied sourly. "Dog killer."

Nicole gasped. "Do not say such a thing." She turned her head sharply to rebuke him but fortunately saw the twinkle of humor in his eye before she spoke.

"How quickly you rush to my defense, Miss Paget," Miles declared in an interested tone. "Why do you do that, I wonder?"

"Because no one else will." She ceased walking and gave him a pointed stare. "Especially you."

"I am humbled by your faith," he said softly. "Misplaced though it may be."

His quiet tone brought on a rush of emotions. Nicole's throat went strangely taut. *'Tis because I love you, Miles,* she wanted to cry out. But the gallant Reggie rescued her from making a complete fool of herself.

A spray of dirt flew onto the gravel path and landed on Captain Nightingall's perfectly polished Hessians. "What in the world?'' He glanced away from Nicole and the spell was broken.

"Get out of the flower beds, you damn fool dog, before the gardener takes after you with a shovel,'' Miles ordered.

The sheer timbre of command in Captain Nightingall's voice gave the dog pause. He ceased rutting in the soil and raised his round face to stare at his liberators, his black nose covered in dirt.

"Oh, dear,'' Nicole remarked with a merry giggle. Her initial frustration at being interrupted vanished at the comical sight. "We might have to clean him up a bit before bringing him back. Lady Beachamp will succumb to a fit of the vapors if she sees her beloved Reggie in such a state.''

"Lady Beachamp is an idiot,'' Miles said forcefully. "He is an animal, not a toy. 'Tis past time that she acknowledged that fact.''

Miles whistled for the dog and he obediently joined them. The smudge of dirt remained on his nose, and his paws were caked with mud.

"Perhaps we can wash him off in one of the ornamental fountains,'' Nicole suggested. "I remember there is a rather large one in the south garden.''

"Absolutely not,'' Miles said. "Reggie wears his dirt as a badge of honor. Besides, have you forgotten what a wet dog smells like? Anne will have our heads if we bring him into her drawing room after he has had a bath in one of the fountains.''

"An excellent point,'' Nicole agreed, before bursting out into laughter, imagining a wet Reggie, a hysterical Lady Beachamp and a stern Anne together in the earl's very formal drawing room.

The trio continued their walk, strolling beyond the roses, and entered yet another of the earl's many outdoor rooms. The silence at first was comforting, familiar, but soon the tingling awareness began to creep into Nicole's heart and her stomach and her knees.

It was as if she could feel Captain Nightingall's magnetism pulling her toward him. And she did nothing to resist. Both her eyes and her thoughts wandered in a most improper manner. She deliberately did not make conversation. But, compelled by a deep yearning, Nicole could not resist placing her hand upon his arm.

She felt him momentarily flinch, but he made no remark. Nor did he attempt to remove her hand. Nicole slowly let out her breath.

"You have resided in the country for several weeks now, Miss Paget," Miles remarked. "What is your opinion of country life?"

"It can be dull being in the same company day after day, but to be fair, in London the society is often the same. The fashions are not as current and the gossip not nearly as interesting. Yet I find that I am surprisingly well contented. I enjoy being with my family, and Lord Mulgrave has an extensive library that he has kindly allowed me free use of so I may indulge my passion for the written word."

Nicole paused. "I will, however, confess my biggest complaint." She leaned in and whispered mischievously, "There are too many animals."

He laughed, just as she intended he would, and it made her feel strong and powerful. *I can make him happy,* she told herself fiercely. *If only he will allow it.*

"And what of you, Captain? Are you tired of rusticating? Will you soon return to the excitement and frivolity of London?"

"I shall return to London eventually," he stated confidently. "For now I shall enjoy the dullness of country life. 'Tis peaceful here."

"You seem a man who is in need of a little peace, sir."

His head turned sharply. She could tell he was startled by her comment.

"And you, Miss Paget, seem like a girl in search of a kiss."

Nicole's heart leapt with anticipatory joy. Putting his words into action, Miles placed his hands on either side of her face. Her eyes closed as he bent his head and pressed his lips upon hers. His kiss was soft, feather light. He stroked her cheek with his thumb, and she shifted restlessly until he kissed her deeper, harder.

Her mouth clung to his, her hands slid up along the softness of his coat to join together behind his neck. Nicole could feel herself starting to melt as her senses soared. No man but Miles could bring her to life with such practiced ease. He tore his mouth from hers, trailing a line of hot kisses against her throat and neck.

She gasped, then boldly kissed the line of his square jaw. His shudder was followed by a deep moan. She did it again. And smiled slyly at his answering moan.

Then suddenly he pulled away. She cried out in distress and tried to bring him back but he resisted. Her knees quivered and nearly gave out but she somehow managed to stay on her feet.

"I will not marry you," he declared vehemently. He sounded more as if he were trying to convince himself rather than her, but Nicole was too distressed to think upon it. "I will not marry you," he repeated.

She nearly blurted out that she did not care. Pressed close to his warmth, feeling her breast rise and fall against his strong muscular chest, Nicole wanted only the chance to be with him. To become one with him. At this moment in time marriage was the furthest thing from her mind.

But he withdrew from her. Physically. Emotionally. His kisses were now gone, a faint mocking memory, leaving her lost and cold. Slowly, gradually, she regained her senses. Straightening, Nicole met his gaze. To keep her voice from trembling, she spoke calmly and deliberately.

"I have been taught that men will not value what is so easily given for free. And so I will tell you, Miles Nightingall, that my regard for you comes without expectation or obligation, but to claim my body and my soul you must pay the price."

He lifted his brow. "A price, Miss Paget?"

"Marriage, sir. Respectability."

"And if I deem the price too high?"

"Then you are a fool," Nicole whispered through her teeth. "And do not deserve such a prize."

She turned and ran from him then, feeling deep within her heart as though she were also running from herself. She could hear the anxious clicking of Reggie's nails against the stone path as the little dog struggled to keep up with her. But she did not slow down.

Her goals had taken a drastic turn over the course of the past few weeks. Where she had at one time hoped only to lure Miles into an impetuous marriage proposal, she now longed for something more permanent, more concrete. It was no longer enough that he allow her to love him. She wanted, nay, needed, him to love her in return.

In the coming week there were changes at Cuttingswood Manor. Slowly, steadily, the Paget family began to take over, putting their indelible stamp on all aspects of life on the estate. The quiet, sedate country life the earl had so carefully orchestrated was now gone, perhaps banished forever.

Childish laughter was heard throughout the house at odd hours of the day and night. Meals were elaborate, boisterous affairs, with neighbors and friends in constant attendance. There was music and dancing in the evening, stimulating conversations on literature, the arts and even politics, along with cards and good-natured wagering among old and new friends.

Miles and Ian seemed to be permanent fixtures, staying late in the evenings and appearing again in the early morning. One day Richard remarked jokingly to the pair that he wondered if they were secretly sleeping somewhere in the manor, returning only to Ian's house to change their clothing.

They informed him with lofty smiles that visiting his home was far more enjoyable now that he had a wife. And at Anne's urging they continued calling.

This was not the typical tedious round of country soirees the earl's mother had often complained about when in residence at the manor. In fact, Richard and Anne rarely left Cuttingswood. Instead, friends and neighbors came to them in a series of well-planned, carefully orchestrated evenings, faultlessly supervised by Anne.

The earl resigned himself to his fate with little sign of outward concern. True, his in-laws could be beyond irritating at times, but for the most part he found their generally high spirits and frivolous attitude toward life a tolerable antidote.

Yet what fascinated and frustrated him most was Anne. She was never the center of attention at these many gatherings. Quite the contrary. She stayed deliberately in the background, allowing Nicole that honor. But it was clearly Anne who arranged these evenings, who worked tirelessly to ensure that all the guests felt comfortable and welcome.

She had an uncanny knack for broaching topics that brought on lively debate and interest yet avoided stirring up controversy. When she was only in the company of her family, she occasionally scolded or lectured them, but for the most part kept her thoughts to herself.

He should have been pleased with his wife. She had taken to her duties as his countess with vigor and dedication. He could find no fault. Except one. In the odd moment when he caught an unguarded glimpse of Anne, she seemed as miserable as he felt.

Unfortunately, Mr. Quimby, the painting instructor Ian had recommended, was unavailable and had sent an underling in his place. Anne, never a woman to suffer fools gladly, sent the foppish Mr. Dane packing after just one lesson.

It distressed Richard that he had been unable to provide her with the one thing he had promised—art lessons. The earl took small comfort in the knowledge that he had at least provided her with a large room to paint in. Anne shut herself up in the studio at some point nearly every day, spending many long hours with her paints and canvas.

Anne was always polite and proper toward him, but distant. He felt it more keenly each time they were together. The growing friendship and regard they had begun to develop before their marriage seemed to have fallen apart almost immediately after they were wed.

He didn't understand it. He didn't like it. Most importantly, he didn't have a clue how to change it.

The sound of female voices and high spirits brought the earl away from the many papers on his desk. He walked quickly to the hallway to investigate and discovered his wife and daughter preparing for an outing.

"I shall have a green bonnet made to match my new riding habit. And I shall tell Mrs. Wilder to put three feathers on my new hat, one higher than the next," Alexandra exclaimed, lifting her arms into the air to emphasize her resolve.

"You will topple over if the bonnet is too high," Anne remarked with a smile as she tugged on her gloves.

Alexandra giggled and Anne joined her. Richard moved forward to greet them. Yet at the sight of him Anne's laughter abruptly ceased.

To Richard, it felt like a slap in the face. Anne glanced away from him, her long dark lashes shielding her eyes. It was as if his unexpected presence had taken all the joy out of the moment. Fortunately, Alexandra's enthusiastic greeting covered the awkward moment.

"Papa! Anne says I may buy a special bonnet today in the village since I have been so dile . . . dile . . ."

"Diligent," Anne supplied softly.

"Yes, diligent in my studies. And I have saved my allowance

for the whole week," Alexandra said with emphasis, impressing upon her father the great sacrifice involved in this endeavor.

"I am very proud of you," Richard proclaimed, glancing sideways at his wife.

He was about to remark that he could easily afford to buy Alexandra as many bonnets or gloves or gowns as she wished, but Anne's stoic expression stopped him. He realized that today's afternoon visit to the millinery shop was far more than a reward for being a good student. This was a life lesson on thrift and economy. A topic near and dear to Anne's heart.

He deliberately came closer. Anne appeared paralyzed by his sudden nearness. For an instant he would have sworn she looked wary.

"We are expected at the milliner's and must not be late. It would be rude and inconsiderate. Come along, Alexandra. Good day, my lord." In her confusion Anne dropped a hasty, prim curtsey.

"Damn," Richard muttered under his breath as he watched his wife and daughter scurry away. Was the distance so wide between them that she now felt compelled to resort to formality in both address and manner?

He blamed himself. After making such an ass of himself the night she was unable to share his bed, Richard had waited for an invitation to hers. None had been forthcoming. So since that unmentionable night a week ago, he had absented himself from his wife's bed.

As he tossed and turned at night unable to sleep, he told himself he was respecting her wishes. He told himself that Anne only needed a bit more time to accustom herself to being his wife. He told himself that in time things would improve.

Richard glanced out the window. There was a thin layer of fog visible in the distance, hanging low over the fields. It looked dense and oppressive. Rather like the weight inside his chest.

It hadn't escaped his notice that Anne was both kind and attentive to Alexandra. She seemed to genuinely like his daughter and made a special effort to spend time each day alone with Alexandra, allowing the child to choose the outing or activity they undertook.

Richard was heartened by his wife's interest in his daughter and her obvious regard and affection for the little girl. Yet he envied the ease they shared in each other's company, for it too closely resembled the type of relationship he had shared with his child and had so hoped to establish with Anne.

Richard frowned, perplexed to admit that the idea rankled him. He was jealous. Alexandra had always been his alone for these many years. He did not mind sharing her, for he recognized her need to have female guidance and companionship. Yet he felt a definite twinge of sadness at the thought of no longer being needed.

The many papers waiting in his study held little appeal. Richard admitted that what he really wanted to do was go into town with Anne and Alexandra. But he hadn't been invited and he wasn't going to force himself upon them.

Force himself upon them! Egad, he sounded like a spoiled little boy. Shaking his head at his juvenile thoughts, the earl turned, but instead of going to his study he found himself climbing the grand staircase and following the long gallery to the west wing of the house.

With his permission, Anne had set up her studio in this seldom-used section of the great house. She pronounced the light excellent and the location private.

It was there he walked now with such purpose. 'Twas high time he learned more about his wife. And the earl knew precisely where to search for the answers. In her paintings.

Chapter Eighteen

Set in his determination to learn more about his mysterious bride, Richard turned the handle of her studio door, glad it wasn't locked. He entered cautiously, feeling very much like an uninvited guest at a party. The smell of paint and turpentine assaulted his nostrils, but the moment he caught a glimpse of the beauty of the work spread before him, Richard barely noticed the unpleasant smell.

He first went to the large table on the far side of the room where a pile of pencil sketches were haphazardly scattered. He shuffled through the papers, selecting several for closer study. He recognized his gardens, his stables, even some of his servants. Country life depicted with realistic accuracy and whimsy.

He reached for another pile and saw the sunny smile of his daughter mischievously looking back at him. Rosalind was in the drawing also, sitting on a cushioned chair, with Alexandra informally posed on a stool near her feet.

They looked impossibly young and innocent. Alexandra's elbow was propped against Rosalind's knee, her chin resting on her hand while her head was turned in a typically coquettish angle.

Anne had somehow captured the essence of his daughter's personality. Though only a sketch in shades of black and white, it looked so real that Richard half expected to hear his little girl's happy giggle.

Wondering if Anne had also made paintings of this marvelous scene, Richard abandoned the sketches, after first carefully placing the one of Alexandra and Rosalind off to the side. Hands on his hips, the earl then surveyed the many canvases, in varying stages of completion, carefully lined against the wall. He reached out for one, turning it around gently so as not to disturb the others next to it.

It was not Rosalind and Alexandra but a far more intriguing subject. Hoisting his prize toward the light, the earl studied the painting with intense interest. Against a pearly overcast sky on the crest of a grassy knoll Anne had painted a man and a woman, their nude bodies sensuously entwined.

The passion and eager anticipation of the couple were brought to life with color and texture, and clearly illustrated in the tension of their straining muscles and the placement of their hands so lovingly upon each other's bodies.

Richard smiled faintly. Perhaps the lack of intimacy that now existed between them was distressing Anne. Maybe his bride had missed his presence in her bed this long week. Though the male depicted in the painting was in a reclining position, Richard could see that he was tall, with broad shoulders and a muscular back. The female was also tall, but pale and slender.

He had always suspected that Anne had a romantic, sensual soul. Now he had proof. Although the features were not yet defined by the stroke of the brush, there was no mistaking the identity of the couple. It was him and Anne.

Yet these lovers were free. Free to express their emotions and needs. Oblivious to the elements, carrying on their tryst in a steady drizzle. He could almost hear the rain pattering softly against the leaves and dripping onto this ardent pair, could almost smell the damp fresh scent of rain and earth blowing gently in the breeze.

Eager to see more of his wife's extraordinary work, the earl moved among the many canvases. There were pastoral scenes, a brilliant sunset over rich, fertile fields, and a series of intricate floral designs that reminded Richard of a medieval tapestry.

After finishing his examination of the paintings on the perimeter of the room, the earl turned his attention to the center of the room, where the natural light was the strongest. Here at center stage, perched on the easel in the middle of the room sat a large canvas covered in cloth.

Richard thought it strange that this was the only hidden work but he suspected it was Anne's current project. He hesitated, but curiosity won out over conscience. Feeling like a voyeur, Richard nevertheless slowly peeled away the covering.

His deep gasp echoed off the stone walls of the cavernous room.

"Lord, what a clever girl I have married." Entranced, the earl stepped closer and leaned forward, taking in every subtle detail of this extraordinary work.

It was an amazingly flattering portrait. Of him. Richard sucked in his breath. He was only partially clothed on the canvas. The light and shadow hid the secrets of his maleness, but his chest was bare as were his arms, legs and thighs.

Was this how she saw him? An arrestingly handsome man in control of himself and of seemingly all around him. Long-legged with narrow hips, muscular forearms and a broad chest, exuding a raw animal power that was dangerous and hypnotic.

Richard stepped back. He looked like an arrogant, invincible male, ready to do battle at a moment's notice. All that was missing was a weapon. A broadsword seemed appropriate. The earl moved to the left, viewing the portrait from a different angle. He appeared even fiercer from that side.

Looking beyond his imposing self, Richard studied what

little there was of the background. It was dark and hazy, but along the edges of the portrait he could make out the distinct detail of green leaves and small spots of red to soften the harshness. They were barely noticeable.

Moving closer once again, Richard studied the design. Roses. Tiny, almost imperceptible red roses. For a warrior? He examined the green leaves with great interest, then excitedly identified them too. Myrtle.

It was completely wrong for the painting, given the manner that Anne had portrayed him, yet it was so cleverly done, so well hidden that unless the portrait was intently studied only the artist would know the roses and myrtle were there.

Red roses and myrtle. Symbols of love. Recalling his schoolboy lessons, Richard remembered well that myrtle was regarded by the ancients as sacred to Venus, who was the mother of love. This manor house, built in the time of the Tudors, contained numerous allusions to myrtle as a symbol of love, as was the custom of the period.

Red roses and myrtle. For him. Was it possible? Had he really discovered the truth about Anne's feelings, or was he being a vain fool? A wishful fool.

He stepped back and studied the painting once more. And as he stared at the arrogant reflection, he realized suddenly that it didn't really matter.

He carelessly flung the cloth over the painting and raced from the room. He would have his horse saddled and ride toward the village to meet Anne's carriage upon its return. He needed to see her. Quickly.

Perhaps this painting and the one of the ardent couple showed that she was far from disliking or feeling indifferent toward him as he had feared. Perhaps her paintings had clearly spoken what her tongue could not. Perhaps Anne was in love with him.

Or perhaps not. The earl sighed. Richard knew he could not merely assume what Anne's feelings were. Nor could he control them. He could only acknowledge his own. He was in love with her. And 'twas high time he told her.

Anne closed her eyes briefly and relaxed against the comfortable squabs of the carriage. Alexandra sat beside her, chattering about the visit to the village and making comments about the changing landscape.

Anne slowly opened her eyes. It had turned out to be a fine day. The early fog that had hung over the fields was now gone, burned away by a brilliant sun. She reclined back in the open carriage and glanced lazily up at the sky as puffs of clouds floated above, coming apart, then drifting together, making new and bizarre shapes.

Perhaps I should do a series of cloud sketches, she thought drowsily. The light, airy, fanciful shapes were fascinating and ever-changing. One reminded her of Pegasus, the winged horse of mythology, while another looked like a medieval castle with pennants flying against a sunny blue sky.

With a deep sigh, Anne continued her fanciful cloud watching. That cluster resembled a large canopy bed draped in white netting, she decided. And those looked like a herd of very fat sheep.

Her concentration drifted, like the clouds, and her eyes grew tired. Slowly she lowered her lids. The warm afternoon sun, the gentle sway of the carriage and the steady crunch of the wheels lulled her into a dreamlike state.

But her languid mood was soon shattered by the ominous sound of hoofbeats. Alexandra shouted with innocent delight and pointed. Anne struggled to an upright position and saw a single rider crest over the hill and approach them at a rapid speed.

She glanced at Alexandra anxiously, her stomach clenched in fear. Though they had both a coachman and a footman for protection, they were riding in an open carriage on a lonely, deserted section of road.

They watched the rider jump a tall hedge at good speed, then turn his mount in their direction.

"Coachman," Anne called out in alarm.

"I see him, my lady," the servant replied, extracting a lethal-looking pistol from his coat pocket. "You and Lady Alexandra have nothing to fear. John Coachman will keep you safe."

Anne put her arm around Alexandra's shoulders and held the little girl protectively against her side. Sensing the seriousness of the moment, the child grew quiet and still.

"Perhaps we can outrun him," Anne shouted to the driver.

"No need for that, my lady. He's close enough now that I recognize his mount. 'Tis Lord Mulgrave."

Lord Mulgrave! Anne huffed out her breath in annoyance. Whatever was he thinking, bearing down upon them like some deranged highwayman?

The coachman pulled the horses to a full stop as the earl brought his horse alongside the carriage.

"Did you have an enjoyable afternoon shopping in the village?" the earl asked cheerfully, tipping his hat in greeting.

Alexandra opened her mouth eagerly to reply, but Anne cut her off.

"You gave us quite a fright, my lord," Anne said sharply, as anger and relief churned madly inside her. She stood up, balancing herself in the unsteady carriage. "We thought you were some evil reprobate out to cause us harm."

Richard appeared to be confused. "This is not London, madame, with footpads lurking in the shadows. You are only a few miles from our property. There is no need to be fearful."

"I exercise prudence at all times, sir, but never more than when I have our daughter in my care."

Richard gestured toward the pistol that the driver still held. "My servants, especially John Coachman, are well trained. And ever on guard."

Anne's hand fluttered nervously to her throat. "That is not an excuse for frightening us half to death."

Richard removed his hat, ran his fingers through his wind-tousled hair, then jammed it back upon his head. He appeared ready to deliver an angry retort but must have changed his mind. Instead, he bowed his head gracefully. "My apologies, madame, for any distress my actions might have inadvertently caused."

Anne squared her shoulders and lifted her chin. She hesitated, wanting to reply with just the right amount of dignity in her voice and manner. But Richard completely negated his conciliatory words by speaking first.

"I will escort Her Ladyship home," the earl informed his servants in that irritating tone of command that grated so fiercely on her nerves.

"I prefer to ride back to the manor in the carriage," Anne said flatly, bending at the knees to resume her seat.

Faster than she dreamed possible he grabbed her at the waist, hauled her from the carriage and lifted her onto the front of his saddle. His horse shied, but he managed to keep the beast under control.

She thrust her hands down and tried to pry herself loose from his grip. "I demand you put me down this instant!"

His embrace tightened. "Careful, my dear," he whispered softly in her ear. "We have a most rapt audience."

Anne's head shot up. Alexandra's eyes were round with curiosity, and the normally discreet servants were also staring boldly. Anne forced her body to relax, but it was difficult. She was pressed so tightly against Richard she could feel the steady thud of his heart. Her own heart was pounding at an equally fast pace.

"You have less than three miles to go before reaching the estate," the earl said to the driver. "I entrust you with Lady Alexandra's safety until she returns to Cuttingswood."

The coachman's chest inflated with pride. "She'll come to no harm nor mischief under my care."

"Good." The earl nodded with approval. He smiled warmly at his daughter. "We'll see you later, Alexandra."

The little girl returned his grin and waved goodbye. Anne gritted her teeth helplessly. She felt foolish entrapped in Richard's arms, all the more so because in part she enjoyed it so much.

They did not wait for the carriage to depart. The earl turned his mount and led the horse back up the hill. They rode for some time. In the opposite direction of the manor house.

Teeth clenched in annoyance, Anne refused to speak to her husband. It would have been undignified trying to shout against the wind anyway. She struggled to keep her body rigid as a stone, but her hips rubbed against him in a most indiscreet location.

It was not a comfortable or companionable silence. Anne could hear his breathing as it whispered past her ear, and feel the solid strength of his thighs holding her in place. They were so close that his musky male scent surrounded her, sending a strange, almost primitive stirring within her.

At last they arrived at their destination. A small secluded glen, carpeted with lush green grass and surrounded on three sides by thick shrubs.

The earl dismounted, then reached up and pulled Anne down from the horse. She didn't bother protesting, knowing they would not leave until he concluded whatever business had brought them to this secluded place.

Anne remained silent as she watched Richard tether his horse to a sturdy tree limb. When he was done, he turned to face her. She stared back at him.

"I apologize for my behavior, but I wished to speak with you and I wanted some privacy. It seems that despite its many rooms our home is always filled with people."

Anne stiffened. "I thought you understood before we married

that I had numerous responsibilities toward my family," she said, trying to keep the hurt from her tone. "I am constantly telling them not to pester you. In future I shall double my efforts to keep them from invading your privacy."

"You misunderstand," Richard replied. " 'Tis not just your family. Actually, I am starting to become accustomed to encountering them. It is the constant and steady stream of visitors we have every day and night that puzzles me."

Anne rubbed her arms vigorously even though she didn't feel cold. "Goodness, I had nearly forgotten. We are having twenty guests for dinner this evening. I need to return to the manor soon."

She noticed a multitude of emotions moving across his face at her pronouncement. He gave a deep sigh but maintained an even expression. "Are you happy being my wife?"

Not at this particular moment, she thought. Anne opened her mouth to reply, but the serious expression on his handsome face held her tongue. She bit her bottom lip, realizing she was incapable of answering such a complicated question with a simple yes or no. Was she happy? "I am not unhappy," she finally admitted.

He sighed again. "I am tired, Anne. Tired of the distance between us. Tired of how you run from me, hide from me. 'Tis long past time that there was truth and honesty between us."

"I don't understand what you mean. I have not lied to you." Anne shifted her feet. He was making her uncomfortable. For the first time since their wedding night, he was paying close attention to her. Anne quickly decided that she liked neither his pensive mood nor his intense stare. "Richard, please, we have guests coming for dinner. I am needed back at the house to supervise the preparations."

"Why?" he challenged.

"Why?" Anne sputtered. "What do you mean, why? I need to make certain the roast beef is properly cooked and the fish is fresh and the accompanying dishes aren't too spicy and the table is properly set and enough bottles of wine have been brought up from the cellars—''

"Why?''

Anne stomped her foot in exasperation. "For heaven's sake, stop this. I am in no mood to play games.''

"I am not playing games.'' He braced his feet apart and folded his arms across his chest. "I want to know why you are doing all of this.''

Anne furrowed her brow. "I am your countess. We are having guests for dinner, and as the hostess I must be certain that all is in proper readiness for our company. That is my duty. 'Tis expected.''

"By whom?'' He pushed his hat back and scratched his head. "I do not remember any specific mention of that in our wedding vows. To love, to honor, to obey. In sickness and in health. Nary one mention of entertaining.''

"Do not mock me, Richard.''

"I am trying to understand you.'' He put his hand over his head as if he were in pain. "Yet you make it so difficult.''

"I warned you,'' she said softly, fear gripping her heart. Had she failed? She had so wanted to be successful in at least one aspect of being his wife. She had tried hard, very hard, to be a gracious hostess, a social success. Could she do nothing right? "I told you that I might not be a suitable wife, a suitable countess. But you would not listen to me. I'm sorry. So very sorry.'' Anne closed her eyes and swallowed fast and hard, just as she did when taking bad-tasting medicine. "You would have been far better off choosing Miss Fraser for your bride.''

"Miss Fraser? Alexandra's governess?''

Dear Lord, had she actually spoken those insecure thoughts aloud? Anne groaned. But there was no point in turning back now. In for a penny, in for a pound, as Aunt Sophie would say. "Yes, Miss Fraser. She is a lovely and refined young woman. Did you know that her great-grandfather was an earl?''

Anne did not wait for an answer to her question. "Miss

Fraser's duties go well beyond those of a typical governess. It has not escaped my notice that you greatly depend on her guidance when trying to solve a variety of estate problems.''

''I do? I hadn't realized.'' Richard rubbed his chin thoughtfully. ''Does it distress you?''

''Yes.'' Her answer took Anne by surprise. But it was the truth. She was horribly jealous. Anne held her breath, wondering how much more of the truth she dared to reveal. ''Miss Fraser is very beautiful, charming and intelligent.'' *All the things I am not,* Anne added silently to herself. ''And she is very much in love with you, Richard.''

''What!'' He turned, paced for several seconds, stopped, then turned back to Anne. His face was filled with surprise. ''Are you sure?''

''Quite.'' Anne reminded herself to breathe. ''Whenever you are in the same room together, she cannot keep the longing she feels for you from her eyes.''

''You cannot believe that I return her affections?''

Anne closed her eyes very tightly. ''Perhaps one day you shall.''

He did not answer for a long time. ''Look at me, Anne.''

She sniffed loudly. Then opened her eyes.

''There is only one woman who I dare to hope will someday willingly accept my love. You.''

Her heart lurched. ''We have never spoken of love, sir.''

''Well, we should,'' Richard said solemnly. He tilted his head. ''I saw my portrait, Anne.''

''Portrait? What portrait?''

''The portrait you painted of me.''

''Oh.'' All expression left her face. ''What were you doing in my studio?'' she huffed, but her heart was not in it.

''Do not try to distract me,'' Richard admonished, yet his tone was gentle. ''I was speechless when I viewed that painting. It swells a man's head to believe that a woman, especially his wife, would view him in such a manner.''

"Does that mean you approve?" Anne asked with a slight blush.

"I more than approve." His lips twitched but he did not smile. "I suspect most people would never look beyond the warrior on the canvas, but I studied every detail of the painting."

"You did?" Anne struggled to keep her mouth from falling open. This was the last thing she expected to hear.

"I noticed the tiny red roses in the background. And the myrtle."

"Naturally," Anne bristled, trying to brazen down his pointed stare. Her heart began thumping wildly. He must have studied the portrait a very long time if he had seen the roses. And been able to identify the myrtle leaves. Could he possibly suspect the truth?

"You are correct, the portrait is a depiction of a warrior. The myrtle is a fanciful notion, a symbolic representation. It stands for victory."

"And the red roses?" he inquired with a lifted brow.

"An experiment in color contrast." Anne felt a cold sweat break out on her forehead. "The work is unfinished. 'Tis the artist's choice, an expression of creativity to paint a variety of items before making a final decision about what is appropriate to the work."

"How interesting." Richard's doubting expression told her he was unconvinced. "The representation of red roses as a symbol for love is universally acknowledged, and if I remember my Greek history correctly, myrtle stands for other things besides victory. It too is a symbol of love."

Drat! How in keeping with her current misfortunes to have fallen in love with a scholarly, knowledgeable man. Instinctively, words of denial sprang to her lips. But something hesitant, hopeful in Richard's eyes gave Anne pause.

It flickered there in the depths of green, a shadow of something so vague she might have imagined it. But it gave her the courage to acknowledge the truth in her own heart. And to draw strength from that truth. "Perhaps the roses and myrtle do represent love. What do you have to say to that, my lord?"

"I love you, too?"

Anne closed her eyes tight. It felt as if fireworks were exploding inside her chest. She felt a dampness on her cheeks and realized she was crying. How ridiculous. How impractical. Why was she crying? This was the happiest moment of her life. Richard loved her.

She felt his arms go around her. Anne hiccupped loudly and pressed her head against his broad chest, huddling into his warmth. He rubbed his cheek against the top of her head and tightened his arms. She sobbed harder.

"Shhhh, don't cry," he whispered against her hair.

Her shoulders shook and her throat tightened and she wept until her emotions finally started to even out. Taking a deep breath, she caught his unique masculine scent subtly mixed with the sweet perfume of the nearby wildflowers.

She heard the leaves rustling in the breeze, felt the warmth of the sunlight on her shoulders and back. Felt the glow of Richard's love surround, engulf, protect her. Here in this enchanted place, full of mystery and hope and fulfillment.

Richard raised her hand to his lips and began kissing her fingers. Anne finally lifted her chin and opened her eyes. The look he gave her was undeniable. Filled with longing and passion and, yes, love. She felt momentarily startled. Then he grinned at her. That heart-melting, boyish smile that always made her feel like the most beautiful, enchanting creature in the world.

"Really?" she whispered. "Do you truly love me?"

"Yes, my lady. With all my heart."

Anne's eyes stung, but she smiled through the well of tears. "I'm glad," she whispered with emotion. "Very glad."

"Good, then you may show me," he said.

She could see the spark of mischief in his eyes. It excited her. Richard brought his lips to hers, sealing their emotions. Her lips parted, his tongue slipped inside, and the magic began.

Pure want swept through Anne. She had been away from him for too long, had missed the feel of his hard body, the thrusting and plunging and possession that bound them together so completely.

She felt his fingers glide gently down her cheek, through the nape of her neck and across her shoulders. Tiny, moist kisses followed; then he set his arm about her waist and led her to a secluded spot, protected from wind and prying eyes by thick shrubbery. To Anne it was the loveliest place on earth.

He removed his hat and tossed it to the ground. Next came his waistcoat and his coat, which he carefully spread on the ground.

"What are you doing?"

"I am making a bed for us."

"How wonderful."

Her eager response earned her another kiss. His lips brushed hers lightly. Once. Twice. The third time, she threaded her fingers through his hair and kissed him back. Hard.

Richard did not bother to remove her clothing. He merely undid enough of the buttons in the front of her dress so he could push down the top of her gown and bare her breasts. Then he pulled off her walking boots and stockings and drawers until she was naked from the waist down.

Anne felt wicked. Marvelously wicked and wanton and free. The brush of her silken skirt rubbing against her naked buttocks and between her legs brought a flush of color to her cheeks, and a rush of warm moisture between her thighs.

Wide-eyed, she watched Richard slowly, deliberately open the fastening of his breeches. His maleness sprang forth, thick and heavy with longing. Anne shivered in delicious excitement.

He slid an arm around her shoulder and drew her close. He

beckoned her with his loving eyes and handsome smile. Falling to his knees, he brought her to the ground and she went willingly, the heat already starting to spread through her body in a marvelous rhythm.

But instead of placing her on her back, as Anne expected, he lay down and pulled her atop him.

"Richard," she exclaimed, trying to keep the shock from her voice at the position he had chosen. "I'm not exactly certain what to do."

Doubt edged her tone, along with the growing voice of desire.

"Don't worry, I'll show you." His hand dipped between her legs, which were open and exposed. "Thank God you're already wet. Since we are trying to forestall a pregnancy, I'll need to pull out before I spill my seed," he explained hoarsely. "I'll have more control this way."

Following his gruffly whispered instructions, Anne straddled Richard's thighs. A shudder of pure excitement racked through her as her naked body brushed against the warm skin of his lower stomach, tickling the sensitive inner folds.

Richard put his hands around her waist and lifted her, bringing her against his hardness. She clutched at his chest for balance as she knelt upright, her thighs hugging his sides.

"Guide me inside," he whispered.

Fumbling, Anne reached between their bodies and positioned him at her opening. Her breathing was low and ragged as she slowly lowered herself.

"Now what?" she asked breathlessly.

He flexed his hips and she nearly screamed. The fullness, the tightness rocked her senses.

"Now you ride me, my love."

She was tentative at first, conscious of his eyes upon her. He reached and brushed his fingers across her breasts. Heat flared inside Anne as his fingers circled her nipples until they hardened and tightened. Her breath caught. She rocked slightly and her body flooded with exquisite sensations.

Richard twisted his fingers in her hair and drew her down so that her face was near enough to kiss. Anne opened her mouth eagerly to receive his hot tongue, loving him with her body and spirit and soul. His hips rose up to hers, thrusting with a frantic urgency.

"Oh, love, I'm sorry, I cannot hold back any longer," he groaned.

His body stiffened and Anne felt Richard's fingers dig into her hips as he tried to pull himself away from hers.

"No!" she cried out in protest, feeling an ache so intense it was pain and pleasure. She could not bear to be separated from Richard in these final moments of ecstasy. The realization left her shaking and struggling to remain joined while he continued trying to remove himself.

"Anne!" Richard gritted his teeth and opened his eyes wide.

"Don't leave me, Richard," she whispered frantically, knowing deep within herself that at this instant they were not two separate individuals but one complete being. "Come with me."

His breath hissed in and he took her at her word. Their gazes locked and Anne could see the tension grip his face as his body began to shudder.

"My love," she whispered softly, tears blurring her eyes. She had never felt more alive in her life, in body, mind and spirit.

The gush of his hot, warm seed pulsing deep inside her triggered her own release. When it was over, Anne bowed her head and laid it against Richard's chest, hugging him as if she would never let go. She felt totally sated, not only with the release of her physical tension but with the peace of her soul.

The man turned, staggered and fell to his knees. He had not meant to watch the couple, but once he saw them it had been impossible to look away. Recognizing the intense expression on Richard's face, he had followed the pair the moment he saw the earl lift his wife from the carriage.

It had been childishly simple to remain undetected even though he kept only a discreet distance. Richard was so intent upon the woman who rode in his arms he was oblivious to the fact that he was being tracked. The earl then chose a well-secluded spot for his confrontation and forced his countess to dismount. She had seemed most displeased.

Anxious to hear their conversation, the man had taken cover in the nearby brush. He had hoped to hear them argue with each other. Cold, nasty words flung between a feuding man and wife.

But the anger in their voices had never been very strong. Soon the stiffness of their bodies had eased, and before long they were entwined in each other's arms. Articles of clothing were discarded, pushed aside, rearranged. Heat had spread from his loins to his face as he watched Richard and Anne's carnal mating, heard their words of love and devotion.

The man pressed his thumbs against the pounding ache of his temples and tried to think. Tried to plan. He had gone to the village with the intention of surprising Anne and Alexandra, hoping for the chance to steal a few precious moments with his beautiful daughter. But he had been too late. They had left the millinery shop before he arrived.

Riding hard, the man had caught up to the slow-moving coach that conveyed his little girl and Lady Mulgrave. He was preparing to join them and gallantly offer to ride escort for the remainder of the journey to the manor when Richard had arrived. To abduct his wife for an afternoon of heated love-making.

To abandon Alexandra to the unsafe roads and harsh elements. To subject her to all manner of harm, all sorts of unmentionable dangers. What would happen if the carriage was driven too fast or recklessly and overturned? Or worse, waylaid by ruffians? Who would save her, protect her, keep her from harm?

Were Richard and Anne really so selfish? Did they care so little for their wonderful child, their precious jewel?

Apparently so. A choked cry escaped his lips. 'Twas time, he decided, while an almost frantic panic beating inside his chest stole his breath. 'Twas time to rescue his little girl.

He untied the reins and lifted himself heavily upon his horse. Slowly, carefully, he trotted away, knowing he must not make a sound. Discovery at this stage would only lead to a nasty, perhaps even deadly, confrontation.

He swayed slightly in the saddle, then quickly grabbed the pommel to straighten himself. He had slept little these past weeks, his mind filled with worry and concern and the ever-present jealousy.

It was a relief to finally be taking the action he had contemplated for nearly a year. His conscience gnawed briefly at him, but he pushed it away, burying it beneath the thick layers of love and longing that dwelled within his soul. It was joy to finally release the overpowering need to become a true father to Alexandra. It would bring them both peace. And everlasting happiness.

The ride to the manor passed in a confused blur of emotion. The servant took his horse and bowed politely. He was welcomed inside, and his query about Alexandra's whereabouts was cheerfully answered.

No one stopped him. No one challenged him. The ease of his task gave him strength. His steps no longer faltered, because he knew in his heart he had set upon the right course, the true course.

He found her easily. Skipping around the garden fountain and singing. A silly, charming, childish song.

Tears swam in his eyes. His beautiful little girl. She was alone. All alone. It was almost too perfect.

Taking a deep breath, he stepped from the shadows.

Alexandra ceased her singing. Her head turned sharply, her body tensed.

"Hello, Alexandra," he said softly.

The brief startled look of surprise vanished from her eyes. She smiled sweetly.

"Hello, Uncle Ian."

Chapter Nineteen

Miles slowed his mount to a walk, then pulled back on the reins and drew the animal to a complete stop. From his hilly vantage point he had a clear view of Richard's sprawling lands and a faint glimpse of the manor house off in the distance.

He had been invited for dinner this evening, but he would not be attending. Nicole would be there. In all her shimmering, flirtatious glory. Miles gritted his teeth. Five days. He had managed to stay away from the manor house and Nicole Paget for five days. And it was killing him.

He should leave Devon. Return to London. To the late-night parties, the gaming hells, the actresses. The mindless oblivion of a carefree life filled with no responsibilities, no cares, no conscience.

Each morning he told himself he would leave today. Each afternoon he prepared for the journey. Yet by early evening he still remained in Devon. Caught in a limbo of indecision and frustration.

When the urge to see Nicole became too strong, Miles would

ride the borders of Richard's estate and steel himself against the weakness until it passed. These rides had become more frequent and of longer duration over the past five days. Yet Miles remained steadfast in his determination.

Nicole was too young, too vain, too selfish, too impulsive, too *alive*. He fought hard against succumbing to the feelings she awoke in him. He preferred the deadness and dullness. It was safer, easier, oddly comforting.

The stallion whinnied. Miles abandoned his obsessive thoughts and gazed down toward the meadow to see what had suddenly interested his horse.

Riding hard across the flat open field were two riders. He raised his arm to shield his eyes from the afternoon sun. Squinting, Miles realized he could identify these too reckless riders. Ian and young Alexandra. Riding hard and fast. Perhaps in one of the horse races Alexandra so enjoyed challenging other riders to try?

Miles continued to watch as they rode full tilt. It must be a very long race, for they showed no sign of stopping. Miles whistled. He saw Ian's head lift at the sound, but instead of gazing about in curiosity, Ian hunched his shoulders and appeared to increase the speed of his mount.

Alexandra's horse matched the gait of Ian's stallion, hugging dangerously close. It was then that Miles noticed Ian holding the leading rein of Alexandra's mount. How very odd.

Whatever could Ian be thinking, leading her on such a reckless quest? Fearing for the little girl's safety, Miles calculated the quickest point of interception and galloped down the hill.

Like an apparition, a third horse and rider appeared on the horizon. For a moment Miles feared this stranger might be in pursuit of Ian and Alexandra, but the long, fluttering skirt flying in the wind indicated the third rider was a woman. Hardly a threat.

Ian gave no word of greeting when he met Miles. In fact, Miles had to position his horse in such a way that there was no other choice for Ian but to pull up. For a split second it almost seemed as though Ian was going to try to run around him, but there wasn't enough room.

Within minutes the third rider joined them.

"Thank goodness you finally stopped, Lord Rosslyn," Nicole declared. She was flushed and out of breath, her bonnet was missing, and her braid was not coiled neatly at the nape of her neck but hanging down her back. The sweaty coat and labored breathing of the mare she rode attested to her prolonged pursuit. "I have been trailing you for ages and calling out in a truly undignified manner asking you to stop."

"The wind must have swallowed up your cries, Miss Paget," Ian commented irritably. "You should have returned to the manor. It was foolish of you to continue following us. Very foolish."

Nicole did not reply but took a long, shaky breath. Miles felt an uncomfortable undertone of tension. A jolt of unease rose at the back of his neck.

"'Tis getting late," he interjected, puzzled by Ian's odd attitude. For the first time it occurred to Miles that even though the manor house was faintly visible, they were quite a distance from it. "I suggest we all return to Cuttingswood together before Richard and Anne begin to worry about their daughter."

"Lord and Lady Mulgrave are not at home. They are currently occupied elsewhere." Ian narrowed his eyes. "Besides, we haven't finished with our ride, have we, Lady Alexandra? You and Miss Paget go on ahead, Miles. We shall join you shortly."

"But I want to go home," Alexandra whined in a high-pitched voice. "Will you take me home, Uncle Miles? Please? I told Uncle Ian again and again that I wanted to go back but he wouldn't listen. I am very tired and I want to tell Rosalind all about the new bonnet Mrs. Wilder is making for me."

"I told you we will return soon, Alexandra," Ian said in an even tone. "There is no need to trouble Captain Nightingall."

"I want to go home," Alexandra insisted, rubbing her eyes petulantly. "Now."

"Alexandra," Ian warned in a chiding tone, as tension stiffened his features.

The little girl folded her arms across her chest. "Right now!"

"Be silent!" Ian yelled.

"Ian!" Miles cried. What the devil was going on? Alexandra's young face was set in rebellion. And Ian—Ian looked frantic. Eyes unnaturally bright, almost feverish, shoulders stiff and rigid, expression thunderous.

"Captain Nightingall and I will escort Lady Alexandra home," Nicole began, but her words were cut short.

Ian swore an oath and rounded on her. His eyes held a dangerous determination. "I said that I will see to Lady Alexandra. And so I shall."

Before Miles had time to consider Lord Rosslyn's agitated words, Ian slashed his riding crop down on the rump of Miles's horse with a vicious wallop. Nicole shrieked, the horse reared, and Miles fought to keep his seat.

It took a moment to calm his stallion. In anger Miles turned to confront Ian, but Lord Rosslyn had already turned his mount and was leading Alexandra away.

"What in God's name are you doing?" Miles shouted, trying desperately to determine Ian's intention. This was insane. Ian was acting like a madman.

"Do not interfere, Miles," Ian bellowed across the meadow as his and Alexandra's horses broke into a fast gallop. "This is where Alexandra belongs. With me. The truth was bound to be revealed sooner or later. She is my child. My daughter. Juliana loved me. Only me."

A trickle of unease shot through Captain Nightingall. Was it possible?

"What is he saying?" Nicole inquired in an anxious voice. She brought her horse closer to his, fighting to keep the skittish mare under control. "Lord Rosslyn is acting most peculiar. I don't understand."

Miles frowned. "There has been some bizarre misunderstanding—"

"No!"

Nicole screamed and launched herself at Miles the same moment he heard the pistol shot. And felt the stinging pain of a ball striking his upper arm.

The force of Nicole's jump combined with her weight knocked him from his horse and they hit the ground together with a loud thump.

Miles saw stars. Bright bursts of colors behind his eyelids melded the pain in his body to his mind. Sweat broke out on his forehead and he couldn't seem to breathe.

"Miles!"

He heard Nicole call for him, fear and panic in her voice. He felt her crawl to him as he lay immobile, sprawled upon his back like a floundering sea creature beached upon the shore.

"Miles, are you hurt?" She made a small sound of distress and ran her hands gingerly over his torso. "Can you hear me?"

Her questing fingers brought him pain of another kind. Sexual desire, long denied, too long unfulfilled, tightened his body. Miles smiled grimly. Well, at least he knew he wasn't too badly injured.

With difficulty he raised his head. "Why the hell did you do that?" he croaked out.

"Oh, Miles, thank God." She gathered him in her arms and gave him a bone-crushing hug. "I was so frightened. Lord Rosslyn had a pistol. I saw him draw it from his coat. He was going to shoot you. To kill you." Nicole's lower lip quivered. "Why? What have you done? And why has he taken Alexandra?"

"I do not know." Miles shut his eyes. It was all too much to take in. Ian proclaimed himself to be Alexandra's father? And he was willing to defend his claim with deadly force if necessary? Almighty God, if not for Nicole's selfless act of bravery . . .

Miles opened his eyes abruptly. Nicole might have been seriously wounded. Or even killed. His brows pulled together in an angry frown, realizing he was furious that she had endangered her own life. For his sake.

"You little idiot." Miles struggled to a sitting position. Nicole immediately reached out to help him. He accepted her assistance, then shook off her hands as he continued his lecture. "The moment you spied the pistol you should have taken cover, Nicole. Ian's shot might have missed me and hit you."

Nicole rocked back on her knees. "Better to face a bullet from the unsteady hand of a gunman than to live with the horror of watching you die, Miles Nightingall." She tilted her chin and huffed out a breath. "Though you choose to ignore it, I care a great deal about you. Apparently more than you care about yourself."

Something twisted painfully in his chest at her words. He had fought so hard to keep his emotions from being touched, and in turn refused to acknowledge Nicole's feelings as anything more than a temporary aberration.

But he had failed. He finally admitted it was useless to continue to deny it. Nicole was in love with him. It was not a girlhood flirtation. Or a childish infatuation. It was love. Real, complete, unselfish.

And she had just proved the depth of her feelings by saving his ungrateful hide.

Guilt mingled with joy inside Miles, fearing he didn't deserve her love, thinking he was wholly unworthy of it. Yet when he looked into her beautiful blue eyes, he didn't feel unworthy. He felt humble. And proud.

"My goodness, you're bleeding," Nicole declared with great concern.

Miles glanced at his arm and saw the small red stain. It hurt like fire, but he had received enough wounds to know the ball had not penetrated but merely grazed his flesh.

"'Tis nothing," he said softly as he watched her search frantically for something to stanch the steady trickle of blood. Finding nothing at hand, Nicole reached beneath her riding habit and without hesitation ripped a good portion of her petticoat.

Miles raised a rakish eyebrow. "Tearing your unmentionables for me, Miss Paget? That is highly improper."

Nicole clucked her tongue and gently wound the bandage around his arm. "I'll wager I'm not the first woman whose torn undergarments you have seen, Captain Nightingall."

"No." He reached up with his other arm and smoothed her hair from her brow. She had lovely hair. Like fine spun silk. "But I vow that you will be the last, my love."

Her hands went perfectly still. She lifted her eyes to his, then quickly glanced away. "Do not tease me, sir," she whispered.

His heart turned over. She looked so young and vulnerable. So sweet and fragile. He noticed her hands trembling as she tried to finish tying his bandage.

"I don't have a noble title, just an honorable family name," he said hoarsely. "And along with it an estate in Yorkshire. It isn't as grand as Richard's but 'tis a fine property with a steady income. My brother appointed a dedicated, hardworking steward to oversee the running of the place while I was in the army, so the house and grounds are well maintained. It truly is the perfect spot to bring a young bride for a prolonged, secluded honeymoon."

She swallowed so hard he could see her throat move. "I have heard that it can be barren both in terrain and population in certain northern counties. Is there much society in the community that surrounds your estate?"

"Hardly any," he replied honestly.

"Perfect." She took a deep breath and then smiled at him. The flirtatious, enticing grin he was quickly coming to adore. "I have discovered that I dislike the rigid rules that govern a small community. I prefer to make my own. Living in the North could well provide me with that opportunity. Therefore I might very well consider becoming your wife, Captain Nightingall. That is to say if I am properly and *romantically* asked.''

He gave a short laugh, then came up on his uninjured elbow, leaned over and pressed a soft kiss on her mouth.

''I love you, Nicole,'' he stated clearly. ''You stir in me all the feelings I thought no longer existed. When I look into your beautiful face I am filled with such a sharp pang of longing it nearly takes my breath away.

''I shall honor and love you with every ounce of strength I possess, because at long last I have come to realize that the rest of my life will be incomplete without you to share it with me. Marry me, Nicole.''

''Are you sure?'' Her lovely blue eyes swam with tears and emotion. ''I really can be frightfully difficult at times. Mother says I'm spoiled, and Anne is always scolding me for being childish. I'll probably make a horrible wife.''

''I'm counting on it.''

She gave a weak giggle, and a tear spilled onto her cheek. ''Well, don't count too hard, I might just surprise you.''

''You always surprise me.''

He wanted to lean over and kiss her again. To press his mouth against the softness of her lips, to absorb the sweetness of her breath into his body. But there was no time to celebrate the joy of their hearts. Alexandra was still in danger.

Gingerly Miles regained his feet. The pain in his arm had dulled to an occasional ache. Nicole stayed pinned to his side, supporting him as he carefully walked out the stiffness in his legs and back.

''My little mare has bolted but your stallion remains nearby,'' Nicole observed. ''Are you well enough to ride?''

''I shall be fine,'' he assured her. ''We cannot linger here.''

''I'm frightened,'' Nicole admitted, burying herself in his

chest. Her arms went around his waist and she held him so tight he nearly winced.

"I don't believe we are in any danger," Miles replied. "But I'm worried about Alexandra."

"So am I," Nicole said uneasily. "Lord Rosslyn was acting so strangely. I didn't understand half of what he was saying. Who is Juliana?"

"She was Alexandra's mother. We all knew her when we were in Spain, fighting the French. Her husband, a brother officer, was killed but after his death Juliana stayed on the Peninsula." A muscle ticked in Miles's cheek. "Apparently Ian has some twisted notion that Alexandra is his child, not Richard's."

Nicole pulled back and starred at him in horror. "Is it possible?"

"Given Ian's skill with women, I don't doubt that it could be true." Miles took a steadying breath. "Yet even if it were, why has Ian waited all this time to say something? He was present when Juliana gave birth. Why did he not claim Alexandra as his daughter then?"

"This is very confusing," Nicole said softly. She nuzzled her cheek against his chest. "I imagine Lord Mulgrave will be most upset when he hears of this. And so will Anne."

"It will be far easier for Richard to listen to this tale if he has Alexandra safely in his keeping. I must hurry and find them before Ian takes her too far away."

"You cannot mean to say that you are planning on chasing after them right now," Nicole cried out. "You are injured, Miles."

"This fine bandage you have fashioned has stopped the bleeding. I cannot delay, I must follow Ian," Miles insisted. "We have already wasted too much time. I have an idea where he might be headed, but if I have any hope of catching him I must leave immediately."

Miles walked stiffly toward his horse, who was feasting on

some sweet grass under a tree. He grabbed for the reins, but the beast promptly danced back a few steps. Miles swore under his breath, then gave a low command.

This time the animal remained in place. He grabbed the reins easily and prepared to mount. Nicole rushed forward.

"I'm coming with you."

Miles shook his head vehemently. "I feel this is an impulsive act on Ian's part, yet he has proven that he is dangerous. You are safer here."

"Alone?" Nicole whispered, her voice catching.

A pang of guilt followed quickly by fear assaulted Miles. Would she be safe? He would never be able to live with himself if anything happened to her. Yet all his instincts told him Nicole would be in far more danger accompanying him.

"You will be perfectly safe." Miles saw the doubt in her eyes, but he continued. "Once your mare returns to Richard's stables without you, servants will be dispatched to search the grounds, fearing you have been injured. If Richard has returned to Cuttingswood I am certain he will be among them.

"Once you are found, you can explain what happened. Tell Richard I suspect Ian has taken Alexandra to the old hunting lodge in the southern woods and I have followed them there. Richard will know where to go."

"No."

"Nicole."

"No." She regally inclined her head. "I will not be left behind. I hesitate to state the obvious, Miles, but my horse ran off when I leapt off him in order to save you from a nasty bullet. Since I lost my mount aiding you, by rights I am entitled to your horse."

"You expect me to give you my horse?" he asked incredulously.

"Certainly." She gave a toss of her head and her already untidy braid loosened further. "However, I am far more generous than you and will gladly share my ride."

His lips twitched. Perhaps it would be better to bring Nicole along. She had shown both a quick head and fast reflexes when faced with danger.

"You are a very maddening woman," Miles declared as he boosted her up on the horse, then climbed behind her.

"Well, you had best become accustomed to it," she replied, settling herself in a comfortable sidesaddle position in front of him. "I have no intention of changing after we are wed."

He shook his head. "I'm still amazed you didn't break your neck jumping off that mare."

Nicole turned her shoulder to face him and smiled impishly. "I had you to cushion my fall. You are a rather large man, you know."

"With an apparently very small brain," he retorted as he directed the stallion toward the open meadow.

As they rode, Miles forced himself to think and plan. Ian seemed desperate. And a desperate man could be deadly. If they had any chance of succeeding in enacting a rescue, he would need Nicole's complete cooperation.

"When we arrive, you must do precisely as I command, Nicole. Our lives could very well depend on it."

"I will do whatever you say," Nicole replied sincerely, snuggling closer. "I trust you, Miles. To keep all of us safe."

Richard and Anne took a slow, circumspect route to the manor house. The earl's horse was practically walking as it carried the two lovers. In front of Richard, Anne leaned back against his broad chest and closed her eyes. Every now and again she would lift her face for a heart-melting kiss.

She felt languid and sleepy and utterly contented. Their interlude in the magical glen had brought peace to her heart and joy to her body.

I love you. I love you. The words that had sung in her head for weeks miraculously had an answering chorus. *I love you too.*

"If we continue traveling at this slow gait we shall arrive very, very late to our own dinner party," Anne remarked.

Richard bent his head and pressed a delicate kiss at her temple. "Do you care?"

"No." A small well of laughter bubbled up inside her. "I invited Mrs. Havlen this evening. 'Tis her first invitation to Cuttingswood since our marriage."

"Mrs. Havlen? The pretentious old cow who dared to shun you for your scandalous behavior at Ian's Waterloo ball?"

"The very same," Anne answered with a louder laugh. "Whatever will she think of me after I arrive rudely late, disheveled and grass-stained?"

"If she is intelligent enough to surmise you have been making love for the better part of the afternoon, she will be riddled with jealousy."

"Ahh, but knowing how Mrs. Havlen's small mind works, she will be suitably aghast and attempt to discover *who* has been engaging me in this most scandalous activity."

Anne felt Richard's arm tighten. "You are mine," he said fiercely. "If anyone ever questions your love or devotion or dares to doubt your honor, they will have to answer to me. That I promise."

Anne felt a gentle warmth steal into her heart. It was a unique experience having someone so readily defend her, so quickly support her. She decided she liked it.

"Perhaps we should sneak in through the servants' entrance," Anne suggested, "to avoid the possibility of detection."

"I refuse to sneak into my own home," Richard declared. " 'Twill be a sad day in England when it is considered a crime to love your wife—"

A sudden, sharp noise shattered their conversation.

"Is that—?" Anne began in a frightened voice.

"A pistol shot," Richard finished grimly. "Hold on."

Anne adjusted her position and gripped Richard's arm tightly. He maneuvered the horse through the wooded path and rode for the meadow.

"Richard, there in the distance." Anne pointed to a single horse galloping through the open field.

The horse and rider were traveling on a parallel course with theirs. Richard changed direction and headed toward them. Within minutes the rider waved his arm in the air, gesturing wildly.

"He is anxious to get our attention," the earl remarked.

"Richard! Anne!"

"Apparently he knows us." Anne squinted. "Do you recognize him?"

"I'm not sure." The earl lowered his shoulders and peered intently over the top of his horse's head. " 'Tis Ian!"

They met in the middle of the field.

"Richard, you must come quickly," Ian insisted. "There has been an accident. Alexandra is hurt."

Anne's finger's tightly clutched Richard's hand. "Is she badly injured?"

"I don't know," Ian replied. "She was thrown from her horse. We must hurry."

The earl reacted without hesitation. Protective instincts screaming, they set off at a clipping pace, with Lord Rosslyn in the lead.

Anne could do nothing but hold on tightly and force herself to be calm. The minutes seemed interminable and her mind had little to do but speculate and worry. Sternly she commanded herself to cease imagining the worst. Yet when she was able to finally hold her fears momentarily at bay, she began to wonder at the circumstances that might have brought this accident to pass.

What was Alexandra doing so far from home? Had the little girl been alone when Ian found her? Did he see this accident occur? Although an impetuous and curious child, Alexandra knew better than to go riding without permission and without a servant. Besides, the little girl had been tired from their afternoon outing. It made no sense that she would have gone riding at this time of day.

Now riding abreast, Anne glanced over at Ian. His expression was impassive. A tingle, an unnerving touch of unease, slithered down Anne's spine. Despite Lord Rosslyn's apparent concern, all did not seem right. There was something very strange about this entire incident, yet Anne's mind was too cloudy with concern to clearly decide what that might be.

At last they reached the spot. Ian dismounted quickly and rushed forward.

"She is here," Ian called out, glancing wildly down at the ground in front of him and then back at them.

Richard scrambled off the horse, lifted Anne down, then turned and ran after Lord Rosslyn. Anne shivered. There was no sign of Alexandra nor her mount.

Staving off panic, Anne followed the men. The terrain appeared sloping and innocent, but Anne noted larger stones and crumbling rocks on the edges of her vision and realized there were several places where someone might be lying concealed on the ground.

"She has tumbled into some sort of pit," Ian declared. "It is narrow and deep. I cannot reach her without help."

"How could she have possibly fallen down there?" Anne questioned, but Richard did not hear her. He had rushed to the edge to stand beside Ian.

Anne moved to join them but heard the snapping sound of a brittle branch breaking. She whirled around and came face to face with Captain Miles Nightingall. And found herself gazing into the smooth-barreled end of his drawn pistol. It was aimed directly at her heart.

The blood drained from Anne's face. She opened her mouth to shriek but no sound emerged. Miles motioned for her to move out of the way, then brought his finger to his lips, indicating she should remain silent.

Their eyes locked. *What in God's name was he doing?* Anne drew breath in her lungs, determined to scream a warning to Richard, even if it was the last sound she ever made, when suddenly Nicole emerged from behind a tree.

Her sister's eyes were big and alert. Nicole repeated Miles's gesture, imploring Anne to remain quiet. Before Anne could blink, Miles had gone past her.

"Ian!"

Miles's shout forced Lord Rosslyn to turn around. He stiffened, then dropped his head wearily. "Put that pistol away, Miles. Alexandra has been injured. She has fallen into this sinkhole. We must rescue her."

"Pistol?" At the mention of a weapon, Richard also turned. And frowned. "What is going on?"

"Is Alexandra really there?" Miles wanted to know. "It isn't some sort of trick?"

"Trick?"

"Her horse bolted," Ian insisted, "and she rode away from me. Somehow she ended up here."

Captain Nightingall rushed to the edge. Anne and Nicole quickly followed. What appeared to be a small dip in the earth was actually a steep drop. It was deep and narrow, easy to miss until one had practically fallen into it. Alexandra lay on her side at the bottom, curled in a small ball. She was not moving.

"Be careful!" Ian warned as bits of soil and rock trickled down onto the child. "The ground is soft and unstable. If you come too close, the entire lip might collapse on top of her."

"We need a rope," Miles insisted.

"Well, we don't have one," Richard said in a frustrated voice. "And I have no intention of leaving her down there until we can find one."

He flung off his coat and dropped to his knees, preparing to ease over the edge of the large hole. Ian positioned himself behind the earl and grabbed his ankles. Anne cried out in alarm.

"The space is too narrow and deep, Richard. You cannot reach her, and if you fall inside you might land on top of Alexandra and injure her further." Anne quickly threaded her loose hair into a tight braid, yanked a satin ribbon from her gown and tied it around the end. "There's just enough room for me inside that hole. Once I'm beside her I can lift Alexandra. You should be able to reach down and pull her the rest of the way out."

Richard pressed his booted foot experimentally against the edge. The soggy ground instantly gave way. "It isn't safe."

Anne reached out and gripped her husband's shoulders. "You just said we can't leave her down there. Let me go, Richard."

The earl glanced down in the pit, then back up at his wife. His handsome features tightened. "Be careful."

All fell silent. Her pulse quickening, Anne gathered her skirts around her legs. She sat gingerly on the edge of the drop. She lifted her arms in the air and Richard held them tightly, guiding her carefully as she slid down the side.

Anne could feel sharp rocks and damp earth pressing against her back, but she gritted her teeth and held back any cries of distress. Her palms were damp with sweat, and for one panicky instant she feared Richard would lose his grip and she would fall, but she managed to hit the bottom standing upright. She landed beside Alexandra's feet.

"I'm fine," Anne called up to the anxious faces peering over the edge.

It was narrow and close and the earth beneath her feet was damp and muddy. It smelled musty and dank. Anne carefully inched her way over to the small prostrate form. A sob caught in her throat as she knelt beside Alexandra. Oh, dear God, please let her be all right.

With a trembling hand, Anne stroked the little girl's soft

cheeks. Her face was pale, but her breathing was deep and even. Anne could see no visible signs of bleeding, no obvious cuts or bruises. Gently she brushed back a curl and smoothed her hand over the crown of the child's head. Alexandra's eyes popped open. Anne nearly screamed in fright.

"Anne?" Alexandra's voice quivered as she clutched onto Anne's sleeve and raised herself slightly off the muddy ground. "Has Uncle Ian gone away?"

Reflexively, Anne looked up to see the four faces standing above them.

"Is she badly hurt?" Richard asked with great concern.

"I don't think so," Anne answered. Turning back to Alexandra, she tried to smile reassuringly. "How do you feel?"

"I'm fine." Alexandra lowered her voice to a tiny whisper. "I was hiding from Uncle Ian. He took me riding with him and I was having a lot of fun but then I got tired and he wouldn't take me home. I asked him and asked him and asked him, but he wouldn't take me. Then Uncle Miles and Nicole came, and Uncle Ian shot his pistol."

Alexandra frowned deeply. "It scared me. So when Uncle Ian dropped the leading reins on my horse I rode away. I thought this would be a good place to hide, but after I started to climb down, I fell and couldn't get out."

What was the child saying? Ian had fired at Miles? Was that why Captain Nightingall had arrived at the scene with a drawn pistol? Anne glanced up. All three men, Richard, Miles and Ian, showed great concern. But was there an edge of desperation to Lord Rosslyn's features, or was her imagination running away with her common sense?

Anne's shoulders began to shake. Was Richard in danger? She looked up again. "Captain Nightingall?"

Miraculously, he seemed to understand her unasked question. "If necessary, I have your husband's back covered, my lady," Miles answered. "As always."

Despite the good captain's reassurance, a chill stole down

Anne's spine. Something ugly was about to happen. She could feel it in her bones. Gingerly she helped Alexandra to her feet and hugged the little girl tightly. Then she called out for help.

"Alexandra is . . . uninjured," Anne said loudly. "I shall lift her as high as I can manage. Will you be able to reach down and pull her out, Richard?"

After much shuffling and mumbled debate from above, Richard lay at the edge of the pit and reached down with both hands. Anne bent at the knees, laced her fingers tightly together and gave the little girl a leg up, much the same as when mounting a horse. On the other end, Richard stretched his hands toward his daughter.

Anne smiled with relief and exhaustion when she heard the chorus of relieved cries above her. Thank God. Alexandra was safely free of this damp, gloomy prison.

Taking a deep breath, Anne waited for her turn. It took several tries, but after finding a toehold in the soggy earthen wall she too was able to reach Richard's outstretched hand.

But her arrival was not greeted with the same joy. There was a palpable tension between the three men. Captain Nightingall coolly checked his pistol. Anne was relieved to see that Nicole had taken Alexandra a fair distance away and was cuddling the little girl in her lap.

"Put that damn pistol away, Miles," Richard said, "before someone gets hurt."

"Unfortunately, I thought it was necessary. Tell him why, Ian," Miles commanded as he put the weapon into his waistband and adjusted his coat over it. "Or else I will."

The planes of Lord Rosslyn's handsome face shifted. Misery and bitterness lined every curve. "This horrible accident was my fault. I coerced Alexandra into going on a ride this afternoon because I was planning to take her away. To Plymouth. Where we would have caught the first ship sailing out of the country."

"You were going to kidnap my child?" Richard asked with an angry scowl. "Are you out of your mind?"

"Alexandra is mine," Ian retorted, spirit returning to his voice. "My child, my daughter. I could no longer bear the weight of the lies. For too many years the burden of my secret has eaten away at my conscience." Ian paused, his chest heaving. "Alexandra is my daughter, Richard, not yours. Juliana wrote to me as soon as she discovered her condition. She sent me several letters, in fact."

Anne gasped and turned to look at her husband. The earl's face was dark as a storm cloud, etched in anger and confusion.

"You're lying," Richard said at last in a deep, tight voice.

"No, Richard, I am finally facing the truth," Ian declared, looking the earl straight in the eyes. "I was in shock when I received Juliana's letter telling me that I was about to become a father. Me, a father. I couldn't even properly care for myself, how was I to take on the challenge of a wife and child?

"I never answered that letter. Nor the ones that followed. I tried to tell myself that she was better off without me. I was an army officer fighting in a struggling war, what could I offer her? I had no title, no home, no security. I figured she would return to England and later, if I survived the war, perhaps I would see her again. And meet my child."

Ian bowed his head a moment before continuing. "I never dreamed she would run to you, Richard. Perhaps I should have known. Everyone respected you, looked up to you. The wise and brave Earl of Mulgrave. No matter what the crisis, you were always clear headed. It made sense that Juliana would turn to you in her hour of need. And once again you did not disappoint."

Mired in disbelief, Richard stared at his lifelong friend. "Why? Why didn't you say anything?"

"I never knew the reason you sent Miles and me searching for a clergyman that horrible day until I entered your bedchamber and saw Juliana take her last breath." Desolation twisted Ian's face. "How I ached to beg her forgiveness, to try to make her understand my fears, but it was too late. She was gone, and she had chosen you to raise the child. Above all else I felt I had to honor her dying wish."

"And now you no longer feel it is necessary?" Richard said through his teeth.

Ian gave a sharp nod. "Circumstances have changed. I have a title, equal to yours in rank. A stable home, a healthy income. And you have a wife."

"A mother for my daughter," Richard said defensively.

"A wife," Ian repeated, "who will give you other children."

"You bastard!" Richard lunged at Lord Rosslyn, but Miles stepped between the two men. "I'll kill you before I let you take my daughter from me."

Anne moved toward her husband. She groped for his hands, found them clenched tight. She brought them close to her heart.

"Despite what Ian has told us, Alexandra will always be your daughter," Anne whispered frantically, squeezing the words past her lips with difficulty. "Our daughter."

"Bloody hell, Ian, how could you do this?" Miles exclaimed in anger. "Your selfish obsession put Alexandra in grave danger. What kind of a father does that to a child he is supposed to love?"

Anne stared at Lord Rosslyn, searching too for answers. His face was closed, his expression odd. He kept glancing over at Richard, but the earl refused to even acknowledge him. Anne again looked to Ian. There was a sense of total anguish about him. His once handsome face held the look of a person who's been careless and only just noticed the damage.

"The truth remains. She is my child," Ian said tonelessly.

"How dare you!" Richard roared, turning on his former friend in a fit of rage. "You never cared for her, never even acknowledged her as your flesh and blood. You gave up, willingly, any claim you had to Alexandra the day she was born."

A muscle jerked in Ian's cheek. "Juliana died before the priest arrived, Richard. You did not marry her."

"You will never be able to prove that, Ian." Richard's green eyes were turbulent with emotion. "I made a vow, a promise to Juliana that I shall always keep. Legally, morally, emotionally, Alexandra is my child and I shall never, never relinquish her to you or any other. You held your silence that day, and by God, Ian, you will hold your silence for the rest of your days. Do I make myself clear?"

Lord Rosslyn seemed to crumble as he stood there, acting as though he wanted desperately to say more, yet seeming to know there was no defense for his actions. Something desperate and sad flickered in his eyes. Finally he nodded his head in agreement.

"Get him out of my sight, Miles," Richard ground out viciously. "Before I do the unthinkable."

Anne felt a stab of sympathy, despite her anger at Ian for the hurt and worry he had caused Richard. Yet he had knowingly betrayed them all, first with his secrets and now with his obsessive need to reveal them.

"Come, Richard," Anne intoned, her arms wrapped around her husband. "Alexandra needs us."

They walked together to the area where Alexandra lay, cuddled in Nicole's lap. She smiled eagerly at the sight of her parents and held out her arms to be hugged.

"Where are Uncle Miles and Uncle Ian going?" Alexandra asked as the two men rode away.

"They are getting horses for us to ride back home," Anne lied cheerfully.

"Oh." Alexandra squirmed out of Nicole's lap and settled into Anne's. "I was very mad at Uncle Ian."

Anne felt Richard stiffen at her side. She held out a hand to steady him. "Did Ian frighten you?" Anne asked sympathetically, snuggling the child close to her breast.

"Some." Alexandra bit her lower lip. "I didn't like it when he shot the pistol. And he wouldn't listen when I told him I wanted to go home. I shouted and screamed ever so loud, even though I know it is rude to yell at grown-ups."

Richard reached out and stroked his daughter's hair. "Uncle Ian did not mean to upset you, Alexandra."

"I know." The little girl sighed happily. "I hope he comes to my birthday party next week. Will you tell him that I'm not mad at him anymore?"

"Never fear, Alexandra," Richard said in a brittle tone. "I shall tell Uncle Ian."

Anne turned to stare into her husband's confused eyes. A variety of intense emotions crossed his handsome face. She was relieved that Alexandra seemed so willing and able to forget this bizarre incident. She only hoped that someday they all could do the same.

Chapter Twenty

Cuttingswood Manor
Two months later

"Nicole, I vow if you do not sit still, your wedding portrait will be the most unflattering painting imaginable. Future generations will scoff at the tales of your legendary beauty when they view this likeness," Anne admonished.

"It is not my fault," Nicole retorted, stiffening her back. "You failed to tell me how exceedingly boring it would be sitting here for hours and hours when you offered to paint this picture of me."

"I thought it would make a lovely wedding gift," Anne replied, peering around the large easel. "Even with all his restless pacing, Miles was not half as difficult to paint."

Nicole huffed out a breath and glared at her sister. Anne smiled. In truth, Nicole had been far more patient than Anne thought possible. Still, with the wedding less than a week away,

Anne needed one more sitting to do justice to the radiance of her sister's happiness.

As Nicole reached up to straighten the spray of flowers in her hair, Lord Mulgrave entered the room. Moving behind his wife, he leaned down and wrapped his arms around Anne's waist.

"My, what a pretty picture," he whispered in her ear.

"It won't be if the artist's concentration is continually challenged," Anne said in a mockingly stern voice.

The earl laughed and blew a gentle kiss in Anne's ear.

"Thank heavens you have rescued me," Nicole intoned. She tossed her bouquet on a nearby table and scurried for the door. "Miles is most likely down by the stables with Father. If I hurry I should be able to change out of this dress and meet him before he goes riding."

"I expect you to sit for me again tomorrow," Anne called out as Nicole ran from the room, waving a hand noncommittally in her direction.

"You appear to have lost your model, my dear," Richard commented.

Anne sighed good-naturedly. "It was bound to happen sooner or later. Miles came in a few minutes ago. I knew the moment he arrived I would have only a few short minutes until Nicole thought up an excuse to leave."

"It is becoming more and more difficult to keep them apart," Richard agreed. "Thank heavens the wedding is coming soon. I think the strain of waiting is starting to wear thin. On both of them."

Anne smiled in agreement and started packing up her paints and brushes. Reaching into the pocket of her smock, she pulled out a wrinkled mass of paper.

"There was another letter from Ian," Anne told her husband softly. "He sent it to Miles in hopes that you might read it."

Richard arched a brow. "And Miles gave it to you?"

"Yes. Miles knew I would have the best chance of getting

you to at least look at it before you tossed it in the fire.'' Anne held out the letter accusingly. '' 'Tis past time, Richard.''

He glanced away. ''My darling wife, forever the peacemaker,'' Richard grumbled, but he took the missive from her hands.

Anne smiled. He was right. For most of her adult life she had been cast in that role. First with her family, now with her husband. But she no longer minded. It was something she did well and it seemed to make everyone's life happier. Including her own.

''Aren't you going to read it?''

Richard shifted his gaze and focused on some distant object. ''Not yet. Perhaps later after I have set my mind to being in a more congenial mood toward Lord Rosslyn.''

Anne said nothing but nodded her head. She wouldn't push him. In time forgiveness would come. Richard was not the sort of man who would hold a grudge, especially toward Ian.

''So what have you been up to this afternoon?'' Anne asked as she gathered the last of her art supplies.

''Since this wedding has finally afforded the entire family an opportunity to gather together, I have spent the better part of the day enclosed in my study with all of your sisters' husbands and Miles and your father.''

Anne's hands stilled. ''Discussing finances?'' she whispered as a thread of worry ran through her.

''Anne, please don't fret,'' Richard said gently, sweeping her into his arms. ''We have devised a plan, a fair one I believe, where each of us will assume part of your family's outstanding debts. More importantly, we will be able to return control of the family estate back to your father by the end of the year.''

''And then what?'' Anne muffled into Richard's shoulder. ''Who will pay the next round of debts?''

''No more debts.'' Richard backed away from her, lifted her fingers and pressed a soft kiss into her paint-stained palm. ''We have suggested a variety of ways that your father can make the estate profitable, and after a bit of persuading he has agreed to give it a try.''

''Really?''

''Yes.'' The earl grinned. ''Apparently the steward you placed in charge of the estate several years ago is a bright fellow. When your father started acquiring some rather splendid horse flesh, instead of selling all these animals the agent took the initiative to keep a few of the very best for breeding. Your father has a fine start on establishing a first-class stable.''

Anne raised a skeptical brow. ''Buying horses and breeding them are two entirely different activities.''

''Exactly.'' Richard kissed the tip of her nose. ''Which is why your father will have lots of advice and support from each of his sons-in-law. After all, we do have a vested financial interest in his success.''

''I will feel totally responsible if he makes a complete muddle of it,'' Anne said fearfully.

''We won't allow that to happen. We are a family, Anne. All of us. The burden will no longer unfairly fall to you alone.'' Richard put his arm around Anne's waist and she automatically slid her arm around his. ''There is more good news. Madeline's husband has found a new post for Miss Fraser. I have already spoken with her. She leaves immediately for Cornwall.''

''Richard, are you sure? Alexandra is devoted to her governess.''

The earl pressed his lips together. '' 'Tis best for all of us. We will all be far happier if Miss Fraser takes another position.''

The earl was right. It was the best solution. Anne felt a thankful thrill at the closeness she and Richard shared. Theirs was a strong union, growing more so each day. She no longer feared revealing a part of herself, a part of her soul to this wonderful man, because he cared about how she felt and would do anything in his power to make her happy.

They moved together arm in arm toward the door. ''I like these men your sisters have married,'' Richard said. ''They are each honorable and kind and devoted in their own way to their wives. You did an excellent job in guiding their choices. They should feel grateful indeed for your able assistance.''

Anne bowed her head modestly. ''I did the very best I could by my sisters, but I must confess, my lord, I feel horribly guilty.''

''Guilty? Why?''

She lifted her head. Emotion choked Anne's throat and her eyes shone with love and joy. ''Because I saved the very best husband of all for myself.''

Epilogue

The afternoon sun was at its height, yet Anne felt no compelling urge to work on the canvas set before her. She swiped languidly at the painting, but the pastoral scene held only limited appeal. Instead her eyes kept turning to the chubby baby sleeping peacefully on the blanket beside her.

William Maxwell Edward Cameron, heir to the earldom of Mulgrave, beloved son, perfect baby.

Anne stared down at her child and her heart swelled with love and pride. It seemed impossible to imagine but with each passing day she grew to love this baby more and more. Who knew, who could have possibly suspected, that this small, perfect creature would have the power to so quickly capture her heart? Her soul?

Though only a year old, the little boy had become the undisputed prince of the household. Everyone adored him, including his father and older half-sister. But no one loved him as fiercely as his mother.

Anne put down her brush and stretched out beside the sleeping child. The air was fragrant with the scents of wildflowers and trees, alive with the sound of singing birds and chirping insects. She felt safe and contented here in the sunshine.

Tenderly she stroked the tight curls of the baby's soft brown hair, gently she traced the curves of his tiny ear. Her fingers brushed against his rosy cheek and she realized she had never felt anything as soft as her baby's skin.

Her familiar touch woke him. The baby rolled over onto his back and alertly lifted his head. He gave her a wide, happy smile of recognition and Anne felt moved to tears. At times such as this she could only wonder at the intensity of the bond they shared. And be humbly grateful that thanks to her husband, she at last understood the power and joy of a mother's love.

"Ahhh, so this is where you have been hiding."

Both mother and son turned at the sound of the familiar male voice. William spied the tall presence of his father and started jabbering, his pudgy legs pumping excitedly in the air.

The earl knelt beside his wife. Anne watched him pick up their son with ease and toss him in the air. The child squealed with delight and clutched at his father's shoulders. A lump of emotion formed in Anne's throat.

How dearly he loves our little boy. The notion that had been hovering in the back of her mind for weeks took root and held. Yes, it was the right choice. She smiled, anticipating the moment she would tell Richard of her decision.

"I saw Trent kissing Rosalind in the rose garden," the earl announced with a casual smile. He settled the giggling baby gently in his lap. "I expect the young marquess to be making an offer of marriage. Soon."

"Really?" Anne's head shot up. "How interesting. I suspect my mother will be over the moon at the news. At long last she has a daughter who will one day become a duchess."

For a brief moment Anne felt an odd pang of wistfulness. Rosalind, a married woman. It was the final piece in the plan she had devised so long ago. The plan to win her freedom, her independence, her individuality.

"Any regrets?" Richard inquired in a mild tone.

Anne's lips curved in a small smile. How well he knew her, this man she loved beyond distraction. She watched as her son, so very much the image of his father, thrust out an eager hand and pulled on the shiny gold chain of Richard's watch fob. "Actually I do have one small regret."

The earl cleared his throat. "Oh?"

Anne bent her head to hide her widening smile. He almost sounded worried, but she knew he was not. Over the past three years they had built a good life for themselves. She had blossomed as an artist. Her work was being taken seriously by art enthusiasts in London, most of whom did not know, at her request, that she was either a woman or a countess.

They had been blessed with healthy children, good friends and neighbors, a boisterous extended family. Nigel had married a Scottish noblewoman last Spring and seemed happy with his choice. There was even talk of Ian returning to the county, and Anne was thrilled that Richard was not opposed to the idea. It was a life far richer than she had ever dared to dream. Yet there was one small missing item.

Leaning forward, she ran her forefinger lightly over her husband's lips. "I have been thinking that my darling William deserves a very special gift for his first birthday next week. You spoil him so much, 'tis not easy trying to decide on a proper present. However, after much thought and consideration I have decided I shall do everything in my power to ensure that he becomes an older brother."

Richard's brows drew together in puzzlement, but as awareness dawned, his eyes went soft with tenderness. "Another baby? You want us to have another child? Dearest Anne, are you certain?"

"No." She laughed even as she felt the tears welling in her eyes. "Being pregnant is not a very enjoyable way to spend a good part of the year, but the end result, oh, Richard, that is worth any amount of temporary discomfort.''

''I vow I never in my wildest dreams thought I'd hear you say those words. When I think back on how long I campaigned to have William.'' A smile touched the earl's lips, then without warning he pulled her close for a breathless kiss.

Anne melted in his arms. As always her body yearned for his touch, her heart craved the sincerity of his love, her spirit longed for the completeness that only he could bring to her soul. Giddy with excitement, they kissed harder, coming up for air a minute later, ever mindful of the baby the earl held.

''I take it you are pleased with my suggestion, my lord?'' Anne asked with an impish grin, most pleased with her decision and her husband's delighted response.

Richard gave a sigh of exaggerated resignation. ''If you so dearly wish it, then I suppose we can manage another child.''

Then gently holding his son in one arm and his wife in the other, the Earl of Mulgrave threw back his head and laughed with pure joy.

ABOUT THE AUTHOR

Adrienne Basso lives with her family in New Jersey and is currently working on her next Zebra historical romance set in the Regency period—look for it in 2001. Adrienne also writes short contemporaries for Zebra's Bouquet line and her newest will be out in November 2000. Adrienne loves to hear from readers and you may write to her c/o Zebra Books. Please include a self-addressed envelope if you wish a response.

BOOK YOUR PLACE ON OUR WEBSITE
AND MAKE THE
READING CONNECTION!

We've created a customized website just for our very special readers, where you can get the inside scoop on everything that's going on with Zebra, Pinnacle and Kensington books.

When you come online, you'll have the exciting opportunity to:

- View covers of upcoming books
- Read sample chapters
- Learn about our future publishing schedule (listed by publication month *and author*)
- Find out when your favorite authors will be visiting a city near you
- Search for and order backlist books from our online catalog
- Check out author bios and background information
- Send e-mail to your favorite authors
- Meet the Kensington staff online
- Join us in weekly chats with authors, readers and other guests
- Get writing guidelines
- AND MUCH MORE!

Visit our website at
http://www.zebrabooks.com

Put a Little Romance in Your Life With
Fern Michaels

__Dear Emily	0-8217-5676-1	$6.99US/$8.50CAN
__Sara's Song	0-8217-5856-X	$6.99US/$8.50CAN
__Wish List	0-8217-5228-6	$6.99US/$7.99CAN
__Vegas Rich	0-8217-5594-3	$6.99US/$8.50CAN
__Vegas Heat	0-8217-5758-X	$6.99US/$8.50CAN
__Vegas Sunrise	1-55817-5983-3	$6.99US/$8.50CAN
__Whitefire	0-8217-5638-9	$6.99US/$8.50CAN

Call toll free **1-888-345-BOOK** to order by phone or use this coupon to order by mail.

Name_____

Address_____

City _____ State _____Zip_____

Please send me the books I have checked above.

I am enclosing $_____

Plus postage and handling* $_____

Sales tax (in New York and Tennessee) $_____

Total amount enclosed $_____

*Add $2.50 for the first book and $.50 for each additional book.

Send check or money order (no cash or CODs) to:

Kensington Publishing Corp., 850 Third Avenue, New York, NY 10022

Prices and Numbers subject to change without notice.

All orders subject to availability.

Check out our website at **www.kensingtonbooks.com**

LOVE STORIES YOU'LL NEVER FORGET . . .
IN ONE FABULOUSLY ROMANTIC NEW LINE

BALLAD ROMANCES

Each month, four new historical series by both beloved and brand-new authors will begin or continue. These linked stories will introduce proud families, reveal ancient promises, and take us down the path to true love. In Ballad, the romance doesn't end with just one book . . .

COMING IN JULY
EVERYWHERE BOOKS ARE SOLD

The Wishing Well Trilogy:
CATHERINE'S WISH, by Joy Reed.
When a woman looks into the wishing well at Honeywell House, she sees the face of the man she will marry.

Titled Texans:
NOBILITY RANCH, by Cynthia Sterling
The three sons of an English earl come to Texas in the 1880s to find their fortunes . . . and lose their hearts.

Irish Blessing:
REILLY'S LAW, by Elizabeth Keys
For an Irish family of shipbuilders, an ancient gift allows them to "see" their perfect mate.

The Acadians:
EMILIE, by Cherie Claire
The daughters of an Acadian exile struggle for new lives in 18th-century Louisiana.